Conflict:
A Civil War Sea Saga

A Navy Gray Novel of the Civil War at Sea

Hibberd V. B. Kline, III

One-Time
Colonel of Marines

*To Judy & Peter,
Real Virginian!
(A am only beg desire)
Hibberd Kline*

Conflicting Loyalties

Cover: a 19th century painting of *U.S.S. Jamestown* in heavy weather

ISBN: 9781620301685

Additional copies of this book may be ordered from:

http://www.thebookpatch.com/BookStore.aspx

or

as an e-Book from

Amazon
Barns & Noble

ISBN:

MOBI: 978-1-4756-0044-5
ePub: 978-1-4756-0050-6

Visit our website at:

http://www.adventures-in-time.com

To My Father

Hibberd Van Buren Kline, Jr.

1913 – 1988

PhD.
Phi Beta Kappa
Commander, USNR
Office of Strategic Services
Office of Naval Intelligence
Fulbright Scholar, Fourah Bay College, Sierra Leone
Chairman, Department of Geography, University of
Pittsburgh
Author & Director of Peace Corps Training Program for
Liberia

Who introduced me to West Africa

&

So Much More

Acknowledgement

My thanks to my wife, Christine, and my sons, Hibberd IV and Charles, for tolerating my fixation upon a project that was supposed to take six months and became my principal focus for several years; to my late Uncle, Captain George H. Kline, USMC 1942 - 46, for critiquing the early drafts and keeping my morale up; to the selfless mentoring and sage advise of Jerry Gross - my freelance editor; to the wise guidance and persistence of Jonathan Silbersack – my agent; to Yvonne Nicholson, Bill Vaughn, Nick Nicholson, and several others who critiqued the early drafts; to Michael T. Marcotte, Esq, whose eagle eye copy edited the final draft; and to my War Between the States reenacting comrades in "C" Company, Confederate States Marines/U.S. Marine Guard, *U.S.S. Galena*, particularly the late Sgt. Anthony Bernecchi one-time corporal of U.S. Marines, for help in "researching by experiencing" the life of an 1860's Marine.

Hibberd V. B. Kline, III

INTRODUCTION

This book attempts to reproduce the actual attitudes, conflicts, and challenges of the people of the 1860's by immersing the reader in the politics, machinery, activities, attitudes, and speech patterns of the mid-nineteenth century. Actual persons, places, and things are incorporated throughout. The common understanding in the 1860's was that a proactive, omnipotent God choreographed the smallest details of daily life to accomplish His plan for humanity. Creationist beliefs dominated the world of 1861, although Darwin had just published *On the Origin of Species*. To the educated mid-nineteenth century American, the ascending order of life reflected God's intentional order culminating in Caucasian man and his culture (at least according to Caucasian man). Given the Euro-American monopoly of the industrial revolution at that time, even non-Caucasian, non-Euro-centric peoples accepted this belief to varying degrees. These attitudes permeated the life of the period and thus the views of the characters in this story, although they confront and respond to their contradictions in varying ways and to varying extents.

Most descriptions and many events and personages are historical, thanks to Sir Richard Francis Burton's *Wanderings in West Africa* describing his 1862 trip along that coast. I have drawn upon my own experiences in West Africa to present its ambiance in terms of language, smells, and vistas. Where possible, direct quotes from original documents or publications are incorporated. For example, the resignation letter is modeled upon that of Raphael Semmes, later Captain of the *C.S.S. Alabama,* and the British Admiralty dispatch describing the Confederate First National Flag is *verbatim.* So also are the quotes from newspapers and the quotes from William Rawles' *Views of the Constitution.* Historical figures' personalities, political positions and statements may have been adapted or modified either to represent what the author assumes they may have thought or said, or to advance the plot. The same is true of historical places and things, such as the presence of certain ships off West Africa at the dates given in the story. General attitudes, beliefs, and facts of daily life are authentic as understood by the writer.

In addition to Burton's book, numerous works from diaries to academic tomes to original manuals have provided historical and technical details. Particularly valuable have been Hugh Thomas' definitive history *The Slave Trade*, Howard Chapelle's *The American Sailing Navy*, the Kennedy brothers' *The South was Right,* Eric Foner's *Free Soil, Free Labor, Free Men* and E.A. Pollard's *The Lost Cause.* Obviously many other sources as well as experiences have contributed to this tale. For those readers wishing more detail concerning certain people, places, and things than reasonably can be included in the text, a reference section "Who's Who and What's What," has been included at the end of this volume.

Welcome to *Conflicting Loyalties*.

Hibberd V. B. Kline, III
Colonel, USMCR (Ret.)

CHAPTER ONE

"Quickly, Mr. Sweet, or you'll spend next watch sharpening your eyes at the main truck!" Lieutenant Trueman lowered the speaking trumpet but kept his gaze fixed upon the white-clad figure eighty feet up the mainmast. He almost smiled at the thought of Midshipman Charles Sweet, Naval Academy Class of 1859, spending four hours clinging to the "truck," the very tip of the mainmast 135 feet above the deck, as U.S.S. *Jamestown* pitched and rolled in the Atlantic swell. The vision was some consolation for his suspicion that the Captain's pet snotty was toying with him. Trueman did not give a two-penny Dutch *dam* if Sweet was Pennington's pet; he would be obeyed, and smartly.

Struggling to conform to *Jamestown's* motion, Sweet braced his feet against the crosstrees, horizontal wooden arms spreading the rope shrouds that steadied the main topgallant mast as it rose from its junction with the topmast. The hatless twenty-two-year-old was having difficulty focusing the telescope upon the sails just visible above the northern horizon. He felt the warm wood through his stockinged feet as he flexed and relaxed alternate legs trying to keep the glass steady. The sun was hot on his ears and the wind whipped his sandy hair against his cheeks, but the young Virginian's biggest distraction was the harangue through the speaking trumpet. He tried to disregard the Lieutenant's threats, but Trueman's pestering kept drawing his attention back to the quarterdeck.

Trueman was a severe man: dark, thin, taller than most at five feet-eleven inches. Something over forty years of age, his perpetual expression was one of petulant frustration. He was easy to spot in his dark blue cap with patent-leather visor, matching frockcoat, and white drill pantaloons. Navy regulations required that uniform for the officer of the deck, the senior watch officer responsible to the captain for all that happened aboard the ship during his "watch," his tour of duty. Everyone else on deck, excepting of course Lieutenant Bonney of the Marines, obviously preferred white cotton or canvas in the tropical heat. For a fleeting second Sweet fantasized "dropping" the heavy spyglass at the man twenty-five yards below. Probably miss, he thought dismissively, and "an officer and a gentleman" does not do such things, certainly not if he intended serving a full career in the United States Navy.

A frown creased the clean-shaven face of the young officer in white duck trousers, fully buttoned navy blue wool frockcoat, and matching kepi who was standing by the lee rail. Second Lieutenant Aaron Claverton Bonney, United States Marines, observed with distaste the little drama unfolding between quarterdeck and crosstrees. Despite his ingrained respect for his seniors, the twenty-six-year-old Baltimorian despised the very sound of Trueman's voice. Life on the sloop-of-war had been tolerable while the

First Lieutenant was alive, Bonney thought, but now Trueman was senior lieutenant, his peevish pickiness less restrained. "mastheading" for example, Bonney reflected, the Massachusetts martinet loved the old punishment. Bonney could accept a lad of twelve, fourteen, even sixteen banished to the masthead for a spell. Midshipmen used to be that young; why they still were nicknamed "snotties." But, for today's midshipmen, Naval Academy graduates in their early twenties like Charlie Sweet, it was degrading, insulting … he searched his mind unsuccessfully for a third epithet … and, well, just poor form.

As the only Officer of Marines aboard *Jamestown*, it was not Bonney's position to intervene in matters among officers of the United States Navy. Except for the Captain, and the First Lieutenant until his death, the Navy officers were polite, but generally left the Officer of Marines to himself. Marines aboard a man-of-war were part of the ship's company, but a separate part; the Captain's police force and little land army, should he need to project sea power ashore beyond the range of his guns. Like most enforcers, Marines were avoided by the general population and as a defense to the ostracism considered themselves an exclusive elite. Sailors and Leathernecks maintained a mutual cordial aloofness, officers included.

Still, Bonney could not help wishing that the pickle-faced Trueman would ease up on the youth. Sweet was a good lad, Bonney reflected, intelligent (he was two years younger than most members of his graduating class at Annapolis), but impetuous. And the youngster simply could not keep his thoughts from showing all over his face, plus erupting from his mouth. If Trueman continued badgering, there would be a clash that Trueman inevitably must win, and Bonney opposed Trueman winning anything.

Sweet rested the telescope on the cap, the apex of the main topmast that overlapped the bottom several feet of the main topgallant mast "stepped" or attached to its forward side. Finally, he had the rhythm. Through the lenses he watched the distant ship turning, its masts coming into line until there seemed but one pillar of sails above the hull that Sweet could only imagine out of sight beyond the curvature of the earth, "hull down" in naval parlance. With increasing speed, the stranger's foremast reappeared to Sweet's left, west, as she reversed direction heading away from Africa. Her masts blossomed with new sails. Apparently on the run, she now was classified as a "chase," a vessel under pursuit. Sweet forgot his resentment and excitedly reported her actions to the quarterdeck.

Trueman turned, parroting Sweet *verbatim* to the graying man in the straw hat, double-breasted white jacket, and matching pantaloons who had just come on deck. Captain James Pennington, USN stroked his full beard and frowned irritably at his senior lieutenant's penchant for repetition, yet he would demand it of a quartermaster. Mentally, he admitted to himself that he did not like the fellow. For a second he questioned his motives in keeping Trueman a watch officer after the First Lieutenant died. The expected eventuality would have been easier, giving Trueman the executive duties of First Lieutenant, rather than adding them to his own. He had valid reasons for not promoting the acerbic martinet, he reminded himself. Ending his reflections, he ordered Trueman to set all sail to intercept the chase and grimaced as the Lieutenant echoed his words.

At the crosstrees, Sweet watched the chase gather way on a course converging slightly toward the sloop-of-war, shortening the separation in her effort to get to seaward, out of the Bight of Benin. Hull-down, her sails looked like a flock of water birds skimming the edge of the infinite over a silver-flecked sea. For a second Sweet thought of geese startled into flight by *L'Audace,* the little gaff-rigged cutter he and his brothers had used for boyhood adventuring along the Nansamond and James rivers and out into Hampton Roads. Well, he thought, *Jamestown* was no cutter, but she certainly had startled the unknown vessel into flight. Dismissing the daydream he reported the new heading.

As the distance between the ships lessened, the chase appeared "hull up" above the horizon. Captain Pennington hailed Sweet through cupped hands requesting details. Sweet hesitated, straining to pick out national characteristics in her lines, sail-to-hull ratio, placement of the masts, anything to indicate the black-hulled stranger was American, thus subject to *Jamestown's* inspection as a possible slaver.

"*Damn you!* Answer your Captain!" Trueman barked through the trumpet.

Bonney cringed. Pennington despised unnecessary harassment, especially, the Officer of Marine knew, when the victim was a family friend assigned to his ship at the Captain's request.

"Look to your sails, Mr. Trueman," snapped Pennington. "I can handle my midshipman." There was none of the usual softness in Pennington's Virginia drawl.

"As you wish, Sir," Trueman replied icily.

One step too far, Mr. Trueman, Bonney thought. Pennington would not let that pass.

"Lieutenant Trueman, a moment," Pennington said smoothly. "What I wish is an accurate report; not some whatever-pops-into-a-man's-head, because an officer's bellowing at him. Lead, Lieutenant; don't drive. Scared men make mistakes, lots of 'em."

"As you wish, Sir."

Pennington's anger flared. "Listen carefully, Mister. I do wish it. And before I can, *or will* certify you as ready for command, you'll learn the difference. Not a whole lot of ships in this Navy, and a passel of officers hankering after them. My duty, Sir, is to recommend *only* those officers capable of making those ships perform to the highest of standards." Pennington held Trueman's gaze for a moment. "Now bend-on that sail, Lieutenant."

3

Trueman turned angrily away. This captain was lax, he fumed; even wore that slovenly white jacket and ridiculous straw hat. Why the Navy authorized such a rig, Trueman could not fathom. "Lead, don't scare," Trueman thought with contempt; "coddle, don't demand" more like.

As the topmen scurried aloft to set more sail, Sweet studied the chase. Towering tiers of canvas on aftward-raking masts told him she was Yankee-built, the swaggering freshness of her country written all over her. Before he could report, Pennington ordered Sweet to the deck. Exuberantly, the midshipman hiked his white trousers, grabbed a backstay and slid the giddying distance to the port rail, careful to keep the thickly tarred rope that stabilized the mainmast from soiling his clothes.

Pennington could not contain the smile. "Like doing that, don't you, Charlie?"

"Yes, Sir," Sweet grinned.

"I did too, once-upon-a-time," Pennington said almost wistfully. "Now, Mr. Sweet...."

Sweet reported, offhandedly mentioning the unadorned black hull. With a sudden realization he blurted, "Maybe the one we're after, one the Brits call '*Black Jonathan*.'"

Trueman overheard and grimaced, much to Bonney's amusement. He knew that the thin-lipped New Englander hated the term "Jonathan," British sailors' slang for Americans. Pennington, however, merely raised questioning eyebrows at Sweet's excitement. Bonney suddenly wondered if the Midshipman were deliberately goading Trueman? No, he thought, the youth was not that reckless.

Pennington's brow furrowed thoughtfully. After a series of diplomatic mini-crises over seizing American slave ships, the British had concluded that it was not worth the bother. For two seasons a brazened Yankee slaver had operated in the Gulf of Guinea, flaunting her actions under the protection of the Stars and Stripes and the nose of the Royal Navy. The impudent Yankee had confined her activities to well north of the American squadron's concentration off the Congo River. Not wishing another diplomatic crisis, the British christened her "*Black Jonathan*," chided the Americans, but left her alone. By April 1861, Commodore Inman, commanding the American anti-slaving patrol, had had enough of British barbs and sent *Jamestown* to find the wraith.

The wind's power against *Jamestown's* additional sails passed to her masts and fed down into her hull. As the deck inclined further before the wind, Sweet's shoes, white jacket, and straw hat, abandoned for his scramble aloft, went sliding toward the scuppers. He lunged to intercept these items, nearly impossible to replace on the West African Station, before they slid through the drain. Pennington chuckled and Trueman snorted. Charles Sweet heard neither. Bonney fought to control a smile.

Mr. Cherry bent his graying head over the long black tube, squinting through the brass rear sight at the stubby iron blade on the cannon's muzzle flare. The lay was right he told himself stepping back from the breech; now for the elevation. Trueman's goading hail, metallic through the speaking trumpet, interrupted his concentration. As Gunner of the ship, Mr. Cherry received great respect from almost all aboard. Trouble was, he consoled himself, Lieutenant Trueman did not respect anybody, not even the Captain.

A long-mile away, the black ship was crossing *Jamestown's* bows at, Cherry calculated, well over twelve knots. The sloop-of-war might make that running fair before the wind with every stitch set, but the chase was under plain sail, excepting staysails. *Damn,* reflected the grizzled Gunner, but that ship could fly. He had to bring her to with the gun. That was why the sloop-of-war carried four of the great 64-pounders, eight-inch Paixhans shell guns that could throw their 51.5 pound explosive shells 1770 yards at 5 degrees of elevation in 6.32 seconds. Under the eyes of the gun crew, 14 men and a boy, the Gunner slid out the quoin or wedge beneath the fat black breech, rotating the tube upon its trunnions, causing the muzzle to rise. He gave it a tad extra, cold guns fire short.

The Gunner made no reply to another tinnish hail. He pocketed the brass rear sight and waited for the pitch and roll. As *Jamestown's* bows rose and her hull tilted to port, he smoothly pulled the lanyard. The piece tongued flame followed by a belch of smoke that pistoned out above the sea, then blew back across the deck, a great wobbling smoke ring shimmering upward to bounce once against the concave canvas of the foresail before disintegrating. Nostrils filling with the sulfurous scent of black powder, Cherry moved aft clear of the smoke to spot the fall-of-shot.

Observing from the quarterdeck rail, Bonney believed the shot was "over," impacting beyond the target. The 64-pound solid shot would not explode, merely splash, showing that the vessel was within range and encouraging it to heave-to or more projectiles would follow. He examined the chase for any information that would be helpful if he had to send a boarding party to take possession of the black ship. She seemed high in the water, her buoyancy not yet affected by the weight of a hold packed with chained humanity. That would make for a more difficult mission, if his Marines had to scramble up the black ship's side, especially if there were resistance. Bonney was certain she was a Yankee slaver, built for speed. The only perishable West African cargo valuable enough to make such a craft profitable was a load of "woolly-heads" or "black sheep," slaves bound for Cuba.

Something fluttered to the tip of the chase's mizzen gaff, the long spar that supported the ship's fore-and-aft spanker sail above her stern. As Midshipman of the Watch, Sweet was responsible for reading and reporting signals. He put the big glass to his right eye, steadying it on one of the horizontal ropes in the shrouds, the great triangular ladder-like sets of rigging, which supported each of the three masts and gave access to the work stations of the topmen – sailors who manipulated the complexity of spars, ropes, and sails that captured the wind and converted it to *Jamestown's* motive power. Again Sweet tried to harmonize his body's sway with the combined rhythms of the two hulls. The eyepiece suddenly filled with scarlet bloomers.

"Well?" demanded Trueman.

"Maggie's Drawers, Sir; flying a pair of lady's unmentionables ... red ones."

Bonney had to hand it to the slaver for brashness; "Maggie's Drawers," usually a red flag, was the accepted signal for a miss in gunnery. The slave ship captain had used the real thing to insure his pursuers got the message. The man must have a sense of humor, the Marine reflected, or the intent to highly perturb *Jamestown's* officers.

Trueman's face reddened. "By Heavens! ... Gunner, give her a shell!"

"Belay that!" snapped Pennington; his head cocked back angrily as he looked up at Trueman who stood three inches taller than his Captain.

"*Sir!*" exploded Trueman. "That is an insult to the Navy and the Nation! Will you let that pass?"

"I'll decide at what and when this ship fires, Mr. Trueman, thank-you-very-much," the Captain answered with intimidating calmness.

Pennington moved to the rail silently relieving Sweet of the glass. It took him a moment to focus on the black ship a long-mile away. As Charles had reported, Pennington found the black hull remarkably unadorned, no figurehead other than a Corinthian swirl. It well could be the "*Black Jonathan.*" Plain as she was, he mused, she probably did not even exhibit her name; no wonder the Brits had to give her an epithet. She was pulling away from *Jamestown,* increasing the range for Mister Cherry's next shot, if there were to be one. Pennington weighed the likelihood that the slaver, for he was convinced that was what she was, had seen the Gunner's shot fall short. He doubted any slaver captain within range of *Jamestown's* broadside would worry about hoisting bloomers rather than maneuvering his ship away from certain destruction by those guns. Firing again only to have the round splash short, Pennington reasoned, would merely reinforce the slaver's cocky sense of security and frustrate his own crew. Trueman's impertinence tipped the balance. At the moment he would not venture another shot.

"Make to the chase, Mr. Sweet," Pennington ordered an answering signal, "'Please Advise; Short or Long?'" If they were going to make light of Mr. Cherry's gunnery, at least they could tell him on which side of the black hull his shot landed.

Sweet could hear Trueman snort behind him. The signal went up swiftly. They waited briefly for the reply. "'Request too much of a good thing,' Sir."

Pennington chuckled. "That I do, Mr. Sweet, that I do."

*　　*　　*　　*　　*　　*　　*　　*　　*　　*

For three-and-a-half days both vessels surged southwestward before the trade winds. *Jamestown* bent-on every possible inch of canvas. The black-hulled suspect toyed with her, reducing sail to let the sloop-of-war close, then sprinting away until hull-down on the horizon bobbing *Jamestown* after her the way a small boy might drag a toy boat on a string. Aboard *Jamestown* the crew became accustomed to the presence of the chase far beyond the bowsprit. While all aboard did whatever was within their power to eke every bit of speed out of the sloop-of-war's hull, the excitement ebbed and life continued the endless routine of watches, duties, meals, and maintenance of the incredibly complex mechanism and society that was a sail-powered man-of-war.

On the poop Bonney put his Marines through bayonet drill despite the steeply titled deck as *Jamestown* leaned over under full sail. In the shade of the nest of ship's boats on the spar deck, Daniel meticulously cleaned the nine .42 caliber cylinder chambers and the 16 gauge smoothbore barrel of Sweet's LeMat revolver. In the waste the sailmaker and his mates inspected and repaired the storm canvas in anticipation of The Rains, West Africa's monsoon that spawned Caribbean hurricanes. Far below Boatswain Goode led a small party through the cable tier looking for rotten timbers and leaks. In the galley, the cook sweated over caldrons of dried peas and salted pork to produce yet one more bland meal for his unappreciative shipmates. In his cabin so as not to appear anxious by staying on deck staring at the chase, Captain Pennington pondered the strange behavior of his quarry. Why was it pulling *Jamestown* to the west rather than just leaving her behind and getting about its business?

As the lavender dusk of the fourth evening swept westward engulfing *Jamestown* and racing toward the chase, the slaver again was pulling ahead. On *Jamestown's* quarterdeck, Captain Pennington, playing with his chin whiskers, slowly studied his rigging. There had to be a way to get more speed. If he wetted *Jamestown's* sails to increase air resistance…. It worked in a near calm, and would in a wind, but the strain….

Lieutenant Ralph Quincy Appleton's watch had the deck. Shorter than average, with ample girth and fair complected, the clean-shaven, jolly-looking New Yorker was the junior of the two lieutenants left aboard. Captain Pennington considered Appleton a competent watch officer, although not ready for an independent command. Pennington wanted the Boatswain's input on this decision as well as Appleton's. "Boatswain to the

7

quarterdeck" was repeated throughout the ship. Mr. Goode appeared in moments, pulling upon a lock of his thinning hair in salute. For a second the Lieutenant wondered how "Boats" could keep his white jumper and trousers so spotless when his duties took him everywhere in this world of pitch and tarred ropes.

Pennington discussed his notion with the ship's most senior petty officer. It was the Boatswain's daily duty to inspect *Jamestown* from trucks to keel. He was cautious. The masts were old, none too strong. Added weight of the wet canvas and strain of increased wind resistance could cause a mast to "spring," crack longitudinally along the grain so that it could not support a sail without breaking. If that happened, they would lose the chase for certain. Pennington dismissively noted the black ship could have walked away any time during the last several days, and once again silently wondered to himself why she had not. He made his decision. One of Goode's mates shrilled his pipe. The watch below, bare feet thumping on the wooden risers of the ladders, rumbled onto the weather deck. Purposeful chaos spread along the ship as men rigged hoses, rove lines to trucks, and aligned buckets. Goode scanned the foremast and summoned Peck, Boatswain's Mate on duty. Peck shook his head and summoned Thoms, Captain of the Foretop.

"Needs watching, sure," Thoms assessed in a thick Swedish accent. "Foretopmast crack in grain, *Jah*, just short of crosstrees. Mind to report, get any worse, sure I do."

"Reported, Thoms," Boatswain Goode grumbled irritably wondering how he could have missed such a hazardous condition. "Best you get aloft. Keep a sharp watch for increase in the cracking and report instantly, *in person*. 'Old Penn' will want to look you in the eye, you tell him something to reduce sail."

New leathers in the forward pump enabled the hose at the crosstrees to wet all the foresails. Thoms eyed the foretopmast; it seemed to be taking the added strain. "Old Penn's" luck was holding, he concluded; it always did when he pushed his ship. Thoms noted the starboard topgallant studsail spar, an extension tied to the standard spar that enabled an additional "studding sail" to be set outboard of the regular or "plain" sail when running fair before the wind. The studsail spar had begun to oscillate in its lashings. Not the time for that to come adrift, Thoms thought. With a couple of topmen, he moved up the starboard topgallant shroud. The spar secure, he slid down to the crosstrees and examined the chase. Thoms sensed *Jamestown* gaining slightly in the freshening wind; by Jessie, they might just close her. He began to dream of prize money and a certain woman in Portsmouth, a barmaid at a grogshop just outside the main gate to Gosport Naval Yard. How much would it take he calculated for the umpteenth time to buy that bar, so that he and....

Slowly, he became aware of an unaccustomed vibration in the mast. He eyed the timber as *Jamestown* completed her pitch, stopped her downward movement, hesitated, and reversed, rising to the next wave. Geometrically increasing stress spasmed upward from keel to masthead. Thoms thought the crack widened. *Jamestown* completed another pitching cycle. The fissure gapped, did not close, and, alarming, spread longitudinally.

Lashing now, Thoms thought. He snapped orders to the sailors playing the hose across the foretopsail. It took them a moment to comprehend, while the hose continued to pulse adding pounds of seawater to the stresses on the mast. Thoms heard cracking. "Report," Boats had ordered. He grabbed a backstay to slide toward the deck as a crack opened with a rending screech just below the footings and inexorably moved down the mast.

Pennington heard it too, instinctively starting toward the sound roaring, "Hands Aloft! Strike the foretop and gallant! *Lively!*"

As additional topmen raced to the foremast shrouds, there was a sharp report. The foretopmast dipped forward spilling wind from its staysails and jib as they crumpled into the lee of the foresails. The foretopmast wavered, then arched aft under the force of the main staysails and the pull of the hose. With a mighty snap, it crumpled backward toward the deck. The main spar, largest on the ship, received the full weight of the falling mast. Together they thundered down in a confusion of sails, spars, blocks, and lines. Captain Pennington was almost to the mainmast when the cascade of rope, wood, and canvas engulfed him. Appleton was momentarily immobilized in shock, then ordered, "Helm a-lee!" and *Jamestown* swung into the wind.

*   *   *   *   *   *   *   *   *   *

Bonney sat alone at the long wardroom table reading Mr. Dumas' new novel *The Three Musketeers* for the second time on the voyage. The trick, he kept telling himself, was to banish all memory of the plot, making each reading a new experience. Sometimes it even succeeded. From across the compartment Daniel, the wardroom steward, approached with a cup of coffee. Despite the canting deck, the Negro moved with casual confidence. In his early twenties, he was tall and well muscled, with a light *cafe-au-lait* complexion. In addition to being wardroom steward, Daniel happened to be Sweet's lifelong friend and companion - and Sweet's personal slave.

He was almost to the table when they heard the explosive crack as the mast snapped followed by the thundering cascade of rigging. *Jamestown* seemed to shake like a dog shedding water. Their gaze met and for a second Bonney wondered if his own eyes were as wide with surprise as Daniel's. Suddenly *Jamestown* listed sharply in her wild pivot into the wind. Daniel stumbled dumping the coffee intended for Bonney. As the mini-flood spread across the polished table, Bonney twisted out of its path, saving the novel from a drenching. The two men exchanged glances and scrambled for the ladder.

9

They reached the weather deck at the instant Sweet plunged into the chaos of collapsed rigging frantically seeking the Captain. Daniel charged forward to assist his master. Feverishly they clawed at the creaking, shifting wreckage that moved with *Jamestown's* motion like some great, injured beast. Bonney followed, naturally drawn to the disaster. He was aware of shouted orders, racing seamen, axe blows. Goode's voice cut through it all as the Boatswain began to bring order, purpose out of anarchy. Sweet's wild efforts were more in the crew's way than helpful, Bonney reflected. Officers had better things to do than paw at wreckage.

The catastrophe brought Lieutenant Trueman on deck where Appleton excitedly reported what had happened. Trueman immediately took command. His first impression was of Sweet's furious efforts. Trueman sharply ordered him back to the quarterdeck. Sweet glanced over his shoulder in disbelief, then anger. He opened his mouth to protest.

"Do it now, Mr. Sweet," Bonney growled. Trueman's command was a lawful and rational order. Besides, the midshipman and his servant simply were in Goode's way.

Sweet glared at Bonney with an anguished, feral face.

"He right, Marse Charles," Daniel counseled. "Your place the quarterdeck; this here the Boatswain's workin's." He knew his master's moods and had seen that wild look of Sweet's several times before. It always had led to no good, such as the time Charles' disobedience of a master at Episcopal School in Alexandria had got Sweet a switching. Trueman could do a sight worse than that, Daniel reflected. He fixed Sweet with his most severe gaze of disapproval; hoping Sweet somehow would comprehend his intensity and come to his senses.

Trueman seemed about to repeat the order, which could expose Charles to a charge of disobedience. Sweet looked from Daniel to Bonney and back again. The wildness died in his pupils. Resentfully, Sweet complied with Trueman's command. Bonney and Daniel withdrew to the lee rail well aft of the confusion.

"Look to the chase, Sir." Lieutenant Appleton snapped to Sweet whose eyes were still riveted on the tumbled wreckage burying the Captain.

In the fading light the black ship showed some color at her gaff head. Through the glass Sweet read aloud, "Tough luck, friend."

"Nervy Bastard," snapped Trueman. As the *Black Jonathan* gathered way to slip beyond the western horizon, for once Sweet was in full agreement with the Lieutenant.

CHAPTER TWO

From the confusion of collapsed rigging, Goode and Peck had retrieved the Captain, unconscious, bleeding from ears and mouth. Trueman immediately assumed command, improvised ("jury rigged" in naval parlance) a stubby foretopmast from the remains of the main spar so that *Jamestown* could deploy a jib and steer with some efficiency. He set a course for the British colony of Sierra Leone. Under reduced sail, the sloop-of-war limped northeast toward Freetown and the best dockyard in West Africa, her progress marked by an occasional mustering of hands to commit to the deep the bodies of the three topmen mortally injured in the accident.

For the first two days Sweet spent his time off-duty in the Captain's cramped sleeping cabin, witness to the labored breathing and laudanum sweats of the unconscious man whom Sweet had known almost as an uncle for most of his life. James Pennington, Unted States Navy, was the man upon whom Charles had modeled himself from before he could remember, whose walk and manner of speech he had copied, and whom he had imagined being, as he and his brothers had sailed forth from Sweetlands pier on the Nansamond in the little *L'Audace* to engage imagined Barbary corsairs in Hampton Roads or fight their way ashore at Vera Cruz, (which also happened to be "First House" built by the founder of Sweetlands Plantation when Charles II was King); Charles' mentor, a man of power and vivacity, who suddenly seemed so old.

Daniel watched with growing concern Sweet's anguish at the Captain's condition. Charles' attention wandered from his duties when on watch and his obvious grief and foul humor won him what privacy was to be had in the confines of a sloop-of-war. Daniel had tried to warn Charles about his attitude, but was sharply rebuffed. There was no place to take him aside as he would have at home and go into detail about Sweet's behavior and its impact on his performance and his shipmates. Not that it would do a flip of good, the state Charles was in, Daniel admitted. Ordinarily he would have asked Uncle Joshua, Captain Pennington's steward, for advice, but Joshua was more ravaged than Charles by the Captain's condition. All he could do was pray Sweet would snap out of his mood, and Daniel was spending plenty of time communing with The Almighty.

Bonney calculated that Sweet's vigils were not doing the Captain any good and they surely made the Midshipman petulantly morose, verging upon disrespectful. It was obvious to Bonney that Daniel clearly was concerned about his master; it showed in his preoccupied service to the wardroom. Worst of all, Bonney noticed the displeasure on Trueman's face every time he observed Sweet near the Captain's cabin. Against his better judgment, Bonney intervened. As Sweet came on deck on the third day, he placed a hand on the Midshipman's shoulder maneuvering him to the lee rail out of earshot of the others on the quarterdeck. "Surgeon Brooke says it's in God's hands now, Mr. Sweet; naught you can do."

"That's the only option when the Surgeon's a tippler!" Sweet snapped bitterly. "I simply cannot believe … three days ago he was…."

"And now things have changed, quickly, as they do at sea." Bonney had not been this seriously engaged with Charles Sweet during the nearly two years *Jamestown* had been on the West African Station.

Sweet wrenched his shoulder free and glared at Bonney. "He's still Captain, much as *some folks* would wish him dead!"

"Watch yourself, Mr. Sweet," Bonney said sternly. "That's disrespectful talk and Mr. Trueman's not particularly inclined to favor you, any event."

Sweet bristled. "What's his damned Puritan problem, Lieutenant?"

Bonney shrugged. How could anyone possibly understand a character as complex as Elias Welles Trueman, he pondered. Still, Sweet demanded an answer or he would recklessly pursue the question, probably to a disastrous end. "He's jealous," Bonney finally said with exasperation. "Not your fault you're well connected, Charles Sweet, and a Virginian like Captain Pennington. But it doesn't set well with our new 'Captain' who blames his lack of advancement upon favoritism shown to others."

"Captain Pennington showed me no favors, but common courtesies, Sir."

"Not saying he did, other than maybe asking your appointment to *Jamestown* as I hear, but that's a captain's right," Bonney soothed. "Clearly, Mister, Lieutenant Trueman doesn't take to the Captain asking you about other senior officers like they were family." Just maybe, Bonney thought, Sweet would realize how his unthinking behavior could irritate Trueman.

Charles' eyes widened with surprise, then narrowed in indignation. "Sir, my family has a home and business in Portsmouth. As you well know, we supply most of our crops from Sweetlands to the Navy and Gosport Navy Yard is our chandlery's biggest customer. Sweets have been acquainted with naval officers for generations. Captain Lee is a good friend. Captain Du Pont, Captain Buchanan, Captain Penningt…."

"My point exactly, Mr. Sweet," interrupted Bonney, smiling. Just possibly, he thought, young Charles is beginning to see the light. He was wrong.

"But, Sir…." Sweet started to contest his conclusion.

"Du Pont and Buchanan of the 'Immortal Fifteen'?" Bonney interrupted. He had to get Sweet beyond this issue before his increasing ardency attracted the attention of others on the quarterdeck. "And Pennington? Certainly they don't pay their visits at the same time!"

"Sir?"

"Like to have seen that dog fight!"

"They've no quarrel," spluttered Sweet.

12

"You think not?" Bonney smiled. "Listen to your elder, Young Sir…."

Bonney briefly explained that before the actions of the Navy Retirement Board, the "Immortal Fifteen," the youngest captain in the U.S. Navy was fifty-six, while the Royal Navy compelled retirement at fifty-five. Convening at Annapolis, June – July 1855, the Board had been a revolution in the Navy's officer personnel policies instigated by a handful of well-connected reformers including then-lieutenants Du Pont and Buchanan. The Board had replaced an immutable seniority system in the promotion and posting of senior officers with the subjective measurement of merit. It had reviewed every officer for fitness for, and retention upon active service, and consigned those not selected to life ashore on the Reserved List at half-pay. Along with smashing hopes of many timeservers who had confidently assumed that, whatever their shortcomings, eventually they would climb the ladder of command, the Board inevitably made some controversial decisions. It seemed that the resulting animosities would disappear only with the deaths of those involved, an ironic final act for the principle of absolute seniority.

"But Captain Pennington, Sir?" Sweet asked, returning to the cause for the discussion.

Bonney chuckled. "He liked not the lash, Mister, and said as much, while Buchanan and Du Pont held to its efficacy, even after Congress outlawed flogging in '50. It was only through Senator Mallory's efforts that Pennington was kept from a life on the beach instead of a quarterdeck. Maury too being a cripple; outcry in *Scientific American* saved him from the Reserved List at half-pay."

"Lieutenant Maury is the World's best oceanographer!"

"And another of your 'family friends,'" chided Bonney with a wry smile. "Trueman sees you all tied-in with a bunch of Southrons that he perceives as excluding others – such as himself - from advancement. That and something about what a Southron, who was his captain, did that put him in a bad light before the Board." The Marine shrugged. "Rumor has it, but for the intervention of some big dogs like Senator Charles Sumner, Lieutenant Trueman would have been gone from the Navy."

"He must have had some influence to get Sumner to speak for him," Sweet rejoined.

"Well, Mr. Sweet, I'd not make that point with him, were I you," Bonney smiled.

Sweet answered sharply, "I'll say naught to him unless compelled."

"Don't flaunt your hostility, Mr. Sweet," Bonney admonished firmly.

"I am fully capable of deciding my own actions, Sir," Sweet retorted.

Bonney disregarded the hostility. "Be respectful, do your duty, and entrust Captain Pennington to the care of Joshua." To soften his directive, Bonney added, "Lord knows that old uncle has cared for his master more years than you or I have graced this earth." He should understand that,

Bonney hoped; after all, the relationship between Pennington and his servant was the same as Sweet's with Daniel, just several decades older.

Sweet glared at Bonney for a moment, then asked resentfully, "Will that be all, Sir?"

Reluctantly, Bonney dismissed him and tried as well to dismiss his foreboding.

*   *   *   *   *   *   *   *   *   *

Despite Bonney's advice, Sweet's visits to Captain Pennington continued until Trueman assembled the officers in the wardroom to expand upon their obligations as part of *his* command. The Marine was not surprised that Trueman's glare seemed to bore into Sweet as the New Englander pontificated against assuming additional obligations that would reduce an officer's effectiveness on watch.

For a second Sweet wondered if Trueman considered mastheading an additional duty. With a start, he realized Trueman was speaking directly to him, "No officer will keep vigil beside the Captain without my personal approval."

Standing directly behind him, Bonney watched an angry blush spread across the back of Sweet's neck. He closed a hand around the lad's elbow and squeezed just enough to break his focus, to make him think. He hoped that Trueman did not sense Sweet's ire, but Bonney certainly did as the Midshipman jerked his arm free.

What do I care, Bonney wondered. He was not young Charles' guardian angel. Yet, with Trueman in charge, tensions aboard *Jamestown* were high enough and need go no higher. Was that the reason he had this compulsion to save Sweet from himself? Maybe, or maybe he just did not want Trueman to have the satisfaction of blasting the headstrong lad. Or, Bonney had to admit, Sweet simply reminded him of his younger brother in Baltimore who couldn't keep his mouth from working mischief either. Bonney had a sudden pang of anguish at the thought of his estrangement from his family. He had been bound for the law like his father, but one night of hotheaded, alcohol-enhanced bravado had ended all that. He could picture them so clearly, the entire family in the doorway of the large brick house, the rain falling across the gas lights framing the doorway in the pre-dawn darkness as he entered the carriage for the ride to the train station.

Foreclosing any debate, Trueman demanded Surgeon Brooke's prognosis for Captain Pennington. The older man shook his head slowly, his bulbous red nose putting Sweet in mind of some sort of pachyderm. He felt his anger ebb a bit as he reflected that he had seen a couple at circuses and pictures of the creatures in the wild. He hoped to spot one in its natural habitat, before they departed the tropics. He forgot elephants at the Surgeon's assessment: absent improvement in the following 48 hours, the

14

medico feared for Pennington's life. A heavy silence settled upon the crowded cabin.

So the Captain was not about to resume command for an extended period if ever, Truman concluded with a sense of excitement. He would command *Jamestown* for an extended period, possibly for the remainder of the commission.

Trueman was emboldened by the silence, the acceptance of his authority. For a second he reveled in his accomplishment, in command at last! It had been denied him for so long, he reflected, by cabals of well-connected men who had refused to recognize his superior qualities and had conspired to frustrate his advancement. Now, by Thunder, he would have the smartest ship in the squadron, in the whole damned Navy! Then no one could question his merit or challenge his advancement. From reading Pennington's orders from Commodore Inman, he could keep *Jamestown* on independent duty in the Bight of Benin until The Rains started. That should give him time to tighten-up the ship and show his merit, to enable him to retain command until the deployment was over. He would start with those ridiculous tropical costumes the officers were wearing.

"Thank you, Surgeon Brooke, for your report," Trueman said resuming control of the gathering. "It is obvious that I shall be exercising command for the foreseeable future, Gentlemen." He passed his gaze around the compartment fixing each officer in turn. "There are a few improvements I am implementing immediately. Henceforth," he announced, "*all* officers on duty will dress in frockcoats, caps, *et cetera*, Gentlemen. No more damned white jackets and straw hats. Service Dress, Gentlemen; true Service Dress."

An uneasy stirring rippled through the cabin. Only lieutenants standing Officer of the Deck could justify the expense of summer-cloth frockcoats. The rest had one coat of blue wool that could become miserably hot during a sun drenched four-hour watch on deck in the tropics. As approved by Navy Regulations and tradition, most officers wore white cotton or linen as their daily uniform in hot weather. The Marine Corps made no such accommodation, Arctic or Africa, Marines wore their blue wool frockcoats fully buttoned, but were allowed to change to white cotton duck trousers in hot climates.

Bonney flinched as Passed Midshipman Talliaferro cleared his throat and opened a small booklet. He knew what was coming. Henry Lawton Talliaferro was twenty-six years of age, from Wilmington, North Carolina, and, in Bonney's opinion, more hotheaded than he (Bonney) had ever been. Tall at five foot-nine, clean shaven, and redheaded despite the Mediterranean origins of his name, Talliaferro was extremely sensitive of his honor and brooked no slight from anyone regardless of rank. Reticent to speak of his family or past, Talliaferro was reputed to come from circumstances unable to maintain the social position of his august Tidewater name. Bonney had heard rumors that the Midshipman's father had been unaccounted for during much of his upbringing and his mother had married for a second time during his boyhood to a Wilmington merchant. The intercession of distant relatives in Virginia had won him his appointment to Annapolis. Amazingly, Bonney reflected, thus far his temper had not scuttled his career. Having passed the examination for promotion, he was only waiting in order of seniority for a vacancy in the authorized number of lieutenants to assume his new rank. As the senior midshipman aboard *Jamestown*, he was the natural spokesman for the other junior officers.

In his North Carolina drawl Talliaferro began, "Pardon me, Lieutenant Trueman, but *Regulations for the Uniform and Dress of the Navy and Marine Corps*, last page above Secretary Graham's name, it says,

> Jackets. May be worn as "Service Dress" by all officers *when at sea*, except when at general muster, or in charge of the Deck. To be of Navy blue cloth, or *white drill*, lined with the same, double-breasted, rolling collar, same number of small size buttons on breast as for full dress-coat; open fly-sleeve with four small buttons in the opening. With shoulder-straps for the appropriate grade – but without epaulettes.

Talliaferro took a quick breath, continuing before Trueman could interrupt.

> *Straw Hats.* In summer or in tropical climates, officers may also wear, on shipboard, under similar circumstances, white straw hats – the body of the hat to be six inches in height, and the rim three and a half inches in width.

Trueman stiffened, demanding the date of the publication.

"Says, 'PHILADELPHIA: LIPPENCOTT, GRAMBO AND CO. Printed by T. K. and P. G. Collins. 1852', Sir."

Trueman smirked, reminding Talliaferro that new regulations had issued in 1859. His smile vanished when the Passed Midshipman replied that the issuance postdated *Jamestown's* sailing and all aboard had outfitted under the 1852 document.

Trueman gave a dismissive wave. "Obsolete. Not official in any event, *Midshipman* Talliaferro. And Mr. Graham has not been Secretary for some time. I shall decide what uniform best maintains the good order and discipline of my command."

"Wonder what the new Regs say 'bout white drill?" Talliaferro pondered aloud.

Trueman let it pass. He did not have the new regulations either, Bonney concluded.

An awkward silenced again dominated the assembly. Trueman finally broke it, seizing the opportunity to rearrange the watch bill. In command, he should not stand watch and needed to designate an Acting Lieutenant. Although he disliked, *distrusted* the irreverent North Carolinian, Trueman saw no way to bypass Talliaferro, *Jamestown's* only Passed Midshipman, without some formal finding of incompetence or insubordination. He would have preferred skipping both Southerners Sweet and Talliaferro to make Sweet's Annapolis roommate, Philadelphian Harold DePue, Acting Lieutenant, but, absent cause, he was constrained by seniority in the assignment of duties to such junior officers. With rancor in his voice he announced Talliaferro's temporary promotion to Acting Lieutenant and other adjustments to the watch bill. With officer assignments reorganized, he took his leave.

For a moment all in the compartment were silent, immobilized as the tension diffused. Then, with a scuffling of feet and murmured conversation the gathering dispersed. Bonney sensed a general relief among the officers as if a threatened storm had passed over. However, Sweet, eyes blazing, pivoted to face the Officer of Marines.

"In future, Sir, I'll thank you to keep your hands off me and abjure meddling in my affairs!"

Sweet was right, Bonney had to admit, he should not have laid hands on the Midshipman, but his anger simply illustrated how much he needed someone "meddling in his affairs." Aloud, Bonney responded, "My concern, Mr. Sweet, was that you not make a comment resounding to the detriment of all present."

"I am free, White, and twenty-one, an officer and a gentleman, and do not need the supervision of you or anyone else to show me my duty, Sir!"

That is why you do not enter into the Navy's squabbles, Bonney reminded himself. "I apologize for having a care for your well-being, Mr. Sweet," Bonney responded. "Rest assured that in future I shall not give a *dam*!"

CHAPTER THREE

Bonney tugged his sword belt and sash into alignment, then rapped three times upon the hatch of the captain's day cabin. Not ten minutes before, at the conclusion of Captain Pennington's funeral and Trueman's assumption of command, the new "Captain" had directed Bonney's presence in *his* cabin. To Bonney it seemed almost a sacrilege for Trueman to be occupying Pennington's quarters, still fully furnished and stocked with the late Captain's property and attended by his servant, Joshua. Trueman's nasal order to enter grated upon Bonney's nerves. He dismissed his feelings, stepped smartly into the cabin, centered himself on the large table behind which Trueman was sitting, and reported.

Surprised at Trueman's invitation, Bonney seated himself, motivated more by discomfort at the low overhead than a desire to socialize. On some pretense or other he declined Trueman's offer of refreshment from a decanter no doubt filled at the late Captain Pennington's expense and implied that his commander should get to the point. Irritation flitted across Trueman's face as he reflected that there was an implicit, almost challenging arrogance about these Southrons, even ones with an urban upbringing from as far north as Baltimore. However, he had more important purposes this morning than teaching courtesy to this aloof Leatherneck. Surprised, he realized that Bonney routinely still wore the archaic leather stock around his neck that gave the Marines their sobriquet. Trueman turned to business. "Are you a slave owner, Mr. Bonney?"

Bonney was shocked. Trueman made no secret of his Abolitionist leanings and connections with the Radical Wing of the new Republican Party that had so swiftly supplanted the moribund Whigs to win a plurality and thus victory in the four-way race that was the 1860 presidential election. Bonney was immediately on guard and in dread of what interjecting conscious consideration of attitudes toward the "Peculiar Institution" into the daily running of *Jamestown* would do to the already high tensions aboard the ship. He almost stammered, "No, Sir … No, I am not."

"Or your family?"

"No, Lieutenant." With deliberately excessive formality, he used Trueman's permanent rank, rather than "Sir," or the courtesy "Captain" traditionally used to address anyone in command of a vessel.

It was none of Trueman's damned business what he or his family owned, did, or believed Bonney thought angrily. For a second he wondered what Trueman would think if he knew that his father was a major supporter of the Maryland Colonization Society, which sponsored the return of manumitted slaves to Liberia. Not that he had much to do with his family since leaving college near the end of his third year. There had been that one night six years ago when he arrived home in haste and told his father that he could not return to Princeton. Early the next morning he had traveled to Washington City with his father's letter of introduction to an old friend residing in a large white house at 8th and "I" streets, and obtained a commission in the United States Marine Corps. That had been his last visit with the Bonney's of Baltimore. There had been nothing formal, but with hardly any contact with the big brick house or its occupants he was effectively banished, disowned.

"Then your loyalties remain with the United States, the Union, in this disgustingly treasonous display by the Cotton States?" Trueman's words ended Bonney's dreaming.

"Lieutenant Trueman," Bonney spoke slowly, challenge implicit in his tone, "I am an Officer of United States Marines. Your question impinges upon my personal honor and, of greater import, upon the honor of my Corps."

Trueman's eyes narrowed. That was a damned devious response, he thought. Was Bonney trying to wriggle out of answering this critical queston? How stupid did Bonney think he was to try such an obvious ploy, or was this just more overblown Southron balderdash about honor?

"Mr. Bonney," Trueman growled, "these are unusual times that require direct questions and unconditional answers." He paused momentarily. "You will answer mine."

Bonney clenched his jaw until his teeth hurt, then slowly articulated, "I am loyal to my Corps and my country, Sir."

"The United States," Trueman stated rather than asked.

Bonney made absolutely no response, verbally or physically. Let the insulting bastard draw his own conclusions, he thought.

Trueman stared at him for a moment. Clearly Bonney was incensed by the question. If the Marylander were so touchy about his "honor" then he would feel compelled to challenge the specifying statement, were it not true, Trueman concluded. While he did not know the details, Trueman was aware that Bonney had fled from a falling-out within his family to find a new sense of place as an Officer of Marines. He had been at this sea-soldiering long enough to have fully committed to the ethos of The Corps, so his bristling response to Trueman's challenging questions were perfectly natural, even expected. More than one duel between Naval Officers had been fought over significantly lesser insinuations regarding personal honor. Besides, the Navy Lieutenant reminded himself, he needed a presence in the wardroom and the Officer of Marines was the obvious choice, so long as he could be trusted. Bonney sat before him, eyes glaring, jaw locked in an obvious struggle to maintain self-control. Uneasily, Trueman decided to trust him, at least for the moment.

With a dismissive wave of his hand Trueman went on to other matters. Quoting the standard wording of an officer's commission, he said, "I do *not* 'repose complete trust and confidence in the patriotism and fidelity of' some of my officers." Trueman examined the Marine's face for signs of resistance. It was immutable. He continued, "Mr. Talliaferro is an uncertain fellow from Wilmington, North Carolina, a stone's throw across the Cape Fear River from that nest of treason, South Carolina. He has intentionally questioned my authority in front of the other officers of my command and then expressed resistance to my final decision."

Bonney knew Trueman would view the white jackets incident in that light. He had to admit that Talliaferro had pushed matters more than was proper; a Passed Midshipman, he knew better.

"That spoiled snotty, Sweet," Trueman continued, "is impetuous, assumes that he is entitled to unwarranted privileges, such as having his own servant assigned to this ship, and is a budding sea lawyer in Talliaferro's wake."

Bonney had to agree that Sweet's judgment was still maturing, but Trueman was not helping matters the way he rode the lad. As for being a sea lawyer - a sailor who always had an argument justifying opposition to the command's of authority - he had not observed that in young Charles, although he could be hotheaded with more sensibility for his pride than his professional advancement. Aloud Bonney responded, "Neither North Carolina nor Virginia has seceded, Sir. Last we heard, Virginia's state convention overwhelmingly rejected secession."

Trueman gave a dismissive wave. "With the new Republican Administration, the stranglehold of the Southrons' cabal on the national government is broken and those who for so long have stymied their peers must mend their ways. It starts with those two, now."

Bonney saw things differently. The Democratic Party had managed to sustain an alliance inclusive of northern and southern branches that had imperfectly kept together what had become – perhaps had always been - two disparate societies with increasingly divergent economic and social interests. In the Marylander's opinion, the Democrats had done a laudable job reconciling the two blocks during the expansion into the Louisiana Purchase, maintaining a balance (some might say a standoff) in the Senate by admitting slave and free states in equal numbers.

Excellent, Bonney reflected, until Illinois' Senator Douglas in a bid for the Presidency had blown it all apart. His Kansas-Nebraska Act of 1854 mandated "squatter sovereignty," a popular vote by territorial residents before admission to statehood to determine whether the new state would be "slave" or "free;" shorthand for belonging to the Northern or Southern Congressional voting block, thus deciding the Senate's vote upon national policies such as tariffs, trade, and patronage. It had nothing to do with racial attitudes, Bonney knew; Oregon's 1859 "Free State" Constitution specifically prohibited Negroes from residing in the new state.

Douglas' act had created a scramble between the sections to populate Kansas Territory with their partisans. It put Bonney in mind of the competition for dominance of North America between Britain and France during the preceding two centuries. Once the killing started in "Bleeding Kansas," sectional confrontation had escalated uncontrollably shattering the Democrats into three factions, permitting the new Republican Party to win the Presidency with only a plurality of votes almost entirely from the northern states, and triggering secession of the seven states of the Deep South.

"Inevitably, these two," Trueman referred to Talliaferro and Sweet, "will instigate attitudes and talk detrimental to the good order and discipline of my command." Trueman studied Bonney's face for an indication of his feelings and found none. Probably gets that inscrutable visage from his father, one of the leading lawyers of Baltimore, he thought. How exactly did he end as a Leatherneck bobbing about off the West African Coast, Trueman wondered for a second, before continuing, "As the Marine Officer aboard, you are primarily responsible for enforcing order and discipline among the ship's company." Trueman gave a knowing look. "That company includes officers as well as hands." He paused for response; there was none. "I expect you to squelch any derogatory discussions in the wardroom and inform me of the nature, content, and reaction of all officers to the same, should it arise."

Bonney managed to control his contempt. The wardroom was the officers' home. They should be given some leeway there without being spied upon. Politics, along with religion and women, were taboo subjects in the mess in any event. This entire directive was beneath him as a gentleman.

"With particularity, Mr. Bonney, you shall report immediately any suggestion of sympathy for or justification of the treasonous rebellion in the Deep South."

Bonney just caught himself before openly suggesting that an officer's politics were his own concern. That, he knew, would do nothing beneficial and only enrage Trueman. "Will that be all, Sir?" he said aloud.

"Keep to mind that I require your absolute attention to this matter, Lieutenant." Trueman paused, then concluded, "Yes. That will be all."

Bonney rose without another word and departed. Exiting the hatchway he nearly collided with Joshua. The old servant said nothing, but gave Bonney a steely look. Enraged at Trueman's behavior, Bonney did not even notice.

CHAPTER FOUR

Triangular sails towering above clinker-built hulls like vertical vanes of ancient windmills, the two Bullom boats raced toward *Jamestown*. Bonney admitted that the panorama was spectacular: the pilot boats putting forth small bow waves, the flat Bullom Shore to the northeast, eastward the broad mouth of the Sierra Leone River sparkling with reflected sunlight, and southeast the green heights of Sugarloaf Mountain, its peak as usual wreathed in cloud.

Bonney's nostrils caught the first rich sent of land. He would need an honor guard to man the entry port after they anchored. His gaze turned to the forecastle where his senior non-commissioned officer, Sergeant Cullin Banning, already was mustering the detail. Bonney thanked Heaven for the big Irishman. An immigrant child, Banning was reared in the Pennsylvania coalfields working in the mines from the age of eleven. His father had enlisted for the Mexican War and never returned. After his mother's death, young Banning and another brother had fled to Philadelphia and joined the Marines. The Corps gave him acceptance, self-respect, and purpose for the first time in his life, which he repaid with absolute devotion.

Signal flags fluttered up the longer spar on each boat. The northerly craft flew two. The glass to his eye, Sweet read the signals to Talliaferro who had the deck. The matching flags read, "Pilot." The windward boat also flew the mail flag.

Amused, Bonney noted Acting-Lieutenant Talliaferro's assumed severity, appropriate to his new though temporary rank, as he ordered Midshipman DePue, idling on deck, to make himself useful by informing Lieutenant-in-Command Trueman of the pilot boats. Talliaferro began to say something to Sweet about being at sea thirty days, but stopped in mid-sentence as a uniform cap rose through the aft hatch.

Like some rigid stalk breaking the spring earth, Elias Welles Trueman emerged onto the weather deck. Although instantly aware of the situation, Trueman peremptorily demanded the appropriate formalities, "Mr. Talliaferro, *Report!*"

Standing with Lieutenant Appleton by the lee rail, Bonney exhaled in disgust. If Trueman had given Talliaferro the chance to take a breath, he would have made the customary report to a commander newly on deck. Instead, at Trueman's biting command, Talliaferro stiffly recited location, course, weather, and approaching pilot boats. Trueman nodded curtly. The sudden tension on the quarterdeck was as grating on the nerves as a wailing tom cat.

Behind Trueman, Lieutenant Appleton opened his mouth, then shut it rapidly. Caught himself before another familiarity with his erstwhile messmate, concluded Bonney. "Captain" Trueman had visited a devastating correction upon Lieutenant Appleton when the hapless New Yorker offered, "Best of luck, Eli," at the conclusion of Pennington's funeral and Trueman's formal assumption of command. Trueman's gruff order to bring aboard the pilot ended Bonney's musings.

Although the leeward boat was ahead, its rival flew the mail flag. Perhaps the men moved with extra speed in backing the main topsail, or the order to heave-to was somewhat early, or the helmsman was a bit excessive rounding *Jamestown* into the wind. Whatever the cause, as the warship abruptly lost way, the lead boat overshot, and the windward craft with its two flags, rounded-to hooking the sloop's chains.

A broadly smiling African hopped from the boat to *Jamestown's* cleats, an evenly spaced column of timbers nailed to her side as a permanent ladder. As he did so, a loud wail arose from the losing craft. Halting his climb, the African swung around and bellowed, "*Ahyee*, Pa Elliott, I *done-catch* the fare. You no go *jam head* the lawyerman; no *go bob* this time for *cut yamgah*. This be Jonathan gunboat!"

"Sir!" Trueman snapped at the pilot.

If he heard, he paid no attention while focused upon Elliott's response, "Johnson, you one thief. I go for *jam head* lawyerman, *one time*!"

Raised amidst the Gullah of the Carolina Coast, Talliaferro fought to stifle a grin. Trueman obviously lacked all comprehension of the pilots' bluster. Johnson had crowed of winning the pilotage ("*done-catch* the fare"), told Elliott he had nothing to gain by consulting ("*jam head*") an attorney ("lawyerman") to create a conflict ("*go bob*") for not being paid ("*cut yamgah*"), because *Jamestown* was a United States warship ("Jonathan gunboat") immune to libel in Sierra Leone's courts. Elliott retorted by calling Johnson a thief and promising suit immediately ("*one time*").

Trueman nearly bellowed at Pa Johnson to get aboard and proceed to port.

"*No agree for go*, the Queen money," Johnson replied casually.

"What?" Trueman snapped.

"Whyfore, no go, the Queen money, Pa Johnson?" Talliaferro intervened.

Trueman looked at the North Carolinian contemptuously. Damned Southrons probably learn this gibberish from their mammies before their own peculiar English, he concluded.

"Ahhh," responded Johnson. "Jonathans make *big bob* between theyselves, I savvy. No go, save have Queen money, 3 pound, 10 shilling."

Trueman tempestuously demanded an explanation.

"Says Americans are having a "*big bob*," a *big disagreement*, among themselves and he wants to be paid in 'Queen's money,' British sterling," answered Talliaferro.

"No great surprise, a bunch of damned slavocrats won't accept an election," responded Trueman. "Mr. Appleton, get the *gentleman* 3 pounds, 10 shillings."

Bonney winced as Talliaferro inhaled preparatory to countering Trueman's editorializing, but the North Carolinian was preempted.

"It be true, Captain." The speaker was a second African dressed in frockcoat, porkpie hat that out of respect for the Americans he now held across his chest, off-white pleated shirt, and gray cotton breaches. "I be the mail, Sir. I have the news." Finished, he replaced his hat on his tightly curled head.

Bonney struggled in vain to stifle a smile. He was uneasy nevertheless. *Jamestown* had not touched land since April 17, 1861, a full 30 days. Silently he reviewed the last tense but hopeful American news, received via a British paper handed off by a passing Portuguese barque. While the Cotton Belt states had seceded protesting Lincoln's election, disunion had not spread to the Upper South. Bonney recalled Sweet's relief upon reading that on April 4th the Virginia State Convention had rejected an ordinance of secession 89 to 45. There were numerous proposals in and out of Congress to return the seven seceded states to the Union with their internal institutions guaranteed. If none of them came to fruition, Bonney had read with relief, Northern public opinion overwhelmingly favored letting the seven leave without a fight. A professional soldier committed to his Corps, Bonney should not be affected by either outcome. Still, he worried, the standoffs at Charleston and Pensacola, where small Federal garrisons occupied fortifications controlling the harbors, presented potential flash points. What had happened in the last thirty days, he questioned with an intensity that surprised him.

The "mailman," introduced himself as Nathaniel Cabot, late of Greenville, Sinoe County, Liberia; now proprietor of the American Hotel in Freetown, serving "American meals" to the likes of *Jamestown's* crew, all of whom were welcome at his establishment. He proceeded with his garbled "news." After long bombardment, Secessionists had seized Fort Sumter in the mouth of Charleston harbor. Lincoln immediately had called for 75,000 state troops to "enforce the laws." The Upper South, which so recently had rebuffed secession, adamantly rejected the demand to dragoon the seceded states back into the Union. Cabot reported two days of bloody rioting as troops from Trueman's state of Massachusetts moved through Bonney's home of record, Baltimore, *en route* to Washington City. Cabot ended the "mail" by angling for a *dash,* the customary West African gift betokening gratitude, amity, or submission to blackmail.

Under backed main topsail, *Jamestown* lay hove-to. Across the water Pa Elliott continued his threats. The entire crew, whether watch-on-deck or watch-below, seemed to be topside within hearing. Trueman's color rose as he fumed inwardly that the last thing he needed was this damned black-amoor spreading rumors of national dissolution. Icily he ordered the Liberian to the transom rail at the extreme aft end of the ship.

In a state of barely controlled apprehension, Sweet followed Cabot aft. The Liberian had said that other states had refused Lincoln's demand for troops, he reflected; was Virginia among them? Virginia was the cradle of the Republic, the home of presidents. Virginians had penned the Declaration of Independence, much of the Constitution. The vast majority of her free citizens were strongly attached to the national federation. Yet, Virginia was a sovereign state, her people strongly committed to constitutional principles and determined never to bow to an outsider's *dictat*. What had Virginia done in answer to Lincoln's demand? What of Gosport Navy Yard? What of his family? What of his future in the Navy?

Sweet joined Cabot at the transom looking down over the stern into the blue-green Atlantic and asked him if he had access to newspapers. Indeed, Cabot admitted to amassing a great quantity, "*borku* the papers," at the American Hotel. He indicated that the effort to enlighten his "fellow Americans" had given him "the thirst." Sweet thought it a nicely put request for a *dash* and motioned to Daniel in sailor's white jumper and matching trousers leaning against the lee rail. The steward moved toward them on bare feet.

"Marse Charles?" Daniel asked, stopping three feet from them.

As Sweet ordered port for Cabot's "thirst," the Liberian's face flooded with curiosity.

"Dan'l is Wardroom Steward, a Volunteer, a member of the Navy for most purposes, aboard with the Captain's permission," Sweet explained. "It's most common carrying officers servants as 'volunteers' so they can be berthed and fed as crew." Sweet failed to mention that he owned the man.

Jamestown again underway, Trueman turned to the Cabot matter. His face hardened upon seeing Daniel descend the aft companionway. At the transom, he ignored Cabot and addressed Sweet. "Interesting, Mr. Sweet, to see what temptations present themselves to your Nigra this time in port. No slaver for captain, he may take advantage of British law."

"Doubt Dan'l will maroon himself in Freetown, Sir," Sweet answered Trueman deliberately. He sensed that Trueman's words had confirmed Cabot's assumptions.

"Ah, you slave owners always overestimate the loyalty of your property," Trueman replied smirking. "Our late Captain used to have the same delusions. That the Limeys, at Pennington's request of course, would hold Daniel a deserter and return him to the ship might have bolstered his *loyalty*, don't you agree?"

"And Joshua, Sir?" Sweet knew he was courting disaster. Trueman was availing himself of the late Captain's personal steward who had served Pennington from childhood.

"Joshua is a Volunteer fulfilling a critical role aboard this ship until we return to the United States, where he will be free to decide his future," Trueman snapped.

"Captain's heirs, Sir?" Sweet shot back. "You've no more right to deny them Joshua than to keep the Captain's sword or sextant." Trueman had been making free with both.

"Depends where we make landfall, don't it, Sweet?" Trueman growled.

"Not after *Dred Scott*, Sir." Sweet knew Chief Justice Taney's recent decision that the Constitution guaranteed property rights in slaves in all states had inflamed Abolitionists across the country. That Taney himself opposed slavery and put his duty to the Constitution and the Supreme Court above his personal beliefs had not saved him from Abolitionist attacks. One look at his "Captain's" face told Sweet that Trueman obviously held with the Justice's detractors. For a moment Sweet regretted the statement. Too late he recognized that it had been a stupid bit of bravado that could only worsen his relationship with the man who held absolute power over his life aboard *Jamestown* and could decisively affect his naval career.

"Dismissed, Sir." Trueman was unwilling to debate a junior in front of an African.

"Aye, aye, Sir." Sweet fingered the bill of his cap. "Good day, Mr. Cabot."

Trueman rounded upon Cabot before the surprised Liberian could acknowledge Sweet's farewell. "As for you, I shan't suffer strangers insinuating themselves upon my decks spouting unconfirmed gibberish tending to the disorder of my command. You will remain here until we anchor; then remove yourself from my ship. Do you understand?"

Cabot stepped backward in confusion. "All be truth, Sir, hear? We Americans…."

"You are no *American*, you uppity…." Trueman just caught himself. "You will stay here in silence until you leave my ship."

Striding forward, Trueman intercepted Daniel carrying a stem glass on a silver tray. "Belay that, Boy! Throw that drink over side and get below where you belong. This is a quarterdeck, not a promenade."

*　　*　　*　　*　　*　　*　　*　　*　　*　　*

Bonney hurried below as soon as Trueman ordered Cabot to the transom rail. He strode across the wardroom and into his miniscule cuddy or cabin barely large enough for him to stand beside the bunk built against *Jamestown's* hull. It provided no real privacy as the side toward the wardroom had spindles instead of solid bulkhead from slightly above waste level to the overhead or deck above. Judas Priest, he thought, was there no place for privacy aboard this ship? Baltimore a battleground! His little brother would be in the thick of it, the damned fool! Willie, he pictured the sandy haired twelve-year-old with green eyes, the hothead with dreams of glory who idolized Patrick Henry and the firebrands of the Revolution. "Pitched battle" that African had called it; for two days – that meant many casualties, so what of Willie, now eighteen? What of the rest of the family he had disgraced?

Bonney cocked his fist to strike the bulkhead, thought better of it, and looked quickly around the wardroom to see if anyone were watching. He was the Officer of Marines aboard, supposedly the stoic pillar of discipline and obedience to Honor and Service and he had to get himself under control. He shut his eyes, leaned against the flimsy aft bulkhead of his cuddy and forced himself to take a half-dozen deep slow breathes.

He should have stayed in correspondence, he chastised himself for an unnumbered time, but it would only have continued the hurt his father felt at his eldest son's changed future. So he simply had not written, had not answered the letters until they became fewer, then almost none but for Christmas. But Samantha Prewitt had kept him informed and sent him clippings from the newspapers that kept him aware of his family. Miss Prewitt whose day school he had attended as a small boy had continued to encourage his academic career after he left her little school to attend more formal education. She had been as upset as anyone by his departure from Princeton, but she had freely forgiven him and for some unknown reason he could correspond with her without the anguish always generated by contact with his family. She would let him know of Willie. He would write that evening.

Bonney opened his eyes, straightened his shoulders, and turned to the cuddy door as Daniel steamed down the ladder into the wardroom, lips pursed and eyes flashing. Bonney started to speak, but caught himself. From Daniel's carriage he was having as contrary a day as Bonney.

*   *   *   *   *   *   *   *   *   *

"What riling you, Boy," Joshua asked Daniel as he stomped into the wardroom pantry.

"How y'all stomach that man, I cain't figure, Uncle Joshua, surely not." Daniel was livid at the way Trueman had addressed him and ordered the wardroom's port tossed overboard. It was running low and not to be wasted on fish.

The older servant shook his graying head in resigned sympathy. "Don't pay that peacock no-never-mind, Dan'l," Joshua instructed. "He just a Damned Yankee, don't know no better."

"But what's his problem, Uncle Joshua, that he hate Southrons so and don't have no breeding come to Nigras, neither?"

"You don't know, Boy?" Joshua asked, shocked by the realization that Sweet and Talliaferro probably did not know either. The happenings

28

were long ago. "He got no time for Southrons, slave or master, Dan'l, so just stay clear, much as you can."

Daniel demanded an explanation. Joshua gave it in an apprehensive whisper. Trueman had served under a Southerner aboard a sloop-of-war based at Charleston in the early 1850's. The captain had an old body servant who had trouble with rheumatism and malarial sweats. The old slave's shuffling presence occasionally impeded activities on the vessel in minor ways. At times seamen had to detour around him while trimming sails, or he would spill gravy on the deck, or not clear the ladder quickly for Trueman hurrying between decks. Trueman found him a festering irritant; his impatience grew with time. While serving dinner at the captain's table the old slave had sloshed hot soup on Trueman's best uniform. Trueman snapped, striking the old man fracturing his jaw. Irate, the captain had confined Trueman to his quarters, returned to Charleston, ordered Trueman off the ship, and sued him for damage to his property.

Trueman had avoided the jurisdiction of the civil court by arranging a summons to Washington. Once beyond the reach of Carolina's writs, he publicized the matter as an example of the evils of Southerners, slavery, and the supposed Southern dominance of the national government. The tale changed in the telling, so that the slave's owner rather than Trueman had delivered the blow and had taken unjustified punitive actions against Trueman for protesting. The story had won him favor among Abolitionists and founders of the nascent Republican Party, including the protection of Senator Charles Sumner of Massachusetts.

"Still don't like us Coloreds, slave or free," Joshua concluded shaking his head. "I oughts to know, working for him these times." The old man sighed. "Weren't for that old uncle, he'd a never had no trouble, to his way of thinking. Like saying it God's fault his ship run on a rock 'cause God ain't had put it there, he hadn't of hit it." Joshua shook his head again in amazement. "Ain't never his fault, you can lay to that."

Both stewards laughed, but Daniel dreaded the rest of the cruise, especially, he thought with a grimace, with Marse Charles' mouth talking before his head figured.

CHAPTER FIVE

Sweet stared unfocused through the shimmering heat waves toward the Bullom Shore, hardly distinguishable across the sparkling seven-mile width of the Sierra Leone River. *Jamestown* lay anchored in St. George's Bay, stressed quiet enfolding the ship. Each man aboard was processing Cabot's information: Charleston, Fort Sumter, Lincoln's call for 75,000 state militia, refusal of the Upper South, moves toward secession, Massachusetts sending twice her quota…. One did not speak politics in the wardroom, but….

He wanted to discuss it all with someone, but after Daniel relayed Joshua's warning about Lieutenant Bonney spying for Trueman, Sweet had been more careful of his speech. He had warned Talliaferro and nursed his resentment at Bonney's earlier false expressions of concern for his well being. Was Bonney trying to entice him into some remark that he could report to Trueman? Officer and a gentleman, my….

Boatswain's Mate Peck challenging an approaching boat snapped Sweet from his reverie. The answering hail, "*Jamestown,*" meant Trueman was returning. Sweet resented the instant loathing that seemed to surge up his spine and neck to give his mouth a copper taste. It simply was not right to detest anyone so, let be a superior officer, he admitted. He felt guilty, "un-Christian," his mother would have said. Sweet nodded thanks to the petty officer as the small honor party formed to receive their "Captain." When Trueman appeared in the entryport, the boatswain's mate squealed his pipe, the half-dozen Marines presented arms, and Sweet saluted, revealing a sweat-darkened underarm.

Trueman experienced a moment's gratification at the ceremony and, he admitted, at Sweet's sweat. The snotties, including Acting Lieutenant Talliaferro, certainly looked more like gentlemen in Navy Blue, he thought with satisfaction; shame they had not acquired summer-cloth frockcoats before sailing from Gosport. He knew it would have been extravagant, even for spoiled little rich boys like Sweet. Still and all, they should have been prepared for any eventuality. A little sweat would teach them a good lesson, he concluded.

Acknowledging the honors, Trueman demanded, "Lost your voice, Mr. Sweet?"

"No, Sir." Trueman had not missed his failing to hail the gig.

"You Southrons should have no challenge being alert in this heat," Trueman sneered.

"Yes, Sir." Sweet kept his eyes fixed unfocused on Freetown's irregular skyline.

"All officers, my cabin, ten minutes," snapped Trueman and headed below.

*   *   *   *   *   *   *   *   *   *

Sweltering in woolen vests and frockcoats, the officers shifted uneasily. All were present, except Midshipman Kunstler, standing watch on deck. Trueman pledged to be concise, then launched upon a blistering report of his findings at Government House. The United States was in deepening chaos. Trueman focused upon the revolt of coastal states from Virginia to Texas and the Presidential Declaration of Blockade from the Chesapeake to the Rio Grande. Several United States flagged vessels already had been lost to Rebel raiders. Maryland had been prevented from enacting secession only by Federal troops surrounding the capitol building in Annapolis during the vote. The Naval Academy and its training ship, the venerable frigate *Constitution*, had moved to Newport, Rhode Island. Washington City was under a state of siege. Most appalling was the Navy's destruction of Gosport Navy Yard at Portsmouth, Virginia, across the Elizabeth River from Norfolk, scuttling numerous vessels there including the powerful steam frigate *Merrimack*.

Bonney heard Sweet gasp; his family's economic position was premised upon sales to Gosport. "Sweetlands" Plantation on the Nansemond River west of Norfolk had been a colonial shipping point for area tobacco farmers. From selling supplies to vessels calling at Sweetlands wharf had emerged Sweet & Sons Ship Chandlery now supplying nautical needs from warehouses in Portsmouth adjacent to Gosport Navy Yard. After the Revolution, the Sweets had converted farmed-out tobacco fields to growing foodstuffs for the Navy. The Yard's destruction meant loss of the Sweets' primary customer for both commodities.

Trueman continued, "Treason is even within the Navy. The sanctimonious Captain Buchanan resigned command of Washington Navy Yard to leave the Service. The posturing Rafael Semmes also has left, as has that cripple, Maury, all to join the rebels doubt not." Trueman sneered, "Good riddance; disgusting behavior nonetheless." Trueman's eyes flashed around the cabin looking for hostile reactions, seeking signs of rebellion.

In the sweltering cabin, Sweet became numb, then livid. Buchanan, a Marylander, was a distinguished officer and family friend. Matthew Fontaine Maury, the world famous oceanographer, like Sweet, was a Virginian and had endorsed his attendance at Annapolis. Semmes had been a guest at Sweetlands. True, he liked theatrical poses and made much of his moustache, but he had more than proved his mettle in Mexico. The term "traitor" simply did not apply to these men.

Bonney had re-established his self-control and was outwardly expressionless as Trueman detailed events in his home city. Baltimore had been the scene of a two-day pitched battle between poorly armed citizens and Massachusetts troops who had fired pointblank into the crowds, crowds that must have included Willie. He thought of the one volley fired in the "Boston Massacre" ninety years before, where New Englanders' resentment at troops

32

of a national government which they considered alien had erupted into violence culminating in the Revolution. By comparison the earlier event seemed almost insignificant. Now, from a promontory beside the Inner Harbor to be known ever after as "Federal Hill," Massachusetts cannon threatened Bonney's city, Bonney's family. Did the Bay State Boys, so proud of their Revolutionary heritage, recognize the irony, he wondered?

Family and emotions aside, Bonney was an Officer of Marines bound by that mystic devotion to his Corps. For the first time since the crisis began, he felt uncertain, torn by conflicting loyalties, "patriotism and fidelity," but to what exactly? His Corps was the creation of a Federal Union of Sovereign States. He was a Marylander born and bred. His state, his city had been invaded, its people shot down in their own streets, its government intimidated by troops from far away, strangers with no attachment to the state or its people. Obviously Captain Buchanan saw Maryland resisting and had resigned, rather than side against his state. What did honor - his Corps, his home, his oath - require? "Reposing complete trust and confidence in the patriotism and fidelity of Aaron Claverton Bonney ..." was how his commission read, but to what entity, what people did he owe that patriotism and fidelity? The dreamlike nature of the crisis up to this point evaporated in the humidity of the sweltering cabin and became painfully personal. He hoped that he did not look as confounded as young Sweet and composed his face to hide his feelings.

Bonney's focus returned to Trueman who was announcing that the West African Squadron inevitably must be recalled to enforce the Blockade. It would take *Jamestown* several days to refit, water, and vittle. Looking pointedly at Talliaferro, Trueman continued, "We must preserve order among the men. Any comments disloyal to the United States or the Navy will be dealt with as mutiny, perpetrators treated accordingly." Talliaferro returned the gaze with steady coldness. Trueman added, "Obviously, this applies to all hands, officers included." An awkward silence followed. "Am I understood?"

"Captain Buchanan could not have said it better," Talliaferro carefully enunciated.

Hair-trigger quiet pressed upon the cabin. The Navy's internal politics should not be Bonney's concern, but Trueman had dragged him into them by ordering him to spy on his messmates. And it was Bonney who would take overt action against his fellows, should Trueman order punitive measures. Bonney hoped for a quick Atlantic passage.

At least Sweet had not added to the confrontation, Bonney observed. The midshipman had hardly said six words to him since Captain Pennington's funeral. Not that he cared, Bonney told himself, so long as the youngster did not add to the tensions aboard *Jamestown*.

For a second, Trueman thought of his late wife. Melissa had died in childbirth in Charleston, the baby also, and he blamed the Southern climate for the loss of both her and the baby. She had possessed an unerring ability to undercut him with a superficially innocent phrase as Talliaferro had just done. He did not recognize that, although she had been dead nearly a decade, she had so completely conditioned his response. It had become his inevitable instinctive reaction to pass over such challenges.

Disregarding Talliaferro, Trueman finally, spoke. To prevent the men hearing wild rumors, only officers and petty officers were allowed ashore, excepting working parties, which were to be observed closely and discouraged from communicating with the local populace. The officers had been invited to Government House the following evening, Trueman announced. Refusing would give an exaggerated sense of crisis. Therefore, they would attend. In addition to the usual officials, officers and their ladies, Captain English of the African Steam Ship Company's vessel, *Blackland*, and some of his passengers were expected. Trueman concluded, "I shall tolerate no disloyal statements in the course of the evening. Understood, Gentlemen?"

Sweet glanced around the cabin. Talliaferro's eyes flashed outrage. Lieutenant Appleton of New York seemed uncertain. The Master and the Surgeon were old Navy professionals who long ago had surrendered any ties to a particular location ashore. They would go along with "Captain" Trueman of Massachusetts; the Navy was their only home. Bonney ... well, Bonney was Trueman's spy. Even if he weren't, he was a Marine and would remain faithful to his Corps. The other midshipmen and master's mates were Northerners. Turning to Philadelphian Harry DePue, Sweet had the sensation of a fist-sized lump of lead settling into his stomach. His Annapolis roommate clearly agreed with Trueman.

*   *   *   *   *   *   *   *   *   *

The colorful panorama of Freetown before them, the two midshipmen sat, legs dangling, on the landward side of the main fighting top, the platform near the apex of the mainmast where it attached to the main topmast. It served the same purposes as the main crosstrees further up where the topmast attached to the topgallant mast. In combat the fighting top also served as a post for Marine snipers. Sweet pared a slice from the square plug of Navy tobacco, pressed it against the penknife blade, and extended it to DePue.

"Thanks," Harold said flatly. Before putting it in his mouth, he asked, "What *does* this all mean for your family, Charles?"

"*Thunder*, Harry. How'd I know?" Sweet paused. "Gosport *burned*, for mercy sake."

Chewing, DePue tried to respond. "What will you do?" came out as "Werl ewe d'?"

The humor was lost on Sweet. "Don't know, Harry, surely don't." Sweet drew a deep breath. How, he wondered, could this insanity be taking place? Life had been predictable, secure. He would follow a career in the Navy. The family businesses would expand along with the United States as always. Some day he might transition to the chandlery trade - his eldest brother got the plantation - or he could try politics. Maybe that was what had drawn him and DePue together, Charles reflected fleetingly. Both were junior sons who would not receive the family businesses unless some catastrophe occurred to their elder brothers, so each had sought their futures in the Service. In reality, Charles could not see Harry running his family's New York City furniture factory any more than he could see himself satisfied at Sweet and Sons Chandlery in Portsmouth, outfitting ships, but never putting to sea. Suddenly Sweet's future putting to sea seemed in considerable doubt. How could life have suddenly come asunder like this? "Why *burn* the place?' he wondered aloud. "What in Billy-Blue-Blazes they all thinking of, do that?"

"Awh, Charlie; all those states seizing Federal property, Navy can't just walk away."

"Minute, there," Sweet answered. "Not been seizures, Anderson had not grabbed Sumter, middle of the night; Christmas Night, for Mercy sakes." In the wee hours of December 26, 1860, Major Anderson, senior Federal officer at Charleston, South Carolina, had concentrated his few troops from indefensible mainland locations at Fort Moultrie and Castle Pinckney to previously un-garrisoned Fort Sumter on its artificial island in the mouth of Charleston Harbor.

"Charles, Sumter is clearly Federal property, as are Moultrie and Castle Pinckney, for that matter. Anderson merely repositioned his men."

"Not hardly!" Sweet snapped back. "Harry, you clear forgot the Coastal Defense Plan we spent so long on at Annapolis?"

"No," replied the Pennsylvanian with an edge, "Federal monies plainly built the forts."

"Passel of State funds too, as it's to be *State* troops garrison them in time of trouble. Federal Government can't keep enough soldiers in peacetime to garrison all those forts. Time they raise and train them, Brits'd be burning Washington, *again*, just like 1814."

"Still no excuse for seizing them," responded DePue firmly.

"'Seizing' a bit over-says it, Harry. You know most were just manned by civilian caretakers who did the joint inventory, had the State people sign for the property, *as the plans have always called for*, and gave over the keys as they headed for Washington, paperwork in order." Sweet tongued his tobacco from right cheek to left. "Never needed any other authority."

"But always in the face of a *foreign* enemy, Charles, not insurrection."

"Now wait one minute...." Sweet protested, nearly swallowing part of his tobacco.

35

"And the other facilities?" DePue cut off Sweet's protest. "What about them?"

"Arsenals same as the forts, Harry; arm State troops on *State authority*, in an emergency. Just what happened."

"And the regional mints, post offices, revenue cutters, customs houses; Heck, Charlie, even a naval hospital?"

Sweet gave a sheepish smile. "Grant you, some of that might be a smidgen hasty, but what do you expect after Anderson breaks the word of the *President* for land's sake, that all is to stay *in situ* until agreement can be reached?"

"Despite all this, Charles, those facilities all are Federal Property and cannot be taken under State control in defiance of the national government."

Sweet spat into the small silver flask he carried for the purpose, then extended it to Harry. "Going to become State Property in any event, states out of the Union. Can settle the reckoning before or after; makes no-never-mind."

"*That's the issue!*" snapped DePue, nearly choking on his juice. "Secession is il...."

"*Glory on High!*" barked Sweet. "Federal Government is a creature of the States...."

"'*We the People*' created this Union...."

"*Sovereign States* accepted the Constitution, *specifically reserving* the right to leave...."

DePue held up his hand. "Two middies fifty feet above an African bay cannot change what is done. I have more concern for your family than the New Orleans Post Office."

Sweet grinned slowly. "You're right. We're piddling small fish in this net." He paused a moment before adding, "You know, Harry, I *don't want* secession, but...."

"*Mr. DePue!* Lay on deck this instant!" ordered the foreshortened figure of Lieutenant Appleton peering up from beside the taffrail.

"Must have legions of things to entertain us," observed DePue. He turned his gaze back to Sweet. "Charles," he said firmly. "We cannot let this come between us. We've too much time together."

"Closer than brothers. Don't be loony, Harry," Sweet responded. "Next news we hear, this will have all blowed over. Nothing will come between us." Sweet paused, then grinned. "Balance of the plug, I beat you to the deck!"

CHAPTER SIX

Sweet was "sea-lawyering" and he knew it. He was not about to deprive Daniel of a run ashore just to placate that pinched-faced Puritan. Plausibly, Trueman's prohibition against seamen ashore excluded servants. Alternatively, a steward on a mess member's business was a one-man working party. Squeezed between Bonney and Sweet in the sternsheets, Daniel, the one-man working party, was under the supervision of an officer, as Trueman required, a midshipman named Sweet. Sweet settled on the working party argument as the gig pulled for Government Steps between the Commissariat and Haddle's Warehouse. The three passengers were embarrassingly silent. Sweet harbored a combination of hostility and suspicion toward Bonney that made him enjoy snubbing the Lieutenant and Bonney was at pains to evidence his indifference for the headstrong Midshipman. Daniel stared dead ahead, staying clear of this White men's hostility.

"Ship Oars!" The coxswain's command brought Sweet back from his ponderings as the gig coasted toward Government Steps cut into the 80-foot cliff that ringed St. George's Bay. As the gig neared the jetty, a crowd of Africans eager to serve as porters magically materialized. Finally convinced that there was no luggage and Bonney was not about to relinquish the canvas bag tucked under his arm, they opened a path for the Americans to ascend the stone steps to Water Street, where two large Africans again blocked their way, this time competing to serve as their guide. Both men stood over six feet, were ebony black, in their mid-thirties, powerfully built, and better dressed than the would-be porters. The more forceful salesman of the two, "General Jackson," wore an off-white course cotton shirt and tan breeches that ended several inches above his ankles and bare feet. His martial name was reflected in a navy blue vest with brass buttons of varying sizes and patterns. His competitor, "Jumbo" was slightly larger, sporting a white shirt of finer weave, black string tie, and nearly full-length trousers separated from leather sandals by bare ankles. Both were talking rapidly trying to drown out the other with assertions of how necessary it was to have a guide and how far superior to all others, including those present, each happened to be.

Sweet was hot, impatient at the jostling by the would-be porters, uncomfortable at Bonney's semi-presence, and preoccupied by having sounded to DePue like a secessionist, which he certainly was not. The competing boasts and deprecations of the two giants irritated him. He saw no need for a guide; Freetown was not a major metropolis. When "General Jackson," as a fellow "American" from Liberia, asserted he was entitled to guide them, Sweet had enough. He directed the other giant, "Jumbo," to take them to the American Hotel.

With a victorious grin, the large man turned down Water Street paralleling the shore toward St. George's Cathedral and the great Cottonwood Tree. He silently commended himself upon not claiming also to be an "American." He could have; his great-grandfather had been a slave in the Carolinas until he ran off to serve King George in unsuccessfully trying to suppress rebellion in the 1770's. The Loyalist former slaves had been settled in Nova Scotia and suffered terribly from the climate, so a grateful sovereign had embarked them for Sierra Leone via Britain where they added some prostitutes from England's jails to the disproportionately male colonists. The mixed-race progeny of these settlers were the Colony's "Creole" elite, among whom Jumbo proudly included himself.

To Sweet's agitation, Bonney's route paralleled their own. He was apart, yet too close to politely be treated as such. It grated upon Sweet's Virginia sense of hospitality and good breeding. Finally he turned to the Lieutenant and said, "I would enjoy being left to my privacy, Sir." The formal address implied not subordination, but challenge.

"And I as well, Sir," Bonney snapped back. "Regretfully, we are constrained to share the same street, since apparently our destinations lie in the same direction." He gave Sweet a contemptuous look and added, "As gentlemen, I would expect that we both could suffer in silence."

"Agreed, Sir," Sweet replied, "gentlemen should mind their own affairs." He was disappointed that Bonney did not respond to this allusion to spying upon his messmates.

They passed Gloucester Street, the main route from the shore to Government House on Tower Hill, where Bonney turned-off. He headed toward the top of the street, where a conglomeration of sticks and timbers arched the thoroughfare. Jumbo misread Sweet's intent stare after Bonney as curiosity and explained the celebratory arch. "Highness come visit Sierra Leone. Savvy?" He spoke slowly, as if to dullards or small children. The American had no response. Disappointment crossed Jumbo's face at this rebuff of his tour commentary and he silently continued southeast.

"You know, Marse Charles," Daniel began, "that Lieutenant Bonney ain't no spy for Trueman. He just tryin' to keep you from givin' that Trueman reason to do you evil."

Daniel had observed Bonney closely since Joshua's warning. The Marine Officer had plenty of opportunity to report Mr. Talliaferro for his constant caustic comments regarding the American situation. Joshua was certain that Bonney had not done so at any time. And it was clear to Joshua and Daniel that Mr. Bonney had no time for Trueman. "Man just wants keep the lid on 'til we home," Joshua had summarized. Daniel almost regretted warning Charles in the first place and was embarrassed by Sweet's unmannerly responses to Bonney. His mama surely be ashamed, the slave reflected.

38

Sweet shot Daniel an angry look. "None of your affair, Boy." Even if Bonney were not a spy, and he was undecided upon that point Charles reminded himself, the Marylander had no business trying to dictate his behavior.

Daniel snorted in dismissal. "How I explain at home, lettin' y'all ruin yourself by your stubborn head and too-fast tongue?" He smiled, adding, "Lord, your mama and my mama both have my soul to the Devil, I let you act so stupid!"

Sweet smiled despite himself. Daniel was right. Celia, Daniel's mother had raised him as much as his own mother. Daniel and he had been inseparable and in the same trouble all their lives. Explaining their relationship to Harry DePue, he had described Daniel as his "brevet older brother," responsible for minimizing the dangers he could not keep Charles out of all together. Sweet grinned at memories from stolen pies to more serious scrapes, as he answered, "Right about that, Dan'l, but I'll not be chivvied about by Mr. Bonney. I'll stand clear of his life and he damned well better bear-off from mine."

"Just don't be burning ships we may be wanting to use at future times, that's all," Daniel counseled as Jumbo led them further along Water Street.

They passed the newly constructed brick market building and the butcher yard on the shore cliff opposite, their senses accosted by the bleat and bellow of animals mixed with the smell of blood, the crack of machete on bone, and the yells of hawkers. Sweet turned his eyes from the carnage back to the market, a sea of color and activity. Most sellers were women dressed in wraparound skirts, "*lappas*." They encased their upper torsos in "*boobas*," long cloths wrapped tightly around the body at armpit level leaving the neck and shoulders bare. Obviously the brighter the cloth, the better; Southern cotton via Manchester mills, Sweet thought. The women squatted flat-footed behind their *blies*, round woven baskets containing merchandise ranging from plantains to imported pins. Scattered among them were a few male tailors and one or two male letter writers asked to, "*make book*," West African patois for any writing.

Beyond the market stood a double row of two-story frame structures, the ground floor reserved for trade, while the second-story ("first" here in keeping with British usage) provided living quarters. Sweet wondered where this style of architecture, common to the Caribbean, the South Coast of the United States and West Africa, had originated? Was the slave trade the common link, or just the climate? In front of one of these buildings flapped a faded Union Jack and a weathered United States gridiron designating the American Hotel. Above the door a hand scrawled signboard proclaimed, "Lunch-house."

"Pa Cabot there," Jumbo announced. "You *chop* there, *Jonathan yam*." Jumbo read the confusion in their faces. "You *eat* there, *American food*." Ah, understanding, he thought with relief. "Jumbo *chop* ... *eat* same. You *cut yamgah,* 'til we go boat. Savvy?"

Sweet understood that the large man would eat at the "lunch-house" and expected Daniel and himself to do likewise. He had no idea of the meaning of, *"cut yamgah."*

Foreclosing further interpretive efforts, Pa Cabot appeared wiping his hands on the skirt of a large bibbed apron before profusely pumping Sweet's hand in welcome. He ushered all three inside demanding they eat from his menu. There was no escaping the toughest piece of beef Sweet had ever tried to chew, Navy "salt horse" included.

Anxious to discuss happenings across the Atlantic, Pa Cabot produced a handful of smudged newspapers and spread them across the largest of the several tables of varying shapes that along with a variety of chairs and benches constituted the furnishings of his dining room. Most were copies of the *Sierra Leone Times* featuring re-printed North American dispatches to British papers. Sweet tried to keep his host happy with occasional comments as he skimmed through the stack, reading with some difficulty thanks to the poor light filtering through the opaque windows shaded by the building's veranda. The thought occurred to him that unwashed windows might be seen as reducing the heat in the building. One quotation starkly clarified how matters had changed. Reprinted in the *Sierra Leone Times* was a quotation from the *London Illustrated News,* in turn quoting the *New York Times* of April 13th:

> The reverberations from Charleston Harbor have
> brought about what months of logic would have been
> impotent to effect—the rapid condensation of public
> sentiment in the Free states. The North is now a unit.
> Party lines have shriveled, as landmarks disappear
> before the outpouring of volcanic lava. The crucial test
> of this is New York City – the spot most tainted by the
> Southern poison ... [of] lifelong Democrats. There will
> be no "fraternal blood" shed unless it be the blood of
> men who are willfully and persistently in the position of
> traitors.

Etched in Sweet's memory was the final line of an editorial from the November 7, 1860 *New York Tribune,* "We hope never to live in a republic whereof one section is pinned to the residue by bayonets." Now the bayonets were fixed. Why had the South Carolinians fired on Fort Sumter? That one act had destroyed all will for compromise.

Despite the sweat running in rivulets down his backbone, Charles Sweet felt a definite chill reading of Virginia's overwhelming vote to secede. It couldn't be true, he hoped more than believed. Somehow this would all be resolved; it had to be. He was proud-to-strutting, he admitted, to be an officer in the United States Navy. It was what he had always wanted to be, *expected* to be since he'd worn baby dresses. Life without the United States, without the Navy, without Gosport Navy Yard was incomprehensible, yet the print before him said that it was all coming asunder. He felt adrift in a great void and realized this must be what it was like to fall overboard at night. Overwhelming loneliness engulfed him; how he missed Captain Pennington. He had been so accustomed to simply following his mentor's lead when confronted with such momentous issues. Well, that no longer was an option. You're on you own, Lad, he concluded. He needed an immutable reference, a fixed point from which to chart his course, like the bricks in the courtyard of the Royal Observatory marking the Greenwich Mean Line. With such he could resolve his conflicting loyalties, but, he pondered, what was the immutable truth?

First it was God; "Thy will be done, On earth…." Such momentous events could not happen without the concurrence of Providence, he was certain. Second it must be his people, his culture, his…. Sweet searched his mind for a description of the concept he sensed more than intellectualized. Society, he thought; Hell, his *tribe*, those he identified with by blood, by circumstances, by outlook, by … by being who he was, by being a *Virginian*. If these third-hand stories were correct, the Virgin on the State Seal had resolved her conflicting loyalties by following her motto, *Sic Semper Tyrannis*. If the crisis were to be resolved by reasoned compromise, her loyalty to the federal union was unshaken. If others tried to trammel the Constitution, in large part the creation of Virginians, and compel her or others to remain by force, she owed them no loyalty, just one hell of a fight.

Sweet felt immeasurably better. He had found the polestar by which to navigate his personal passage through this crisis. The principle was consistent with the tenets of patriotism and fidelity, with his oath to uphold the Constitution, with his most basic loyalties, and the outcome was in the hands of The Almighty. What more could "patriotism and fidelity" mean? What more could a gentleman ask for, he reflected with a sigh of relief.

*   *   *   *   *   *   *   *   *   *

"This is even half true, Dan'l, Virginia will be as fought-over as the Plains of Troy." Sweet and Daniel were following Jumbo back to Government Steps as the Midshipman grappled with the revelations in the papers. Random thoughts pinwheeled through his head, skipping from shells bursting above Sumter to the African *restaurateur* adamantly refusing payment for the all-but-inedible beef, but accepting with pleasure Sweet's *dash* of a crown for his courtesy. It more than covered the cost of their meals. Sweet pursed his lips at more important concerns. "We must be home soonest we can."

41

"How we do that?" the slave questioned. "Trueman ain't about to let us go."

It was hard to think with this drained sense of unreality pressing upon his skull like a shrinking cap. Sweet shook his head and suggested Talliaferro might have an idea.

"Mr. Bonney might too," Daniel suggested. He had seen enough of Past Midshipman Talliaferro's hot-headedness to hope Charles would not follow the North Carolinian's advice.

"I'll not ask his interference, thanks all the same," Sweet answered sharply.

"May needs it, all the same," Daniel responded emphatically.

They walked on in silence for a while, each lost in his own internal grapplings with the sudden collapse of the accepted order of life. Passing Gloucester Street Daniel suggested they write home to let those at Sweetlands know that they were safe … for the moment at least.

Jumbo answered Sweet's question about a post office by turning in mid-stride and pointing up Gloucester Street. That was where Bonney was going, Sweet realized. The Officer of Marines had been carrying a sack under his arm; it must have been the Marines' mailbag. At Sweet's request for paper, pens, and ink, Jumbo led them further along Water Street to a low building, its back extending beyond the bluff and projecting downward 80 feet to the tidal flats. The proprietor, Mr. Sibyl Boyle, greeted them. (Later Sweet would learn that a vessel named *Sibyl*, commanded by a Captain Boyle had foundered south of the harbor mouth. He never discovered whether Pa Boyle or his parents had appropriated the names.)

Boyle's establishment was a cornucopia. Wax-encased Dutch cheeses promised a good combination with tinned English biscuits. Bolts of colorful cotton faced a wall from floor to ceiling. Without apparent system, tin ware, tools, even musical instruments were strewn about or hung from hooks on the rafters. Gold and silver jewelry glittered dully beneath a dusty glass-topped counter. Daniel noticed the butt of an English Adams revolver barely visible at the edge of Boyle's obligatory shopkeeper's apron. The merchant proffered a variety of pens, inks, and parchments. Sweet made his selection. Boyle stated the price. As he reached for his wallet, Jumbo seized Sweet's wrist.

"*Ayee*, Pa Boyle, this be thievery! We no pay such for book things!"

Five minutes of heated palaver followed, ending with Boyle reducing his price by one-third. Jumbo proudly squired his Americans into the brilliant sunlight of Water Street and led them southwest. He stopped at the foot of the giant Cottonwood just beyond St. George's "Cathedral," a bedraggled stone English country church showing the depredations of extended exposure to tropical weather. The Cottonwood stood at the top of the Slave Steps rising from the Bay to Water Street. Under its canopy, agents of Her Britannic Majesty had removed the shackles of innumerable slaves spared the

42

Middle Passage by the good offices of the Royal Navy. Sitting side-by-side upon one of the elevated roots of the ancient tree, master and slave wrote families at the same address. The irony did not occur to either of them, though Jumbo shook his head in amusement; he had taken a liking to these two young foreigners.

Half an hour later, Sweet stood, examined his watch, and set off purposefully. Surprised, Jumbo momentarily became the follower. At the Post Office, a throng of Africans milled about in what, only with the greatest exercise of the imagination, could be considered a queue. Sweet suggested the Americans find their own way to the jetty, if Jumbo would post their letters. The next issue was Jumbo's fee.

"Two shilling," Jumbo demanded.

Daniel's jaw dropped in mock horror. "Two shilling no good. Pay three-pence!" he challenged, not wanting his master to lower himself to haggling with this African.

"You no *cut yamgah* by Jumbo! He go charge you at law!" Jumbo threatened.

Sweet suddenly understood, "*cut yamgah*," it meant, *not pay*. He also respected Jumbo's threat; Sweet was well aware of Freetown's notoriety as the most litigious port in Africa. The last thing Sweet wanted was to be embroiled in the Freetown courts.

Daniel persisted, haggling to one shilling-three pence asked, eight pence offered, where it stuck. A crowd gathered, enjoying the entertainment. Sweet did not want to alienate the increasingly frustrated Jumbo to the point that he would not post the letters, let alone actually seek legal action. The midshipman stepped between the two hagglers.

"Pa Jumbo, I'll pay you ten pence for guide; for posting letters and for your good work, I'll *dash* you two more." A shilling a day was exorbitant pay in Freetown, reflected Sweet, so a shilling for the few hours Jumbo had spent with them was robbery, but he was tired of being the afternoon's street entertainment for the locals.

Jumbo looked down at Sweet and smiled. "And for *jam head* time, three pee!"

The very audacity of adding three-pence for his time haggling over the price, struck Sweet as humorous and he broke into a broad grin that Jumbo automatically reciprocated.

"Too much of a good thing, Jumbo," Sweet drawled.

"Too Good thing," Jumbo replied, then laughed loudly. Smiling broadly, he pocketed Sweet's shilling, and, letters in hand, trotted toward the Post Office. Halfway up Gloucester Street, he turned and called, "You make Jumbo all-time your guide at Freetown!"

Still smiling, Sweet waived in agreement. Then he and Daniel hurried to Government Steps. Emerging onto the pier they beheld, anchored alongside U.S.S. *Jamestown,* the African Steamship Company's vessel *Blackland,* the Royal Navy steam sloop *H.M.S. Falcon,* and the gun-vessel *H.M.S. Tourch,* the latter two constituting the Northern Division of the Royal Navy's West African Squadron. There would be quite a turnout at Government House that evening.

CHAPTER SEVEN

Government House was a two-story villa hinting of Mediterranean influences within a walled compound on a hill behind Freetown. It was an easy walk gently uphill along a route between tall grasses and occasional trees that had been spared during the deforestation to build Freetown and "make farm" to feed the colony's population. The route was more properly described as a broad path rather than a road. Most of Sierra Leone's thoroughfares were on the narrow side, since there was hardly a horse in the country thanks to the deadly tsetse fly spreading equine encephalitis. The few attempts to introduce horses had ended in the beasts dying within months, although a few lasted an entire year. If conveyance were required, native bearers would transport important personages in hammocks suspended from poles. To Bonney's eye it was too much like carrying a large dead animal back from the hunt and he was pleased that Trueman showed no interest in arriving like a dead boar. Still, there was no breeze as they trudged along between the better than ten-foot walls of vegetation. Bonney felt the perspiration irrupt over his face and across his back. Deliberately he slowed his pace and the others conformed.

Inside the compound at the foot of the steps to Government House, Captain Lindsey Page-Norton, 2nd West Indian Regiment, Officer Commanding Freetown Garrison, ran his left index finger along his mustache insuring that the hairs were properly aligned. He could feel the perspiration on his lip beneath and felt a trickle down his spine. Where were the blasted Jonathans, he wondered, and why had Governor Porter asked him to greet them at the front of the house rather than let them find their own way to the receiving line? Something His Excellency had concluded after their commander (Lieutenant Trueman, Page-Norton reminded himself) had paid the required visit upon the Governor the previous day. The American had been most agitated by the news of that incredible business in Charleston, as who would not be, Page-Norton reflected. Governor Porter obviously felt that the officers from *Jamestown* required special handling to ensure things went smoothly. Jolly good, the Captain concluded, but he wished the guests would hurry so he could return to the breeze in the public rooms above rather than sweltering in the dead air behind the compound walls at ground level.

Bonney was impressed by the way the two Negro soldiers in black shakos, red tunics, and white trousers slapped their muskets to "Present Arms" as the Americans passed through the gate. Page-Norton did not miss the compliment in the way the American Marine returned the salute of his sentries and smiled slightly as he tugged the hem of his tunic to insure he too looked smart. The officers exchanged salutes, then shook hands while introducing themselves. Courtesies completed, Page-Norton ushered the

Americans up the steps, passed houseboys who took their headgear, and to the receiving line.

Bonney kept his distance from Sweet. After the confrontation on Water Street, he had resolved to let the arrogant whelp be, in the phrase of a favorite Princeton professor, "hoist on his own petard," Shakespearian for blown-up by his own bomb. Still, he did not relish being Trueman's enforcer when the inevitable clash came.

As they queued to shake hands with the Governor, Bonney overheard Talliaferro whisper to Sweet that this was the first of many long lines in Sweet's inevitably distinguished naval career, though it might not be in *this* navy. To Bonney's surprise, Sweet responded with an angry glance. Daniel must have counseled his master, Bonney concluded; Sweet might even have listened.

Bonney saw Talliaferro as powder looking for a spark. In a state of agitation ever since Trueman's report the previous day, Talliaferro's expression, posture, set jaw all screamed defiance. He was seeking confrontation with their "Captain" and Devil take the consequences. To Bonney's and Sweet's relief, Talliaferro abstained from further comments as they exited the receiving line, paused at the punch bowl, and stepped onto the veranda as the sun set with a green flash beyond the Atlantic.

Bonney found the meal excellent, with the exception of the beef, driven down from Foullah Country according to the Captain of the 2nd West. Local barracuda and guinea fowl satisfactorily filled the requirements for fin and feather. The cheeses were a fine collection from Britain, as were the sweets. *Jamestown's* officers enjoyed the excellent wines along with everyone else at the table. Portuguese, Bonney decided, probably from The Azores, possibly Cape Verde, good, but strong.

He was pleased to see his shipmates, even Talliaferro, relax a bit, enough for him to hope they might make it through the evening without incident. He gave silent thanks to Bacchus for the benefits of the fermented grape, noting that it was not affecting "Temperance Trueman" who abjured all spirits. Bonney actually was enjoying himself for the first time since Pennington's death. With each glass Sweet was increasingly effusive about the wine, the food, the company. He could not possibly realize how loudly he was speaking, Bonney was certain.

"Mr. Sweet," Bonney spoke across and down the table, "a glass with you, Sir." He raised his goblet in salute and waited for Sweet to respond. Sweet hesitated; still smarting from their last exchange, Bonney wondered?

"Your health, Sir," he finally replied raising his own glass suspiciously.

"But lightly done, Sir," replied Bonney, "for the night is warm and the spirits strong."

Anger flashed across the Midshipman's face. "And those not up to it, should mind their own affairs, Sir!" Sweet roared defiantly, then tossed back the entire goblet.

Studiedly, Bonney sipped in response, cursing himself for doing more harm that good. Why couldn't he leave the snotty to his fate? He just seemed to spur Sweet to greater self-destruction. Thinking of his college experience, Bonney admitted self-destruction seemed to be his specialty.

Sweet attacked the wine with gusto in obvious defiance of Bonney, but not to the extent of Lieutenant Appleton whose cheeks were flushed by more than the heat. If Appleton kept up this pace, Bonney figured he would have an interesting meander to the jetty. The New Yorker had been outdone, however, by several of the *Blackland's* party.

The table rose as the governor's wife led the ladies' departure in a rustle of silks and sparkle of jewelry. With the tablecloth removed ("pulled" was the British phrase, Bonney recalled) and the lamps trimmed, the port and cigars made their counter-cyclical rounds. Visibly relaxed after his first inhalation, Governor Porter sat back in his angled chair, looked down the table, and breaking the silence observed how marvelously peaceful was the evening. A murmur of agreement encompassed the table, when one of *Blackland's* passengers, an older gentleman who had clearly enjoyed his wine, loudly observed, "Bit confounding for you young bloods, eh? Small glory here, biggest excitement chasing some poor sod with a load of wooly-heads intended for slavery in Cuba, or shooting up damned mud huts. Disappointing, what?"

There always had to be one to put a spanner in the works, the Governor regretted, a slight scowl furrowing his high forehead and dipping the ends of his moustache. Aloud he answered, "Yes, Mr. Swinton, we enjoy the age of the diplomat, not the soldier. At least among civilized nations, I dare say we shall see no great bloodbaths."

Swinton was not to be deterred. Looking fixedly at the Governor he carefully enunciated, "Ah, Governor, depends how you define 'civilized,' don't it? Jonathans bound to go at each other; could be *damned* bloody." Porter nearly gagged on his port. He had been thinking of African chiefs, not Americans.

Bonney sensed a flickering movement along the table as all eyes shifted to Trueman. "I assure you, Sir," The Lieutenant-in-Command rasped, "the United States is as civilized as any nation on earth and we shall have less trouble disposing of these miscreants than your government does with your rebels in Ireland." Trueman's jaw was set, his eyes afire.

Before the Governor could turn the subject, Talliaferro's voice resonated from the lower end of the table. "The *Hell* you say, Sir!" He was on his feet, his chair just saved from a backward crash by timely intervention of an African houseboy.

Bonney frowned in despair. Confrontation between the truculent Carolinian and the petty New Englander seemed unavoidable. With faint hope he looked to the Governor.

Damn Swinton, Porter thought. "Gentlemen, please," he calmed. "I believe you Americans share our tradition of not discussing politics in the mess."

"Sir, my apologies," Trueman rejoined, his voice steely. "I cannot sit here and have my country insulted or my officers condone treason."

"'Captain' Trueman," the Governor hurriedly replied, "Certainly Mr. Swinton meant no insult to the United States." Would the drunken old fool apologize, he wondered? "It is my understanding that your rather unique governmental structure accommodates alterations in the relationship among the various states, even to include states withdrawing from your federation." Bonney caught a hint of condescension as Porter continued, "Thus, I do not see how any of your officers have condoned treason."

Who in *Hades* was this Limey to lecture on the United States Constitution, Trueman fumed? Fighting to control his building rage, he rose deliberately from his chair while replying, "Your Excellency misconstrues our Constitution. There is no right to sunder the country. President Lincoln won the election fairly and these Southron cabals resort to treason, rather than accept defeat like gentlemen."

But Trueman was incorrect, Sweet thought rather blurrily. The constitutional principles were well known. This was an opportunity to clarify constitutional matters, to explain them and end the squabble; to best that damned Bonney at his own busybodied game. Sweet surprised even himself when he began to speak.

It was as if someone else were reciting how at the Naval Academy, they spent considerable time studying the nature of the United States. Sweet realized that somehow he was standing as well. Trueman must recognize, he continued, that many states, including Sweet's own, explicitly reserved the right to depart the Union as a condition to ratifying the Constitution. Trueman must recall the Virginia Resolution penned by President Madison and the Kentucky Resolution by Mr. Jefferson. New York and other Northern states had made similar declarations. All states had recognized this right. Why, the first serious suggestion of secession, Sweet observed with an obvious touch of glee, was made by Trueman's own Massachusetts and three of her New England sisters at the Hartford Convention in response to Mr. Jefferson's Neutrality Acts. On three subsequent occasions, Massachusetts had made to leave the Union. These were the adjustment of state debts, the Louisiana Purchase, and the Annexation of Texas.

"States are irrelevant, Sweet," snapped Trueman. "The Declaration of Independence was made by 'One People,' not a pack of petty states!"

Trueman had entered the Navy before the Academy existed, Sweet realized and determined to enlighten his commander with what he had learned at Annapolis. He explained how William Rawles' book, *Views of the Constitution,* the text at both Naval and Military Academies, stated, "Since, in all cases, the people retain the right to determine how they shall be governed, the people of a state possess the inalienable right to determine that their state shall leave the federal union." Amazingly, he realized, he had quoted *verbatim.* If he could do that, why could he not remember the name of the Captain of the 2nd West seated beside him?

Sweet was flabbergasted when Trueman rounded upon him like a cat upon an impudent mouse. He had only been trying to correct erroneous misunderstandings, so why was Trueman so irate, he questioned, recognizing he best have no more wine.

Trueman was the leader, Bonney thought. It was upon his shoulders to avoid such a display, but instead he was fueling it. Sweet seemed simply to be arguing a reasoned interpretation of recognized precedent as if this were a classroom discussion. Was he really that naive, Bonney wondered, or simply tipsily insensitive this evening? It did not matter. Trueman was about to eviscerate him. Whatever he said would goad Talliaferro into action. Bonney felt he owed a duty to his ship, his country, his Corps to stop this foolishness.

A quick glance along the table told him that Brooke, Appleton, Kunstler and the rest of *Jamestown's* officers were staying out of the affair. Perhaps, Bonney speculated, if Trueman were met with a calming voice of reason, that at the same time did not ignite Talliaferro, the situation could be salvaged. Sweet was right in any event.

"It also reads," Bonney heard himself say, "'the secession of a state from the Union depends on the will of the people of such state. The people alone … hold the power to alter their constitution.'" One look at Trueman and he wished he had not intervened.

"Impressive, Lieutenant Bonney," Trueman replied contemptuously, "to hear a Leatherneck quote *verbatim* from anything other than 'Rocks and Shoals.'"

Royal Marine First Lieutenant Robert Paltier's face turned as red as his tunic, his jaw clenching until his great muttonchop sidewhiskers twitched. He did not understand Trueman's references to "Rocks and Shoals," slang for the U.S. Naval Articles of War, a list of offenses and mandatory punishments allegorically as dangerous to seamen and Marines as rocks and shoals were to ships. Paltier did understand "Leatherneck" equaled the British term "Bootneck" – both services traditionally wore leather stocks – and that Trueman was insulting Marines, Royal or not.

Shocked, Bonney realized how far he had crossed the line in his impulsive rescue of Sweet. What had he been thinking? All Trueman's built-up anger at Talliaferro and Sweet, at Southerners in general now focused upon him. But he simply could not let this insult pass unanswered. "While, *like you*, I did not attend Annapolis," Bonney spoke deliberately, "I was fortunate enough to spend some three years at Princeton College."

"Three; bit short, eh, Mr. Bonney?" Trueman replied contemptuously.

Bonney felt his heart race, his breath shorten, yet he controlled his emotions. This was a battle of wits. "In answer to your question, Lieutenant," he stated deliberately, "pressing demands did not allow me to remain longer in New Jersey."

"Covers myriad of sins, that phrase," Appleton slurred.

Disregarding the drunk, Bonney explained how during a late night student discussion of the 'Peculiar Institution' of slavery, "A young man shared your position, Mr. Trueman." Bonney fixed his commander with a level stare concluding, "immediate, uncompensated, total emancipation of all persons held in servitude."

Governor Porter caught his breath. "Uncompensated? By Gad, West Indies emancipation cost the Crown twenty million pounds in 1833."

"Would save 'em twenty million!" slurred old Swinton.

Bonney explained that he had reminded his New Jersey schoolmate that northern states sold-off slaves as the process of ending chattel servitude. In fact, in 1804 New Jersey had enacted gradual emancipation that freed not a single slave, but provided that offspring born into slavery on or after the first of January 1805 were to be emancipated upon reaching the age of twenty-one years. New Jersey had been noted as a particularly eager exporter of slaves beginning in the early 1820's, Bonney had observed. "I merely asked how many his family sold south," Bonney added. "Gentleman took exception that, next morning, proved fatal. Circumstances dictated my departure from New Jersey."

Sweet was flabbergasted. Bonney had always been rather aloof; Sweet qualified his conclusion, except lately when he started sticking his nose where it did not belong. He was not exactly on the run from the law - New Jersey's criminalization of dueling only applied within her borders – but....

"The issue, Lieutenant," Trueman sneered, "is not how this vile institution was abolished in the past or even how it is to be abolished today, but rather the unlawful, unjustified, and treasonous behavior of the oligarchies at the South. Our sacred Union came into existence of the Will of the People, not of parochial state governments dominated by cabals whose members count their wealth in human flesh."

"*Enough!* By God, Sir, *Enough!*" Talliaferro smashed his fist on the table rattling the stoppers in the decanters. "If any oligarchy owes its wealth to the slave trade, it's the ship owners, masters, distillers, weavers, manufacturers and merchants at the North. A double-eagle says that rake-masted black devil hails from a day's sail of Boston!"

Governor Porter seized the opening. "So, 'Captain' Trueman, you've chased the *Black Jonathan?*" Before Trueman could respond to the Governor's unfortunate use of "Jonathan," His Excellency continued, "Captain Jennings,

I'm sure you have some questions for 'Captain' Trueman concerning that fellow, eh?"

Captain Jennings, *H.M.S. Falcon,* took the Governor's cue, "By Heaven, yes; playing blind-man's-buff with the sod on and off this year past. Not that raising her would do much good. I've not the slightest doubt she is American. Were we to overhaul her, damned fine trick the way she sails, we should inspect her papers and bid her fair winds. I'm not about to raise a diplomatic donnybrook like poor Moresby when he seized the *Pachita* red-handed and packed her off to New York, what, four years back?"

"Right, '57 it was," Governor Porter confirmed. "Your minister in London, 'Captain' Trueman, brushed aside the entire topic of slaving and protested most forcefully that seizing the vessel was solely a matter of the violation of your sovereignty."

"Then there was that business of the *Cortez* one of our gunboats seized off Cuba." Captain Jennings eyebrows rose in mock consternation, "Nearly had a war."

Hastily Porter explained, "Serious enough for Lord Napier - you recall him, 'Captain' Trueman, our ambassador to your government at Washington City - to suggest to Sir Houston Stewart commanding North American Station that his ships not bother with Jonathans."

"Still visit to confirm entitlement to your colors" injected Jennings. "Not actually search, you get my meaning, but young officers might sniff 'round a bit, eh?"

"You must understand that the excuse of suppressing the slave trade cannot be allowed to permit open contempt for the protection of the American flag or the freedom of our commerce," Trueman replied. "As for war...."

"Ah, 'Captain'...." Jennings began to respond, but the Governor cut him off before the "war" erupted at his table.

"Seen him, eh, 'Captain' Trueman, the rake-masted fellow?" Porter made repeated use of the courtesy title; clearly Trueman relished it. "Actually given pursuit? Please tell, 'Captain.' The full story, if you please."

Trueman realized that his behavior was beyond accepted limits for the ranking American at the Governor's table and Porter was offering a graceful way out. "Why yes," he replied after a deep breath, "fell in with her off the Niger. I doubt she had taken on cargo. Any event, she stood out to sea. We gave chase...."

Self-conscious in their defiance, Sweet and Talliaferro sat down. Bonney had remained seated with an air of detached bemusement. Trueman could have classified Bonney's pose as "Silent Disrespect" punishable under Rocks and Shoals.

"Good on you, Lef'tenant." Lieutenant Paltier of the Royal Marines was not an accomplished whisperer. His comment to Bonney, heard well up the table, broke the embarrassed silence among the junior officers. Even Talliaferro managed a slight smile.

Lieutenant Sawyer, of *H.M.S. Falcon* asked, "Nightly occurrence in your mess?"

"Thank God, no," answered Bonney. "As His Excellency observed, we share your tradition of abjuring discussion of women, religion, and politics in the mess; for good reason, as you can see."

"*Rather!*" responded the Englishman.

"Senior officer opens the subject, is fair game," interjected Talliaferro defiantly. "Besides, these are not ordinary times, and I shall not have my state, friends, and family slandered."

"You do have rather strongly held, and, if I may say so, most divergent opinions," volunteered Lieutenant Ryder of *H.M.S. Tourch*. "Don't envy you the voyage home. After tonight, rather strained, I shouldn't wonder."

"No wonder about it," Sweet agreed. He eyed Bonney inquisitively. Maybe Daniel was right; maybe Bonney was not Trueman's puppy and only trying to keep the lid on things until they could return to America? To his surprise, Sweet felt stirrings of respect for the Marine, almost enough to forgive his repeated interference in Sweet's affairs.

At the moment Jennings was holding Trueman's attention, but Governor Porter knew the discussion inevitably would strike some nerve evoking a further eruption. Reluctantly abandoning his cigar, His Excellency led the gentleman to rejoin the ladies.

*   *   *   *   *   *   *   *   *   *

Lady Porter needed only a glance to recognize the agitation; she had heard the louder statements through the flimsy tropical walls. Like an athlete bracing for an event, she stepped forward to make *all* her guests at their ease. The Americans were in several groups, congenial within themselves. She merely had to dilute these emotionally charged centers by mixing-in affable Britons.

Smiling, she placing her arm inside the right elbow of Captain English propelling the merchant captain toward several blue-coated Americans. *Blackland's* captain had visited America, she recalled aloud. Perhaps, she suggested, some of the guests might bring him up to times on those ports? As English rumbled confirmation through his salt-and-pepper beard, Bonney understood Lady Porter's intent. Remorseful at the display in the dining room, he quickly supported her, asking exactly where the Captain had called?

The Briton smiled. Yes, he had been up and down America's coasts rather thoroughly and found each port to have its own peculiar charm, English admitted, trying hard to avoid any suggestion of regional preference.

Did Bonney not agree as to the uniqueness of each of the Republic's major ports? Bonney assented, maintaining the banality. Lady Porter volunteered that the variety must be absolutely fascinating; why, from the Scandinavian coasts of Maine to the exotic tropics of New Orleans, America had nearly as much diversity within the immense country as Britain did within the Empire.

"Ah, New Orleans, now there is a wondrous town," English rumbled. "Bet our friend Louis Napoleon wishes old uncle Boney'd not sold it to you lot!"

"At the time the Royal Navy made keeping it rather awkward," responded Bonney. "We are grateful for the assistance in convincing the Emperor to let Louisiana go."

"Just might need y'all's help again," observed Talliaferro joining the group. "Appears others might need convincing to 'let Louisiana go.'"

Captain English blinked, mistrusting his hearing. Disregarding Talliaferro he mumbled something about the magnificent variety of goods from the vast middle of the continent, otter pelts to orchid blooms all in one town. Bonney raised his voice inviting Sweet to join them, suggesting the Midshipman could bring Captain English up to date on New Orleans. And help dilute Talliaferro's infernal tendency to trigger confrontation, he thought. Bonney explained to the Captain and Lady Porter that Charles' family owned a prominent ship chandlery business with close ties to a firm in the Crescent City.

With Harry DePue, Sweet was talking to two British officers, amused that Sweet had met Sybil Boyle. The Captain of the 2nd West laughingly explained Boyle's story to the American midshipmen. What was this captain's name, Sweet demanded of himself, disgusted at his poor recall. Chuckling, all four stepped to Lady Porter's gathering.

"When were you last at New Orleans, Captain?" Sweet could not name him either.

"Heavens, my lad, decade, I shouldn't wonder," replied English with a chuckle. "But, I recall full well the amazing variety of goods available."

"Yes, Sir," agreed Sweet. "It is the natural outlet for the entire continent between the Appalachians and the Rockies. The Mississippi receives goods down the Ohio, the Tennessee, the Missouri, the Arkansas, the Red, the Yazoo…. All the rivers feed down to New Orleans. It's the natural flow of commerce for the continent, despite the best efforts of the North to divert everything east to their ports and factories."

"How so?" asked Captain English innocently, then wished he hadn't.

"Ever since the National Road, the North has been fighting against nature to have the bounty of the heartland move east – west rather than down the Mississippi."

"Now wait a minute, Charles," interjected DePue. "That rather overstates matters." What in Tarnation had come over Sweet these last few days, Harold wondered? It seemed every chance he had, Charles was attacking the national government or those sections loyal to the idea of nationhood.

"Really, Harry? Just look at the record. First off, Massachusetts nearly secedes opposing the Louisiana Purchase. Then the codfish aristocracy at the North can't stop westward expansion, so they try shanghaiing it with projects pulling commerce their way: National Road, Erie Canal, Ohio and Erie Canal, now all those east – west railroads…."

"And rightly so, Charles. Infrastructure, that's what makes a nation strong."

"And keeps a region artificially rich at the expense of its fellows, Harry."

"How so, Charles? There's some pretty extensive levee work by the Corps of Engineers along the Mississippi and of course the national funds in those fortifications the Southrons are helping themselves to right and left."

"Hardly a fair return on what's paid into the National Treasury, Harry. Only federal revenue source worth mentioning is the tariffs and seventy-five percent of that's been paid by Virginia, Georgia and the Carolinas. South pays the lion's share and gets the kitten's milk."

"Don't be a fool, Charles." DePue snapped. "What makes Britain 'Great'? *Industry,* the means of producing goods from ribbons to railroads. Northern industrialization makes the United States strong and transportation is *absolutely mandatory* to that industry and the ability to apply strength where needed. It *makes* us a *nation!*"

"*Us,* Harry?" Sweet replied with growing frustration. "Where you get this 'Us'? We at the South pay the federal piper and you at the North do all the dancing. Right wearisome being victimized Peter to benefit your Paul!"

Sobering, Sweet was aghast at what he had just said. It sounded like some firebrand secessionist, which, he reminded himself, he certainly was not. It was just that some things needed to be corrected and some folks needed better understanding of the Constitution. Wasn't that the oath they'd taken, he asked himself? That meant upholding it against sectional interests or fanatical do-gooders prying into other folks' affairs, which seemed to have been a Puritan propensity since Plymouth Rock.

Fully engaged neither Sweet nor DePue realized all present were gravitating toward them. It had gone too far for Bonney to stop. He just let it roll.

"Federal Government hardly paid all the cost, Charles," observed DePue. "State bonds and heaps of *private* monies helped fund this *national* investment."

"All subsidized by taxes on Southern economies, Harry; admit it."

"Admit what, Charles; that we at the North invest in the betterment of the nation rather than tying up funds in human chattels?"

That made Sweet mad. Harry hadn't seemed so self-righteous when visiting Sweetlands. "Low blow, Harry!" he snapped. "You know, well as I do, New England got the Federal Government to assume state debts after the Revolution and they were paid off by taxes on Southern imports or, same thing, too high prices for goods we could have cheaper and better from somebody else." Sweet looked around. "Like the British, perhaps?" He took a step toward DePue adding, "And don't be so high and mighty about 'human chattels' either. It's the Southron agricultural system that produced the taxes to bail Yankeedom out from the Revolution debts, pay your too high prices, and give you the cussed money to try to divert commerce from New Orleans."

"*ENOUGH*, Mr. Sweet!" Trueman's voice cut the air as Sweet paused for breath.

Talliaferro fixed Trueman with a direct stare and drawled, "Yes, Sir, Yankees done right well out of slavery. Y'all made the trade goods, built, owned, and crewed the ships, carried the darkies to America, sold them at one hell of a profit, taxed and still tax the Sam Hill out of the goods needed to make them pay. Then y'all got the effrontery to get all high-and-mighty moral about it, when it was good part Southrons worked the end of slave importations into the nation. Never mind. Y'all just carry them to Cuba."

"*TALLIAFERRO!*" bellowed Trueman.

"Hell, I'd rather be a darkie in a Wilmington rice patch, than some poor Patty Irish debt slave in a Yankee factory or mine. Be shut of y'alls' holier-than-thouing makes secession damned attractive."

"*Mr. Talliaferro!* You will consider yourself under arrest!" Trueman's face now flamed with color. "You will return immediately to *Jamestown* and confine yourself to your quarters." Trueman's eyes flickered across the faces. "Mr. DePue, assume the duties of Acting Lieutenant in place of Mr. Talliaferro."

"Sir, I believe I am junior to Mr. Sweet." Harold DePue's response was automatic. His appointment to Annapolis had been dated four days after Sweet's.

"By Heaven, Sir! Do you contest my orders?" For a second Bonney wondered if Trueman would arrest DePue as well. He did not get the chance.

"Therefore I assume, Sir," Sweet instinctively intervened deflecting Trueman's wrath from DePue to himself, "that I also am under arrest?"

Trueman pivoted toward Sweet. "By God, Sir, you are. Mr. Bonney, escort Talliaferro and Sweet to the ship and confine them to their cabins … *under guard!*"

A sensation of shock, rather than an audible sigh or physical movement, rippled through the gathering. Even Trueman sensed it. With it came the realization that he had effected a disastrous embarrassment to himself, his Service, his country. Gentlemen were not put under guard. Had he just tacitly admitted that American officers could not be taken at their honor? The Limeys must be absolutely chortling behind their stoic expressions. He had to extricate himself, but the Marine Lieutenant would not let him.

"Mr. Talliaferro and Mr. Sweet are *gentlemen,*" Bonney challenged deliberately.

Trueman knew that all present agreed. "Treason removes that status, Lieutenant."

For a second Bonney thought of defying the order, but that was out of the question for an Officer of Marines. Instead, he made no response to his commander, but, looking in turn at Talliaferro and Sweet, simply said, "*Gentlemen* ... If you please."

Somehow Trueman kept from exploding at this affront; Bonney at least was obeying his orders. Instead, Trueman turned to Governor Porter apologizing for the behavior of his officers, asserting he had not realized the putrification of treason had spread to his wardroom. With the Governor's permission, the remaining Americans would withdraw in hopes that the others might yet receive some peace and enjoyment from the evening.

Porter denied any need to apologize. Indeed, while no one took enjoyment from the travails of America, the discussions had been most informative. For all present His Excellency wished Trueman and his officers a speedy crossing and a peaceful resolution to the present state of affairs. If anyone might assist in *Jamestown's* departure, including the Governor himself, they were anxious to do so. Should Trueman meet with any impediments, he was to contact Porter directly. Understanding Trueman's need to return to his ship, His Excellency bid him good night.

Thus relieved of the obligation to pay their respects to Lady Porter and take their leave of the other guests, Trueman and his officers exited the room without further comment. Descending the steps of Government House, the Americans heard Swinton's voice, loud with drink, announce, "*Damned bloody!* Mark my words. What it will be; damned bloody. But Porter is right; it's diplomat days among *civilized* nations."

CHAPTER EIGHT

Sweet twitched into consciousness in the sweltering confines of his tiny cuddy. Indifferent to the sweat-soaked nightshirt sticking to his skin, his mind focused upon the disastrous evening at Government House. Whatever happened at home, he was positive that the last twenty-four hours had put paid to his career in the United States Navy. He doubted a court martial would sustain Trueman's allegations of treason and mutiny; lesser offenses like disrespect or conduct unbecoming perhaps. But, the affair would follow him through his career, likely cutting it short of command. Influence could start you on the promotion ladder and perhaps move you ahead of your peers. Influence was much less effective in overcoming negative reputation. He worried about informing his family, the reactions of Governor Wise, Captain Buchanan, and others who had assisted his matriculation at the Naval Academy. What was he thinking? The realization shocked him. If Virginia had seceded, hadn't they all just done similar things? He had no career.

He swung out of his bunk, stooping as the timbers of the deck above, the "overhead," brushed his hair. He pushed outward on his cuddy door. It moved less than two inches.

"Sorry, Mr. Sweet. Can't come out." The voice belonged to one of the Marines, older man over thirty, "Orrin," Sweet thought his name was. Sergeant Banning was not chancing a younger guard being influenced by his prisoner's rank.

"Now listen here, Orrin, I need to use the head."

"With respect, Sir, you're to use this." The louvered door opened slightly; the sentry proffered a bucket. "I'll pass word for Dan'l when you want it out, Sir."

"Where's Mr. Talliaferro?" Sweet was exasperated. The officers' quarter-gallery was not ten paces from his cuddy.

"Mr. Talliaferro's cuddy, Sir, but not to talk. Orders. Sorry."

"*What?*"

"Not Orrin's fault, Charles." It was Talliaferro. "Be patient; 'this too shall pass.'"

"Now, Sir, enough of that." Orrin was not to be overawed. "Orders is both of you Sirs to be quiet until we raise Boston. Captain going straight there, so to try you for treason and not have some court martial with Southrons let you off."

"How y'all know this, Orrin?" Talliaferro's voice was icily ominous.

"Heard him say direct to Mr. Appleton, Sir, just before watch. To give matters to Federal Persecutor, Sir, so it be jury of citizens, not Rebels protecting they own, Sir."

Orrin's misstatement probably had more truth in it than he knew, Sweet thought. If Trueman reflected Boston's mood it would be more of a persecution than a prosecution. It occurred to Sweet that, under present circumstances, Freetown would not be such a bad place to leave the ship. After using the bucket as intended, he quietly raised the lid of his sea chest and retrieved pencil and paper. In small block letters he printed, "MR. T & I MUST NOT SAIL W/ SHIP. IDEAS? WHOM WE TRUST? CAN'T TALK, WRITE. TELL MR. T. CS."

It took two minutes after Orrin boomed out, "Dan'l to the wardroom," for the young man to knock on Sweet's cuddy. Orrin stepped aside allowing the door to open, but prevented Daniel from entering. "No visitors, Sir, sorry."

"Orrin! He's my *servant*, not a social guest. Don't be ridiculous."

"Sorry, Sir; orders."

Sweet held up the bucket by its rope handle using both hands. As Daniel's golden-brown fingers closed between Sweet's fists, he felt the tube of paper against the underside of the hemp. A glance of understanding pass between them and Daniel was gone. Staring at the closed hatch, for the unnumbered time Sweet silently thanked his father for having the foresight, technically illegal though it was, to teach Daniel to read.

*　　*　　*　　*　　*　　*　　*　　*　　*　　*

"Deuced sorry, Lef'tenant," sympathized Commander Bounce, Royal Navy, the portly middle-aged Captain of the Port of Freetown. "Old tub watered Nelson, I shouldn't wonder. Stands condemned. Any water taken into her comes out brackish right as not."

Bonney greeted Bounce's statement with resignation. Short of officers, Trueman had tasked the Marine with replenishing *Jamestown's* water supply. At least he was removed from opportunities to run afoul of his "Captain," Bonney admitted with some relief.

Bonney and Bounce stood in the window of the Commissariat looking eight stories down upon an aged water hoy riding low in the water at the foot of the cliff. The stubby little barge might well have seen service in the Napoleonic Wars, Bonney reflected. If the caulking in her seams was in the same disrepair as the rest of her, Bonney had no doubt that the incoming tide would infiltrate her tanks contaminating the fresh water she was designed to carry to ships in the roadstead.

"Most inconvenient for all." Bonney turned to face the speaker, Lieutenant Robert Paltier, Royal Marines, approaching from the door. "We've had to put casks in the boats and run a hosepipe from Sanders Brook uphill of the Colonial Hospital to the beach. We make quite certain to draw from well upstream of the hospital. No telling what the natives drop in the water, eh?" Obviously, Paltier also had commanded a watering party. "Were I

58

you," he continued, "I should wait until morning. Try aught this afternoon means running hose through the fish market below King Jimmy's Bridge. All costs, avoid battle with the market women." Paltier's smile was genuine.

The Port Captain readily agreed assuring Bonney that every barrister in Freetown would bless him for the flood of litigation disrupting the fish market would engender.

Paltier offered to show Bonney where to draw water. Why not, Bonney thought, observing aloud that clearly Paltier had avoided the wrath of the magistrate as well as contagion among his crew. The two Officers of Marines took their leave of the Port Captain, stepped into the merciless sunlight of Water Street, turned right, and moved at a respectable pace past Mr. Heddle's establishment toward the center of town.

*　　*　　*　　*　　*　　*　　*　　*　　*　　*

Jamestown's deck was organized chaos. Topmen dismantled the jury-rigging, the makeshift foretopmast pieced together from the remains of the main yard that had enabled *Jamestown* to limp to Sierra Leone. Just forward of the taffrail the Cooper examined hoops and staves and reassembled water casks. By the starboard entryport, Mr. Brooke, the Surgeon, and Mr. Flint, the Purser, mustered several hands. Daniel moved forward in hopes of catching their attention. It was not long in coming. He was swept up into a working party the two were taking ashore for meat and fresh produce.

At Dougan's Wharf, a frowning Jumbo scanned the Americans. Making eye contact, Daniel sensed the big man's desire to talk. As the working party move off toward the market, Jumbo followed.

In front of the "Bazaar," as the new market building popularly was known, the Surgeon selected three sailors and turned right to the slaughter yard. The Purser with Daniel and four others proceeded into the market. They stopped before a grinning *ma*, as the market women were called, with several large *blie* of oranges. Mr. Flint asked the price, seemed taken aback by the response, and attempted to negotiate a discount for purchasing her entire inventory. Daniel, now familiar with Sierra Leonian commerce, nodded to Jumbo. It took little convincing for Flint to retain the giant as negotiating agent and to rely upon Daniel to interpret the more alliterated patois. The little group moved on to a lithesome young woman selling greens. Daniel reconciled himself to a long morning.

For more than two hours Mr. Flint, Daniel, and Jumbo worked their way among the stalls buying out *ma* after *ma*, their progress preceded by an inflationary spiral. Flint, perspiring heavily, called for a rest shortly before midday. Jumbo suggested the American Hotel. Joined by the Surgeon, they passed between Pa Cabot's faded flags into the shade of the Liberian's taproom. Messrs. Flint and Brooke took a table and paid no notice as Daniel and Jumbo went to the rear of the premises.

After seeing to the officers, Cabot finally entered the pantry through the bead drape. The flimsy divider only partially blocked observation and minimally inhibited sound.

"Hear Sweet got plenty big *bob* ..." Pa Cabot began, wiping his hands on his soiled apron. He noticed some question on Daniel's face and elaborated, "big *trouble* with Trueman, savvy?"

Daniel nodded, not surprised that the confrontation at Government House was common knowledge. Few secrets existed at Big House, regardless of the continent.

"He in *Jamestown* jail?" Cabot continued. Daniel nodded. "How much time, that boat stay at Sierra Leone?" Daniel held up two, then three fingers. Cabot nodded. From the taproom came the Surgeon's voice reading aloud from the *London Illustrated News*.

"Sweet not want to go America?" Jumbo interjected. His voice had a tinge of incredulity.

"Not by that Navy ship," responded Daniel.

"Trueman not want Sweet rest at Sierra Leone?" the innkeeper continued.

"Trueman wants Sweet and Talliaferro in America for hanging," Daniel responded.

"*Enty*!" Cabot exploded in the universal West African expletive that could mean surprise, emphatic truth, or scathing disbelief, depending upon the context. "I savvy Talliaferro. He talked good to Pa Johnson, the pilot." Cabot grinned.

"Indeed," Daniel replied with the root word for *enty*. "He ain't no friend to Trueman."

"*Enty*! I savvy. Talliaferro, Sweet, not want to sail away with Trueman." Pa Cabot was almost gleeful. "They be gone off that boat tomorrow. We fix it so, *one time*."

*　　*　　*　　*　　*　　*　　*　　*　　*　　*

The two Lieutenants of Marines set a brisk pace along Water Street. Between the Bazaar and the slaughter yard, Bonney stopped the boatswains mate in charge of the Purser's working party and printed a note warning the ship of the circumstances. "WATER HOY UNSERVICABLE. MUST FILL CASKS FROM STREAM. MAY REQ. HELP RN. MAKING RECONNAISSANCE OF WATER POINTS. LT. BONNEY." Bonney instructed the petty officer to give it to the Officer of the Deck. Coordination accomplished, they continued toward the watering point.

Perspiring profusely, at last they halted above the single masonry arch of King Jimmy's Bridge and looked inland along Sanders Brook. Paltier indicated a pool near a large mango tree about 75 yards above the hospital, explaining that its depth allowed hoses to be well submerged for good suction and was above any point where they would pick up dead fish or other trash. Both *Tourch* and *Falcon* had drawn water there.

Bonney ran his eyes along the stream to where it passed underneath the single stone arch of King Jimmy's Bridge and down to St. George's Bay, a considerable distance. Aloud, he doubted *Jamestown* carried enough hose. Paltier looked pensive, recalling he had used hose from both *Falcon* and *Tourch*. Captain Jennings should be agreeable to assisting, he ventured, but compatibility of British and American couplings was uncertain. Bonney suggested they leave that to the sailors.

Paltier raised his gaze to *Jamestown*. The jury-rigged foretopmast was unshipped and slinging the new main spar well advanced. "Seems all good harmony from here."

Bonney shook his head. "Would to God it were so."

"I dare say. No offence by observing that your country's divisions are fully reflected in your ship's company, at least among the officers. Ehr ... understandable of course."

It was no secret after last evening, Bonney admitted wryly, observing that the division had been long in coming and had more layers than an artichoke. Still, Paltier mused that it was startling to an outsider; they tended to see America as a uniform mass, a "people."

Bonney pursed his lips. How to explain the mysteries, the confusion of an imperial republic that had been united more by resistance to the British Crown eighty-five years before than by true commonality of interests or even beliefs? Some of it was the ancient competition between agrarian and urban societies, he explained. Last evening, Paltier had heard the debate over whether the great wealth of the continent would flow toward the Northeast or down the Mississippi and the reliance of the national government upon tariffs on Southern imports for the lion's share of its revenues.

There also was the great fear of the laboring classes of the North and the immigrant Germans and Irish of competition from slave labor, mostly stirred up by the abolitionist press, and the same fear by the laboring Whites of the South if the slaves were freed. They could not both be right Bonney opined with a humorless chuckle.

Then there were real fears of slave uprisings instigated by radical abolitionists, Bonney observed, like that murderer John Brown. The revolts at the end of the last century of the Jamaican "Maroons," some of whom had been transported to Sierra Leone to join the Creoles, sporadic slave revolts in the South such as Nat Turner's in Virginia, the massacres of Haiti, and the very recent Sepoy Mutiny in India all gave good cause for alarm.

"Slavery" as a cause was a misnomer, Bonney continued. "Slavery" was shorthand for whether new states entered the Northern or Southern Congressional voting bloc. The North would raise the issue, then make concessions in exchange for Southern concessions on protective tariffs or federal projects or immigrants to nurture Yankee industry. Except for an extremist few, Bonney explained, most Americans, North and South, wished all slaves, all Negroes gone from America. That was the impetus for the colonization societies encouraging free Negroes to return to Liberia. Reportedly, Lincoln himself favored the policy.

Truth was, observed Bonney, dominant Northern interests could not afford to overturn the South's economy by abolishing slavery or drive it to independence. Were the South's cotton economy to collapse, the biggest protected market for Northern goods and only significant tax base of the Federal Government would disappear. Were the Cotton States to be independent, Yankee mill owners would have to compete with Europeans for Southern cotton, Yankee bankers and insurers for Southern borrowers and insureds, and Yankee captains for the Southern carrying trade. "North and South, like Jefferson said," Bonney summarized, "we got 'the wolf by the ears and can't figure how to turn loose.'"

Bonney paused for a moment. Paltier waited without comment, so he continued, "The real issue that will not go away, and upon which it appears now that there can be no compromise, is what powers are held by the Federal Government and what powers are retained by the States. And" Bonney said wryly, "the belief seems to change depending upon whether one is in power in the national government or not. Five years ago, Northern abolitionists like William Lloyd Garrison were demanding New England and New York secede, rather than enforce the Fugitive Slave Act. Now, after Sumter, they claim never to have heard of such a right."

He looked to Paltier for comment, saw there would be none, and continued, "Comes down to how close a man is to those who decide his fate. If a man doesn't talk like you, doesn't feel the same breezes, hear the same songbirds, worship in the same way, fear the same fears, hope the same hopes, and dream the same dreams, should he have the power to rule over you? I guess it comes down to what you think the Founding Fathers, sort of our Barons of Runnymede, understood when they created the United States and just how much you think one man's entitled to meddle in another man's business ... and that seems to change with who has the big end of the stick."

Bonney kept his gaze fixed toward the water, but Paltier knew full well that he was not focusing upon *Jamestown,* the harbor, or even the Bullom Shore seven miles distant. They stood in silence for an indeterminate time. "And you, Lef'tenant Bonney?"

Bonney continued to gaze through the African heat into some unknown. Finally, he turned slowly to the British officer. "Paltier...." He hesitated before interjecting, "and I do not believe that I could say this and be understood by anyone in the whole damned world, other than an Officer of Marines," and then continued, "I shall do my duty to my Corps. I shall see the ship home, despite her commander, not for him, not for some abstract of country, but for the Honor of my Corps. Once there, I shall do the most painful thing I'll do my entire life, resign my commission and go South. First,

I believe my state, Maryland, my *home*, will secede despite Federal troops invading the legislature. Baltimore's citizens already have taken-on Federal troops and are living under the muzzles of Federal cannon. The place is one great prison camp. Second, I'm not about to take orders from a lot of people who don't breathe my air, fear my fears, and dream my dreams. But I'll *never* disgrace my Corps."

They stood in silence for an uncertain time. Then, without comment or expression, Lieutenant Paltier slowly extended his hand to Lieutenant Bonney. They clasped rather than shook. Finally, Paltier said, "Marine to Marine, I do so understand."

*   *   *   *   *   *   *   *   *   *

Cabot watched from the doorway until Jumbo and the Americans disappeared around the corner returning to the market, then bolted his door and hurried to an ochre-colored house near the Police Courts. The ground floor housed the offices of one of Freetown's most flamboyant Creole barristers, Halcyon Nevis, Esq. He was friend, counselor, and financial backer of Cabot and the brains behind everything that the Liberian refugee did. Cabot's news energized the lawyer, for it held the possibility of advancing his plans regarding certain unpleasant trends in Liberia affecting both their interests. Now, he reflected, he merely had to decide how best to exploit the Americans.

*   *   *   *   *   *   *   *   *   *

"Half of states leave, ain't no more nation, like was we signed," Thoms whispered hoarsely, his walrus-like mustache twitching.

"I tell you, Thoms, won't be no chance to say 'I'm walkin'' and just sashay off of this nor no other Navy tub," replied Boatswain's Mate Peck in an equally vehement semi-whisper. "Either you stays or hang a deserter." Peck sported a full beard around his chin, rather like the new President, except for the copper glint. "Besides, you dumb Swede, you're not even a Southron."

"Yah, nor Northerman neither, I'm thinking," Thoms snapped back. "Besides, I got family to Gosport."

"Family?" snorted Peck. "As the Bible says, I 'knowed' your 'family' before you did, as did half this and most other crews. That floozy's pulled an oar for most the fleet."

"You shut God damned trap, there!" snapped Thoms, menacingly rising from his stooped position by the forward hatch.

"Easy, All," commanded Sergeant Banning coming up behind the sailors with Corporal Dyer, both perspiring freely in fully buttoned navy blue wool frockcoats. "What's the fuss?"

"Dumb Swede thinks he can walk account of the secesh business," snorted Peck.

"Why not?" demanded Thoms. "No United States, no Navy of United States, sure."

"Only reason he thinking of walking is a strumpet in Gosport," harrumphed Peck.

"Damn you, Peck. Good Girl!"

"Steady, Thoms," ordered Sergeant Banning. "No cause to fight over a woman five-thousand miles away."

Dyer thought he noticed the hint of a smile at the corners of the big Sergeant's mouth. Banning was clean-shaven and unlike a bearded man, had to struggle to keep his quick emotions from expressing themselves on his visage.

"Well, I still right. Country change, Navy change, I can change too, I'm thinking," Thoms responded.

"Won't let you," rejoined Peck. "Right Banning? I'm right, ain't I?"

"Holy Trinity, Peck," replied the Sergeant, "I don't know. And I ain't paid to know. Do your duty, both. We get back across the pond, then we find out what's what." Banning was uncomfortable with such talk.

"Seems fair, at least they let the Southrons go home to their states," Dyer observed.

"Well, that do seem fair, Dyer," responded Peck. "Like as if you were Jack Tar and come the Revolution? Wasn't that what British impressments was all about?"

"That were later, Peck," replied Sergeant Banning, wishing the conversation would end.

"Same idea, Sergeant. Man's home leaves an empire, he got a right to leave too."

"All I know, Peck, is you and Thoms and Dyer and me all took the oath and bound to live by it, least until the Navy says how it reads the tea."

"But who's that oath to, I'm thinking, Sergeant," Dyer mused. "The Swede's got a point, if the South secedes, the people at the South ain't Americans no more and, at least for the Americans joining the Navy," he glanced at Thoms and continued, "you think it's account of them being Americans that they join. So, if they ain't Americans no more, then it's sort of a different deal, see?"

"Yeah, Dyer, maybe." Banning was frowning at the complexity.

"Say you gets married, some fellow makes light of your sister-in-law?" Dyer asked.

"Honor-bound to thrash the clod," observed Sergeant Banning, momentarily forgetting the dangerous nature of the subject matter.

Peck and Thoms shook their heads affirmatively.

"Say your wife dies. Ain't your sister-in-law no more, right?" Dyer continued.

"*Ja,* sure not," answered Thoms.

"Say," continued Dyer, "you never got along with this used-to-be sister-in-law and you really agree with what the Old Boy said anyhow?"

"Married to the sister, you got to thrash him," asserted Peck to general agreement. "Not married no more, she ain't your sister-in-law."

"None of your matter," observed Thoms.

"You saying the Old Union's like the dead wife, and the whatever's left under the Old Flag's the sister-in-law?" summarized Sergeant Banning. "If you ain't related to the sister-in-law no more, she has no right to call on you to fight her fights," he concluded.

"And that's true, even if you took on to before she stopped being your sister-in-law," Peck said with conviction.

"Well, that's the concern, right?" responded Dyer. "I mean, what do you think?"

"You right by me, Dyer. No fighting her battles that happen, specially I don't like her much," concluded Thoms.

"Guess I agree," mused Peck, as if agreeing with Thoms in itself was unbelievable.

"Sensible, sure," affirmed Sergeant Banning. "But, we still are for getting this damned great ship…."

"*Stand where you are!*"

Banning looking up at Lieutenant Trueman's scowling face, automatically came to attention, and saluted. "'Day, Sir." How long had the "Captain" been there?

"*Silence!* You men are all under arrest. *Master-at-Arms!*"

"Christ," Banning heard Peck mutter.

CHAPTER NINE

It was mid-afternoon when Lieutenant Bonney pulled himself up *Jamestown's* side. As his eyes cleared deck level, he froze, incredulous. Arms fully extended above their heads, wrists strapped together, their unnaturally elongated bodies balanced on the balls of their feet, four men were suspended from the new main yard. Barefooted, stripped to the waist, they squinted to block the tropical afternoon sun full in their faces. Two already had sunburn-inflamed trunks, while the others were shielded by mahogany tans.

The images flickered through Bonney's mind without really registering. His attention was locked on the belaying pin forced into each man's mouth and held in place by cord around the back of each neck. The punishment was common in both Naval and Land services for insubordinate or disruptive behavior or speech. Small trickles of blood ran down either side of the men's jaws where the iron shafts protruded from just behind their wisdom teeth. The sunburned men were his Marine non-commissioned officers.

Bonney catapulted onto the deck hurrying toward them, drawing his penknife from his waistcoat pocket. *Damn* Trueman! He fumed. How dare he do this without informing him? Bonney was not even aware of his bellow, "What in *Hell* is this?"

"Mr. Bonney!" Trueman's voice slammed out from the quarterdeck. "Belay that!"

Bonney spun facing his commander who was striding toward him. Except for the click of Trueman's shoes, absolute silence enwrapped the deck. Bonney spoke first as the distance narrowed, demanding the meaning of the insult to his noncoms. There was no deference to Trueman's rank or position in his seething tone.

"These men are under punishment on my *personal* orders." Trueman took up the challenge, flinging it back. "I warned you that I would not tolerate sedition aboard my ship, and *by God*, Sir, I will not!"

"Sedition? Those are *Marines!*"

"Mr. Bonney, I don't give a Dutch *dam* if they are archangels. There will be no treason aboard my ship. And you, Sir, are on the brink of committing it yourself."

From some well of rationality, a cold calmness banked the fire in Bonney's head. "Sir, I know these Marines and I am shocked that any action of theirs could be construed as seditious. Further, I am surprised that, as members of my contingent aboard the Lieutenant's ship, they should undergo punishment without my first being informed."

"As '*Captain*' here, I shall decide what constitutes violation of the Articles of War and of my personal orders. *I* shall determine as well when immediate action is appropriate. And, Mr. Bonney, I shall *not* be questioned by my subordinates. *Am I understood?*"

"*Yes, Sir!*" Bonney barked, then more calmly, "May I know their offense?"

"Later. Since you have taken it upon yourself to diddle ashore, we are behind times in watering. You will join us on the quarterdeck."

Trueman marched aft. Bonney had no choice but to follow. Between the transom and the wheel, stood a group of frockcoated officers. He recognized Lieutenant Appleton, Acting Lieutenant DePue and Mr. Goode, *Jamestown's* Boatswain, the only one in a petty officer's jacket. With them were three officers of the Royal Navy: Captain of the Port Commander Bounce and lieutenants Sawyer of *Falcon* and Ryder of *Tourch*.

Trueman announced that he would not retrace their discussions solely for Bonney who only need know that parties from *H.M.S. Falcon* and *H.M.S. Tourch* would rig hoses from the pool above King Jimmy's Bridge to the beach. "*Jamestownes,*" i.e. sailors from *Jamestown*, were to man the pumps and fill casks in her boats. Bonney would command the American shore party, Trueman paused, assuming Bonney had the time? Bonney nodded, not trusting himself to speak. All boats would be readied that evening. First light, the British would row to the beach and rig hoses and pumps. Bonney was to follow to assist as necessary and assume pumping duties from the Royal Navy. His counterpart ashore was a Lieutenant Paltier, Royal Marines. Both navies seemed to have more demanding duties for *skilled* officers, Trueman concluded, insinuating that Marine officers fell into another category. Bonney nodded. He would not give Trueman the satisfaction of rising to his barbs.

Forward, the routine of ship's work returned. A longboat bumped alongside filled with fresh fruit and vegetables. The great main course lay on deck ready to be bent onto its spar once the four malefactors were removed. The Cooper assembled casks on the forecastle and the Gunner examined lashings on the starboard battery. Activity flowed smoothly around the stretched bodies, sweating and bleeding in the relentless sun.

Bonney was aware that Lieutenant Sawyer was speaking to him, saying his farewells. He asked the Briton how was it he and his compatriots were aboard? Trueman had requested assistance from Commander Bounce, who in turn had asked for help from *Falcon* and *Tourch*, Sawyer answered hurriedly, eager to depart. Clearly, Bonney realized, Trueman had to have received his note. The humiliating public upbraiding for "diddling" ashore was deliberate and contrary to what Trueman knew to be the truth. Was it petty vengeance for challenging his treatment of Talliaferro and Sweet at Government House, or retribution for Bonney's reaction to having his NCOs trussed-up without his knowledge? Bonney hurried below to his cuddy across the wardroom from Sweet's and Talliaferro's cabins. At least he could step outside his, Bonney reflected, but for how long?

Orrin shook Bonney's shoulder, announcing one bell. Four-thirty, Bonney converted automatically. He kept time like he served, on land and sea. After the Marine exited he swung up out of his bunk, squirmed into his trousers, and groped toward the head.

Sweet heard the exchange. It was frustrating to lie there, unable even to go to the necessary, while life continued unaltered all around. Patience, he thought. Daniel's short note indicated that a plan was afoot to get Talliaferro and him off *Jamestown* before she sailed. What troubled him most was being cast up in Freetown without means, without even a change of clothes; in any escape he would have to abandon his sea chest. He suddenly questioned how his letter home would be delivered if the U.S. Mail no longer serviced Virginia? He could be as marooned in Freetown as if left on a desert island.

As Sweet tossed in his bunk, Bonney ascended to the weather deck. Not even the hint of dawn to the east up river, but there was movement about the deck as his shore party was issued breakfast of biscuit, cheese and hot black coffee. Bonney felt steam rising across his face as his nostrils filled with the full, slightly acid aroma from the mug proffered by a shadow at his side.

"Sergeant Banning?"

"The same, Sir, and I'm stretching myself to the limit on account of the old *Jamestown*, so I am, Sir." And I am beginning to understand why my father deserted, Banning realized.

"Well, you've not lost that Hibernian humor. How are you?"

"About three inches taller and a bit tender in the mouth, but fit for duty, Sir." Hanging by the wrists capped hanging by the neck as the U.S. Army had done to his father, Banning reflected. "Dyer, too, though he'll whine if you listen to his yap," he added.

"Which I shan't. How many in our party?"

Eight Marines for the pump, and sixteen sailors, under Boatswain's Mate Peck, to handle boats and hoses, Banning reported, hoping the British pump was in good shape. It would be hot work and Banning suspected that eight men was the minimum number of pumpers required, so there would be no relief.

Peck's inclusion shocked Bonney. "Wasn't he stretched with you yesterday?"

"Aye, Sir, and Thoms' along too, who was dancing the gag with us, like Punch and Judy hanging from the main yard." Bonney was certain the big Irishman was rolling his eyes, though he could not tell in the dark. "Seems 'Captain' figures sweat might improve our commitment," Banning continued. "We done no mutinous talk, Sir. It was but...."

"Later. Ashore," Bonney cautioned. "So we've twenty-four sailors and Marines, two NCOs and two petty officers?"

69

"And yourself, of course, Sir, for a grand and staggering total of twenty-nine souls; assuming the Methodists among them have souls...."

Bonney cut him off. Enough of the Sergeant's blarney, his humor was short this morning. He thought he could discern a slight hint of grayness to the east. He gave Banning twenty minutes for the men to eat and prepare, then into the boats. Boat, Banning corrected. They had the gig for three or four trips; all the rest were full of casks. Bonney nodded in acceptance. He would go in the first load to coordinate with Paltier. The eastern sky was definitely paling. Shapes were emerging aboard *Jamestown*. Across the roadstead, Bonney could distinguish the rigging of *Falcon* and *Tourch* and connect hazy visual impressions with the sounds of boats crews preparing to shove off.

The rapidity of tropical dawns always impressed him. Certainly, there was no true difference in the rate at which the earth rotated toward the sun in the tropics compared to temperate zones. Was it the awakening noises of so many bird and animal species, or the way the breeze picked up with the first suggestion of the warming rays? It was still too dark to read the face of his watch. About 5:00, he estimated. In another hour, hour-and-a-half, the fishing fleet would sortie on the morning offshore wind.

The color party moved aft. Usually Banning or Dyer oversaw the ceremony, but this morning Orrin, just relieved from his duties as jailer, was in charge. The Marine bugler, a boy of fifteen, last in the marching line, moistened his lips, his shining horn tucked under his right arm. The detail halted, faced, and with mechanical movements two Marine privates readied the halyards. The other two stepped up, one cradling the folded ensign while the second tied it to the halyard, then stood motionless. Bonney caught Orrin's all but imperceptible nod to the bugler who snapped his horn to his lips, inhaling deeply. Another slight nod and "Attention" rang out simultaneously with similar commanding music from H.M.S. *Falcon,* H.M.S. *Tourch*, Government House, and the 2d West Indian Regiment's barracks on Tower Hill. Along *Jamestown's* deck all activity ceased as officers and crew faced aft and stiffened to attention. A moment later, to a second cacophony of competing tunes, the folded colors rose rapidly to the gaff and, at a snap of the halyard, burst open in the first rays of the morning sun.

Bonney experienced that momentary, involuntary tingling along his spine. A fleeting shortness of breath replaced the chill as he beheld the flowing folds of his country's flag seductively dancing above him. Holding his salute an instant longer than those about him, he had to admit that the emotion glowing through his being was love, love for his Corps dedicated to that banner; love for the commitment to it as a symbol of the loyalty to each other of those who served under it; love for the ideal, no matter how far short fell the reality, of a nation of free men striving to tame and empower a continent, complementing each other with their differences, rather than

70

attempting to dominate each other because of those differences. Belatedly he snapped away his salute.

Turning back to the tasks at hand, Bonney experienced a crushing sense of loss. Present circumstances rendered his love impossible of satisfaction. The symbol no longer reflected the reality. Columbia, the beautiful maiden, was deathly ill and corrupted. His emotions were for a memory evoked by ceremonial repetition and colored bunting. The fraternal loyalty for which the flag purported to stand now seemed as ephemeral as the river mist being shredded by the morning breeze. Patriotism and fidelity … to what?

The rhythmic swish of water and squeak of oarlocks alongside refocused his thoughts. *Falcon's* boats were passing under *Jamestown's* bows. Bonney could distinguish Paltier in the sternsheets of the leading boat. They exchanged nods; "See you on the beach."

CHAPTER TEN

Bonney could not shake the gloom that had settled upon him at Colors. During the good two hours required to rig the hoses, progressively peevish demands from *Jamestown* to explain the delay did not help his mood. He took small comfort that the signals meant Trueman also was having an early morning. Banning was right; it required eight hands to work the Marines' pump. The exhausting labor began a few minutes before 9:00 a.m.

Engrossed, Bonney did not notice a gig pull from Dougan's Wharf to *Jamestown*. From the veranda of the Colonial Hospital, Paltier did and through his field glasses recognized Pa Cabot in his porkpie hat; Halcyon Nevis, Esq. dressed in white linen frockcoat and trousers, white pleated shirt with a burgundy cravat beneath his olive face, and gray top hat; Jumbo, the guide and man of all trades, whose gargantuan frame was unmistakable; and "E'phant," Jumbo's "brother," distinguishable from Jumbo by his brass-buttoned blue wool bailiff's uniform. Paltier had witnessed such scenes too often to harbor any doubt as to the purpose; process was to be served upon person or persons aboard *U.S.S. Jamestown*. "Happy day, 'Captain' Trueman," Paltier muttered.

*   *   *   *   *   *   *   *   *   *

"My business is with the captain, Sir; kindly stand aside." Halcyon Nevis, Esquire peremptorily ordered as he brushed past Acting Lieutenant DePue.

On the quarterdeck, Trueman was immersed in his telescope studying the beach below King Jimmy's Bridge when a booming voice near at hand caused him to lose the image in the glass. "You are captain, I presume?"

Trueman spun to face Nevis. "And you are?" How dare this fellow interrupt his concentration? Especially, how dare he use that tone?

Without touching his headgear, Nevis proffered his card with bent arm requiring Trueman to extend his reach bending slightly forward as if in obeisance. As the naval officer took the *carte*, the barrister pronounced, "An officer of Her Majesty's Courts, in furtherance of justice. Bailiff," he ordered holding Trueman's gaze, "Do your duty."

The hulking E'phant, in a uniform almost as distinguished as Trueman's, took two forward strides to tower over the lieutenant's usually dominant frame. "Her Majesty summon Misters Sweet and Talliaferro for defend theyselves to court," E'phant boomed, placing two folded sets of legal papers in front of Trueman's chest.

"This is a United States ship of war!" spluttered Trueman. "Your damned writ doesn't run here! What kind of damned monkeyshines is this? *Get off my ship!*"

"Sir, I should be careful how I use the appellation 'monkey,'" Nevis drawled.

"Do you *dare* admonish me on my own deck? Mr. Appleton! Remove these *fellows*!"

Nevis nimbly took the folded summonses from E'phant and in a single motion, gapped a space between the third and fourth buttons on Trueman's coat with his right forefinger, while sliding the papers into the gap with his left hand. Utterly surprised that anyone would dare to touch him uninvited, Trueman was too shocked to react.

"We shall find our own way, thank you," Nevis said with excessive pleasantness. Then he pivoted and, followed by his retinue, strode to the entryport. In the opening, he turned and called, "Please note, while the court date is a fortnight hence, the gentlemen in question are required to present themselves to the Court by 4:00 of-the-clock this afternoon to give assurances. Mere formality, you understand."

Descending into the boat, Nevis did not hear Trueman's explosive oath. It would be a cold day in Hell or Freetown, before he sent those two ashore! He barked at the yeoman to signal the beach party to complete watering by six bells of the afternoon watch, 3:00 p.m. With his main course bent-on to its spar and the foretop rigged, Trueman could depart Freetown as soon as he had sufficient water. He had enough salt horse and ship's biscuit, he calculated; fresh meat, fruit, and vegetables would be healthier and a morale booster, but they were not necessities. The arrogant Limeys just could not keep from stepping on American sovereignty he fumed. Serve some damned writ on his deck, the nerve! Trueman angrily pulled the summonses from his coat and hurled them to the planking at his feet.

From the boat Nevis noted Trueman's gesture. "Pa Cabot, I surmise that more than a writ is required to convince 'Captain' Trueman that the defendants should appear." Nevis turned his gaze upon Jumbo. "My, my. The Jonathans are making a right cock-up of the market. I shouldn't wonder the *ma's* were quite upset by it all."

*   *   *   *   *   *   *   *   *   *

Trueman's goading signals had Bonney at the limits of his tolerance. Four boats were involved in watering: one alongside *Jamestown* as her full casks were lifted into the warship's hold; a second en route to the beach; another pulling from the shore to the sloop; and a fourth beached to fill her casks. To keep it out of the brackish water, the shore party had to run the hose through the shallows on the shoulders of several sailors. The men sweated and swayed as the water pulsed through the casing. At some point Bonney would have to rest them. He flinched thinking of the signal that would elicit.

74

"*Ahyee*, Mister! This be my place for market!" As Bonney looked about, the water surge in the hose dissipated. By the pump stood an ample *ma*, large *blie* on her head and baby strapped to her back, confronting the sweating Leathernecks. "You thief my place!"

Before Bonney could react, another commotion erupted further inland. He carefully had avoided laying hose across paths from Water Street to the beach. Now, disregarding the paths, half-a-dozen women with baskets on their heads were demanding to descend an uninvitingly precipitous route that crossed the hose at several points.

Bonney rounded toward the shallows where a Bullom boat, spars shipped, butted against *Jamestown's* longboat. "This my beach, to land fish for market!" a large boatman yelled at the coxswain. Without fumbling for his watch Bonney knew it was not even noon. The fishing fleet would not arrive for at least three hours. Bonney felt an urge to laugh. He recognized a coordinated attack when he saw one.

Paltier appeared at Bonney's side observing, "Must say I've not had the pleasure of such an experience." He looked about, eyebrows raised. "Usually, we're all jolly … er, no pun intended," Bonney understood the reference to "Jollies," slang for Royal Marines, but declined comment as Paltier continued, "and have our watering over by one in the *post meridian*, to everyone's satisfaction. Something is afoot for such serendipitous confrontations. I believe that the *ma* by the pump usually sells groundnuts at the Bazaar."

Paltier suggested *dashes* might free the beach. Bonney knew Trueman would see that as capitulating to blatant blackmail. Besides, Bonney was damned if he were going to personally pay for Trueman's water. A signal from *Jamestown* interrupted his thoughts, "Explain Delay."

How did one explain the situation in the terse terms of signals, Bonney questioned? "Territorial Dispute," he decided. Trueman took under a minute to respond, "'Repair Onboard, Execute." Paltier looked away; the demand for immediacy was an insult.

*   *   *   *   *   *   *   *   *   *

Confronting Bonney at the entry port before the younger man had both feet on deck, Trueman demanded, "What in the name of all that's holy are you *doing* in there?"

"All was well, until a hank of market people showed claiming we'd blocked their customary pathways, stall sites, beaching points, and all, Sir."

"Brits had this all arranged! Bonney, damn you, your people are wrongly placed!"

"Respectfully, Sir," Bonney's voice was half a pitch lower than normal with a deliberate cadence and clarity, "the British sited all hoses and

75

the pump and designated the beaching point. They are the same they use, according to Lieutenant Paltier."

"*If* that is true, why are these … err, *people* doing this?"

Bonney felt his neck bulging and his vision constricting. How dare this ass berate him in front of the entire crew? Desperate to keep control of his anger, he responded flatly, "Lieutenant Paltier suggests *dashes*, gifts in the right places might clear up the matter."

"Blackmail? The United States will not pay tribute! Clear that beach, Lieutenant."

"Respectfully, Sir, you certain you wish that?"

"Do you question…."

"Would we stand for the Royal Navy doing that in one of our ports?"

Unaccountably, Trueman paused. "Call away the gig. Mr. Appleton, you have the deck. I am going to see the Governor. Lieutenant Bonney, in the meantime, you will take a detail of your Marines along with muskets and accoutrements for those ashore. Present a show of force. Cow those darkies. In so doing, avoid any confrontation with the Brits."

"May I have those orders in writing, Lieutenant Trueman?" Bonney demanded.

"Damn you, Bonney. You may *not*! My orders are clear. This is hardly a trying task to put some respect into a pack of Nigras. At the very least, your request signals a desire to delay our sailing to suppress the rebellion. Is sabotage your purpose, Mister?"

"I call Lieutenant Appleton to witness; Mr. Trueman has refused my request for written orders. To avoid further delay, Lieutenant Trueman, I take my leave to carry out your orders as best I understand them." Bonney crisply saluted his commander, executed an about face, and strode to the main hatch, bellowing for Marine Orrin.

Trueman's mind was made-up. Bonney's defiance was the last straw. He ordered Appleton to identify the loyal hands, the questionable, and any obvious rebels. With most if not all Southern sympathizers ashore, it should not be difficult as they returned simply to arrest them and pack them below. Bonney was from Baltimore, Trueman recalled, where the mob had assaulted Massachusetts troops as they moved across town from one train station to the other. He must be another damned rebel. It really rankled him that he had erred in his assessment of Bonney when he had questioned him just after assuming command. He could not afford more such mistakes. Any indication of disloyalty would be quashed immediately, he resolved. Trueman ordered Appleton to arrest the Marine Lieutenant once he returned aboard and confine him like Talliaferro and Sweet. He had more than enough loyal hands and officers to make the passage without the assistance of traitors.

Appleton managed to croak, "Aye, Sir."

Trueman continued his instructions. Appleton and the other loyal officers and petty officers best unobtrusively arm themselves, as Trueman was doing. He would be back on deck by the time the gig was ready. He headed to the hatch without waiting for Appleton's reply.

Daniel had been standing by the port rail with Joshua. Mess stewards were always unobserved, as though they did not exist, Daniel thought for the thousandth time. As Trueman descended through the captain's hatch, Daniel stepped toward the main.

*   *   *   *   *   *   *   *   *   *

Bonney met Orrin at the foot of the ladder. His instructions were simple. Orrin and four other Marines Bonney designated were to draw light marching order and sixty rounds for themselves, and the eight Marines, two NCOs, and the sailors on the beach. They were to muster by the portside entry port away from the beach and place the weapons and equipment out of sight in the bottom of a longboat. Yes, Bonney clarified with some exasperation, Orrin should take out some casks to make room. Ashore, Sergeant Banning would take charge of arming the sailors and Marines.

"Pardon, Sir." Daniel knew Sweet would be furious at his asking Bonney's help. "May I assist, Sir?"

Bonney caught the urgency in the slave's voice. The two moved through the wardroom hatch to Bonney's cuddy. He pulled his sea chest from under the bunk, extracted his field gear, handed the canteen and tarred canvas haversack to Daniel, and began giving instructions. Bonney stumbled in his speech as Daniel pressed a tiny wad of paper into his hand. "CPT SAY ARREST YOU & SOUTHRONS AS BOARD. MASTER CHARLES AND TALLIAFERRO MUST LAND. ASK HELP." So, Bonney thought, Mr. Sweet needed assistance to get out of what Bonney had tried to save him from in the first place. Bonney was tempted to leave him to his own devices. Instead he nodded his affirmation to Daniel.

Topside, Appleton had a boat standing by, but Orrin's detail was not, so Bonney went below to the arms room. Orrin and four other Marines were waiting to draw ammunition while the Master-at-Arms issued pistols to almost every petty officer not on the beach, or in custody, Bonney reflected. If Daniel's report needed any corroboration, arming the leadership against a threat that could only come from aboard the sloop satisfied it.

CHAPTER ELEVEN

Trueman's appearance at Government House was no surprise to Governor Porter. Just moments before The Queen's Attorney had departed after informing His Excellency of Halcyon Nevis's efforts to summon before the bar of justice certain officers of the United States Sloop-of-War *Jamestown*. Counsel had been most loquacious concerning the finer points of law governing service of process upon alien nationals aboard a foreign ship-of-war in British waters. The Governor found distinguishing among criminal, civil, and chancellery procedures quite Byzantine. Particularly so as it was *postmeridian* and Counsel's fondness for fortifying libations, the cause of his promotion from the counsel's staff at the Colonial Office in London to his present post in Freetown, was much in evidence.

"We all have our sins to expiate," the Governor muttered, shifting his attention to the American entering his office. It did not escape his notice that Trueman was armed. The situation aboard the American warship must be deteriorating, he concluded. Aloud he greeted his visitor, "Ah, *Good Day,* 'Captain' Trueman."

Regretfully, it was not such a good day, Trueman assured His Excellency. He must trouble the Governor with what, ordinarily, should be too insignificant to bring to the attention of the Queen's *alter ego*. No trouble at all, Porter assured his dear 'Captain.' Would he be seated, some refreshment perhaps? Trueman confined his discussion to the situation below King Jimmy's Bridge. His Excellency permitted him to finish without interruption.

Most unfortunate and, Porter had to say, most unusual. The Governor furrowed his brow. He quite understood Trueman's impatience and, as Trueman reminded him, (Governor Porter was too experienced a politician to respond to Trueman's blunt demand that he honor his promise to facilitate *Jamestown's* departure) his responsibilities to a belligerent vessel in departing Freetown were clear. Yet he had responsibilities to the populace as well. If, as Trueman suggested, he were to employ force, it would generate significant animosity between the Government and those it was constituted to protect and civilize. *"Auspice Britannia Liber,"* "Free Under Britain's Auspices," was the motto on the colony's coat-of-arms and Porter intended to adhere to it. "For Her Majesty's Government to simply brush aside these people would appear to our simple sable brethren as no different than the behavior of some savage chief up-country." No, Porter explained, he could not neglect his civilizing responsibilities through such lack of regard for the law. Silently he admitted borrowing the phrase from the Queen's Attorney.

Continuing, the Governor preempted Trueman's reply. No, he would have to close the market properly, giving notice to the population - effective notice, mind you – that they must forego market for a day. People's livelihoods were involved, Trueman must understand. The Governor raised his eyebrows, but did not pause long enough for Trueman to interrupt. It was the twenty-first of May, Tuesday. It was rather late for notice that evening to be effective, which meant the publication would be next day, earliest. Could not possibly expect all concerned to understand and prepare in under … say … 96 hours, so … Thursday, Friday, Saturday … could not count Sunday … Monday; Yes, His Excellency would be able to cordon off the beach on the morning of Tuesday, the twenty-eighth. Governor Porter beamed at a brilliant solution to a thorny problem.

"*Sir!*" Trueman exploded. "*Your Excellency!* That's *six* days!"

"Well, five actually; can't count the Sabbath, you understand," Porter corrected.

"*I must protest!*"

The Governor held up his hand. "There *may* be another means of resolving this situation 'Captain'." Porter smiled reassuringly. "There is a definite hierarchy in Freetown. Were we to involve some of the community leaders…."

Trueman bristled. "The United States will not be held to ransom."

Anything but, soothed the Governor. There was concern among some of Her Majesty's subjects regarding obligations undertaken by certain of Trueman's officers. Trueman stiffened. If he referred to those two traitorous midshipmen, they were under arrest on most serious charges. It was out of the question to release them ashore on the ineffective summons of a civilian court.

"How unfortunate, my dear 'Captain,'" The Governor commiserated. "I understand that Mr. Halcyon Nevis is acting for Pa Cabot and a gentleman commonly known as 'Jumbo.' I've no recall of his given or surname, I'm afraid. All are substantial personages in Freetown with great influence among the market women. However, I quite understand that this situation involves a matter of principle. Perhaps it is best to observe the formalities and close the market through official channels."

Trueman frowned, diverting his gaze. He loathed letting the midshipmen out of his control and had no illusions as to their actions once they left the ship; they would join the rebels if they could get home before this ridiculous secession farce ended.

Perhaps there lay the solution, he reasoned. The revolt of Southern cabals could not last long. From the 1860 census, Trueman knew that only six percent of Southerners were slave owners, less than three percent owned more than five slaves. Those belonging to the small owners were household servants or workers alongside their owners in the master's fields or trade. Along with the leadership of the Republican Party, he could not imagine the overwhelming majority of Southerners tolerating this revolt of the oligarchs for more than a few weeks. Once the national government moved with determination to support the majority, the slave magnates' house of cards would collapse in a matter of days. If Talliaferro and Sweet were left in Freetown, their careers would be ruined as effectively as by courts martial. Additionally, they would not be a disruptive influence on the passage home. Hell, he thought, they might even die on this sickly coast.

"I am torn between conflicting principles, Your Excellency. I cannot let my Government or Service be trifled with in this manner. Yet my duty is clear. I must return my ship to home waters to suppress this treason. Weighing the two necessities, it may be best to put the miscreants ashore to satisfy their obligations here. The Navy can address their other malefactions upon their subsequent return to the United States; assuming of course that by such accommodation persons of influence will be inclined to assist in smoothing the way for my command to complete watering."

"The difficult choices of command, 'Captain.'" Governor Porter smiled his condolences. "You execute them well, I must say."

"Thank you, Your Excellency. Have you any suggestions as to the manner of enlisting the cooperation of these *gentlemen*?"

*   *   *   *   *   *   *   *   *   *

"My, my," Paltier shook his head at hearing Bonney's orders. "Impetuous fellow, your Lef'tenant Trueman; nervy bastard for a belligerent."

"Pardon?"

"A belligerent; surely he knows his obligations as such?" Paltier exhibited surprise at Bonney's confusion. "Lord John Russell, Foreign Secretary, announced in Parliament the sixth instant that vessels of the United States and … the Confederate States is it? … were to be treated as belligerents in British ports. Repairs as necessary for seaworthiness, no alteration in offensive or defensive power, not to sail within 24 hours of a vessel of the other belligerent, no hostile acts; you know the drill."

"The sixth of May this happened?"

"Quite. The Governor informed Lef'tenant Trueman during his initial call at Government House." Paltier suddenly understood. "What? You've not heard?"

"No one in the wardroom knew this to my knowledge, Paltier. Belligerents…." His mind racing, Bonney poured forth his thoughts. Obviously, Her Majesty's Government was obligated to accept the statement of those in question as to their allegiance. If certain Americans were to claim allegiance to the Confederate States, their claim must be accepted, regardless of the views of United States officials, correct? Yes, Paltier agreed, Bonney was correct, as he comprehended matters, but he was no barrister. Bonney understood, but would the Briton pursue this with him? The seamen and Marines Trueman put ashore for the watering party were all suspect in his eyes as potential traitors. He had promised to arrest the entire party as they returned and had taken action in furtherance of that intent. Had he not, on behalf of his government, Bonney questioned, recognized those men as belligerents hostile to the United States? Further, had he not attempted to maneuver them into breaching their obligations as belligerents by constituting them an armed force coercing Her Majesty's subjects?

"I take your drift, Lef'tenant. Devious mind; I could mistake you for a barrister."

"Headed that way at one point."

"I say! Do you contemplate declaring yourselves Secessionists?"

"It would solve our conundrum, would it not?"

"Handily; most handily. I cannot see how your, or rather *not* your, Lef'tenant Trueman could counter it without the collaboration of Her Majesty's forces or a grievous breach of neutrality. Devilish clever." Paltier joined in the gleeful grin. "I've something that may help. Do you know the Confederate States colors?" He retrieved a heavy envelope from the dispatch pouch over his shoulder and proffered it to Bonney.

> *Admiralty, 10 May, 1861.*
>
> *Sir,*
>
> *I am commanded by My Lords Commissioners of the Admiralty, to transmit to you herewith a copy of the flag which has been adopted by the Confederate States of America.*
>
> *It is intended that the Seven Stars in the upper Canton should be increased in number, in the event of new States being added to the Confederacy.*
>
> *I am, Sir,*
> *Your most humble servant,*
>
> *Signed: W. G. Romaine*

The accompanying illustration showed a banner somewhat similar to the United States colors, with a circle of seven white stars in a blue field. The rest of the flag consisted of two horizontal red bars separated by a white bar of the same size.

"I imagine some attachment to the old pattern," observed the Royal Marine. "I am to transmit the packet to *Tourch* on my way out to *Falcon* after we are finished here … if ever we are finished here." Paltier raised his view to the Bay, the scene of stalemate on the beach, and the vessels in the roadstead. "What of your oath, my friend?"

"I must resign before I act." Ordinarily, Bonney explained, he would feel compelled to conclude the voyage and wait for the resignation to be accepted before disregarding his orders. However, Trueman had refused to confirm in writing orders that, were Bonney to obey, would be most detrimental to his Marines, himself, his ship and, indeed, the United States.

82

Trueman had placed him in a position where his duty of loyalty to Corps, country, and command compelled him to actions on their face disloyal to his oath. Bonney looked at Paltier and growled, "Hell, I don't know if I believe it either."

*   *   *   *   *   *   *   *   *   *

Lieutenant Appleton faced a dilemma personified by Sergeant Banning's hard Irish face demanding an immediate answer. Banning had handed him a request from Bonney to land the Marines' field equipment so the watering party could overnight ashore. They would be ashore for hours yet, so the request was reasonable. He dared not make Bonney self-sufficient, but he dared not alert him to the pending arrests.

Midshipman Kunstler interrupted. Why would a Dutchie from Ohio join the Navy, the Lieutenant wondered irrelevantly? Kuntsler handed Appleton a carefully folded paper, a message from Trueman. He wanted Talliaferro and Sweet ashore, Appleton read, quite a reversal from when Nevis left.

"Need shift the gear before them fishin' dories come home," Banning prodded, sensing Appleton was about to turn to the prisoners and leave Bonney's request hanging. "Permission, Sir, I can see to it all. Not to worry. Thankee." Before Appleton could protest, Banning saluted and left; inaction constitutes action, Lieutenant, he thought.

Once Goode understood what had to be transferred, Banning went to find Daniel. He felt uncomfortable passing into the wardroom, "officer country." He had orders, but he could not exactly repeat them if challenged. Daniel was seated at the wardroom table polishing a lamp and singing one of Mr. Foster songs, something about a cabin floor or the like, accompanied by Mr. Sweet from within his cuddy. Banning looked questioningly at the Marine sentry, a pimpled kid from Upstate New York.

"Didn't say nothin' 'bout singin', Sergeant."

Banning gave him a look of contempt; then ignored him. To Daniel he ordered, "Shift your bones, Boyo. There's work for the doin'." With Daniel in tow, Sergeant Banning went forward of the wardroom into psychologically more comfortable enlisted environs.

Sweet felt like he had rolled in mental poison ivy. What did that sergeant want with Daniel? Other questions took precedence when Harry DePue appeared, ordering him to put on his frockcoat and look smart as he was going to court. No, Harry assured him, not a court martial, some nonsense in the local courts ashore, Talliaferro too.

*   *   *   *   *   *   *   *   *   *

From the twelve-foot tall windows of the Queen's Attorney's office in the Police Court, Trueman looked upon the roadstead. At this distance his ship seemed calm, well ordered. By God, he resolved, it would be in actuality as well. The disloyal aboard would soon be cast ashore or confined and he would have done all that he could at present toward crushing this damned rebellion. His gaze shifted to his left, onto the beach below King Jimmy's Bridge, his watering party under that traitorous Bonney. Most in the group would be confined as soon as they re-embarked. What were they doing in the meantime? His attention returned to the room as Halcyon Nevis, Esq. walked in. God, Trueman thought, how he hated that uppity....

"'Captain' Trueman, my clients understand your situation and are obliged that you understand theirs." They were honored, Nevis assured him, to do all in their poor powers to obtain cooperation of the market women. All that was necessary was that Messrs. Sweet and Talliaferro present themselves ashore. Nevis smiled sociably.

They would be ashore in a matter of minutes, once Trueman gave the signal, he promised the barrister, if it would be possible to complete watering that evening.

"Ah, my friend," (Trueman gritted his teeth at Nevis's suggestion), "it is late and the fishing boats are returning. I shall attempt to accommodate your wishes, but...."

"Listen here!" Trueman dispensed with the farcical politeness. "I can have those men ashore now, but you'll open the beach before they submit themselves to any jurisdiction."

"Do not excite yourself, dear 'Captain.' As the boat departs the ship, my clients will be *en route* the beach. We can accomplish much before the fishing fleet returns."

Trueman opened the tall sash. He moved his cap at arms length in a slow circle. The gig pulled from behind *Jamestown* with several passengers in the sternsheets. He motioned Nevis to the opening and indicated the boat's course. Nevis wordlessly turned and left the room. Trueman was about to follow when a longboat appeared from behind *Jamestown*, Daniel in its bows. Trueman smiled. Daniel was seizing his chance for freedom. Good, Trueman thought, Daniel's desertion saved the cost of passage to Liberia or wherever the freed darkies would be taken after the oligarchs' defeat.

*   *   *   *   *   *   *   *   *   *

Sweet sat in the gig with Talliaferro, DePue, four Marines, the coxswain, and six oarsmen. There was no chance for private conversation. All DePue had said was that they had been summoned to appear before the local court. Was this some game of Trueman's, Sweet wondered? With Harry as the escort officer, Sweet's loyalty to his friend negated an escape attempt; it would discredit if not incriminate DePue. Talliaferro might try something and for Harold's sake Sweet was determined to prevent it.

DePue looked miserable, shoulders sloping, head down. Sweet was about to say something to cheer him, when Talliaferro identified Daniel headed for the beach in the prow of one of *Jamestown's* boats. Sweet twisted to look over his shoulder.

"And I told Appleton he'd never run," DePue whined.

"Not running," Sweet answered vehemently, wishing he knew what Daniel was doing.

"If not runnin', Nigra's just stealin' our chests!" spat Talliaferro.

Sweet shifted so violently that he put the oarsman next to him off his stroke. Daniel clearly was perched upon a sea chest in the bow and the top of at least one other was visible over the gunwales. Black lacquer, it was Talliaferro's.

"Damn it, Sweet! We'll be in rags at our courts martial, thanks to your darkie!" Talliaferro snapped. "DePue, can't y'all do something?"

"Prisoners are to keep silent!" Harold ordered with sudden energy. Talliaferro's attempt to dictate his actions had ended his funk at Charles' situation and restored his sense of place. He squared his shoulders and sat straighter in his seat.

Talliaferro seemed about to challenge this, then shrugged and sat silently as the gig approached Government Steps. Ten yards out, the coxswain ordered "Ship Oars!" and the sailors raised the dripping poles to the vertical so that water ran down onto their arms and a few stray drops spattered on the passengers. Just as the bow bumped the stone steps, the forward-most sailor vaulted to the landing with the painter and held the gig against the stone with the little rope. Numerous African hands helped to shift the boat portside to the steps and held it while the Marines landed. DePue motioned Talliaferro to follow them.

Once the Carolinian's back was to them, Harold thrust out his hand to Charles wishing him God's Speed. Sweet took the proffered hand and felt something press into his palm. Their eyes met and Charles understood. Gratefully, he accepted the double eagle. Twenty dollars would not get him home, but the little gold piece would buy a lot of rice. Most of all, it proved that Harold had not abandoned him. Their personal loyalties were intact.

*   *   *   *   *   *   *   *   *   *

Daniel was in the bow with sea chests, so that was the last boatload of gear Bonney concluded, then looked away from the bay, northeast along Water Street hoping to see Paltier. Instead, two massive figures came striding toward King Jimmy's Bridge, the sun glinting from the numerous brass buttons of the landward giant's coat. As they approached the more plainly dressed made a great show of waving toward the beach. Bonney saw Daniel

85

spring from the longboat waving furiously. They loped toward each other and upon meeting burst into great smiles and laughter. Bonney was too far off to hear Jumbo's words, but there was no confusing the commands he bellowed to the market people who stepped back inviting the Americans to proceed with their tasks.

Bonney cursed his luck that Paltier had not returned with word of the authorities' attitude toward the sudden appearance of a Confederate landing force in the colony. Now he must decide between open defiance and completing the watering, destroying any justification for remaining ashore. In actuality he had no choice. He had to string out the impression that all was normal. Marines back at their pump and the signalman standing by, Sergeant Banning carefully selected committed Southerners to handle the hose to the longboats. Bonney nodded, the signal flags waved, and a boat sprang from *Jamestown* toward the beach.

Bonney looked toward the Bullom Shore and the open sea. The water was speckled with varicolored patches of canvas, the sails of the fishing fleet. He had precious little time left for watering. After that, his actions would be dictated by circumstances.

*   *   *   *   *   *   *   *   *   *

From the window of the Queen's Attorney, Trueman watched the longboat beach, the greeting between Daniel and Jumbo, and the resumption of purposeful activity. Daniel had made friends ashore, clever fellow. The boat's cargo caused concern. What would necessitate landing such a quantity of whatever it was, Truman wondered?

Impatiently he scanned Water Street for the prisoners. He drummed his fingers upon the casement and slowly exhaled. Obviously, the Navy would expand. He had to be on the scene to receive one of the better assignments. There was the possibility that, through friends in the Radical Abolitionist wing of the Republican Party, Senator Sumner for example, he might secure more than merely some gunboat. But he had to *be there* before all of the choice assignments were gone. Where were those damned midshipmen?

CHAPTER TWELVE

The small party of Americans pushed through the crowd at Government Steps, the sharp tang of human sweat accosting their senses. Acting Lieutenant DePue led, followed by Talliaferro and Sweet, four Marines bringing up the rear. They passed Gloucester Street and the market and slaughter yard, the Cottonwood, Slave Steps, and St. George's. As they approached the Courts, Sweet observed Trueman frowning from a second floor window. Suddenly he stiffened, his frown contorting into a scowl. To Sweet's left, Talliaferro was recovering from a flourishing, archaic, and blatantly contemptuous bow. DePue hustled them inside.

Halcyon Nevis met them in the foyer followed shortly by a furious Trueman. The barrister let Trueman vent his anger upon poor DePue - something about prisoners not being entitled to exchange courtesies – before ushering all of them through tall double doors into the court chamber. As if cued by their entry, a be-robed and be-wigged light-skinned Creole arose from the high bench and looked down imperiously, a large carving of the Royal Coat of Arms on the wall behind him.

Nevis stepped through the bar. "My Lord, we are here at last."

"And 'At last' is too late, Mr. Nevis," rumbled the judge in a melodic baritone. Seated below and in front of the justice, still elevated well above mere mortals, the clerk stopped rustling his documents. His Honour pulled aside his red robe and fished in his waistcoat pocket for his timepiece. Meticulously, he examined the instrument, closed the lid, and as carefully returned it to his vest. It was three minutes past four-of-the-clock, he intoned, and counsel was well aware that the court did not sit past that hour. Nevis must "catch some time, perhaps on the morrow if the docket allowed," to determine sureties for "these persons." The judge made a dismissive gesture.

"*Nevis!*" exploded Trueman.

"*SIR!*" The judge's voice reverberated from the walls. "Extemporaneous comments by those not called to the bar are not permitted in my courtroom."

Nevis preempted further statement by Trueman, informing "M'Lord" that Americans might not be familiar with the more ancient and developed procedures in Her Majesty's courts. Trueman reddened. Would His Lordship please excuse the outburst? Nevis would school "these persons" before another appearance.

"See that you do," the judge glowered, then looking pointedly at Trueman's holster and the four Marines, he added, "And advise them that armed persons, other than those of Her Majesty, *are not permitted in my court!*"

His Lordship departed down a short stair and through a doorway to the rear of the bench. The Clerk scurried after. Nevis started explaining that the defendants should remain ashore pending their court appearance. Ignoring Nevis, Trueman peremptorily ordered DePue to return the prisoners to the ship. In that case, Nevis expressed grave doubt that watering would continue, such a pity. Trueman scowled.

From the back of the chamber Paltier moved forward accompanied by the Captain of the 2nd West, whose name Sweet could not remember. Paltier announced that Captain Page-Norton had proffered the 2nd West's guest quarters for the midshipmen's use and would vouch for their appearance at their proceedings, whenever they might occur.

Trueman shot the two Readcoats a sharp glance. It seemed just too damned convenient that the British officers had appeared at just this moment to offer a solution to the burgeoning impasse with Nevis. Was he being manipulated, made a fool? Or was he being paranoid, he wondered. After all, what did it matter, so long as he could get *Jamestown* watered and homeward bound? He had come ashore ready to leave the two midshipmen behind. While he was not about to be ordered around by some gussied-up African, it was more important to return to America and the advancement that the revolt must produce. With Page-Norton's assurance that the prisoners would not disgrace their country further, he announced that he had no objection to Sweet and Talliaferro remaining ashore pending the hearing. To Nevis he added that now matters doubtless could be arranged to permit *Jamestown's* crew to finish watering.

"My humble efforts in that regard may bear some fruit, 'Captain,'" the barrister responded.

"In that case, Captain Page-Norton, I entrust the prisoners to you," Trueman muttered.

"It is only a civil matter, 'Captain,'" Nevis interjected pleasantly.

"I refer to their status aboard my ship, Nevis," snapped Trueman. Seething, he turned toward the doors growling, "Come, Mr. DePue."

*　　*　　*　　*　　*　　*　　*　　*　　*　　*

On Trueman's heels, Paltier led Sweet and Talliaferro onto Water Street toward King Jimmy's Bridge. At the head of the path to the beach, they met Bonney, who gave a staccato summation of events since Sweet and Talliaferro had been confined. Sweet at first was furious that Daniel had sought Bonney's help, but his anger cooled as the Marine Lieutenant continued with his report.

"So you weren't spying for Trueman?" Sweet demanded when Bonney finished.

"That, Sir, is a damned insult!" Bonney's explosive response caused Paltier to step between the two Americans, certain that they would instantly come to blows.

"*Sweet!*" Talliaferro blurted in disbelief.

"Uncle Joshua say nary a time," Daniel interjected hurriedly. "Done told you, Marse Charles, times Trueman went to askin', Marse Bonney say, 'Nothin' of the nature we discussed,' and Trueman just had to live with that." The concern on the slave's face was not lost on Paltier.

Sweet gave Daniel a furious glance. Boy's presuming too much upon our closeness, he thought. Then Talliaferro's protest registered and Sweet realized how Paltier had moved to prevent blows. The Royal Marine's expression was of frustration with Charles' tactless accusation. Talliaferro's and Daniel's faces said the same. And, Sweet recognized, between Bonney and Daniel even his sea chest had come ashore.

"So now what?" Sweet's tone still was suspicious, even resentful.

Bonney relaxed with a slow exhalation and, his temper under control again, answered, "We must induce *Jamestown* to depart and find our own way home."

"In for a penny, in for a pound," quipped Paltier. "My word, Bonney, you impose shamelessly upon this 'Fellow Marine' business. However, I've found you billets, allowed you to land your baggage, and now, as your paternal service, I must extricate you from your own navy. What would the Jonathans do without John Bull, I ask you?"

"Be as lost as a Lancaster mill owner without Southron cotton," Talliaferro growled.

Bonney and Sweet exchanged despairing glances; then realized that they had and each looked away. Paltier held up his hand; he had seen Talliaferro's brand of debate at Government House. The British were strictly neutral, he assured the North Carolinian. To issues at hand, he urged. Assuming Bonney might delegate duties at the beach, Paltier believed that a few minutes spent in conversation with the Governor might induce *Jamestown* to depart. To himself he added that a bit of separation between the Lieutenant and the Midshipman would not hurt either.

Bonney was at Paltier's service. First, however, he suggested that the midshipmen resign from United States service. Bonney passed a piece of stationary to Talliaferro.

> *Freetown, HBM's Colony of*
> *Sierra Leone*
> *May 21ˢᵗ 1861*

Sir:

> *I respectfully tender, through you, to the President of the United States, this, my resignation of the commission, which I have the honor to hold, as a Second Lieutenant in the Marine Corps of the United States.*
>
> *In severing my connection with the Government of the United States, and with our Corps in which I have had the honor to serve, I pray you to accept my deepest gratitude for the kindness and*

*fraternity, which has characterized the deportment of yourself and all
your subordinates toward me during my service.*

Col. John Harris	*I have the honor to be*
Commandant of the	*Very respectfully*
Marine Corps	*Your Ob't. Sv't,*
Washington, D.C.	

Aaron Claverton Bonney
2nd Lieutenant
U.S. Marine Corps

They should make appropriate adjustments in composing their own and be
careful not to smudge his document. With that, he turned and followed
Paltier toward the town.

CHAPTER THIRTEEN

Bonney tugged at his coat and straightened his sword belt and sash. Confident of his military appearance, he followed Captain Page-Norton and Lieutenant Paltier through the double doorway into the office of His Excellency, James D. P. Porter, Gent, Governor of Her Britannic Majesty's Crown Colony of Sierra Leone. From the angle of the sun and shadows in the room, Bonney estimated there were at least three hours of daylight left on this 21st of May 1861. It had been one very long day, and was not over yet.

As senior officer, Page-Norton spoke first. "Your Excellency, I fear that we present a rather dicey situation for so late in the afternoon."

"Doubtless involving the delightful 'Captain' Trueman of *U.S.S. Jamestown?*" Bonney's presence made that a foregone conclusion, Porter reasoned.

"Seems Mr. Trueman has attempted an armed invasion of this colony," Paltier replied.

Bonney began to appreciate Paltier's sense of the dramatic. Porter's eyebrows rose.

"All well, at the moment, Sir, thanks to the initiative and sagacity of Lef'tenant Bonney." Page-Norton inclined his head toward the American.

The Governor motioned to the several chairs before the large table that served as his desk, better air circulation, a trick he had learned in India. Perhaps some details, before they commence complimenting each other, Porter suggested. Was he to understand that Lef'tenant Bonney was best situated to supply them, if he felt free to do so, of course? Bonney alone remained standing and proceeded to brief the Governor without emotion or editorializing.

Did Bonney believe, questioned Porter, that had the situation resulted in confrontation between his party and say some of Captain Page-Norton's people, Lef'tenant Trueman would have disowned his actions?

Bonney could not say with certainty.

Why else, Paltier erupted. Trueman had refused written confirmation of his extremely questionable instructions. Once Bonney's party returned aboard, it would have justified confining the lot of them for exceeding their orders. Or, if they claimed to be Southern belligerents, it would have damaged the Confederacy's standing with the British government, press and people, and compelled Porter to take action against the men.

"You have this all on the word of a, err, *servant*, am I to understand?" questioned Governor Porter.

Bonney noted with amusement the Governor's studied avoidance of any direct reference to Daniel's status under American law. "And my own observations, Your Excellency," he responded.

Where did things stand regarding water, the Governor inquired?

Bonney calculated quickly. Gallon a day … say 400 men. Fifty day transit to be safe … twenty-thousand gallons … fifty-gallon casks … 400 casks … ten per boatload … forty boatloads … some water still aboard from before … nineteen boats that morning and another eight or so since … transfer continued uninterrupted, *Jamestown* should have enough water by end evening nautical twilight to comfortably make the transit.

She could make landfall in Brazil or any of the Caribbean islands, so that further lessened requirements, added the Governor, or simply rejoin her squadron off the Congo.

Paltier interjected another factor. Were Bonney's party to declare for the Confederacy, the British should have two belligerent forces on hand. His Excellency would be fully justified in ordering one of the parties to sea to avoid clashes.

The Governor chuckled, rather obvious who that would be, since only one party possessed a vessel. It certainly was preferable to helping Trueman recover deserters. Even absent advice from the Queen's Attorney, Porter was drawn to the approach. Nevertheless, he observed, best tread cautiously when it came to constitution of a combatant entity on British soil, Foreign Enlistments Act of 1818 and all that. To himself he thought that he could not afford a misstep on this matter after his troubles in India during the Mutiny. He was resolved to act conservatively.

"Refugees, more like, cast upon the hostile coast of Africa?" questioned Page-Norton.

"Refugees, belligerents, deserters, or … a party detained for adjudication while their ship is instructed to depart?" suggested Paltier.

"Litigious Sierra Leone," sighed the Governor. "We've more than enough theories to confound poor 'Captain' Trueman." Turning to Bonney, he added with a hint of sarcasm, "Least we can do for one who saved us from armed invasion." Bonney smiled politely.

The next few hours could ruin his career, Porter well knew, but action or inaction the risks were the same. It was better to go down for having *done* something than for abdicating decision and just letting things drift. "If we are to send the Jonathan on her way this evening," The Governor's tone was serious, "and I've absolutely no wish to extend the opportunities for further non-conventional behavior, we've not a moment to lose, gentlemen. I suggest, Lef'tenant Bonney, that you keep the water flowing until events indicate otherwise. Lef'tenant Paltier, would you be so kind as to carry a message to Captain Jennings asking him to attend me at his earliest possible convenience, along with Commander Parker of *Tourch*. Captain Page-Norton, you may wish your officers to join us as well. I shall send for Commander Bounce also." Porter looked around the group for questions. There were none. "Best be about it, gentlemen," he said rising from his chair.

*   *   *   *   *   *   *   *   *   *

As soon as he saw the Port Captain's launch with the large White Ensign of the Royal Navy heading for *Jamestown*, Sergeant Banning assembled the sailors and Marines of the watering party on the beach beneath King Jimmy's Bridge. Lieutenant Bonney stood ten paces behind him, far enough away so as not to reduce Banning's authority over the assemblage, yet close enough to signal his endorsement of his Sergeant's actions.

"Now, listen-up," Banning quieted the group. "Comes a time, when a man's to make a choice with no turnin' back and no second chance." He paused for a few seconds to let the seriousness of the moment settle upon his listeners. The assembly became earnestly silent so that the rustling of banana fronds above the beach was clearly audible. Bonney watched two vultures, Freetown's only garbage disposal system, riding the winds above the city. "One o' them times is upon us," Banning said evenly, but with an earnestness that held the men's rapped attention.

He reviewed the state of events in America that they had first heard when Nathaniel Cabot brought "the News" aboard *Jamestown*. He recited the orders from Lieutenant-in-Command Trueman concerning discussion of those events among the crew and the enforcement of those orders upon himself and the other non-commissioned and petty officers the previous day. Then, as Bonney phrased it, Banning loosed the fox in the henhouse by revealing Trueman's orders that the members of the watering party be arrested for treason upon their return to *Jamestown* that afternoon. Something between a gasp and a growl errupted from the assembly.

I know somethin' 'bout treason, Buckoes," Banning said after the first utterances had subsided. "Me Da' answered the drum to fight in Mexico so to use the bounty to pay the company store and free his family from the coal company and the Allegheny County Sheriff." The hands fell silent, as Banning knew they would; they always loved a good tale. "Bastards did na pay it though and some other peculiarities o' Army life did na set well wi' my Da' so he hooked it to the Mexican side with the *San Patricios*, the Irish lads what quit the Americans an' went over to fightin' against 'em for Santa Anna." He gave them a second or two to absorb that. "Well, they stood when they should o' run and captured they were by the Americans and as the Stars and Stripes broke out over Chipaltipec, me Da' and his mates were hanged for traitors, deserters, and ..." Banning pauses a second for effect "like typical Patties, once again backin' the wrong damned side." There was no laugh, but the perverse humor of the last phrase kept the story from detracting from the present dilemma.

"So," Banning continued after a pause, "we be in a similar kettle ourselves. To go back aboard and like to face a charge o' treason account o' where you hail from or who your mates be, or desert the American cause here and now and risk being stranded in bloody Africa and hanged for certain if the United States ever lays hold o' ye." He waited a couple of seconds for the shock to pass through his audience. "It ain't a pretty prospect, but it is what we face and not me nor the Lieutenant," he said giving a nod toward Bonney, "wants a man-jack o' ye to ever say we did not give ye a choice, especially Orrin and the lads that came ashore late with the muskets."

Surprisingly the men remained silent. Banning continued, "Lieutenant will do his best to get us home to a safe port, but we cannot promise, so you each have a choice to make and not long to make it. But seems to me, Mr. Trueman has made us Rebels, so Rebel I shall be and get back quickest I can to join the Secession." Banning faned an epiphany. "They got t' have Marines, they want to have any sort o' country at all," he concluded.

*　　　*　　　*　　　*　　　*　　　*　　　*　　　*　　　*　　　*

"Enter," Trueman responded flatly to the three raps on the cabin door.

Midshipman Kunstler eased open the hatch, stuck his head around the frame and announced that a boat flying the White Ensign was pulling from Government Steps. Probably some invitation, Trueman observed. He would be right up. Having spent the last hour logging the events of the day, he was thankful for a reason to go on deck. The large White Ensign, banner of the Royal Navy, a white flag quartered by the red cross of Saint George with the Union Jack in the upper left canton, indicated a formal visit. Trueman guessed it to be the Captain of the Port, Commander Bounce, who had been helpful in providing materials for *Jamestown's* repairs. He buckled his sword belt, centered his cap, and passed through the hatchway. Perhaps an hour of sun left, he calculated automatically as his eyes cleared deck level.

Boat, Ahoy!
Captain of the Port!
Proceed!

It pleased Trueman to be confirmed in his assessments, even such little things as this. Mr. Armond, the Master, had the deck and had seen to the courtesies. Two boatswain's mates manned the side and piped as Commander Bounce's heavy frame came aboard. Bounce was in a particularly fine uniform for the end of the day on a Tuesday. He saluted the quarterdeck, turned, saluted Mr. Armond, asked and received permission to come aboard. Trueman watched closely to ensure that Armond knew and performed all customs and courtesies; after all, it reflected directly upon himself as commander.

"Good day, Sir." Armond greeted Bounce.

"And to you, Sir," Bounce returned. "My business is with the commanding officer."

"The 'Captain' is on the quarterdeck, Sir. May I escort you?"

94

"You may, Sir." Bounce indicated two younger officers who followed him aboard. "May I present Reginald Dowling, Subaltern of the Second West Indian Regiment, and Lef'tenant Paltier, Royal Marines, of Her Majesty's Steam Sloop *Falcon*."

What would require such a formal delegation? Trueman caught himself clearing his throat. His palms were moist. The three Britons and the Master crossed the short space between entry port and taffrail. All three visitors saluted with great formality and Armond tugged upon the bill of his cap. Trueman returned the courtesies as formally.

"Lef'tenant Trueman" – no courtesy "Captain" Trueman noticed with irritation - "on behalf of His Excellency, the Honourable James D. P. Porter, Governor of this Colony, I have the honour to present you with these orders for the immediate departure of your vessel, the United States Sloop-of-War *Jamestown*, from the territorial waters of Her Britannic Majesty's Crown Colony of Sierra Leone." Bounce removed a parchment from the large dispatch case under his arm, proffering it to Trueman.

Trueman did not move, ignored the document, and demanded the cause of such peremptory action. The facts were set forth in the document, which, Bounce assumed, Trueman had the courtesy to receive from his hand. Bounce's voice was level and hard.

"Take it, Mr. Armond," Trueman said flatly.

Before Armond could comply, Bounce thrust it to the startled Subaltern, Reginald Dowling. Principal-to-principal, or subordinate-to-subordinate, by Jove, thought Bounce. Dowling caught-on instantly and completed the delivery to the Master.

Trueman informed Bounce that he would be obliged, if the Port Captain could summarize the cause for the order and assured him that any variance from the wording of the document would not be seized upon to undermine the formal statement.

As a belligerent vessel, Bounce summarized, *Jamestown* was permitted to remain in port only long enough to refit and provision, both of which it was obvious she had accomplished. Lef'tenant Trueman had been informed of the belligerent status of his vessel upon his first visit to Government House, so the order to depart should not come as a surprise.

Trueman looked hard and long at the officer before him. But for the splendid uniform and neatly trimmed brown beard, the corpulent commander was a personification of a John Bull caricature in a cartoon from the *Illustrated London News*. "There are a few matters yet to be resolved ere we depart, Commander," he countered.

With evident relish, Bounce pompously intoned that, while it certainly would not do Trueman's career any benefit to have done so, the Governor could have added that *Jamestown* had violated the sovereignty of Her Majesty's domains and jeopardized the peace of Her realm by putting ashore an armed body of men intended to coerce Her Majesty's subjects. In recognition of the amity between their governments, he continued, *Jamestown* simply was ordered to depart forthwith to avoid any future violations of British sovereignty.

"What armed body of...."

Bounce interrupted, "I am not here to debate facts, Lef'tenant. Depart forthwith!'"

The wind and tide were against them, Trueman argued, and he must wait for proper conditions and a pilot. Not so, answered Bounce. Her Majesty's Gunboat *Tourch* had steam up and would tow *Jamestown* out. The pilot was aboard her. Trueman would depart within the hour. 'Waste not a minute!' was the watchword of the Royal Navy, and Bounce commended it to the American. Bounce raised his hat high off his head in parting salute. As he did so, Union Jacks broke out at the batteries on King Tom's Point, Fort Falconbridge, and the single gun position to the northeast of Government House. Simultaneously, *Falcon* and *Tourch* opened gunports exposing their ordinance.

"Very well," Trueman snapped at Bounce's half-turned back.

Paltier extended another large envelope to Trueman. "I place the enclosed documents in your hands on behalf of certain gentlemen ashore, Lef'tenant."

Preoccupied, Trueman automatically accepted it. Paltier was striding to the entry port before Trueman realized what he had done and flung the package to the deck.

"Recall the water party, Mr. Armond," Trueman snapped viciously. "Hands on deck to get underway. Boatswain to muster a party to receive cable from *Tourch*. *Get 'em moving!*" Perhaps an hour of daylight left, he calculated. They would depart in full visibility if they hurried and all went well.

Trueman turned his gaze to the beach, the field equipment. One longboat with partially filled water casks pushed off for the ship. The only other boat inshore was pulling toward the sloop. It only held six men, barely enough to row it. Trueman had a sinking feeling in his stomach.

"Signal from the beach," the signalman reported. "Spelling, Sir. 'A ... D ... I ... E ... U,' Sir. A, D, I, E, U, Sir."

"Gobbledygook," spat Armond.

"Think New Orleans, Mr. Armond," Trueman snapped. "French, Mr. Armond. 'Farewell, Goodbye.' By God, I'll see Bonney hanged for this."

Appleton came on deck as Trueman turned from the rail. "Damn it, Mr. Appleton, get the boats aboard and that cable in from that damned steamer! Anchors Aweigh. *Now!*" At least, Trueman fumed, they would look sharp leaving this damned place.

*   *   *   *   *   *   *   *   *   *

Sweet and Bonney stood apart from the others on the beach focusing intently upon the activities aboard *Jamestown*. How would Trueman respond to their deifying his recall order? The sudden flury of activity indicated that they would not receive a reply. Clearly, Trueman's attentions were focused upon getting his ship underway.

"Cast loose and provide," Bonney mused aloud to no one in particular.

"What?" Sweet snapped in confusion at the Marine's recitation of the first in the series of orders required to bring a naval gun into action.

"Not thinking of the guns this moment, Mr. Sweet," Bonney said with a half-hearted attempt at a smile. "Rather that we are 'cast loose' from all support and shall have to 'provide' for a score of hands with what resources I know not. We may have landed ourselves in a bigger stew than staying aboard *Jamestown* would have been."

"Sufficient unto the day are...."

"But He also helps those who help themselves, Charles, and we best be cogitating on that most directly, we want to keep this collection of castaways together and get them home in good order ... or at all."

Automatically both officers looked to the sailors and Marines of the watering party, every man of whom was transfixed by the activities aboard *Jamestown*. The dejection was palpable. Their home, their only source of sustenance, of identity, of defining their purpose in life was exerting every effort to maroon them on an inhospitable shore. Dispare, both of them knew, rapidly would erode discipline destroying any hope of getting their little party home as a unit.

"LISTEN UP!" bellowed Banning. "There's gear t' shift up to the road afore them bumboats and the tide comes to this here beach and makes a bloody goat-rope out o' all this fine equipment and supplies our Officer of Marines has convinced the old *Jamestown* to leave for us. So shift your arses or you'll be sleepin' in the wet smellin' like day-dead fish!"

Bonney smiled and relaxed. His sergeant already was keeping the men busy, preserving discipline and unity of effort among the hands. They would make it home by the grace of the Almighty and the loyalty of their non-commissioned and petty officers.

*   *   *   *   *   *   *   *   *   *

From the Law Courts Nevis watched *Jamestown* depart with gleeful satisfaction. Instead of two penniless stranded young soldiers of fortune desperate to get home, the Americans were leaving behind a little army in the same predicament. The possibilities were absolutely beyond his wildest dreamings.

CHAPTER FOURTEEN

Governor Porter eyed the dozen off-white tents neatly aligned along the edge of the Parade on Tower Hill. For a moment he had thoughts of tents in Bengal, displaced survivors who had escaped the night of treachery and murder in the Honorable East India Company cantonments. But this was different, he reminded himself. These were not refugees to protect and meld into a force for a counterstrike. These people were a political disaster waiting to erupt. What to do with thirty-odd armed men marooned in the colony? He agreed with Captain Jennings of *H.M.S. Falcon* that whatever it was, it best be sooner than later. The stranded Americans were living on the rapidly depleting personal funds of their three young officers. Marvelous of Jennings, Porter thought, to say the obvious, then stand there self-satisfied as if on his own quarterdeck. The Governor needed a sound proposal before the American officers arrived. He said as much to his assembled advisors.

Muttered confirmation came from all present. In addition to Governor Porter, Captain Jennings and his Royal Marine Officer, Lieutenant Paltier, the group included the Queen's Attorney, the Governor's Secretary Mr. Hornby in white linen and pince-nez spectacles, Commander Parker of *H.M.S. Touch*, Captain Page-Norton of the 2nd West, and Captain of the Port, Commander Bounce, RN. Porter was amused at the way Bounce had relished his central role in sending *Jamestown* packing. After nearly four decades of being in the shadows of others making decisions and taking dramatic action, Bounce had had his moment. Well, good on him, the Governor concluded.

As if to further delay decision, Bounce asked the Queen's Attorney the legal status of the "guests." Showing the heat despite the pleasant breeze on the hilltop, the lawyer declared them foreign nationals clearly, not stateless persons, but declined to say further, the efficacy of their "purported" resignations being a matter of American *juris prudence*.

Whatever their status the Governor observed, it behooved the colonial administration to pack them off to America earliest possible. When was the next homeward bound Government ship due? Transport *Relief* from The Cape would not call for over a fortnight, Bounce answered. Porter's request for options elicited only negative murmurs. Very well, Porter would propose that the Americans accept transport on *Relief*; certainly Hornby could find a way to hide the expense somewhere in the budget. Meantime, Porter observed, Paltier had the closest rapport with the Americans. With Jennings' permission, would he act as liaison? Jennings swiftly concurred.

"Try to keep them engaged in some profitable pursuit, Paltier," urged the Governor. "Otherwise I fear they will be so embroiled legally we shall never be shut of them."

"Could work with my chaps on beach landings or the like?" suggested Page-Norton. Occasionally, the 2nd West was called upon to land from boats on beach or riverbank to enforce Her Majesty's peace. The last couple efforts had been rather awkward.

"My Jollies would participate," Paltier added, a break from the ordinary always was welcomed by his Royal Marines.

"*Falcon* or *Tourch* will be available for such exercises," added Jennings, "and carried as 'volunteers' they could draw rations from our stores."

Jennings' last was helpful, Porter admitted, and Page-Norton's scheme preferable to the Jonathans sitting about. They would cruise with the Royal Navy until *Relief* arrived, if the embarrassing visitors agreed, and logic demanded that they do so.

*　　*　　*　　*　　*　　*　　*　　*　　*　　*

Bonney and Sweet walked in preoccupied silence from Tower Hill to the address near the Law Courts. Constantly gnawing at the edge of Bonney's consciousness was the problem of getting to America now that they had escaped from Trueman. They did not have sufficient funds to buy passage for all of their party, could not even feed them for much more than a fortnight.

At least they were continuing to conduct the affairs of their small band of marooned Americans as if they remained members of the United States Naval Service subject to the Articles of War. The men readily accepted the arrangement; it gave stability and a comfortable familiarity to their otherwise most uncertain circumstances. As part of this continuity, Talliaferro was back at the camp holding "Captain's Mast," an informal tribunal used for most infractions aboard ship. He had delegated Bonney to represent him at the meeting with Nevis to conclude the litigation that had brought Sweet and Talliaferro ashore.

Sweet's thoughts focused upon Bonney. Daniel had persisted in pleading the Marine's case and Sweet finally had admitted that Bonney's help had been crucial to his deliverance from Trueman's clutches. Intellectually, Charles recognized that he had been wrong and somehow needed to resolve their mutual discomfort with each other. Nevertheless, he continued to resent Bonney's uninvited guidance, the more so when it proved correct.

For his part, Bonney was exasperated with the younger man and resolved to minimize their interaction. He had relaxed his aloofness somewhat the previous afternoon when Sweet and he had accepted the invitation of Page-Norton and a couple of his lieutenants to do some target shooting. In the informal setting Sweet had warmed a bit and proved himself both a good shot and a good companion. He even had shown good-humored acceptance when a percussion cap splattered his face with primer temporarily affecting his vision and ending his shooting for the day. Bonney had been amazed with the casual way that Sweet had Daniel shoot in his place and the slave's exceptional expertise with the rifle. Any man who in violation of the law would develop his servant's marksmanship had more to him than Sweet appeared to exhibit.

The walk to the lawyer's home and office gave Sweet and Bonney the perfect opportunity to resolve their uneasiness. Down Gloucester Street and along Water Street they trudged in silence, each waiting for the other to initiate conversation. Neither did so. As a result, they let the opportunity pass.

Halcyon Nevis solemnly greeted them at the bungalow door. The house - a warm ochre color with soft red trim and shutters, capped by a rusting tin roof - housed Nevis's law office on the ground floor, living quarters above. The dormered attic was home to his "wards," children of relations or associates entrusted to Nevis to raise upon the assumption that their own parents would be too permissive. From Bonney's observations, most guardians took full advantage of the labor pool created by the system. He noticed a young boy squatting by the wall absently pulling a cable running to a hawsehole at ceiling level; at least there was a fan in the office.

They passed through an anti-chamber filled with cane furniture. A pigtailed girl of perhaps six in a single-piece dress of colorful floral print held open an interior door, dropping an exaggerated, rather clumsy courtesy as they passed. Sweet's smile at the urchin was answered by a toothy yellow grin before she fled on quiet feet.

As they entered the office, Pa Cabot's patois burbled from the shadows. Nevis indicated several cane chairs before his highly polished spindle-legged desk. The room was dark, the louvered shutters closed against the sun on the eastern wall and the northern windows shaded by the porch where the youth listlessly tugged the fan pull. In the musty heat a stifling lethargy oppressed the room.

Nevis began by observing there were some few matters to put to rest, now that they were delivered from the clutches of that "obnoxious fellow Trueman." First, plaintiffs now realized that all complaints against the midshipmen were ill founded and would be non-suited. Bonney snapped alert at that. Non-suited, not dismissed meant that the claims could be filed again.

"However," Nevis continued, "my clients have gone to some effort to deliver you from your predicament and of course my fees have been significant," Nevis concluded.

They wanted money, Sweet realized, roused from his heat-induced stupor. "Of course we shall pay your fee and…."

Bonney flinched; he knew what was coming.

"You may *not* pay my fees, Sir. You are the opposing party. Such would be most improper." Nevis's tone was one of pedagogical shock. "Settlement with my clients without involving myself, the litigation being ended, is solely amongst yourselves."

"Certainly," Sweet mumbled, chastened.

Nevis leaned forward, elbows on his blotter. "Recall theirs was an act of friendship, not services-for-hire, Mr. Sweet. Opportunity exists to return the favor."

So here it comes, thought Bonney; they were being manipulated into something.

Smoothly, the lawyer explained that Pa Cabot belonged to a distinguished Liberian family of pure "American" blood and had been "well educated" at a mission school. His late father had been Superintendent of Public Affairs of Sinoe County, "Governor" Americans would say. In the natural order of things, Pa Cabot should have succeeded his father when the senior Cabot passed-on three years before.

"However," Nevis explained, "a purported half brother by a tribal woman...."

Cabot erupted, *"Damn Bush Nigger!"*

"Yes, well, this fellow and his savage cohorts seized power rather violently...."

"Enty!" Cabot wailed. " Mammy, wife, pickan, all *done live,* by that *Bush Nigger!"*

"Done live?" "Died," Sweet translated mentally. It had been a massacre, just like the slave revolt in Haiti or the Sepoy treachery in India five years back.

"As Pa Cabot says," Nevis hastily continued, "this fellow - 'Gabriel' he is called - butchered the entire Cabot household, roughly thirty-five souls including wards and servants. Luckily, my client was in Monrovia arranging the orderly transfer of power."

To himself, thought Bonney, as Nevis explained that the Liberian Government, while fully supporting Cabot's ascent, lacked sufficient power to reverse the coup.

Nevis leaned forward across his desk for emphasis, his almond eyes narrowing in concentration. "It occurs that, as a sign of gratitude, you and your compatriots might wish to see justice done and Pa Cabot's fortunes restored."

Bonney and Sweet exchanged wary glances, the most open indication of agreement between them yet. Nevis sat back in his chair waiting for a response. Pa Cabot was quietly animated, putting Sweet in mind of a birddog eyeing a quail. The long silence, heavy in the room's dark humidity, heightened the palpable tension.

Finally Bonney spoke. "Why has not the Liberian Government sought help from its security guarantors? Surely, the United States, the British ... even the French could...."

"No nation wishes to admit that it cannot maintain the rule of law within its own domains," Nevis answered. "Were they to do so, other powers, especially colonial powers, might conclude that Liberia no longer is capable of maintaining its claims to the area. The United States does not even officially recognize Liberia's nationhood." Nevis paused for emphasis. "Is not that the issue confronting His Excellency Lincoln in your own country? You and your men, however, are not in the service of another power. You should help after all Pa Cabot has done."

Interesting idea and fascinating legal issues, Bonney reflected. Just who are we, anyway? Aloud he voiced his concerns: Gabriel's forces were unknown. The Americans had no supplies, no reserves of ammunition, no transport to reach Liberia. How would the British react to an invasion launched from their territory? The Foreign Enlistments Act of 1818, passed by Parliament after several private expeditions consisting of Napoleonic War veterans had left from Britain to support revolts in Spanish America, prohibited exactly such undertakings.

All could be arranged, Nevis assured them. Cabot had a schooner. Gabriel's forces were rabble. Supplies could be had and the British would turn a blind eye. Bonney's skin prickled; it was too easy, and fraught with uncertainties.

Suppose they install Cabot, Sweet asked. What became of Pa Cabot when they left?

"Gabriel dead; *same-same* his wife, his pickan. All then be safe for Cabots."

"Not about to conduct a massacre," Bonney snapped.

"*Ahyee!* No massacre; be justice!" replied Cabot vehemently.

Once order was restored, the Liberian Government could maintain it, Nevis rapidly assured them. The Americans only need chase Gabriel from Greenville until Liberian forces arrived. As they all knew, Nevis observed, it was far more difficult to reverse the order of things than to maintain it once established. Indeed, Nevis pointedly observed, once Mr. Cabot was restored, he would be in a position to facilitate their return to America.

Their predicament must be glaringly obvious, Bonney realized, and it made the Americans subject to the most blatant manipulation. Still, he reflected, a drowning man cannot complain about the coarseness of the rope … or a hanged man either, for that matter. Exactly how would Cabot arrange their repatriation, Bonney asked? Nevis explained that Sinoe County had numerous natural blessings and was a port of call for a few American vessels. Cabot would have at his disposal resources and means to obtain their passage home.

"To a port of our choosing?" asked Bonney.

"Most definitely," responded Nevis.

"Regardless of the status of that port in the opinion of the United States Government?"

"I am confident all can be arranged," comforted Nevis.

This is insane, Bonney thought. He could not envision a Yankee ship sailing them merrily to a Southern port, but maybe Bahamas…. Perhaps they could circumvent the Foreign Enlistments Act by retroactively declaring themselves Confederate forces and presenting their departure in Cabot's schooner as compliance with their obligations as belligerents. What if they simply seized the schooner once at sea and sailed home? Would it be piracy, or an act of war against whatever nation's flag flew over the vessel? Would it create another enemy for the fledgling Confederacy? Bonney could see nothing good coming from the harebrained idea, other than quite probably their only way of getting home. Aloud he said, "Such an undertaking is not entered upon lightly. We must examine the vessel, learn more about the area and the situation, and investigate the British position, before we can agree to such a plan."

"Certainly, my dear Lef'tenant. We expect nothing else. Contingent upon it proving feasible, do we have your assent to participating in the operation?"

"Conceptually, I believe so." Bonney preserved his options. "Any insufficiency in resources, information, conditions, be it weather, attitudes of governments, or opportunity to take more immediate passage to America, we abandon the scheme. Agree?"

"Rather a poor certainty from our perspective," replied Nevis. "At the very least, we should be able to possess your warlike equipment to mount our own attempt."

"We have a frontier saying in America, Mr. Nevis, 'Take it or leave it.' No compensatory conditions. If we pull out, we do so with all of our equipment."

Good try, Nevis consoled himself. "As you say, Mr. Bonney, we shall 'take it.'"

*   *   *   *   *   *   *   *   *   *

Once outside the ochre house and beyond earshot of its inhabitants, Sweet's curiosity overcame his pride and he asked Bonney's views as to why they should even considered such a scheme. Unless Governor Porter had a sane suggestion, Bonney replied, this lunacy might prove their only hope of getting home before their funds ran out. Bonney reminded Sweet of the White former slave traders marooned in Lagos unable to obtain passage back to Europe; he had no desire to join them indefinitely in an area known as "The White Man's Grave."

"You can be a step ahead of me, on occasion, Sir," Sweet admitted.

"My sire was a lawyer, Mr. Sweet," answered Bonney with a hint of a smile. "I am imbued with an instinct for the nefarious."

"Reckon I should be appreciative, Lieutenant," Sweet replied with a grin. "Must say your abilities have been of significance in saving my bacon, last few days."

Bonney grinned back. That was all that needed to be said.

＊　　　＊　　　＊　　　＊　　　＊　　　＊　　　＊　　　＊　　　＊　　　＊

The sun neared the western horizon as the three Americans ascended the steps of Government House. This good weather would break any day, Bonney mused. Then, The Rains, a six-month monsoon moving east-to-west out of central Africa to cross the Atlantic and become hurricanes in the Americas, would render the tent camp untenable and bring the miasmas that caused ague, yellow jack, malaria. In their present situation most of their party were likely to be dead from disease before The Rains ended. Freetown's devastating 1859 epidemic was fresh in everyone's mind. It was imperative they find immediate passage home. Perhaps this was coloring their thinking regarding Nevis's preposterous proposal. However, the Marine Lieutenant reminded himself, that Brit, Brooke, had sailed into Brunei a few years ago with an old schooner crewed by a pack of Lascars and made himself Rajah of Sarawak.

Bonney's musings ended when Paltier stepped through the louvered French doors at the top of the steps and ushered them to the side veranda to join the Governor, Captain Jennings, Commander Parker, Captain Page-Norton and the Governor's Secretary, Mr. Hornby, for small talk over brandy and sodas. Yes, the campsite was quite suitable. Provisions were sufficient for the moment. How considerate of the 2nd West's officers to permit the American officers to occupy guest quarters and participate in their mess. After the obligatory observation of the sun dipping below the Atlantic's rim, they went in to supper, an all male affair. Her ladyship obviously was not interested in another evening with "The Wild Colonial Boys."

Dinner passed with little serious conversation. Over cigars and port, Governor Porter came to the point. "I assume, Gentlemen, you all are anxious to be off home?"

Well put Your Excellency, thought Bonney, suppressing a smile at the Governor's diplomatic avoidance of referencing any nation, or even the geographic term that had become shorthand for the United States. General agreement existed that they must depart before The Rains turned the coast into the malarial deathtrap, "The White Man's Grave." That was why a company of the 2nd West Indian Regiment constituted the Freetown Garrison, Bonney realized; excepting officers, they all were Negroes, commonly understood to be resistant to tropical diseases.

"Best hope," Hornby suggested, "HM's transport *Relief* from the Cape. In England you'll have no problem getting the rest of the way. She's due in something over a fortnight."

"Soonest possible," responded Bonney, concerned. "Morale is a key factor, you understand." The men had a very real and justifiable fear of staying long ashore in Africa.

105

"Preferable to maintain your people as a disciplined unit, certainly," agreed Paltier emphasizing the morale rather than the health content of Bonney's comments.

"I've a suggestion there, really a favor of sorts," Page-Norton began. "Time-to-time my lads get called for some boat work along the coast. Perhaps your chaps would do a bit of training with mine, show them the ropes." He hesitated ever so slightly. "Your people would not bother that mine are darkies?"

"Doesn't appear to have corrupted the Jollies," responded Bonney looking to Paltier.

"We shall require some assistance with logistical support," interjected Talliaferro, trying not to appear over-eager to subsist on Her Majesty's rations in healthy sea air.

"We should accept nothing less," responded Page-Norton.

"Wouldn't hurt to put on a bit of a show for some of the chiefs," Captain Jennings observed. "Porto Novo's a bit far to have had an impact on the headmen hereabouts."

The Americans had only heard mention of the British action at Porto Novo, an African community on one of the mouths of the Niger River. Talliaferro asked for details, which Jennings willingly provided. A local "king" named Soji refused British demands to close his slave barracoon. Commodore Edmonstone, Officer Commanding West African Station, had gone up Victoria Lagoon from Lagos and torched the place, coming off with one killed and six wounded. Soji supposedly had 10,000 men on hand.

"Rather overstated, I'm sure," interjected the Governor.

"Numbers on the native side. Bluster and noise; no discipline," Jennings countered.

"As always, rumors of Whites leading them; doubt it, personally," added Paltier.

"Lord knows, we see Russians commanding every pack of wogs who take a snipe at us, world around," joined in Page-Norton. "At best, might have been a mulatto or possibly one or two of the former slave traders from Lagos who bear us such love." That comment brought a snicker around the table.

"Any event, slaving at Porto Novo is disrupted; respect for Her Majesty's wishes restored," concluded Jennings.

"And the liberal lights of the British press have interpreted it all as an unprovoked assault upon our innocent African brethren," concluded Governor Porter. "Wish they could see the slave barracoons their innocent natives operate." His Excellency glanced at Talliaferro hoping that his last phrase had not set off the touchy American. Porter had no knowledge what slave markets were like in the Carolinas.

"Most interesting; thank you Captain Jennings, Gentlemen," Bonney closed the discussion of Porto Novo. "It would be our honor to do a bit of boat work with the 2nd West and your Leathernecks, Paltier; may well learn some useful tricks ourselves."

"'Bootnecks,' Bonney," rejoined the Royal Marine, "Same idea – the leather stock – but we must maintain some distinctions."

"Rest assured," Governor Porter interrupted with an earnest smile, "Whatever name you wish, you will not have to undergo torture by boredom on the Parade at Tower Hill."

CHAPTER FIFTEEN

Sweet gazed over *H.M.S. Falcon's* port rail across the light swell toward the staysails of *H.M.S. Tourch*, hull-down to the northward. Somewhere beyond was Cape Palmas where the West African coast ceased its southeasterly slant and turned slightly north-of-east, where the Grain Coast gave way to the Ivory; the southeastern corner of Liberia's recently acquired Maryland County. In light winds, the British men-of-war proceeded under sail and steam, preserving both coal and the ability to swiftly accelerate.

Falcon resembled *Jamestown*, with the addition of the tall smokestack just forward of the mainmast and that pervasive scent. *Jamestown* smelled of tar, wood, and salt, smells hidden by the odor of bitumen on *Falcon*. At least her lines were clean compared to *Tourch*, which reminded Sweet of a roast turkey, her great ugly paddle-boxes protruding to either side amidships like the drumsticks of the bird.

Freetown was several days behind them. They had performed three days of boat drill with the 2nd West, ending in a descent upon the Banana Islands off Cape Shilling. Then Captain Jennings returned his small squadron to Freetown, offloaded the West Indians, and invited the Americans on a run along the coast, possibly as far as Cape Three Points, where the Ivory Coast gave way to the Gold. Knowing the men to be healthier at sea, the Americans heartily accepted. Thus, Sweet found himself gazing across the sparkling ocean at the small sails and smoke smudge of *H.M.S. Tourch*.

The thump of a gun ended Sweet's reflections. To instant demands for information, the lookout replied that the wind was streaming *Tourch's* signal flags directly toward *Falcon* making them impossible to read. Sweet's spirits surged. *Tourch* wanted *Falcon's* attention for some good reason, a suspicious sail, a slaver perhaps?

Captain Jennings came on deck as *Falcon* altered course to close her consort. As she turned, Sweet heard an unaccustomed sound; bells, not the clang of the ships bell, but the jingle of the ship's telegraph. The smoke thickened from *Falcon's* funnel as the sloop surged under Sweet's feet. He was fascinated as the British captain trimmed sails and adjusted engine revolutions. The American midshipman imagined Captain Pennington grumbling at the passing of the age of true sailing men, but Sweet sensed the artistry in Jennings handling of his command. He was "sailing" her as much as Pennington ever had *Jamestown*. Time permitting, Sweet could learn much from this officer.

Tourch also must have altered course, for *Falcon* took longer than expected to close the distance to where her signal was visible from the deck, "Suspect Sail." As Sweet stepped aft out of the way, Captain Jennings demanded the suspect's heading. Sweet watched as the message sped aloft, barely aware of Talliaferro and Bonney joining him.

Shortly the midshipman of the watch reported, "*Tourch* sends, 'Hull down, south-southeast-by-south, Sir." Jennings curtly ordered acknowledgement, but the midshipman had his glass up again. "'Believe Black J...O...N...*Black Jonathan*,' Sir!"

Jennings snorted. "Bloody waste of coal chasing after her. However...." Seizing an American ship, slaver or not, would cause a diplomatic crisis.

Bonney looked at Talliaferro and Sweet in their U. S. Navy uniforms. "Beg pardon, Captain Jennings," he said, "She is American; you've U.S. Navy officers aboard."

Jennings turned quickly. "You gentlemen have...."

Smiling, Bonney interrupted, "No formal action upon our status, Sir. We wear the uniform and hold United States commissions. Neither you, nor your Government has grounds to question our 'patriotism and fidelity' as I understand matters."

Jennings grinned, his eyes sparkling like a lad contemplating a prank. "Have the Chief give us all revolutions he can, Lef'tenant Sawyer. Make to *Tourch*, 'Apprehend.'"

Again, Sweet could not help admiring Bonney's ingenuity and audacity, or noticing that Jennings accepted his suggestion enthusiastically without umbrage or argument. Sweet gave Bonney a conspiratorial smile.

As *Falcon's* steam-induced speed increased, Jennings furled his sails to prevent the canvas becoming great wind brakes countering the engines. Under a cloud of bitumen, he set a course that would lose *Tourch* over the horizon and place *Falcon* across the projected path of the unseen chase. It was entirely a matter of mathematics, of angles, Sweet realized, to guess the correct heading to intercept the chase on its southeast-by-south course. Jennings was working by instinct. Still, the winds were moderate, giving the steam-powered vessels the advantage. If *Tourch* could pressure the chase from behind, she might be prevented from altering course to avoid *Falcon*.

*   *   *   *   *   *   *   *   *   *

Sweet's excitement slowly ebbed as *Falcon* surged south-southeast-by-east racing against a phantom across endless sparkling seas. As the sloop charged deeper into the Gulf of Guinea, it became increasingly probable that *Falcon* had missed the intercept. Still, it had been an interesting day. Sweet found the relative freedom from dependence upon fickle winds exciting, but regretted that command of the seas was coming to dependent upon men bent double, twelve hours at a stretch, in the choking darkness of a coal mine half a globe away. Something Bonney was saying ended his philosophizing.

"You actually believe her to be the vessel we chased in *Jamestown*?" he asked Paltier.

"When and where exactly did you raise her?" Paltier responded.

110

Bonney thought for a moment. "Twenty-third of the month past, vicinity two degrees, say 40 minutes east, five degrees, 40 minutes north."

"Heading?"

"North, perhaps north-northeast-by-north, Lieutenant Paltier," interjected Sweet. After all, he had been the first aboard *Jamestown* to examine the *Black Jonathan*.

"In-bound to the Slave Coast, eh? You gave chase for, what … three days?"

"Three-and-a-half, actually, until our foretop gave way," grumbled Bonney.

"Assuming he circled back, that would put him at the same location, with headwinds, roughly the second instant?" Paltier frowned. "Navy has seen the fellow you chased - presumably same fellow - in the Bight of Benin that time for the past two years collecting a last load of 'black sheep' before The Rains. Now, imagine that his barracoon had been disrupted before he could get to it after you put him off schedule…."

Bonney's face lit with understanding, "At a place such as Porto…."

"Porto Novo, which we shot to pieces 22nd April, my dear Bonney, exactly."

"Lured us from the coast, then doubled-back." Sweet realized the answer to Captain Pennington's questioning why *Black Jonathan* had teased *Jamestown* away from Africa.

"Porto Novo in ruins, no woolies there, he must find another source," Paltier observed.

"Could be the same fellow," mused Bonney. "How'd he find another source, Paltier?"

"My dear Bonney, legitimate palm-oil merchants in Lagos, against all natural inclinations, might be induced to renew old contacts. Native chiefs could muster a cargo much faster. They're the slave source for the Lagos chaps, any event. Our friend need but let it be known he'll trade baubles for bodies. Despite abolitionist fantasies, Africa has no wish to end the slave trade. The righteous of the land can gather a cargo in a twinkling."

"But not so quick as our friend would stay at anchor waiting," Sweet observed, surprised at how comfortable he was conversing with Bonney.

"Certainly not. One of those obnoxious British might come along and anchor next to him. Then how can he load cargo? Or, an American cruiser might appear and seize ship and crew. No, gentlemen of The Trade don't stay long at anchor on this coast."

"So," responded Bonney, "Porto Novo the 2nd instant. He perceives quickly…."

"Oh intelligent chap," gasped Paltier in mock amazement.

"Perceives quickly," Bonney repeated, "there's no cargo there, and does what?"

"Try his luck with that great dog, the King of Dahomey, contact sources in Lagos, head either way along the coast looking for another source; he's many options."

"Unless he finds a barracoon that's full, must allow time to fill it," observed Sweet.

"Right you are and the longer the better in terms of quality," responded Paltier.

"Week to arrange things; two, say three to collect the cargo...." Sweet mused.

"And *Tourch* raises him bang on schedule off Cape Palmas," beamed Paltier.

"That being so, where would he be getting his cargo?" queried Bonney.

"Bit westerly for Dahomey or some mouth of the Niger. No need to be at Cape Palmas if he intends something off the Ivory Coast," mused Paltier. "My bet is Liberia."

"But that's *freed slaves!*" protested Sweet.

"And?" Paltier replied. "My Dear Fellow, the Americo-Liberians, colonists of color from your erstwhile country, call natives '*Bush Niggers*' and as soon spit as look on them. Natives hate the Americo-Liberians as conquerors, quite rightly. 'Americans' hold natives in thrall that *I* cannot distinguish from the cane fields of Jamaica thirty years ago. Either bunch would happily ship the other lot off to Cuba and would see naught but profit in packing off some poor sods from the interior. There are chiefs beyond number up-country ready to sell them slaves without limit. My bet, our chap is headed for Liberia."

*   *   *   *   *   *   *   *   *   *

Captain Jennings believed otherwise. *Falcon* maintained course until nightfall, then doubled back at reduced speed, sighting neither chase nor *Tourch*. Mid-morning the following day, *Tourch* re-joined *Falcon* off Cape Three Points and reported chasing the *Black Jonathan* until dusk, when she disappeared. Commander Parker concluded she was bound for the Bight of Benin and sailed in that direction without result. By now she could be anywhere. Far from his patrol area, Jennings made for Freetown without delay to put the Americans aboard *Relief*. Under light steam and sail the two vessels turned west, *Tourch* inshore of *Falcon*, together covering a thirty-mile wide swath of ocean.

After sunset, they proceeded at reduced speed with dimmed running lights. Sometime in the second night, they lost contact. Morning found *Falcon* alone of Cape Palmas. Captain Jennings closed the land until in view of the Cape. When by noon the gunboat had not appeared, Jennings reluctantly turned east again into the Gulf of Guinea.

112

Several hours after *Falcon* settled on her easterly course, the masthead hailed, "Deck there! Ship inshore fine on port bow. It be *Jonathan!*"

Bonney was ensconced against the transom rail with the wardroom's copy of Mr. Dickens' new novel, *A Tale of Two Cities*, when *Falcon* began to reverberate to the double-double-double-beat of the Royal Marine Drummers thumping "Beat to Quarters." Deliberately, he marked his place, closed the book, and headed for the cuddy he was "borrowing" from a junior midshipman of the Royal Navy. Before the temporary walls of his temporary home disappeared, Bonney had to arm himself.

Sweet was touring *Falcon's* machinery with a young engineering officer when the drumming commenced. He rushed to the ladder and snaked his way topside through the confusion of preparing the ship for combat. *Falcon's* ordered world erupted into chaos as screens came down, galley fires were extinguished, decks sanded, and the thousand other little details of "clearing for action" simultaneously performed.

Sweet reached the deck as Lieutenant Sawyer asked Bonney to form the Americans on the poop as boarders. Good God, thought Sweet, my sword and pistol. He hurried toward the wardroom hoping his cuddy had not already been dismantled and his chest hustled into the hold. On the ladder, he met Daniel, Sweet's weapons in hand, announcing that he would load the bulky LeMat revolver, while his master attended to more weighty matters.

Bonney passed Sawyer's request to Banning, then examined the chase. She was in the process of sortieing from the mouth of a river, the San Pedro Bonney concluded, Liberia's eastern boundary. Paltier was right; she had headed for the Negro republic.

The chaos stopped abruptly as Lieutenant Sawyer formally reported *Falcon* cleared for action. Jennings examined his watch, nodded in satisfaction, and ordered Sawyer to fire a gun commanding the *Jonathan* to heave-to. A blast erupted from a carronade near the forecastle. Smoke obscured Bonney's view. When it cleared there was no alteration in course, speed, or actions of the chase. Indeed, a moment later she let fly her topgallant sails. Bonney thought her somehow clumsier than he recalled; natural, he concluded, that there would be confusion with a new cargo of squirming humanity crammed into her hold. He imagined the carnage a shell would produce on her berth deck.

Pursuit continued for another half-hour. The black ship almost cleared the estuary when Jennings ordered another shot, this time with the Armstrong Rifle on the forward pivot mount. The 100-pound shell burst a cable's length ahead and slightly beyond the chase, lashing the water with shrapnel. The black ship showed a flag, the Stars and Stripes. *Falcon* signaled "Heave-To." It was disregarded, prompting Captain Jennings to order Mr. Sawyer to put an Armstrong round through a sail on the black ship. The projectile punched a substantial hole in the fore course, bursting two hundred yards beyond. *Falcon* was gaining on the American in the light wind.

113

Laconically, Jennings ordered the signal, 'End Exercise.'" Shortly after the flag broke out, the slaver rounded into the wind under backed main and fore topsails.

As *Falcon* approached the slaver, Bonney became aware of a low crooning. The telltale stench had not settled upon her; shipped her cargo within the last few days, he concluded. She identified herself as *Ebony Angel*, Port of New York; homeward bound with palm oil, gum rubber, and ivory, bringing a guffaw among *Falcon's* officers.

"She'll have papers to support it, no doubt," commented Sawyer.

"Ask them what is the noise, if you please, Mr. Sawyer," ordered Captain Jennings. The answering hail advised that *Ebony Angel* had shipped cattle for fresh meat. Captain Jennings could not restrain a chuckle. "What cheek. Entertaining fellow, have to admit." Bonney agreed, recalling "Maggie's Drawers" waving at the chase's gaff.

The Third Lieutenant, Mr. MacKay, led the British boarding party. In addition to the oarsmen, the longboats held a half-dozen red-coated Marines and a half-dozen heavily armed Tars in white jumpers and bellbottoms. The Americans on *Falcon* knelt behind the hammock nettings out of view. An officer appeared on the slaver's deck with a leather portmanteau, the ship's papers. Shouting erupted, the man with the valise gesturing wildly. The Royal Marines came to the Ready and the excitement abated.

MacKay hailed, "Jonathan clearly. Suggest is a matter for our American guests, Sir!"

"Stand to!" Bonney ordered. The Americans stood, clearly visible from the slaver.

Talliaferro dispatched Bonney with a half-dozen each of Marines and Blue Jackets to the black ship where he confronted a slender, brown-bearded man in a blue uniform.

"Matter for you Americans, Lef'tenant Bonney," Lieutenant MacKay greeted. "We shall stand-by to assist, if you wish."

"Thank you, Sir. That would be most kind." Silently Bonney took the portmanteau and skimmed the documents. "Let us examine this ivory, Captain ... Hillary is it?"

"No need to go sweating through the holds, now, Lieutenant ... Boney, is it?"

"He was Emperor of the French, Friend; I am an Officer of Marines. It's BONNEY."

"Still no need...."

"Friend, I've always wanted to see moaning ivory. Lead on."

"That's cattle! Already told the Limey here."

"You, Sir, are a liar. *Move*, lest I lose my sense of humor."

Below, multi-level shelves ran the length of the berth deck. They were so crammed with prone humans the occupants could hardly roll over. Two aisles gave access. Light was minimal, ventilation less. Bonney recognized the constant metallic sound, the rattle of chains. "I've seen enough; back on deck," he gagged to Hillary. In the sunlight and fresh air, he formally seized *Ebony Angel* for violating the laws of the United States.

*   *   *   *   *   *   *   *   *   *

Daniel held the lantern for the young Marine, Schmidt was his name, Daniel recalled, from New Jersey and just turned twenty. Schmidt was ladling "cush," a corn meal and dried fish gruel, into the cupped hands extended into the isle from the three levels of shelves on which the captives lay. The air was stifling, drained of oxygen, saturated with the acrid musk of stale sweat, urine, and feces. Only supplicant hands and forearms projecting into the passageway were visible in the dull light. The absence of a pair of hands was obvious. Had *Angel* avoided capture, later in her voyage such a space would mean a captive too weak to eat, to be hustled overboard to sharks or drowning before infecting others.

"*Wait!*" Daniel called.

Surprised, Schmidt looked back and missed the hands extended from the middle bunk. The cush plopped onto the head of a lower shelf occupant who already had buried his face in his ration. Lowering the lantern toward the gap in the row of hands, Daniel did not notice the snickers at this small comedy.

Bending down, Daniel imagined himself to be the prince in that *Sleeping Beauty* book Old Marse Edward, Marse Charles' papa, had read to them years before. On her back, still as death, was a girl whose only indication of life was the rhythmic rise and fall of her breasts. The lantern light produced a kaleidoscope of illumination and shadow, a bewitchingly distorted image that emphasized surfaces toward the aisle. Shoulders, breasts, forearms, hips, and thighs of the same smoothness and tanned-yellow hew as a fine pair of Sweet's riding gauntlets sparked a surging pulse in Daniel. At the change in the repetitious sound of steps, ladle on tin, and plop of cush, along with the light shining into the blackness between the bunks, she tilted back and opened her eyes; then snapped her head aside reacting to the light. That instant, Daniel looked into deep hazel pupils glittering beside a rather delicate nose flanked by tearstained cheeks above trembling lips of unexpected fineness. She moaned despairingly.

"Y'all needs to eat," Daniel said without thought of any language barrier.

"Ain't going to eat," volunteered a male voice.

These people were speaking English, Daniel realized.

"Done give up to die," a female voice abaft the girl added.

"No," replied Daniel. "Y'all been saved. We Americans gone and captured this ship. Free y'all, soonest we can." Excided murmuring spread along the berth deck.

115

"Hush up a minute," interjected Daniel. He leaned back toward the girl, now feebly wriggling against her neighbors in an effort to turn over and face the aisle. She managed to prop herself up on an elbow and looked at him dubiously.

"We'uns sure am Americans," Daniel comforted. "Here." He let the lantern illuminate Schmidt's blue flannel fatigue coat, brass buttons shining in the dull light. "No slaver wear something so comfortless down here sloppin' y'all."

Belief spread across her face, belief and hope. She levered herself the rest of the way onto her belly, and, with the jingle of manacles, cupped her palms for food. "Sorry, all we got," he apologized as the Marine ladled cush into her delicate hands.

"Best get moving, Boy," advised Schmidt. "Need to feed these here others and nothing else you can do for her 'til we make port."

Daniel knew it was impossible to unchain these people. It would be impossible for the shorthanded Americans to maintain order and work the ship, if the captives were allowed to roam about. The most humane action was to make port quickly. In a fog, he followed Schmidt along the line of hands, his eyes open and unseeing; his mind holding the image of a fawn goddess while his pulse raced.

CHAPTER SIXTEEN

"Most dicey, I do say." The Queen's Attorney spoke with more slurred emotion than Captain Jennings could recall. Best give the drunken windbag some credence on this matter, he concluded. Jennings, the Queen's Attorney, Governor Porter, Commander Bounce, Captain Page-Norton, and Mr. Hornby were standing on the seaward veranda of Government House viewing the roadstead. Anchored between *H.M.S. Falcon* and *H.M.S. Touch*, lay *Ebony Angel* of the Port of New York flying the Stars and Stripes. Within her, several hundred naked, prone, chained Africans lay shelved like so many bolts of sweating cloth.

"Dam and Blast," thought Governor Porter. Packing the Americans off to sea until *Relief* arrived had seemed an excellent solution to what to do with the castaways. Not in his wildest imaginings had it occurred to him that they would return with such a diplomatic booby trap. Jennings' cockamamie scheme now had an American vessel seized by the Royal Navy anchored at his colony and his responsibility. How to keep the Yankees from threatening war over disrespect for their flag while placating the liberal press determined to stop The Trade at any cost and crucify those who let minor matters such as war or peace stand in the way? He had visions of the Nabob's palace, the rumors of great change, divine actions, the return of the Moguls, and his decision that the information was too vague to credit. Then the Sepoys had struck in the night murdering their White officers and their families and any Indians loyal to the East India Company. Had he acted he might have warned of it, might have saved thousands of lives….

"Not taken by Royal Navy, not prize for Mixed Commission," slurred the Queen's Attorney. "No jurisdiction." It sounded more like, "Missed Commishon" and "jurisdishon."

His sun's damned well over the yardarm, concluded Jennings, disgusted that a drunken petty-fogger seemed about to decide his future as a sea officer. Jennings knew as well as the lawyer that the three judge Court of Mixed Commission existed by treaty to deal with captures of suspected slaving vessels "north of the Line," the Equator, by warships of the signatory powers: Great Britain, Spain, and Brazil. Panels of the Court with a judge from each of the signatory countries were located in Freetown and in Rio. Slaving was classed as piracy by international law, theoretically making slave ships subject to capture by any navy. However, the United States violently objected to any foreign authority asserting jurisdiction over its shipping. To avoid diplomatic crises, the navies of the signatory powers did not apprehend American vessels. Since over seventy percent of the slavers operating off the West African coast flew the U.S. flag, the court enjoyed a light docket. American registry and theoretical capture by the U.S. Navy were factors placing *Ebony Angel* beyond the authority of the Court.

"The Americans should take her to New York, been their invariable position since John Quincy Adams," argued Mr. Hornby. "Cargo is the issue. Loss of life going to New York would make ugly reading in the *Guardian*."

Everyone nodded in agreement. They all recalled the cock-up in '50 when Captain Denman took a slaver off Rio, Portuguese taken south of the line. Mixed Commission in Rio had no jurisdiction, so, in unseaworthy condition according to Captain Denman, she re-crossed to Africa. No jurisdiction there either, so back she went to Brazil. The few survivors that made it alive through three crossings were sold as slaves at Rio.

Bounce observed that a good quarter to third of the *Ebony Angel's* cargo were Americo-Liberians.

"Treaty bound to send 'em home," rumbled the Queen's Attorney.

"Yanks off-load their Congoes at Monrovia. Pack them all off to the Negro republic for my money," Jennings urged impatiently.

"Rags, rations, and row 'em out! Good! Good!" The lawyer beamed at his alliteration.

"Accomplish the first two under the mandate to suppress The Trade," Hornby added. In fact, he reflected, it would be less costly to the colony's treasury than the passage on *Relief*, which had sailed the morning before *Angel* and her consorts reached Freetown.

"Land 'em immediately or Manchester press will have our hides," sighed Porter.

"Can't see the Jonathans object to landing the poor sods. Even their super-sensitivity must sometime yield to common sense and basic Christian behavior." Captain Jennings was a bit defensive this morning. At sea, the idea broached by the young American had seemed deuced clever. Here at Government House the legal ramifications overshadowed the brilliance of imaginatively ending the *Black Jonathan's* slaving days.

Concerned that the cargo not start dying under the nose of Her Majesty's Government, the Governor concurred and ordered Bounce to provide all appropriate assistance.

"Given her unconventional seizure, her status remains at issue," reiterated the Queen's Attorney.

"Can't see all the fuss." Jennings was tired of being criticized. "Three shots to bring her to. Only showed her colors after the second close aboard. Properly boarded to have her papers examined, Jonathan beyond question. Serendipitously, officers of the United States aboard my ship took charge in the name of their government. Indeed, it was one of them suggested this course. How, I ask you, can the Yanks complain? It's their Monroe Doctrine in miniature; they pontificate and the Royal Navy enforces."

"But were they, to the best of your knowledge and belief, Captain, truly officers of the United States Navy?" The lawyer was not to be cowed by some sailor's bluster.

"Never said else," shot back Jennings.

"The Captain has a point, Counsel." interjected the Governor. "Unlike the American Officer of Marines and the rankers – I believe the term included sailors, does it not? – who disobeyed the recall from *Jamestown*, the Naval Officers were ashore with the permission of their commander. Lef'tenant-in-Command Trueman made no effort of which any of us is aware to contact, let be recall, Midshipmen Talliaferro and Sweet."

"Were not letters of resignation delivered as *Jamestown* departed?" asked Hornby.

"Paltier didn't read 'em to my understanding, Hornby," interjected Jennings.

"Quite," responded the Governor. "No one of importance in this colony has any concrete knowledge of their content. Any opinion would be wildest conjecture. To our knowledge, Messrs. Talliaferro and Sweet are United States Navy Officers still. We've no actual knowledge, have we, Gentlemen, of the cause for Lef'tenant Bonney's inability to return to *Jamestown* at the time of her departure? I see absolutely no basis for concluding that the capture was ought but laudable cooperation between our two navies."

"Still risky, in my opinion," interjected the Queen's Attorney.

"Come, come, Counsel," responded Porter. "Never known a solicitor to say 'have at it' when a question was not absolutely buried in uncontroverted precedent. It's your duty, indeed nature, to press inaction." The assembly broke into laughter, except for the Queen's Attorney, who not only disagreed with the Governor, but heartily resented Bounce thumping him on the back in excessive good fellowship.

*   *   *   *   *   *   *   *   *   *

Talliaferro, Bonney, and Sweet sat at the table in the captain's day cabin assessing their options. The latter two had been cordial, almost informal in their relations since putting to sea with the Royal Navy. Just as well, Talliaferro reflected. Without clear legal authority since departing *Jamestown* their command structure was uncertain, decisions arrived at by consultation. It would have been all but impossible to function like that with two of the three feuding. Talliaferro at twenty-seven was slightly senior to Bonney's twenty-six years and as an Acting Lieutenant on *Jamestown* temporarily had outranked Bonney on all matters, other than internal administration of the Marines. Now nothing was clear, except that Sweet was junior to both. Yet he had become the one to urge resolution when neither of the others wished to press matters.

All agreed they best have a plan. Certainly, Bonney observed, the British were contemplating what to do with them. They could not complain of their treatment by Her Majesty's servants, but they could not expect an indefinite welcome, especially now that they were inextricably connected to the quandary of disposing of *Ebony Angel*. At that moment, Daniel entered with a coffee pot and an oilskin bundle he had found under the seat in the officers' head when throwing out scraps that morning, the ships true papers.

"Anyone checked the cargo?" Bonney asked. No one relished entering the hold.

After a moment of silence, Daniel spoke. "Helped feed afore we made port. They all right, but getting filthy. Some of them Nigras speak fair English. And some them bright girls ain't bad looking neither," Daniel concluded sheepishly.

"Oooh, Dan'l," began Sweet.

"Marse Charles, only natural."

Bonney demanded, "What sort of good English, they speak, Dan'l?"

"Some-like to home, Marse Clave." Daniel used the Marine's middle name, "Clave," short for Claverton. Bonney disliked his given name, Aaron, by which his father had honored Aaron Burr for shooting that leading proponent of centralized government, Alexander Hamilton. "Say they 'Americans,' not '*Bush Niggers*' like them others."

"You said some of them are 'bright,' Dan'l?" asked Bonney.

"Yes, Sir," he answered thinking of the copper-toned girl. "Bright as me almost."

"Best go for a see," summarized Talliaferro.

"First we best decide our approach to disposition of this ship," Bonney responded. Talliaferro conceded to Bonney's priorities, but ordered Daniel to examine the captives' hands. Urban dwelling Americo-Liberians would have soft palms, while laboring tribal people would be callused.

After Daniel left, they opened the oilskin package to discover the true log and ledger of the slaver. *Ebony Angel* had a crew of thirty-two hands, seven officers, and an accounts clerk. Her trade goods included 200 stand of old 1816 model .69 caliber muskets converted to percussion, 10,000 cartridges and 15,000 percussion caps, and a vast quantity of rum. Envisioning unlimited liquor available to his crew, Talliaferro asked Bonney to find and secure the spirits.

Ebony Angel was armed with two artillery pieces on pivot mounts capable of being trained to either side of the ship - a 64-pounder carronade forward, and a "long-nine," a 32-pounder cannon abaft the mizzenmast - as well as half-a-dozen swivel guns. As expected, the slaver had immense water capacity in four tanks, two per side below the waterline. Sweet expressed surprise that she carried little grain. Talliaferro explained it was not uncommon to use the space for trade goods and pick up millet, cassava, and rice on this side of the Atlantic. It gave a better return and the cargo ate native foods better, so they had some flesh at market.

There was a knock at the door and Thoms put in his head. Mr. Peck had the watch and sent his compliments, a boatload of Africans wanted to come aboard.

120

"Compliments to Mr. Peck; be right up," Talliaferro responded. "Wagers?" he asked.

"Hope it's not long lost cousins of the cargo," sighed Sweet.

"Halcyon Nevis, and Pa Cabot, anxious to invade Liberia," suggested Bonney.

"No bet there," rejoined Talliaferro.

At the entryport, Nevis held a scented handkerchief to his nose and Cabot frowned in disgust. Bonney dismissed their acting. There were some stomach-churning odors in Africa to which the slaver warranted no comparison, but it was becoming worse by the hour. Nevis's eyes were in constant motion evaluating the ship and contents. Heaven sent, perfect for the expedition against Gabriel, he concluded, but how to insure that the Americans commit it to that undertaking? Perhaps....

"God done smile on the Righteous!" boomed Cabot. "Devil-man no can beat God-man."

"Indeed," echoed Nevis. "Mr. Talliaferro, rumors are flying ashore, in all of which I put little stock. Where exactly did you take this vessel?"

Sweet interrupted, "San Pedro mouth east of Cape Palmas."

"Liberian waters, then?" replied Nevis.

"Outside the one-mile limit, Counselor." Bonney gave Sweet a cutting look. He did not want matters complicated by some claim of Liberian jurisdiction over the ship.

"International waters, certainly," added Talliaferro reinforcing Bonney's stance.

"Ah, too bad luck," sighed Nevis. "So you must take her to an American port for adjudication; New York, I understand, since that is her home port?"

This gave Talliaferro and Bonney pause. Before either could respond, Daniel appeared. "Hands mighty callused. Say they workin' for the *Bush Niggers*."

Cabot's face snapped toward Daniel. "Who work for *Bush Nigger*?"

Daniel looked to Sweet to reply, but Sweet was not about to put his foot in it again. Talliaferro explained that some of the cargo spoke rather cultured English.

"*Aahyeee!*" Cabot erupted. "Say '*Bush Nigger!*' They *my company!*" Cabot stared at the blank white faces. "*American!* My peoples!"

"Colonists from America, Americo-Liberians," volunteered Nevis helpfully.

"*One time!* We go make free, *one time!*" demanded Cabot, heading for the aft hatch.

Natural light faded quickly in the hold as the group moved away from the aft ladder. Intent upon the packed rows of upturned faces, Nevis forgot his scented handkerchief. Both the lawyer and the hotelier contemptuously dismissed the dark black tribal faces near the ladder. In the

121

darkest area midway between the aft and main hatches, Daniel raised the lantern to a face. The young man snapped away from the painful light.

"How you called?" demanded Pa Cabot. The mumbled response was inaudible. Cabot again yelled his question.

This time the answer was louder, "Munro."

"What Munro?" demanded Cabot.

"Issa…. I be Issa Munro."

"Where home for you, Munro?"

"Jacktown."

"Who be Pa for you?" demanded Cabot.

"Aabrim, father me," the man answered despondently.

"Where you go for to be ward?"

"For Greenville to Pa Cabot."

"How called be this Cabot?"

"'Xander Cabot, certain."

"*COUSIN!*" bellowed Cabot grabbing the man's averted head, eliciting a shriek. "*Aahyeee*! You be cousin to me, certain! I be 'Thaniel Cabot!"

My God, thought Bonney, Sweet was right, long lost cousins. Pandemonium erupted. There was no controlling the chaos; it simply had to run its course. At least they were restrained, Bonney reflected. Once they settled down, action could be taken to free them.

Bonney returned to the weather deck and began working on their release. The captives had to be brought on deck, washed, and clothed. He was confidant that the alacrity with which Mr. Peck and his sailors turned to rigging pumps had much more to do with the prospect of turning the hosepipe on some naked young females than with his authority as an officer. On the other hand, Sergeant Banning's and Corporal Dyer's eagerness gathering canvass scraps to clothe the cargo he attributed to Marine loyalty and conditioned obedience. He banished the momentary thought that his Leathernecks hastened so not to miss the water spectacle, certainly not *his* Marines.

Nevis emerged next from the hold, handkerchief forgotten. The lawyer stepped to Bonney, removing his hat and wiping his brow with his palm. An afterthought, he retrieved the scented cloth from his pocket and repeated the process, while asking a word with the American officer before events got beyond considering what he had to say. They stepped to the port rail away from Peck's hose party.

Noting the evasiveness regarding the location of *Ebony Angel's* capture, Nevis wished to assure that matters had been evaluated from all perspectives. Yes, Bonney admitted, they had possessed the vessel in the guise of American officers. Yes, technically Nevis was correct, as a prize in possession of the American Navy, *Ebony Angel* should be brought before a United States Prize Court to adjudicate the lawfulness of the seizure and to settle ownership of vessel and cargo. Yes, New York, the vessel's homeport was the proper venue.

"You have renounced your allegiance to the United States?" Nevis asked.

"Mr. Nevis, it is not that simple…."

"I suggest significant complexity, Mr. Bonney. As far as the British are concerned, publicly at least, you seized this vessel as officers of the United States. If this is not so, Captain Jennings has committed an egregious breach of British neutrality in delivering an American ship to forces at war with the United States."

"He delivered this vessel to us as serving U.S. officers," Bonney growled.

"In which case, you are bound to deliver the ship to the American prize court at New York. To do otherwise would be treason and desertion, if not piracy, were you to declare her a prize of your new nation, making Captain Jennings either a fool, or a conspirator guilty of violating British neutrality; clearly a result you wish to avoid."

"We'll have to scuttle her at sea, if that is the case…."

"It does not alter the complicity of Captain Jennings and, indeed, the entire administration of Sierra Leone. Think how unenthusiastic British officials will be toward your new nation, if all here are pilloried for their actions regarding this vessel. Beyond damaging your personal honor, you damage the cause of your nascent country."

What did Nevis want, Bonney demanded; pack the slavers on their way with the poor wretches down below? Of course not, the lawyer insisted. Rather, Bonney should review the capture. Was it not in Liberian territorial waters? Liberia, Nevis observed, was bound by treaty to suppress The Trade and had frequently been assisted by both British and American governments in that endeavor. Indeed, the British had given Liberia a small warship, the *Lively Quail*, for that purpose. The United States also had donated a craft, though in such poor condition as to be unseaworthy. Nevis was of the firm belief that the Americans and Jennings had acted in aid of the Liberian Government, in Liberian waters, seizing a ship that was violating international, American and Liberian laws. The offense committed and the culprit apprehended in Liberian waters, Nevis announced, the *Ebony Angel* was best adjudged by a Liberian prize court. American law permitted such procedure, if the vessel were not in condition safely to reach American jurisdiction. By happy coincidence, Nevis added with a conspiratorial smile, once Pa Cabot was reinstated as Superintendent of Sinoe County, he could convene such a court.

Bonney did not know whether to congratulate the preening legal popinjay or throttle him. To get home, all they had to do was conquer a Liberian county. Bonney heard the entryport sentry challenge a boat that responded, "Captain of the Port!" The pumps began clanking followed

123

shortly by high-pitched squeals. Forward of the foremast, half-a-dozen stark naked youthful Africans of both sexes gasped and contorted as grinning sailors directed wavering jets of none-too-clean harbor water onto them. To starboard level with the main hatch Sergeant Banning bent over an anvil wielding a sledge and chisel knocking the irons off more Liberians. Into this chaos Commander Bounce, RN, huffed through the entry port to offer all assistance of Her Majesty's Government.

CHAPTER SEVENTEEN

Bonney and Sweet stood in the center of King's Yard with Nevis, Cabot, and Commander Bounce. The pelting thunderstorm, first of The Rains, had passed exposing the tropical sun just above the western horizon. A thick steam rose from the cobblestone. Bonney felt he should chew the moist air before inhaling. A constant gurgle rose from the open sewers. Moisture dripped from every leaf, roof, and pore.

Pa Cabot had segregated the "Americans" from the indigenous Africans, no great accomplishment given their mutual loathing. From the ship's papers, Bonney knew that of the 287 persons in the cargo, 64 were Americo-Liberian males, 37 Americo-Liberian females, 23 tribal females, and the rest, 163 in all, indigenous males. The oldest of the cargo looked no more than mid-twenties. All appeared in good health; logical, Bonney had to admit, no value spiriting the weak to Cuban cane fields.

With the end of the downpour, the tribal people shed the sodden sailcloth. The "Americans," male and female, wrapped theirs around their waists as rather unwieldy skirts. The total lack of self-consciousness amused Bonney. Baltimore's social mores were incensed if a lady showed her ankle or a gentleman exposed his suspenders in the presence of the opposite sex. At least these people were not wearing woolen frockcoats in this pasty air. Who's the smarter lot, he pondered and decided not to pursue the question.

Cabot was speaking to the Americo-Liberians at the front of the assembly, describing how much his father, the late Superintendent of Public Affairs, had done for the "Americans," how close he had been to President Roberts, the "Father of Liberia" who had just ended his administration. Gabriel had played hardhearted Pharaoh since seizing power, but God in his munificence had spared Nathaniel Cabot, so that, like Moses of old, he could deliver his people from their latter day Egypt.

As God's instrument, Cabot continued, the "Americans" would return *one time* to Liberia and end Gabriel's depredations. (In the presence of the British, he was being appropriately vague, implying the action was sanctioned by the Monrovia Government.) To accomplish this, *Ebony Angel* had to be readied for sea. Thus, the "Americans" must insure that "them *Bush Nigger*" behind them clean the ship. Bonney glanced at Nevis. This was not the understanding. It was to have been the Americo-Liberians who worked. Noting his reaction, Nevis shook his head as if to say, "Do not contest our ways."

Cabot turned to Bonney demanding, "We go to ship, *one time*. Now we go!"

Bonney looked to Bounce, who shook his head. "In the morning, Mr. Cabot."

"*Aahyee*," howled Cabot, "must go Liberia *one time*! No can wait!"

"Have to wait for daylight to get these folks safe aboard," responded Bonney.

"Savvy; but go quick, so Gabriel not make *big bob*, big trouble." Cabot seemed desperate, almost panicked.

"With all deliberate speed, Sir." Bonney dismissed the Liberian with the ambivalent naval phrase. Filled with apprehension, he turned to Nevis. "A word with you."

"Why certainly, Sir, certainly," responded the lawyer. "My office is not far."

"Aboard the slaver, Nevis; now," Bonney growled.

*   *   *   *   *   *   *   *   *   *

"All right, Nevis…." Sweet was still closing the cabin door when to Talliaferro's surprise Bonney launched his interrogation. "I been wallowed around by lawyers and spun yarns by coloreds before, and right now I'm smelling one hell of a big rat, Sir!"

At Bonney's advance, Nevis instinctively retreated, until the large table stopped him. Jaw jutting, Bonney leaned toward Nevis, fully intending to intimidate the barrister. What the Sam Hill was Cabot so scared of in Monrovia, Bonney demanded? Did Gabriel have support of the national government? Nevis damned well better know that they were risking their crew and probably more of the future of the Confederate States than Bonney cared to contemplate, in circumstances they knew diddle about. It gave Bonney the distinct feeling, Hell, he emphasized, *conviction* Nevis was hornswaggling him. So, the Marine concluded, Nevis better tell the full story, and he meant *full*, or by Heaven the lawyer would answer at his peril.

Talliaferro was impressed by Bonney's performance and Sweet realized that compared to this, Bonney had been most restrained in the discussions Sweet had considered offensive.

"Sir," Nevis soothed, "I've been forthcoming. I am uncertain *re* the cause for your mistrust. Perhaps…."

"Aw, *Garbage!*" Bonney exploded. "For a start, just who the hell are you anyway?"

"Why, Sir, as you know…."

"*Nothing!* I know nothing about you, except what you want me to. For starters, how well do you know Cabot?"

"That really is of no relevance…."

"I'll decide that, *damn you!* Answer!"

"Very well," Nevis capitulated. He had dealt with Cabot's family in various business undertakings. Thus, he held certain funds on account for the Cabots. When Pa Cabot arrived from Liberia after his family's massacre, the lawyer provided the money to start his hotel. He had done quite well, Nevis confided, with the lawyer's guidance of course.

126

What was the situation, both in Greenville and Monrovia? In Greenville, Gabriel was viewed as a savage despot, dabbler in the slave trade. And Monrovia? By bribes and intimidation he had influence with certain unsavory governmental elements: primarily Manley, Minister of Trade. Were Gabriel ousted, what would the national government do? Manley, would in all likelihood fall from office. President Benson saw Gabriel as a threat to himself and to Liberia's national integrity and would be relieved.

"So, you're telling me, there'll be no naval or military response?"

"Precisely...."

"It will be viewed with relief and approval by the President?"

"Quite so."

"And what do you get out of this, Nevis?"

"I hope to assist Superintendent Cabot with certain matters calling for his decision."

"I understand fully," Bonney answered contemptuously. "Listen carefully. If things aren't such, if we find the Liberian Government, either through its own means, or through the French or British or somebody coming down on us in force, I shall *personally* pull the rope taking you to the masthead by your neck. Understand?"

Nevis nodded.

"Then, I don't see why we can't have a good relationship, Mr. Nevis, Esquire."

Americans are insane, Nevis thought, but valuable in the games of Africa.

*   *   *   *   *   *   *   *   *   *

Daniel was on deck when the impenetrable wall of rain, rumbling like trains of the Norfolk & Petersburg Railroad at home he thought, surged down the Sierra Leone River, seemed to carom off the steep face of Sugarloaf Mountain, and moved inexorably across the city. As the great drops rattled on the tin roofs, all boats in the roadstead scurried for shelter. No more Liberians would be ferried aboard until it stopped.

The vision of the girl was constantly before him, his mouth dry at the thought of her, his breath shallow. If only she had said something.... Where was she? Why hadn't she come aboard? He remembered Marse Charles that time at Annapolis when he saw that Miss Buchanan, the old Superintendent's niece. "Be still my heart." That was what he'd said. "Well, 'be still my heart!'" Daniel whispered.

CHAPTER EIGHTEEN

Sweet's mouth was dry, his stomach queasy. Close hauled on the port tack, *Ebony Angel* was headed into the Sinoe Estuary, the culmination of a respectable river flowing generally southwesterly from the interior until it hooked to the northwest for its last descent to the Atlantic creating a long, low peninsula on which the town of Greenville was situated. It was just past two bells of the afternoon watch, 1:00 p.m. Last of the morning squalls had passed out to sea an hour before. Under the borrowed coat, Sweet was sweating despite the pleasant breeze. Everyone visible on deck was wearing an outer garment from the original crew over his uniform. In the attack, *Angel* was plugging along at an effective speed, considering the river flow, of only two knots.

Sweet hoped fervently that the ship and those aboard her were ready for what awaited them. It had taken a good seven days to traverse the slightly over three hundred miles from Freetown to the Sinoe's mouth. Partly it had been the hammering of The Rains that marched in regular succession out from the coast to blind the watch on deck and drive below all those not absolutely required to be in the weather. Mostly it had been the layover at Turtle Island to land the "Congoes," tribal members of the cargo. There they would remain during the Greenville expedition. Turtle was a small landmass off the tip of Sherbro Island, home of the famous Caulker family, who for decades ran one of the larger slave barracoons on the Coast. Sweet smiled recalling how Bonney had left the Caulker fox guarding the "Congo" chickens, but had made clear that the fox would be held to account. He was confidant *Angel's* "Congoes" would be there when they returned. And if they did not return…. Sweet shook his head banishing the thought.

Sweet reflected for a moment upon how his attitude toward Bonney had changed since Captain Pennington's disappearance under the fallen rigging. The Marylander certainly was competent, clever and audacious, traits Sweet held almost as high as honor and loyalty. He almost regretted his resentment at Bonney's interference in his affairs and recognized that the Marine had been trying to steer him away from disaster. Still, it had been meddling where he had no business. But, as Daniel had pointed out, Bonney had Sweet's best interests in mind and Bonney had been right. He owed Bonney a debt for his efforts, something more than merely being congenial, but he was uncertain how to honor it without looking a fool.

*　　*　　*　　*　　*　　*　　*　　*　　*　　*

Daniel sat on the deck out of sight below the port rail. He was captain of one of the six swivel guns, oversized carbines with the bore of small cannon mounted in pintles whose pins would be thrust into iron-reinforced sockets in the ship's rail. His crew of two Liberians sat beside him cradling the stubby weapon. On order, they would stand, mount the gun, and discharge a package of musket balls into whatever targets they saw.

That *Angel* was taking her own sweet time in getting to Greenville was all right with Daniel. He was happy to sit on the deck watching the steam rise out of the caulking. He truly had enjoyed the passage from Freetown. Once again, he lost himself in re-living every moment spent with her.

She was the most exciting person he had ever known. Her name was Delcina, Delcina Draper. Her voice was like those little chimes old Captain Buchanan had brought back from The Japans that hung out back of the Superintendent's Quarters at the Academy, especially when she laughed.

Daniel sighed in his reverie.

He had watched for her when she first came on deck in Freetown. He had been the bashful one, whereas she had shown no embarrassment as the sailors played the hose on her. He had held back. Suddenly, before he could speak, she had disappeared over the ship's side headed for King's Yard.

He had learned his lesson. When the Liberians re-embarked he had sought her out, introducing himself with a lift of his cap like Marse Charles did. He had tried that once in Portsmouth with a housemaid and been teased unmercifully for being too uppity, he recalled. He had not done it again until now, when it just seemed right. To his pleasure, Miss Draper had dropped a quick curtsey accompanied by a warm smile.

Talk had started slowly, beginning with self-introductions, names. Daniel quickly realized that Delcina had two at least. He had responded with "Dan'l" and experienced a sudden panic; slaves simply didn't have last names. He had hesitated, fought to control the bile rising in his throat, the cloud of paralysis that fogged his brain, and had blurted out, "Sweet ... of the Nansemond County Sweets of Virginia." Praying that she only thought him shy, he had plunged ahead with some ludicrous observation about the rain stopping or the wet deck or something equally as bumbling. She had picked up the idea and kept the conversation alive.

130

Speech came ever more naturally until simultaneously they recognized that they had been talking at once not really comprehending the other. They laughed and Daniel was transported by the way her eyes sparkled. His breath came short in his tightened chest, his pulse raced, and he knew he was grinning like a madman. He felt awkward, yet graceful enough to float above the deck.

Oh Heaven, don't let me do something stupid to send her away, he prayed coming out from his reverie.

*   *   *   *   *   *   *   *   *   *

Delcina was with the rest of the Americo-Liberian women in the main hold amidships below the waterline where it was unlikely that harm would come to them if *Angel* came under fire. Talliaferro could not convince the Liberians to leave the women on Turtle Island, but he had insisted, successfully this time, that they remain in the safest location on the ship during the coming battle. Delcina was not participating in the general buzz of speculation, punctuated by an occasional raucous laugh as the women gossiped and teased to dispel their apprehension. Instead, she thought of the way she had become involved with that American sailor, Daniel, Daniel Sweet, though he seemed shy about that last part. She felt a hot blush spread across her face as she recalled their time together on the trip from Freetown to Greenville.

Delcina was fascinated by the powerful, exotic young man, who had come out of the blackness of her despair with the message that had given back her life. Of that she was certain, for she had resolved to starve herself, rather than face life on Cuba. She knew how Lazarus must have felt.

She caught herself in this thought and followed it with the prayer, "God forgive me, I don't mean to blaspheme."

She knew this exciting stranger had brought her back from the dead. He was so gallant, so … how should she describe it … so *himself* without the strutting of the self-important youths at home. What was *himself* like? He *cared* for *her*; that was the difference. He listened to her and talked *to*, not at her. Just to be in his presence was like dancing, the civilized way of dancing

131

she clarified. She longed for him when he left her. He was magic for her, but would he understand?

*   *   *   *   *   *   *   *   *   *

Talliaferro struggled to contain his impatience; would this tub ever reach Greenville? In case a glass examined them during the approach, Hillary, the former captain, stood glumly beside him on the quarterdeck. He had been pleased to hear from Hillary, and have it confirmed by checking the magazine and the manifest, that, while Gabriel had received the 200 old muskets as partial payment for the Americo-Liberians *Angel* loaded at Greenville, all but a dozen rounds per weapon had been retained aboard as surety for the delivery of the tribal cargo up the San Pedro and for the majority of the provisions that Hillary was to load upon his return. Talliaferro smirked to himself. It was all security against a double-cross: muskets without ammunition in exchange for a partial cargo; the remainder of the cargo, but without sufficient food to reach the market; a final exchange of food for final payment including the ammunition to give the muskets value. Everyone was happy; no one trusted anyone. "*Ahyee, Bo!* This be Africa," he muttered.

It gave marvelous validity to *Angel's* return to Greenville, though a trifle late. Gabriel certainly knew of *Ebony Angel's* seizure and that she, like most slavers on the coast these days an American vessel not subject to condemnation by the three judge Court of Mixed Commission at Freetown. Once the lawyers brought the Royal Navy to its senses, *Angel* rightly should be released. Talliaferro prayed Gabriel would not have heard that American officers actually took the ship. That would put paid to any surprise. He came out of his reverie. *Angel* was at the end of this reach on her tack into the estuary. "Hands to the braces!" he bellowed. "Prepare to wear ship!"

*   *   *   *   *   *   *   *   *   *

Aft of Talliaferro and Hillary, Bonney was dressed in the hat and coat of *Angel's* First Mate. Forward, out of sight below decks, were his dozen Marines, thirty Liberian musketeers (Heavens, he wondered, what would D'Artagnan think?) and his thirty Liberian swordsmen. Corporal Dyer commanded the musketeers, replaced by Orrin as acting corporal with the Marines. Cabot had appointed his young "cousin," Issa Munro, to lead the swordsmen. Sergeant Banning, in charge below decks, would land with the musketeers, and, once ashore, would assist Bonney in coordinating the entire "goat-rope," Banning's phrase for a chaotic event that Bonney subconsciously had adopted.

Creating this rag-tag "army" had been frustrating. While the "Congoes" were establishing camp on Turtle Island, the "landing force" had spent two days on the triangular bit of earth practicing musketry, basic drill, and, Bonney had fervently hoped, respect for authority. He had demanded that the thirty Americo-Liberians Cabot selected to be his infantry drill with the muskets issued from *Angel's* arms room. Bonney had also drilled his Marines and attempted to maneuver the two groups together with minimal success. Bonney's "third maneuver element" as he had phrased it, consisted of the remaining thirty Americo-Liberian males armed with the slave ship's cutlasses.

Bonney had warranted nothing beyond one good volley. Nevis had confidently answered that that was one more than could be expected from Gabriel's men. He prayed that the lawyer was correct; they had no sensible assessment of Gabriel's strength.

Bonney studied the approaching area of operations. Cabot had given only the most general description. It was unlikely that much had changed in the three years since the refugee had seen it, not the way of Africa. The dominant structure was the "Mansion House," a walled (Bonney hesitated to say "fortified") compound, half warehouse, half Superintendent's palace. Here Cabot had grown up and had expected to pass his days before Gabriel scotched his plans. It sat upon a slight rise at the end of the shoreline along the northwest side of the estuary. Cabot recalled two old brass six-pounder field guns at the Mansion, but never had seen them fire and doubted there was any ammunition.

Northeast of the Mansion was an open space, the "Common." At its northeastern edge stood the church, a one-story clapboard affair with a small bell cupola over its southern gable. Once whitewashed, it was splotched with weathered-gray exposed wood. Beyond the church, the town paralleled the shore. Two streets deep from the water, it consisted predominantly of single-story bungalows with several two-story structures of the ubiquitous tropical design interspersed along the shore. Numerous royal palms majestically shaded the community and stood in grand solitude or small clumps throughout fields north of the village. Further inland a significant oil palm plantation confirmed Greenville as a source of West Africa's second most valuable export.

The critical question was, Bonney told himself, would Gabriel come down from the Mansion House to the shore to greet them? The trick, he knew, would be to keep Gabriel and as many of his henchmen as possible from breaking northward. The last thing Bonney wanted was to pursue the fellow inland. If that happened, he resolved with pursed lips, Cabot would just have to paddle his own canoe.

Except for the small Mansion House rise, the shore was low and flat, terrain where the many could easily overwhelm the few. Surprise, he resolved as the ship came about to settle close-hauled upon the starboard tack; it all depended upon surprising the bastards. Patience, he thought; *Angel* had to make another reach to starboard before closing the town.

*   *   *   *   *   *   *   *   *   *

Nevis looked through the porthole at the low shoreline, hardly believing his participation in this uncertain undertaking. But there was no one else competent enough to trust with managing this desperate gamble. Strange how this had evolved, he reflected. With the late Superintendent Cabot he had conducted a low profile slave exporting operation for several years. His contribution had been tracking the movements of the Royal Navy, warning Cabot when Her Majesty's ships were headed toward Greenville. He had managed negotiations with slave ship captains, and had manipulated funds to avoid suspicion in both Monrovia and Freetown, until the late Mr. Cabot had balked at continuing to pay Nevis his cut.

It had been so clever, his arrangement with Manley, Liberia's Minister of Trade, and Parkins, Minister of Interior. Together they connected all aspects of Liberia's slave trade. Parkins was in a position to negotiate with the chiefs up-country to market the captives of their incessant raiding back and forth. Manley controlled foreign commerce and more importantly commanded Liberia's one-vessel navy. Thus, they could ensure the closest thing to a monopoly anyone could reasonably expect to achieve.

It was Nevis who had suggested that the ministers join him to replace the Cabots with Gabriel. For a second he mused about the unknown poison that "Devil" or priestess of the Bundu Society had concocted to dispose of the Superintendent; a vapor he had breathed, Nevis thought. He made a note to be aware and beware of the leadership of the powerful tribal women's society with chapters throughout West Africa.

Self-satisfied, Nevis recalled maintaining good relations with Nathaniel Cabot in Freetown both to learn of plots to reestablish Cabot control at Greenville and, should it become in the lawyer's interest, to advance such action. He was grateful he had done so. A year earlier, Manley had ousted Parkins and Nevis from their triumvirate. Once the supply chain was established with the up-country chiefs, Parkins was of little value to the operation. Controlling foreign trade, Manley did not need Nevis to conceal suspicious financial transactions. Controlling Liberia's one-ship navy, he coordinated with the Royal Navy and knew its movements, making Nevis's naval intelligence unnecessary.

Nevis had planned a countercoup, but Nathaniel Cabot, now a successful Freetown hotelier, was reticent. Practical preparations had been minimal. Then, Nevis recalled with a smile, Providence had dropped these crazy Americans in their laps. He positively *knew* he could have convinced Sweet and Talliaferro that their only way home was by training and leading Cabot's motley mob of mercenaries in a Greenville coup. Instead, Providence had stranded a small American army in Freetown and the same logic applied. Finally, there was the unanticipated Divine gift of this magnificent ship. He chuckled; Gabriel even expected *Angel's* arrival at Greenville at a time when a dispute with the Spanish tethered Liberia's (and Manley's) only warship to Monrovia. What had Cabot said in Freetown? Nevis remembered, "God done smile on the Righteous!"

In power, Cabot would convene a prize court to condemn the ship. Nevis would purchase *Angel*, take the Americans home to their own power struggle – there now were too many of them to dispose of more directly and they had to be put out of the picture - and become the true power in both Sinoe County and the slaving operation. Parkins would control relations with the Monrovia Government and Cabot would be an expendable figurehead. Except for the imponderables of combat, it was too perfect.

*   *   *   *   *   *   *   *   *   *

"Usually fire-off a swivel gun 'bout now," Hillary announced.

Angel settled again on the port tack. The breeze had veered to onshore, enabling *Angel* to sail six points large with the wind on her port quarter. The tide had turned from ebb to flow, canceling the effect of the river current. Talliaferro believed they were making a good four knots under topsails and jib. "Anything else, you forgot?" he demanded.

"No … Err … Pop the Liberian colors at the forepeak along of firing the gun."

"I swear by my mother's headstone, Hillary, we're found out before we let them have it, *very* first thing I shall do is have that Nigra over there slit your belly and twist your guts around a marlin spike." Talliaferro's voice was venomous. "*Anything* else?"

Hillary shifted uneasily, fidgeting a glance at Daniel, then averting his eyes.

Sweet heard. He had a seaman sifting *Angel's* flag locker for the *Star* and Stripes of Liberia, ordered the forward-most of the six swivel guns prepared to fire announcing *Angel's* imminent arrival, and, almost as an afterthought, sent Daniel to warn Sergeant Banning about the salute and *not* to let his party on deck.

Peck made the best use of his few sailors. The main and fore yards were not in use, so he had lines rigged to lift out the boats as soon as the sails came in. Talliaferro wanted them in the water before their true intentions were discovered.

Angel was moving well, faster than Talliaferro had estimated. "Take in your mizzen topsail, if you please, Mr. Sweet."

"Aye, Sir. Mr. Peck!"

Half the crew ran aloft to furl the sail, and there were none too many strung along the yard. They required more hands to cross the Atlantic, Sweet reflected. He doubted they could convince some local Krumen to sign-on. Renowned as seamen, the Kru tribe expected to serve a specified time and go home, where their earnings made them the wealthiest of their community.

135

Sweet smiled at the Kru saying, "Nigger for ship; King for country," their home country. Kru had little stomach for other people's fights. "Have one life only and want see we country again," was another Kru saying. Some other solution had to be found.

"Maintop at your convenience, Mr. Sweet."

"Aye, Sir. Mr. Peck!"

At the swivel gun's discharge a rapidly growing crowd, mostly women, filled the shoreline. A gentle undulation began among them, the rhythmic shuffle of a welcoming dance into which they seemed to transition unconsciously. *Angel's* arrival naturally would be cause for celebration, Bonney realized. She was bringing significant riches for the community, even if they came as a consequence of perfidy toward some of their own.

There! Bonney raised his spyglass to study the procession emerging from the Mansion House. It was no march of disciplined troops. He imagined what Paltier's commentary would be if he could see the mob. A richly dressed figure, Gabriel for certain, was borne on an elaborately draped chair supported upon the shoulders of numerous bearers, like the Madonna in Roman church processions, Bonney reflected. Swarming around the bobbing throne a large mob of men in no particular uniform, brandished weapons that sparkled in the sun. Obviously *Angel's* trade muskets; newly issued, they had not yet gone to rust despite their undisciplined owners. Chanting and singing were audible now. As the mass neared the shore many in the throng fired their weapons into the air. Bonney saw no effort to reload and smiled, each puff of smoke meant one less shot at his landing party in the crucial first moments.

Bonney ran his eye up the shoreline. There were several boats and numerous dugout canoes pulled up onto the beach. Usually they surged around an incoming ship. At the slightest sign they would not be forcefully repulsed, the welcomers would swarm aboard to pilfer all they could. It was not about to happen to *Angel.*

"Don't like coming aboard slavers," Hillary croaked to Bonney. "Stupid bastards afraid they might just get taken along." His phlegm-filled laugh ended in a cough. "Besides, got a deal with Ole Gabe to keep them off the ship. He enforces real good." Hillary glanced at Talliaferro, adding "About the same as you," nodding at Daniel.

Talliaferro calculated *Angel* had enough way on to carry her to his selected anchorage. "Foretop, Mr. Sweet."

"Aye, Sir. Mr. Peck!"

The handful of topmen hurried aloft to furl the one remaining driver. Now only the jib was drawing to provide steerage as *Angel* coasted toward the beach. Sweet wondered if she had too much way. He would hate to ground in present circumstances. Peck's seamen had un-catted the anchor ready to let go, others stood by to strike the jib. Behind the rail the swivel crews fidgeted. Bonney moved forward toward the main hatch.

"Stand by the anchor," ordered Talliaferro and Sweet repeated it.

As the whirling mass around Gabriel danced toward the water, the women parted to let them through, but the swaying dance never faltered. Bonney did not need his glass now. Gabriel was a huge fellow, tending to fat, thirty or so Bonney guessed. He wore a flowing yellow robe, like some exhibitionist judge, and a porkpie hat, a trifle small perhaps. His fingers sparkled with numerous rings. Around his neck hung a great gold chain similar to a British Lord Mayor's. Dark-complected, a wisp of beard on his chin, he was without the indigenous peoples' keyloid ritual scarring. How they could make a pattern of incisions in the skin, insert and burn a piece of straw, rub in citrus juice, and insert a small pebble over which the skin would grow to "beautify" their bodies, Bonney could not understand.

"Down and easy, men," cautioned Talliaferro. Then to be heard on the forecastle he bellowed, "Let Go!" With a loud splash *Angel's* best bower disappeared into the Sinoe's murky water.

"Jib there!" roared Peck.

"Bring her round," added Sweet and the helmsman spun the wheel to turn the bow into the stream, port side parallel to the shore less than fifty yards away.

As their various tasks of seamanship finished, sailors hurried to the boats. The first longboat jerkily rose off the nest of spars between main and foremasts and swung over the starboard side hidden from the shore. Orrin's twelve Leathernecks crawled from the main hatch to the starboard entry port. Four sailors and a coxswain would follow after launching the other three boats. Unbuttoning his borrowed coat, Bonney moved casually to the entryport, dropped the garment, and followed the Marines over the side.

On deck a dozen Liberians under the direction of an American officer - Sweet forward at the stubby carronade and Talliaferro aft at the long-nine - eased the pivot guns to port. The Liberians had drilled repeatedly and now performed the task satisfactorily. Hillary waved evenly to Gabriel as Daniel smiled menacingly from below the bulwark.

Ashore the rhythmic chanting increased. Sweet noticed more energy in the dancing. The third boat was over the side, one to go. Corporal Dyer's musketeers crawled after the Marines. Talliaferro stepped back to Hillary's side.

Hillary swallowed hard and moistened his lips several times before raising the speaking trumpet. "Ahoy Mr. Gabriel!"

The potentate raised a similar trumpet. "Whyfore, you come past time?"

"Had problems. All good now."

"*Catch* bullets? *Catch* rum?" Gabriel was not interested in Hillary's troubles, so long as he "*catch*," i.e. *had* the goods.

Sweet was aware that the fourth boat was in the water. Sailors completed individual tasks and moved deliberately over the side: four boats,

137

four rowers each, slow movement, yet competent. Banning was in one of the boats with Dyer's musketeers and Dyer in the other. Bonney was with the Marines in their under-occupied craft. Another minute and they would appear around *Angel's* bow and stern pulling for the beach.

"Have *yam* Mr. Gabriel?" Hillary queried, showing appropriate concern. While *yam* included all edibles within its meaning, he clarified, "Have rice, millet, ground nut?"

"You *catch*; I *catch*. All good."

"Where is the food?"

"*Ahyeee*! Gabriel no go *cut yamgah* on Hillary, certain! Trust in me, Bo."

"*Cut yamgah*," made Sweet think of Jumbo and their negotiations in Freetown.

"I have trust, Mr. Gabriel. Not many boats. You bring food to the beach. Boats will carry bullets, rum to you, bring *yam* to me."

"*Ahyee*, you be *close my stomach*, Hillary," Gabriel used the West African metaphor that placed the seat of endearment in the stomach rather than the heart. "You savvy. Me savvy truth. *Ma* tote *yam* to boat, *one time*!" already some women were head-loading baskets to the shoreline, walking with that exotic immobility of the upper torso and rhythmic oscillation of the hips that was the continent's primary means of transport.

At the starboard entry port, Peck looked to Talliaferro and nodded broadly. By the carronade, Sweet motioned the crouching gun crew to angle the stubby weapon a bit more toward the stern, training it on the dancing mass of armed men, rather than the swaying women. Talliaferro stood by the long-nine trained forward. Gabriel's followers would be in a crossfire of canister, a couple-hundred musket balls converging upon the mass of dancing men and their gaudy monarch on his elevated throne.

Talliaferro thrust out his arm, pointing to a slender Liberian youth crouching by the ship's bell. Its rich tone reverberated across the deck, over the water to the masses on the shore, and crisply penetrated the wall of human voices rising from the throng.

After a millisecond's hesitation, Daniel sprang to his feet. He helped his struggling crew to fit the pintle of the swivel gun into its sleeve in the rail. Along the deck five other little groups did the same.

Sweet and Talliaferro kicked outward on the unlatched sections of bulwark in front of their artillery pieces. Sweet leapt behind the carronade's breech checking the alignment. Furiously he motioned the Liberians to heave the slide a bit to the right until the great mouth of the barrel-like contrivance centered on Gabriel. Sweet hooked the lanyard into the primer ring, leapt clear of the breech, and gave the line a steady pull.

*   *   *   *   *   *   *   *   *   *

The swivel gunners were not to fire until after the cannoneers. The psychological impact and the carnage would be significantly greater, if the men on the beach did not react until the canister from the big guns was among them. Amazingly, all six swivel crews complied. As a result, Daniel's view was clear of smoke. He had never seen such a sight. A tongue of fire jabbed across his vision from the right, from Sweet's gun. The undulating mass of humanity was spun, pitched, splattered, and shredded as if by some massive unseen flail. Daniel was positive that a red mist, like a shot of steam from a safety valve, spurted into the air. The sounds of bell, voices, sea, of all creation were smothered in the belched thump of the carronade. The throng on the beach seemed to stagger a step or two southward toward the Mansion House. Then from his left Daniel felt before he heard the eruption of the long nine 32-pounder. The swath it cut was narrower than Sweet's carronade, but equally merciless. The throng on the beach staggered the other way, north toward the fields and the plantation of oil palms.

"Swivels! Fire! Fire *Now!*" Talliaferro bellowed.

Some detached segment of Daniel's brain registered the vultures taking awkward flight throughout the village in response to the crash of the great guns. The swivels seemed almost inconsequential by comparison. Smoke obscured Daniel's vision, but he heard the wail from the crowd, an anguished paean of misery and unbelief he knew he never could forget. With an inexplicable anger, he spun the gun muzzle inboard to reload. His two Liberians were jumping about in glee, duties forgotten. The noise of the other swivels drowned speech, so Daniel cuffed the closer of the two, who shoved his compatriot. Sobered, they looked to Daniel for guidance, but received none.

The slave froze in horror at the chaos where the carronade had been. It had recoiled with much more than normal momentum, crashed through the stop at the end of the slide, reared up, toppled backward off its mount wiping away the ship's bell and the youth beside it, landed first on its side and then rolled onto its back, skidded across the deck through several of the swordsmen, and hurtled through the starboard bulwark over the cathead into the water, creating a wave that sent one of the boats rocking violently to the consternation of the embarked musketeers. All Daniel could see was scattered bodies, parts of bodies. With a howl of "Marse Charles!" he stumbled forward.

*   *   *   *   *   *   *   *   *   *

As soon as the long-nine fired, Talliaferro leapt aft to see around the smoke. Ghastly mangled bodies lay in a great "X" vibrating as the horribly maimed writhed in their gore. If they were screaming Talliaferro could not distinguish it from the general howl as the panicked crowd disintegrating into flight. In the midst of the carnage the gaudy throne was upended, but a

139

yellow-robed figure was scrambling toward the Mansion House. "Damn it!" Talliaferro muttered; they had *not* got Gabriel.

He saw the disaster where the carronade had been, the gouged deck, shattered bulwark, and Daniel dropping to the deck beside a figure who had to be Charles Sweet. Any effort expended upon that situation would not add a wit to their success against Gabriel. Talliaferro turned back to the long nine and put Sweet and the carronade from his mind.

A spitting of uncoordinated firing from his left drew his attention, Dyer's boat. The corporal was standing gesticulating at the musketeers, who, unbidden, had delivered a ragged volley into the massed women fleeing the beach. Like most green troops, the Liberians had fired high. With one exception, the balls had passed harmlessly over the mob to impact somewhere beyond the settlement.

North of *Angel*, Bonney's boat moved toward the beach as quickly as it could with only four oarsmen. Talliaferro saw the Marines put down their muskets and man oars to help the rowers. Bonney was doing all that he could to prevent brigands escaping inland. The second boat of musketeers trailed after the Marines. That should put enough men ashore to continue the pursuit, Talliaferro concluded. From the way that Gabriel's forces were running, he doubted that they could be rallied even behind the compound's low walls. There were so few of his men; he forced himself not to imagine what could happen if the locals did manage to regroup. But, he reminded himself, action ashore was Bonney's responsibility. Talliaferro turned to his gleeful gun crew and began the laborious task of getting them to re-load.

*   *   *   *   *   *   *   *   *   *

Cabot and Nevis came on deck, Cabot in a reverie at the carnage ashore. Nevis seemed strangely indifferent, bemused by Cabot's glee, but otherwise unaffected. In fact, he desperately searched the fallen Gabrielites to find their leader's body. Gabriel's death would assure his victory over Manley.

*   *   *   *   *   *   *   *   *   *

Daniel found Sweet dazed in the scuppers, blood running from above his left eye, a superficial cut. Gingerly he tested Sweet's skull; it was intact. He pulled out his own handkerchief trying to staunch the bleeding, or at least absorb the blood. He knew who would have to get the stain out of Marse Charles' shirt.

*   *   *   *   *   *   *   *   *   *

No one noticed Hillary furtively descend through the forward hatch. He had kept careful tally of the Americans aboard. The entire crew, except

140

for the two officers, the boatswain's mate, and one sailor at the helm, were involved in the landing. This was his best chance to retake the ship. With that junior midshipman down, even that pretentious servant, Daniel, was preoccupied. Hillary sneered. The ship back under his command, he promised himself, he would settle who would disembowel whom, by God!

He moved forward along the main deck to the crew's quarters. The hatch was closed and bolted, but there was no guard. Bastards did not have enough men to afford one, he calculated. In a confusion of haste and stealth accomplishing neither, he fumbled aside the bolt and pulled open the hatch. Before him sat his thirty-man crew, ankles and hands manacled to a series of eyebolts newly secured to the deck.

Hillary looked around hastily. "Where's the key?"

"Sergeant's got it," answered the First Mate.

Sergeant would be ashore, Hillary thought and searched for some way to free his crew. He recalled the firefighting station by the forward ladder, a couple of axes there. It was a mere five strides to the fire equipment. He wrenched free an axe, started for the crew space, stopped and returned to the rack. Might as well take both, he thought.

*   *   *   *   *   *   *   *   *   *

Amidships, the Liberian women were making their way to the weather deck through the main hatch. Anxious to know what was happening, it did not occur to any of them how unwelcome their presence would be.

Passing through the main deck, Delcina glanced forward. A White man with an axe in his hand was headed toward the front of the ship. Suddenly he stopped, hesitated for a second, turned and retraced his steps to take the second axe from the fastenings by the forward ladder. The light down the ladder well illuminated Hillary's face.

Pushing past several women, Delcina propelled herself to the weather deck. Frantically, she looked for someone in authority; Talliaferro, she rushed to him. "Mister! Mister!" she shouted grabbing his sleeve.

Talliaferro was intent upon stopping the vent of the long nine 32-pounder to prevent a rush of air through the touchhole that could ignite any smoldering residue in the bore and explode the new powder charge as the untrained crew rammed it home. He had no time to answer female questions. "Get away, Girl!" he bellowed and jerked his arm from her grasp, catching sight of more women emerging from the main hatch. *Damn it!* he thought. He had no time for this. Contorting into a half-turn from the gun, still keeping his right thumb in the leather thumbstall firmly pressed over the touchhole, he shouted, "All of you! Get back below *NOW!* Do it!"

The women looked startled, hesitated, then continued to emerge heading to the port rail. Furious, preoccupied, and powerless to stop them, Talliaferro turned back to the gun.

141

Delcina was equally as furious, preoccupied, and powerless to change Talliaferro's focus. She had no real experience with White Americans, but this one was proving what her grandmother had said, "Too damned proud to listen for they own good." She looked frantically around the deck for someone to tell of the danger. Forward, there was a terrible mess with confusion, blood, some screaming and several what looked to be parts of men scattered about. It held her gaze. She saw Daniel kneeling on the left side of the ship with a body propped against his left knee. She sprinted forward.

*   *   *   *   *   *   *   *   *   *

"Sure your tompions are out!" barked Bonney at the line of twelve blue-uniformed Marines facing southward some thirty yards from the water. Sure enough, Schmidt still had the wooden plug in the muzzle of his weapon. "Check your caps!" It was not uncommon for a percussion cap to slip off the nipple of a musket at half-cock as troops maneuvered with loaded weapons. Even one misfire would significantly reduce the effect of the Marines' first volley. Bonney was determined to maximize the psychological impact of his first blow.

They were well ahead of the other boats. Bonney decided not to wait. A small, well ordered force could accomplish more by pressing the rabble now, he reasoned, than by waiting for a few more undisciplined bodies while giving Gabriel's men a chance to realize how badly they out numbered their attackers. Drawing his sword, Bonney checked the alignment. "Detail … Forward … Double Quick Step … MARCH!"

The Marines automatically came to "Port Arms," muskets held diagonally across their chests from right hip to left shoulder, rather than the "Right Shoulder Shift" of regular infantry. "At the Port," they were less likely to foul their weapons in a ship's rigging and thus had adopted this modification to *Hardee's Tactics*, the standard infantry manual of the day. They stepped off in a rapid shuffle, not quite a run, of approximately 170 steps to the minute. The little line came to the carnage where the ship's guns had splattered Gabriel's legions. Without breaking step or slowing, they moved across the dead and maimed, gaining on the mixed bag of stragglers and women fleeing southward. Slower fugitives turned aside out of the Americans' way. Bonney had to decide whether to halt and deal with the potential threat to his rear, or press after the larger mass surging toward the Mansion House. He kept his men going, personally stepping slightly to the side and lashing one of the male fugitives across the throat with his sword. The blade bit deep and grated against the man's vertebrae as an instant stream of blood projected from the severed carotid artery. Bonney did not hear the gurgle as the runner collapsed.

142

Behind the Marines, Sergeant Banning tried to get the first boatload of Liberian musketeers into a line. They were too excited to obey. One leveled his musket at a small group of women running toward the village. The report shocked his fellows into an instant of frozen silence, while the ball crashed through an upper story window. The sergeant seized his opportunity with a massive bellow terrorizing his little band into obedience. Banning fought to suppress a grin as he ensured that weapons were capped, tompions removed from the muzzles, and the men attentive. In a clump only somewhat more linear than circular, they started southward in trace of Bonney's dozen Marines.

*	*	*	*	*	*	*	*	*	*

The first boatload of Issa's swordsmen landed as Banning's party passed through the "X" of slaughter from the ship's guns. Miraculously, they stumbled out of the longboat without capsizing it and huddled at the water's edge. As the four oarsmen somehow managed to extricate the boat from the beach, Issa focused on the writhing wounded felled by the crossfire. With a long wail, he raised his cutlass and led his band charging up the shore to hack gleefully at their stricken foes.

*	*	*	*	*	*	*	*	*	*

South of Issa's landing site, Dyer formed his musketeers, slowly putting them through the procedure of "Load in Nine Times" to recharge their weapons. He was amazed that none of the muskets burst in the volley from the boat. The tompions had remained in the muzzles and been blasted shoreward along with the balls. Indeed, it was a tompion that felled the one victim of the ragged volley. Dyer saw without registering that she was bestirring herself. "Draw Rammer!" he bellowed at the clump of musketeers.

*	*	*	*	*	*	*	*	*	*

Hyperventilating, Delcina dropped to the deck beside Daniel. He glanced at her and returned to bandaging Sweet's forehead.

"Dan'l! Trouble! Hillary downstair with an axe to loose them slaver men!"

Daniel snapped his head up to face Delcina. "Certain?"

"As Heaven, *enty*!"

He rolled Sweet from his knee settling him against Delcina. "Help him," he ordered, "I go fix Hillary." As he shifted his unconscious master to her lap he fumbled with Sweet's holster flap and extracted the giant LeMat revolver. He got to his feet shaking his tingly numb right leg; he could not have that in the coming fight.

*   *   *   *   *   *   *   *   *   *

As the head of the rammer cleared the muzzle, Talliaferro jabbed the primer through the cannon's touchhole and into the powder bag. Two of his crew not needed in the loading process already had dropped the section of transom bulwark that was the rear gunport. By example, the Carolinian got his men heaving on the lines to move the gun forward to the end of the slide. He leaped up behind the breech to sight the weapon, giving verbal and demonstrative directions to move the pivot carriage counterclockwise so the tube would bear on the open Mansion House gate. Satisfied, he snapped the lanyard onto the primer ring, hopped down from the carriage and was about to fire, when he froze and let the lanyard slack. Stepping level with the right trunion Talliaferro bent forward and examined the large compressor screw attached to the upper part of the gun carriage. When tightened along with its mate on the left side, the compressor screw clamped a steel-shod block of wood against the iron track on the pivot platform. As the gun slammed back with the recoil, the friction of steel-on-iron dissipated energy and kept the weapon from flying off its mount. My Lord, Talliaferro realized, that must be what happened with the carronade! He tightened both screws and rechecked the lay of the gun.

*   *   *   *   *   *   *   *   *   *

Bonney's men were less than fifty yards from the Mansion House gate, which was plugged by panicked tribesmen jostling to be first through. "Detail ... Prepare to Halt ... HALT!" thundered Bonney. In one step the men came from Double Quick to full stop and brought their muskets to "Shoulder Arms," gripping the trigger guards, the weapons vertical along their right sides supported by right arms fully extended. They stood rigidly, but their chests heaved as they fought to control their breathing. "Fire by Company ... COMMENCE FIRING!" bellowed Bonney as if he had a full hundred men. "Company ... READY...." The muskets inclined forward from the shoulders to be caught by left hands between the first and second barrel bands, the wrists of the pieces gripped by the right hands level with the Marines' waists. "AIM...." Hammers clicked back to full cock as the pieces arched forward and upward until butplates pressed into the hollows of right shoulders. Each man instinctively took in a full breath, half exhaled, closed his left eye, and centered the stubby front sight blade upon an African struggling to press through the gate.
"FIRE!"

144

The twelve Model 1842 Springfield smoothbores crashed out with a single report obscuring the miniscule line of Marines in a cloud of smoke and propelling twenty-four .69 caliber balls and a mass of .00 buckshot into the crowd. Expecting to engage a massed target, Bonney had ordered his men to double-shot their weapons with the standard shipboard charge of "buck and ball." The effect was a repetition in miniature of the artillery crossfire. Striking the packed mass, each .473-grain ball passed through at least one body before coming to rest in another. The mass seemed to lift, then collapse; like a rugby scrum, Bonney thought absently of Princeton. The survivors' shocked immobility yielded rapidly to panic. Discarding weapons, they fled, most outside along the walls in either direction, while a few stumbled through the gates.

"LOAD!" he ordered. The musket butts thumped the ground in unison. Without further instruction, the Marines snapped the pieces in front of themselves, automatically proceeded through the nine loading steps, and returned them to the "Shoulder" signifying that the loading process was completed. When movement ceased, Bonney commanded, "Fix ... BAYONET!" After a pause, he continued, "Charge ... BAYONET" and the men came to the "Ready" position, this time with the long three-edged blades extending from the muzzles of their weapons. "Detail ... Forward ... MARCH!" The Marines stepped through the hanging smoke. From the direction of the Mansion House the first thing visible was a line of twelve shining bayonets moving in unison. As the grim blue-clad automatons behind the needle sharp points emerged from the cloud, the will to resist ebbed from all in Gabriel's band looking in their direction.

*   *   *   *   *   *   *   *   *   *

Cabot had seen enough; it was time to go ashore, to go *home*. He joined the second party of swordsmen as they clambered down *Angel's* sheltered starboard side into the longboat. Nevis remained at the port rail, observing, but not anxious to set foot on land, not yet. His instincts told him that, with Gabriel unaccounted for, the game still was in the balance. He was not a swimmer and abhorred involvement in too many struggling for too little of anything, at least on an equal footing. He would not expose himself to contending for a seat in a boat returning to *Angel,* should the landing fail.

*   *   *   *   *   *   *   *   *   *

Daniel stepped from the forward ladder onto the berth deck, holding the great pistol at full cock, hinged hammer bent down to fire the 16-guage shotgun barrel. Ahead of him the hatch to the crew's compartment was partially open. He swallowed nervously.

*   *   *   *   *   *   *   *   *   *

On deck, Delcina knotted the bandage around Sweet's head as he stirred into consciousness. She was startled to see his eyes focusing on her. "You awake now." He only groaned in response. "You stay awake. Hear?" In her haste she none-too-gently shifted Sweet's weight to the bulwark. "Y'all stay put; I going help Dan'l!"

*   *   *   *   *   *   *   *   *   *

"Stand Clear!" Talliaferro bellowed at his novice gunners. He gave a steady pull on the lanyard. The blast hid the screech of the compressor screws. Smoke obscured the target as the ball streaked toward the Mansion House.

The Marines were a bare thirty yards from the gate when the projectile came ripping overhead, punched through the mud apex of the archway just before impacting in the yard spraying sand over several panicked Gabrielites, and on the bounce demolishing a small outbuilding. While Bonney's little band could not see much through the gate, it was apparent that all in the yard who remained mobile were swarming into the Mansion for shelter from the threat that had literally burst among them. Not about to storm into the courtyard with only twelve men, Bonney stopped at the despoiled gate and looked impatiently over his shoulder for Banning's Liberians.

*   *   *   *   *   *   *   *   *   *

Daniel drew breath, hesitated, then with a bellow threw his shoulder into the partially open door. It shot around on the hinges sending a sailor staggering. Several of the crew turned toward the doorway with startled stares. Hillary had an axe raised to strike at a seaman's fetters. Cat-like he pivoted toward the hatch redirecting the blow.

Daniel pointed and fired, the report deafening in the confined space. Flame lanced toward Hillary as six double-ought buckshot pulverized his face, smashed through his brain, and exploded out the back of his skull. Bits of bloody bone, brains, and scalp splattered the men chained on the deck behind the crumpling corpse.

Hillary's grip released, flinging the axe. The bit struck the hatch combing, pivoting the hickory handle into Daniel's cheekbone and nose before falling to the deck and slithering aft. Stunned, Daniel toppled backward onto the deck as the burley Mate crashed into him. Together they sprawled through the hatchway.

Delcina stepped from the ladder as the axe slithered toward her. Instinctively she stopped it with her foot as Daniel and his attacker crashed

146

to the deck in front of her. Grabbing up the instrument, she sprang forward. The Mate came to rest on top of Daniel flattening the big pistol painfully against the boy's solar plexus. The larger man lifted himself slightly upon his left hand spread across Daniel's face, reaching for the pistol with his right.

Half focused upon striking Daniel's attacker, half concentrating upon not hitting her savior, Delcina swung the axe like a croquet mallet. Glancing up, the Mate had an instant of recognition before the bit sliced into his forehead and eye just right of his nose. Sounds like a machete into a melon, Delcina thought with a detachment that amazed her.

The impact shifted the Mate off Daniel, freeing his left hand to snap up the end of the pistol hammer. As the body rolled further, Daniel extended his right hand and fired a ball into the stomach of a sailor attempting to jump over the fallen men to grapple with Delcina. The impact of the shot sent the seaman back into the several unchained men behind him, slowing their movement toward the doorway. Daniel discharged two more shots into the group before their screams for mercy registered in his racing brain.

Propped up on his left elbow, blood running from his nose, the side of his face hurting unbelievably, Daniel shrieked into the compartment, "Don't none of you move!" God! he thought, he had blood all over his face, in his nose and mouth, and he was shaking like a dog shedding water. Suddenly he was certain that his heart had exploded into his throat. Hands were gripping him under the armpits from behind.

"I help you up. Don't look 'round," Delcina grunted lifting him from the planking. She knew how to lift, he noticed with a vague detachment, bending at the knees and using her legs. Daniel was surprised how little effort he had to contribute to the process.

The smoke cleared from the ghastly scene. Hillary's faceless – almost headless – corpse lay oozing among chained seamen. The Mate's cadaver was propped against the hatch frame, blood puddling from the cloven face. A sailor lay squirming amid his fellows clutched an expanding blotch of red on his abdomen, alternately moaning and cursing the mortal wound. Another, bleeding from the thigh, lay dying of a severed femoral artery, while a third on his knees rocked back and forth clutching a heavily bleeding shoulder.

Daniel felt light headed. He had never killed a man before. "God help me!" he gasped. "I done killed a bunch of White men."

"What needed it," exclaimed Delcina behind him. "What we to do now?"

"Plenty more chain on the wall. Chain them back again."

"Hurt ones too?"

"Hurt ones too."

*   *   *   *   *   *   *   *   *   *

"Finally!" Bonney hissed as Banning's musketeers loped up. Dyer's group was close behind. Bonney felt he had been waiting for hours, while his men maintained a rolling fire into the compound. Actually less than five minutes had elapsed. With forty men, it was time to enter. Bonney was grateful beyond expression that none of Gabriel's supporters had counterattacked. From the noise in the compound, they were doing a superb job of panicking themselves. At that moment a second ball from Talliaferro's long nine ripped overhead, smashing to a stop somewhere in the Mansion House.

"Enough of that!" muttered Bonney. They should have agreed upon a ceasefire signal before starting this business, he admitted. Hastily he unwrapped his sash and knotted it to his sword hilt. Holding the bloodied blade, he arced the streaming red silk from side to side above his head. A dip of *Angel's* colors acknowledged, or at least Bonney assumed that it acknowledged his message.

His Marines discharged another volley through the gate. Then Banning and Dyer urged the Liberians through. Bonney coldly calculated that the Africans should have the honor of taking the likely higher losses in the fight in the building. Then he realized that, at least to his knowledge, there had been no friendly casualties. With his Marines reloaded, Bonney strode across the courtyard and into the Mansion House.

The building was a large plantation-style structure, two stories of deep verandas on the three sides away from the yard. The south side facing the yard had a matching roof and supporting pillars, but lacked a second level veranda. French doors, opening through the walls instead of windows, were covered with louvered shutters rather than glazing. Entering the 36-foot long center hall, Bonney focused on the large staircase all but cut in two by Talliaferro's second shot. From the rooms to either side emanated much shrieking and struggling as the Liberians subdued Gabriel's supporters. Bonney decided to secure the second level before any nest of resistance could be established there. Sheathing his sword, he drew his revolver and led his Marines single file up the shattered staircase.

The second level was quiet, lifeless. The stairs ascended through a central opening surrounded by a balustrade. Four rooms opened off the hall. At the back of the house more French doors gave access to a veranda. Apparently, any defenders of the upper floor had abandoned their post, but Bonney was going to make sure. Doors to both rooms on the west were open. He motioned the first two pairs of Marines to search them. The doors on the east were secured by great bars obviously recent additions to the décor.

"Schmidt!" Bonney pointed at the bar of the southern door with his pistol.

Leaning his musket in the crook of his left arm, the Marine seized the bar. On Bonney's nod, he ripped it through the keepers as Orin hurled himself against the door hurtling into the chamber. Bonney was on his heels. Female shrieks greeted their thunderous entry. Inside were several startled Liberian women ranging in age, Bonney guessed, from perhaps six to forty-something. Their once elegant European clothes were disheveled, their toilettes unattended, and their wrists and ankles manacled. For a moment everyone froze. Then the senior female demanded, "Who be you, Sir?"

"Lieutenant Bonney, United States Marine Corps at …" he responded automatically, hesitated a moment, and continued, "your service…."

Haughtily, the woman announced, "I be Felicitous Benson Draper, young man." She held forth her linked hands toward her three younger companions. "And these my daughters, Conscience," the eldest of the three – probably 20 or 22 – dipped a tired curtsey, "Freedoma," the middle girl – 15 to 17 Bonney estimated – mimicked her sister, "and Chastity." Chastity, about six by the lieutenant's reckoning, delivered a curtsey worthy of an introduction at the Court of Saint James. "Pleased-meet-you," she mumbled.

Bonney fought a grin. Averting his pistol, he bowed low. "And I you, Missy."

Schmidt who had just entered, was grinning ear-to-ear. At Bonney's gaze, his face blanked.

"My husband be next door, Lieutenant. He need be free, *one time*!"

Bonney nodded and left followed by Orrin and Schmidt. The entry procedure was repeated without the shrieks. Chained to a great deadeye driven into the floor, a solitary gray-haired Liberian of perhaps forty-five years wearing the remains of a light blue linen suit introduced himself as "Mr. Justice Draper, Liberian Supreme Court."

All Bonney could say was, "I'll be damned."

CHAPTER NINETEEN

They were gathered in the Mansion House parlor: Bonney, Talliaferro, Nevis and the Drapers. Through the night, strains of celebratory drumming and singing came from the Common. The flickering flames of a substantial bonfire shot up above the compound wall to the north dimming the glory of Africa's stars. Occasionally, a feral roar erupted from the unseen crowd, accompanied by tortured shrieks. At such moments, Bonney would take an angry draught from the tumbler of neat Cuban rum. He had not tried to intervene. With only a dozen Marines, there was nothing he could have accomplished, other than to anger their "hosts and allies," Talliaferro's words.

It had begun with some poking and clubbing as Gabriel's people were rooted from cellars, corners, and crevices or trapped at the end of the low peninsula and herded to the Common. Bonney had been amazed at how the ranks of Cabot supporters grew when the Mansion House fell. Clearly the Americo-Liberian male population, those who had not been sold to slavers like Hillary or conscripted to forced labor in the fields north of Greenville, had been in hiding during the fight. Once the outcome was clear, they emerged to augment the victors. They tended to be older men of what must have been the "better sort" in pre-Gabrielite society, circumspect with a quiet yet deeply vengeful hatred for their tribal oppressors and any collaborators. After the first hour, younger men from the labor gangs began to appear fiendishly energizing the games of vengeance.

Expectedly, Gabriel was the center of attention. His passion began with his discovery hiding in a grain store, a small thatched structure raised on poles approximately six feet off the ground. At his understandable reticence to descend, a fire was set under the little building eventually igniting the thatch. After several smoky minutes, Gabriel attempted to come down, but his tormentors delayed him with various pointed instruments until he was roundly singed. Once apprehended, they hustled him to the Common and splayed the pudgy former tyrant upon a makeshift cross after the style of Saint Andrew. Cabot became personally involved wielding a sailor's dirk. Facing the bonfire in a parody of Golgotha, the naked Gabriel intermittently received physical expressions of hostility – some red-hot, others razor-sharp, a few blunt but emphatic - from Cabot and select favorites. Progressively Gabriel lost bits of his anatomy including both his ears, an eye, and his rings with their supporting fingers. His wounds were swiftly cauterized to prevent loss of blood prematurely ending the festivities. Bonney tossed his head to banish his memories and took another tug of rum.

Across the room, Nevis pompously explained why the national government had not intervened. Every time the story was slightly different, the latest one included the Drapers as a reason for Liberian inaction. Why,

Bonney wondered, didn't Nevis just admit that the Cabots did not have enough clout to get the government to act?

First, Nevis pontificated, Liberia's only operational warship, the small schooner *Lively Quail*, was required in the area of Monrovia because of tensions with the Spanish over the recent seizure by *Quail* of the *Buenaventura Cubano*, a Spanish vessel taking-on slaves in Liberian waters in the mouth of the Gallinhas River. There were few roads in Liberia, so communications and commerce travel by sea. Thus, the government was without means to intervene in Greenville. Second, the captivity of the Honorable Justice Draper and family effectively discouraged any hostile act toward the brigand.

"No disrespect, Judge Draper," Talliaferro said with a nod, "but surprises me that one official and his family being hostages should paralyze the national government."

"I be cousin to President Roberts and sister to President Honorable S. A. Benson," interjected Mrs. Draper with hauteur.

"Like the Carolinas, Talliaferro," observed Bonney. "Everybody's kin to everybody."

Nevis smiled and to Bonney's surprise seemed as if he might actually laugh, observing that colonizing societies, whatever their color, tended to be closely knit and to intermarry to the point that Bonney's observation was fairly accurate.

"Not marry *Bush Nigger*," confirmed Justice Draper. "All family to rule here."

So the Liberians were unable to have a go at Gabriel, Bonney mused, but Nevis had no quibble at sending Americans stumbling in risking the tyrant killing the Drapers. It did not add up. Then, Bonney reflected, Nevis probably was as unaware as he had been of the Drapers' situation and of the unavailability of the *Lively Quail*. Had he seen *The Prince* on Nevis's bookshelves, Bonney tried to recall?

"All this is no matter," interjected Justice Draper. "We safe. You here. Gabriel get righteous fate he deserve. All is proper." The Honorable took a swig of rum; then ordered, "We go Monrovia tomorrow."

Ignoring the Justice, Talliaferro demanded who in Monrovia supported Gabriel? Bonney noticed an uneasy squirming among the Africans at Talliaferro's question.

"Certain elements," started Nevis.

"Some got American face, *Bush Nigger* soul!" spat Mrs. Draper.

"Manley is the major problem," Nevis tried to regain control of the spin.

"Manley *done catch* us here, the first place!" snapped Mrs. Draper.

Nevis hastily began reciting how the Minister of Trade had a long-lived hostility toward the Cabots and had opposed all efforts to address Gabriel's usurpations.

"Manley, he done send us here for a trap!" spat Mrs. Draper.

152

Several months earlier Gabriel had invited President Benson to Greenville. Wisely, he stayed in Monrovia and had the Drapers represent him on a mission that was half state visit, half investigation. At the bottom of it all, Justice Draper explained, was Benson's growing uneasiness with reports, fed by Parkins the Minister of Interior, that Gabriel harbored ambitions for an independent Sinoe Republic. The Drapers had traveled on *Quail*, which, on Manley's orders, had suddenly abandoned them at Greenville to intercept the *Buenaventura Cubano* on the Gallinhas River. The President's sister as Gabriel's permanent guest forestalled any action against him by the national government.

Talliaferro and Bonney exchanged dubious looks. Thanks to Nevis and friends, Bonney observed, they had stepped plumb into the middle of a nascent civil war; damned nice way to introduce themselves to Liberian society. Nevis replied that they also had delivered the Chief Justice and his family, close kin to the President, from imprisonment and imminent peril of their lives. Bonney wondered who held the upper hand in this Machiavellian labyrinth. All Bonney and his companions wanted was passage home. Had they created more problems than they had solved? It all depended upon transport.

"Now, about the prize court," Talliaferro began.

"All be done at Monrovia," responded Justice Draper.

Talliaferro and Bonney shot sharp glances at Nevis.

"Technically that is correct," the lawyer began.

"Lawful it be so," interrupted the Chief Justice.

Bonney realized that Nevis would not have enticed them to attack Greenville with the prize court ploy, had he known the Drapers were Gabriel's hostages.

"So a prize court in Greenville would be no account?" growled Talliaferro.

"Under emergency powers, the Superintendent could convene … " Nevis started.

"No account at all," rumbled Justice Draper. "Only valid jurisdiction at Monrovia."

"Nevis, you're a damned lying gutter rat!" spat Talliaferro.

"*Sir!*" answered Nevis, "An emergency court would be most proper under applicable precedent. I cite the decision of the Privy Council in…."

Bonney snorted, "Privy Council won't bind Yanks keen on hanging us, Nevis!"

"Enough," interjected Justice Draper. "All never-mind. Now bed and go Monrovia of the morning." The Drapers rose and started for the hall. Nevis scurried at their heels.

*   *   *   *   *   *   *   *   *   *

Daniel awoke with a start; movement at the cuddy door, though he was surprised he heard anything over the drumming downpour. Sweet breathed rhythmically; again, the low knocking. At Daniel's invitation, the door opened. Delcina hesitated, gathering courage. Daniel started to rise and gasped at the pain from his bruised ribs. She was through the door instantly settling him back into his chair.

Delcina snapped her hand away, "Hurt you?" she whispered adamantly.

"No … just my rib." He did not want her to move away just on account of his pain.

As if in agreement, she moved closer, putting her hand on his brow. No fever, she concluded, leaving her hand gently in place. They stayed unmoving, relishing the warmth. Finally, she slid her hand to his jaw, gently facing him toward the light.

"Let me see that thin little nose of yours." After a moment she sighed, "Well, ain't going to be so thin nor so straight, but not bad looking. How be your head?" His head ached and his cheek was swollen, but nothing was mortally wrong.

"And him?" inquired Delcina nodding toward Sweet.

"Sleeping good, breathing steady. Can't feel no broke ribs. What y'all figure?"

"I figure, whatfore you care 'bout him? You say he your 'Marse.' Pray God he die, I be you," she said matter-of-factly without animosity, only curiosity.

"Girl, y'all talk crazy!" Daniel replied frustrated. "Me and him together, long as we been. My Mammy suckle him after weanin' me. He itch, I scratch, and other way round."

"Just damn *buckra*," Delcina snorted, using the West African patois for White man. "We keeps them mostly out of Liberia."

Daniel gave a small snicker. How did Liberia do that? Laws prohibited Whites from being Liberian citizens and from owning land, Delcina explained, and her daddy as Chief Justice was the leader in enforcement. Whites came on missions and as diplomats, but not as residents. "*We* the law hereabouts." Delcina blossomed with defiance.

"Damned lucky Marse Charles and them come enforcing it for y'all," Daniel's smile broke the sting of what Delcina could have taken as a challenge, or worse, an insult.

Without reply, she stepped to Sweet's bunk, wordlessly raised his shirt, and probed his torso. He stirred, his eyes meeting hers. She whispered assurance and smiled. Sweet smiled and closed his eyes. Nothing broken that she could find.

Returning to Daniel, she knelt beside him. Before he could object, she had his shirt up over his face. Her fingers were warm, smooth down his sides, his body tingling to her touch. She probed his ribs and abdomen. "My

154

Grammy," she whispered, "right good at the bone fixing. Done past it along to me and passel of other stuff too."

He was like a high-shine copper pot Delcina mused and gave a low chirping giggle. Her touch and sound made Daniel light-headed. Automatically, he moved his hand around her waist pulling her against him. His right hand caressed the back of her neck and drew her face....

Suddenly his chair flipped backwards spilling him painfully against the bunk. Pain knifed through his ribs. He lost his breath. Delcina, propelled against the opposite bulkhead by the sudden force of her struggle, sank sobbing to the deck.

"Cina! What I do?" Daniel struggled to extricate himself from the chair, his face a mask of perplexity, clownish with his swollen nose.

"*Nothing!* Y'all didn't do nothing!"

Daniel was in total confusion. "Then what's wrong?" He took two steps to kneel beside her. "Come on, Girl. I not about to hurt you; last thing I do." He lightly stroked her head, calming her as he would a colt; the way James, his father and Head Groom at Sweetlands, had taught him and Marse Charles to do. She responded, turning slightly away. Correctly, he read it as an act of face saving that meant, "Comfort me." He lifted her out of the corner into his arms. "Now ... what's riling you?"

"Dan'l, you don't want me; *nobody* want me!" she sobbed burying her face in his shoulder. "Gabriel done had me 'til I *catched* his pickan."

He barely felt the pain shooting through his ribs. Daniel's shock was not at the fact of her pregnancy, but at his own reaction, an overpowering rush of protectiveness.

She choked through her tears, "Have *Bush Nigger's* child, ain't nobody want me," and slumped in his arms sobbing deeply.

Through her blouse he felt her heaving warmth against his chest. His mouth was dry, his eyes moist. For an instant he pictured the First Mate's face opening to the axe, Delcina steadying him on his feet, her moving to chain the slaver crew. He saw her breathless and excited kneeling beside him to warn of Hillary's attempt to retake the ship. He did not realize how crushing was his embrace as he whispered, "I want you, Cina, I want you forever and always; baby, no baby, I promise."

CHAPTER TWENTY

Bonney was relieved to put some sea room between *Angel* and the savagery of Greenville, where Gabriel's eviscerated corpse still hung from its low cross by the bonfire's sodden ashes. A score of his henchmen's less august cadavers lay scattered nearby in various stages of dismemberment as the vultures wheeled lower and closer. Many more of his followers still bleeding from whippings and mutilations, presumably would be enslaved to replace the Americo-Liberians in the fields. The wheel turned….

Sweet's appearance on deck ended Bonney's musings. His greeting to Talliaferro seemed uncertain, and that was out of character. Was he unsure of his standing after the carronade catastrophe? Bonney guessed that it was another matter. Earlier he had caught bits of a whispered conference between Charles and Daniel in a corner of the wardroom.

Talliaferro politely asked after Sweet's health and received a pat response. So much for the civilities, Talliaferro announced seriously, how did Charles really feel? Much better, the youth responded. The headache and double vision were gone and, thanks to Miss Draper's bandaging he freely admitted, he could breathe with the sensation of only a couple knives sticking his ribs. He calculated he would be fit in a week or so. Talliaferro allowed he best be, for he was needed as a watch stander on the Atlantic crossing. Sweet nodded, then stood in awkward silence.

Talliaferro sensed his tension, waited, and finally coaxed, "What else, Charles? Y'all aren't standing there gulping like a landed bluegill without something to say."

"Well … er … yes, Sir."

"And it is…."

"About Dan'l, Sir." Sweet stopped again.

After sufficient pause to permit Sweet to continue, Talliaferro nudged, "And about Dan'l, it is…."

"That Mr. Sweet's boy is smitten dumb by the sweet Delcina" announced Bonney, "and Mr. Sweet is sweet on the match, but uncertain how to further it."

Sweet felt the blood rushing to his head, his breath catch, and his muscles tense. Bonney was playing upon his name with a mocking petty cleverness that embarrassed and infuriated Charles. This was none of Bonney's damned business! Couldn't he ever keep from meddling?

"Well …" twanged Talliaferro, "can't buy *her*, Charles, so I guess y'all just have to free *him*."

Sweet's stammered, "Dan'l won't stay in Africa, Heaven's sake! Too smart by half to do a damn fool thing like that." He looked daggers at Bonney.

Talliaferro and Bonney chuckled at Sweet's earnestness. "He is your Nigra and it's your decision, Charles; personal matter, not a naval one," Talliaferro announced.

"Brotherly advice?" questioned Bonney looking at Talliaferro with raised eyebrows.

"To me or him?"

"Not quite sure. Both, I guess." Bonney had a devilish twinkle. "'This be Africa,' correct?" Sweet squirmed as Bonney observed that in the absence of Daniel's father, it was up to Charles Sweet to approach Justice Draper to arrange the marriage. Talliaferro grinned, even chuckled at Sweet's discomfort until Bonney sank his second barb. "That done, there's a marrying to do, 'Captain' Talliaferro."

Their spluttering reactions more than fulfilled Bonney's expectations. In the spirit of the moment, Bonney fervently argued his position. Shortly, he convinced himself that he was correct. As *Ebony Angel* proceeded out to sea under control of Boatswain's Mate Peck, the other two officers grudgingly agreed in earnest to what had begun in jest.

*　　*　　*　　*　　*　　*　　*　　*　　*　　*

A Chief Justice, whatever his hue, should have the captain's cabin, Talliaferro reasoned, especially if he were about to decide the fate of their transportation home. After all, "this be Africa," and the world was changing; look at Perry in The Japans. The same was true for messing. The first meal at sea, a late dinner in lieu of supper, found the six Drapers and the three American officers at the main cabin's large table. Most unusual, Daniel, all nerves, sat beside his master in Sweet's extra white trousers, white collarless shirt, and brass-buttoned navy blue jacket. Dressed like a *buckra*, Daniel thought deliberately using the West African expression. There was something uncomfortable, almost wrong about all this, he concluded, but did not know what. That was it, he realized, he still felt somehow unworthy to sit at this table, that it was *wrong* for him to be there. Did Justice Draper feel the same, he wondered?

Nevis was absent, claiming *mal de mare*. Just as well, Bonney concluded. At Greenville, Nevis had insisted upon going to Monrovia, but aboard *Angel* had hidden in his cuddy or in isolation above the transom. Bonney could not explain the transformation from the confident Machiavellian of Freetown to the uneasy recluse of today. Clearly Justice Draper made Nevis apprehensive. What was going on?

The Chief Justice's beautifully rumbling three-minute grace relaxed Daniel. The soup, served by two Draper domestics liberated from the palm plantation, passed without incident. Daniel thanked God for a light swell and constant wind. Seated across and one down from Delcina, her presence made him feel awkward. Delcina stared boldly at him. She smiled at the way his

158

cheeks flushed as he avoided her eyes. As he studied his soup, she sank into reminiscence:

>The afternoon had been different. With that Charles Sweet's approval, Daniel had approached her. The formal proposal was the easy part. Effectively, it had been made and accepted the previous night in the corner of Sweet's cabin. The devil was in the details.
>
>Raised to equate the return to Africa to the Israelites' repatriation from Babylon, she had been terrified. He had struggled to explain his privileged position, assuring her that she would remain a free woman, even married to a slave. She had begged him to stay in Liberia, but he had allowed he could not. For a moment all had seemed an impasse. Then she had recalled the life coalescing in her womb. Normally, she could have had her pick of Americo-Liberian youths eager to accept paternity as the price for admission to the powerful Draper clan. Gabriel's whelp was different, she had reflected, bad evil there. No eligible Liberian would have Gabriel's bush bastard. She couldn't even tell her family.
>
>*Damn it!* she had fumed. He should have let her starve. She *hated* him. No she *loved* him. If only she were shut of that *thing* in her belly, what a good life they could have. *If* Daniel would stay. She could not fathom why he would willingly continue a slave. She could not stay without him as father to the *thing* and he refused to grasp the future in Liberia. She would be showing shortly and any person who could count would know it was Gabriel's. Her fellow sufferers among the cargo would certainly report how he had used her. She admitted that she did love this man who came out of the despairing dark and gave her life. Who, like his namesake, strode into the slavers' den and worked God's will. Who *did not abandon her* after knowing she incubated Gabriel's evil seed. He cared for *her*, without considering her family or the alien life expanding in her belly. Jacob had been a slave in his youth, her grandparents also. I do and I shall love him wherever, whatever, she had concluded … and said, "Yes."

As the fowl – several scrawny semi-feral chickens appropriated in Greenville – were served, Daniel felt a brush, then a constant pressure against his left shin. Automatically he looked left, his gaze met Delcina's. She gave a coy smile, inhaling deeply, blossoming her olive bosoms in her square-necked dress. Daniel stirred restlessly. She smiled triumphant. Damn, Girl, he thought, bad enough without you doing that.

To Daniel's relief, Justice Draper demanded everyone's attention, rising to offer a toast. "On behalf of the Dra…." As *Ebony Angel* lifted to the swell, the large man, stooping in the low clearance, overbalanced and stumbled against the table spilling a fair portion of his wine. Embarrassed confusion covered his face. Talliaferro and Bonney sprang out of their chairs, serviettes extended.

"No matter," insisted Talliaferro. "Should have told you, Mr. Draper, aboard ship we stay seated for toasts and all."

"Pardon … for the wine," mumbled Draper regaining his seat. "Try again. On behalf of the Draper family, I toast the brave gentlemen who deliver all us from the torment brought by our sins and that Satan's *Bush Nigger* Gabriel." He raised his glass to his family's accompanying "amen's."

The meat was either goat or sheep. Bonney could never tell the difference on the hoof or on the plate between the goat-like West African pendant-tailed "sheep" and the erect-tailed goat. Whichever, it was excellent, served in a highly spiced "soup" as the Africans called the sauce and accompanied by a great mound of rice. The remainder of the dinner was more Euro-centric, consisting of stores embarked by the late Captain Hillary. A tinned nut cake and English cheese and biscuits made an excellent impression upon the Drapers. To Bonney's amusement, Daniel exhibited no guilt at enjoying the delicacies of the man he so recently had killed. Apparently, it did not enter his mind, clearly focused upon not embarrassing himself in front of Delcina.

Matters became a bit awkward at the point where the ladies customarily withdrew. Mrs. Draper was enjoying herself and gave no indication of leaving. Several hints, such as Talliaferro's, "There are some tolerably good cigars aboard," or Bonney's "After the ladies are gone, I've some political questions, Judge Draper," failed to move her. Finally, Talliaferro requested Daniel take the ladies on deck to view the constellations used for navigation. Daniel noted the favorable impression this had upon the Drapers. They were coming to understand he was more than just a servant.

When the females had departed, Hillary's brandy was decanted and the cabin quickly filled with cigar smoke. For forty-five minutes the conversation shifted between Draper's deep curiosity for the troubles in America and the Americans' concern for the disposition of *Ebony Angel*, both delicate subjects. They danced around slavery as a factor in the conflict across the Atlantic and avoided implying there was any possibility of influencing the decision of a court over which Justice Draper obviously would preside.

Before the pleasantries ended, both parties had, as Bonney thought to himself, in Shakespeare's words, "by indirection, found direction out." Grander designs accomplished, Talliaferro excused himself to check matters on deck, asking Bonney to assist him. In particular he was concerned for the lashings of the carronade barrel that Peck had been able to raise from the riverbed before their departure from Greenville. It was secured near the foremast and now that *Angel* had been rising and falling to the ocean swell the lashings could have worked loose.

"Best we out, so Ma Draper and girls make ready for bed," suggested the jurist.

"Certainly, Sir," Sweet agreed. "But first could I have a moment?"

Draper resettled himself in his chair. "Course, young man."

"Never done this, Justice Draper. Bit on the young side to be doing it now. So I hope you bear with me." Sweet felt a twinge of anxiety at Draper's questioning expression. "Presume your daughter, Delcina, told of how Dan'l found her, freed her and all; 'bout things two of them did during the Greenville fight?" Draper was expressionless. Sweet swallowed. "Well, both did a lot to save you folks and me too. Hillary, the slaver captain, would have this ship back and done for all of us, but for Dan'l and Delcina."

An awkward silence followed, finally broken by Draper. "I have some knowledge. Your point, Sir?"

Here goes, thought Sweet. "Only natural ... her ... well ... Dan'l and your Delcina ... well, they come to think right highly on each other." Draper's face froze, his body stiffened. "Dan'l has asked my permission to marry Del...."

"*NO!*" bellowed Draper, pushing his large frame up from the table, only to thump his pate into the overhead. He winced and seized his scalp with both hands. "No!" he hissed, closed-eyed through gritted teeth. "My Cina not marry no damn slave *buck*!"

"Sir, Dan'l ain't exactly a 'damn slave *buck*,'" Sweet snapped. "He's a Landsman Volunteer of the United States Navy."

Draper guffawed. "For just how long, Mr. Sweet? Until y'all back at Old Virginia? Until y'all go fighting that United States Navy?" Draper grew calmer. "What *buckra* Americans do, your own business. Want be killing each other, ain't no affair of Liberia. But want make a slave of my child, that be my damned business, and you damned sure ain't about to do that!"

"On my solemn oath, Judge Draper, nobody would make a slave of Delcina. She'd be a free woman of color and with Dan'l wherever we go," soothed Sweet, adding after a pause, "except afloat, times like that."

Despite his outrage, Draper smiled with a trace of humor. "Well, leastwise you honest in your soul ... and not much count as a lawyer. 'Free woman of color!' What the Hell that mean at *buckra* country? *Think* Mr. Sweet! Y'all send your kin be 'free woman of pale' married to slave at Japans

161

or Arabia? And just admit you and Dan'l be gone a bunch! What she do by herself, free woman of color at Virginia?"

"Sir, I promise, she'll be with my family and Dan'l's family. Sir, it's the *same* family. We all look out for her. On my oath, we would."

Draper sat down and shook his head, this time in communication, not pain. "You intend good, I know, Mr. Sweet, but y'all see my side, surely. She always the odd one don't belong. No way for person to be livin'. No; I shall *not* consent."

Above their heads in the darkness Daniel and Delcina sat by the skylight, supposedly studying the constellations. Across from them, Talliaferro and Bonney exchanged stricken glances. Had Sweet scotched *Ebony Angel* as their passage home? Delcina felt her stomach heave. Once she had decided to go with Daniel, she was fully committed. She swallowed her panic. Hissing for attention, she motioned them to the transom.

"I fix all this, no worry," she whispered. "Y'all hear hollering, let be. Pa Draper don't know all he need know, and I gots to tell him; he not about to be pleased, *enty*." She took a deep breath. "All be right in the end. Hear?"

The three men nodded agreement. As they did so, Sweet dejectedly came on deck followed by a barely controlled Justice Draper. Without ceremony, the Justice ordered his family to the cabin, stiffly nodded his respects to Talliaferro, and followed after his women.

"Well," sighed Sweet, "bollixed that. Sorry, Dan'l, truly am."

"We heard," replied Bonney. "No way not to."

Sweet recognized that his sudden anger at Bonney's comment was due to his own anger at himself for the disaster in the main cabin. Deliberately he stifled his response.

Would Draper hold to the Southerners getting the ship, was Talliaferro's concern. Sweet was certain that he would, but, to Bonney's surprise and approval, Charles admitted that he had been wrong before. Daniel mumbled apologies for bringing about the entire mess.

"Not your fault, Dan'l," replied Talliaferro. "Y'all helluva lot better man than she'll get on this God forsaken coast."

"Draper ain't never been at Virginia," rejoined Daniel. "Nigras to home live whole lot better over these here…. Don't chop each other up, neither."

As one they swiveled toward the skylight, obvious source of a bellow of rage. The drama was worthy of one of Mr. Dickens' new novels, thought Bonney. In the middle of the skylight taking advantage of the additional headroom, stood the Justice. Beside him was Mrs. Draper. Facing them, head out of sight, was a female, obviously Delcina.

"Don't sass me, Girl!" Draper bellowed, his remark ending with a resounding slap. "You a Draper and you ain't about go be no slave at no Virginia!"

"Ain't about be no Lady at Monrovia, neither," Delcina replied.

"How figure?" It was Mrs. Draper who asked the question.

"I gone with child."

"*God Damn!*" burst from Justice Draper, as his wife demanded, "Who child?"

Daniel was sure Delcina was fighting to keep from smirking. "Gabr'l's child, Papa."

"*Ahyeeee*," wailed Mrs. Draper. "No *Bush Nigger* child! *Ahyee!*"

"Hush, Woman," ordered the Justice. "All that be fixed right by Auntie Roth." He turned his head from his wife to his daughter. "How long?"

"Don't make no never-mind," insisted his wife. "Make God take back first pickan, He keep back all." She hesitated. "Ifin' He don't take back mama too." Clearly, she believed the taboo against aborting a first pregnancy, adding, "What Auntie Roth say herself!"

"That old Voodoo Roth got *juju* for that too, Felice," Father Draper said turning to his wife, "Y'all want us have Gabr'l's *Bush Nigger* pickan about our house?" he demanded. "Want Cina be dragging 'round such?" He turned to his daughter. "Ain't your fault, Girl; that damned Manley's fault, certain."

Mrs. Draper bristled. "Forget Manley!" adding at higher decibels, "And forget Auntie Roth make *juju* so pickan go away!" Suddenly she reached beyond the observers' view and pulled Delcina to her ample bosom adding, "What we do for your daughter?" Tears streamed down the cheeks of both women.

"I love Dan'l, Mama, certain do. And he love me, pickan and all."

Mrs. Draper cocked her head, "That Dan'l know 'bout this?"

"Yes, Mam."

"You tell American slave *buck* a'fore tellin' your family?" demanded Justice Draper.

"Awh Hush!" Mrs. Draper commanded. "Way y'all carry on, she be right to tell most anybody a'fore she tell you." She turned back to face her daughter. "He want to marry you, y'all be havin' Gabr'l's pickan?" she asked so softly that it was barely audible to Daniel on his knees, ear next to the skylight frame.

"Yes, Mama. He asked me for marry him tonight; he know all everything. And Mr. Sweet agrees the same. He going to talk to Papa, since Dan'l don't have father here."

"Done talk."

"What you say?" demanded Mrs. Draper.

"My daughter not marry no slave *buck*."

"Sometime, Pa Draper, You a damn fool!" snapped his wife. "That boy ain't no common slave *buck*, as a body that ain't sure enough blind by sinful pride and blasphemous contempt for the Lord's working could figure!" She looked daggers at the Justice while stroking her daughter's hair. "That boy more bright than most; probably much Sweet as that *buckra* Sweet. Cina

163

be bunch better off at Virginia with Dan'l, than drag around Monrovia Gabr'l's *Bush Nigger* bastard." She paused for breath. "What all you figuring do else? No Draper girl can hide at Liberia, not at Greenville, not at Harper, not nowheres. Y'all going send her Sierra Leone?" Mrs. Draper snorted in contempt. "That no place for a Draper. Best life she about could have be with Dan'l."

"Cina did help nurse that *buckra* Sweet." Pa Draper assumed a resigned look. "And he seem honest enough for White man and promised to watch out for her."

"What time you and him talk?"

"'Fore I come on deck."

"Pa Draper, you a damn fool by times! Y'all go fix that, *one time!*" Ma Draper broke into a broad grin. "Sugar," she beamed at Delcina, "Y'all first Draper to go America a free married woman on a boat her daddy done adjudicate to the purpose."

CHAPTER TWENTY-ONE

The water flowed down the windowpane like ranks of breakers undulating toward the shore. Beyond, only wavering outlines were distinguishable in the gray noon light of The Rains. Admitting he could observe nothing more, the Honorable Roland P. Baston, United States Consul at Monrovia, hobbled across the bare floor of his second-story office to his desk, barely discernable in the yellowish light of two nickel-plated whale oil lamps. Damned things burned the local palm oil well enough, he admitted, a great concession for a New England Yankee from a whaling port. He hated The Rains, now hammering furiously on the tin roof. They meant mildew in everything he wore, occupied, touched; air so humid that walking felt more like swimming; sickness from the fetid vapors and miasmas; and, most of all, the doldrums as a prisoner, not only in this despicable land abandoned by the Almighty, but in this flimsy structure that would not serve for a cow shed in Mystic.

So much for being a loyal Democrat, for delivering the votes of the old Connecticut whaling port for now *former* President Buchanan, he reflected. "Head-up some diplomatic mission," had been the promise. "Issie will love being the *grand dam*, Roland, and her father will be pleased." They had expected a German principality; dreamed of castles along the Rhine. Now, Isabelle lay in the sodden ground outside the Protestant Episcopal Church four blocks away and her banker father blamed him for the loss. Not a word from the tight-fisted old curmudgeon since the response to Baston's letter telling of the death of his only daughter. Baston sighed, no future for him in the Merchants' and Seamen's Bank of Mystic. If only *one* of Issie's three babies had lived, the old scoundrel could not turn his back on his motherless grandchild and her widower father.

No future in the Diplomatic Service either with the upstart Republicans in power. Who delivered Mystic for Lincoln, Baston wondered? "May the bastard be appointed United States Consul at Monrovia," he angrily muttered, "some prize!" The "Consulate" in Monrovia was unique. The United States, although not formally recognizing the Liberian Republic, maintained extensive interests there. Above all, Liberia was America's Sierra Leone, port of debarkation for slave cargoes seized by the U.S. Navy. With all the goings-on at home, was Monrovia so out-of-mind the Republicans might leave him at his post, he questioned? Did he want that? For that to be, he best *do something* about that dratted slaver in the roadstead flying the American flag.

*   *   *   *   *   *   *   *   *   *

In the foyer of the President's House, the guests surrendered their sodden cloaks to bumbling doormen, then divided instinctively: the four Draper daughters aside and to the right, Chief Justice and Mrs. Draper centered upon the louvered double doors leading to the main section of the house, and Bonney and Talliaferro several paces behind.

Bonney hoped that his concern was not evident. He and Talliaferro were extremely uncertain as to the disposition of the slave ship. It had seemed to be all understood when they had arisen from the table in *Angel's* main cabin. After the excitement over the anticipated wedding of Daniel and Delcina, Justice Draper had not addressed the topic. Presumably, Mrs. Draper's conviction that the newlyweds would go to Virginia aboard *Angel* had the assent and support of her husband, but no overt confirmation had been forthcoming. Bonney had no inkling who would acquire the vessel after her condemnation as a slaver, whether she would be available for a voyage to America, or, absent *Angel's* availability, how they would make their way home. Their fate seemed completely dependent upon the good offices of the Chief Justice of the Liberian Supreme Court. Hopefully, the next hour would provide at least some answers.

The doors opened dramatically admitting a procession led by a tall, light-skinned Negro in claret-colored coat over light-blue trousers. His high forehead and receded hairline added length to his face, dominated by almond-shaped, slightly protruding eyes above high cheekbones. Close on thirty-five, concluded Bonney, probably the higher side. Without checking his stride, The Honorable S. A. Benson opened his arms and embraced his sister. "Praise God, Felice! You delivered from the clutches of the Evil One!"

With a resounding "Amen," Mrs. Draper gathered His Excellency to herself in an overwhelming hug. The elegant woman, obviously Liberia's First Lady, and the squad of youths behind her, swept forward, she to affectionately kiss her sister-in-law and the Benson children to enwrap the Draper daughters. Justice Draper was as forgotten as the other male visitors.

At last the President extricated himself from his sister. "*Ahyee,* Jefferson!" he beamed seizing Draper by both biceps. "You not die by that *Bush Nigger.*"

"*Enty,* Mr. President. He not able to kill me."

"*Ahyee,* I forget myself," exclaimed Benson turning to the Americans.

"Bonney?" President Benson asked with surprise at Draper's introduction of the Marine Lieutenant. "I am mindful of some Bonney's in Maryland, very helpful in the Maryland Colonization Society's support of repatriation to our newest county."

"My father, Your Excellency," Bonney replied circumspectly.

The two men exchanged long glances of mutual assessment and seemed to approve of what each saw in the other. How lucky can we be, Talliferro thought?

166

Following Draper's introductions, the President led the men through the entryway and left into the spacious Presidential Parlor. The two women and the young people turned right into the Ladies Parlor. Bonney was impressed at the number, if not the efficiency of the servants who quickly produced coffee. To Bonney's amusement, the Liberians drank in the old style, decanting their coffee from cup to saucer and drinking from the latter.

It took nearly an hour for the Justice to recount the Drapers' saga as the President maintained stoic neutrality regarding the various political factions. This changed abruptly when Pa Draper said, "Ah, Stephen, best from all this be Cina *done-catch* to marry sure-enough American sailorman."

"*Buckra?*" Benson demanded in instant disbelief. To President Benson, "American sailor" meant White man. Not only was it unthinkable, but if true, it would present some dicey questions under the Liberian racial exclusion laws.

The temptation was too much for Justice Draper to resist tormenting his brother-in-law. He was careful to assure him that the groom-to-be was "*swanga*," meaning "powerful" or "important." Draper laughed. "*Ahyee …* He be *swanga buck,* no *swanga buckra!*"

Relief mixed with confusion on Benson's face. After an instant's satisfaction at his joke, Draper launched into a detailed description of the heroic Daniel. Neither Bonney nor Taliaferro bothered to correct the omission of Daniel's condition of servitude, nor Draper's strong implication that Daniel was some sort of officer.

"Dan'l want to be an officer at Liberia?" asked Benson. Such an accomplished sailor, warrior, and family member would need an appropriate post; *Lively Quail* perhaps?

"*Ahyee,* They go America for live."

"Cina *close-my-stomach*," Benson said with deep seriousness. "Before God, I wish she stay." Then with a knowing smile he added, "They go to New York for prize money?"

"*No can go* New York by that ship," replied Draper.

Talliaferro recognized his cue, "Unseaworthy, Mr. President."

"*Enty?*" responded Liberia's Chief Executive.

"*Enty,*" agreed Draper. "Bad hurt in Greenville fight; Court to libel her tomorrow."

"And when Cina to marry?"

"When Mama say," the Chief Justice replied. From Ma Draper there was no appeal.

Rain hammered the metal roof, as the conversation turned to living arrangements. The Drapers would be the President's guests until their home was habitable. It would take some time to expel the inevitable intruders, snakes in particular, and prepare the premises for the family's return. Person or persons unknown had made off with a large portion of the structure's rare and expensive tin roofing and many furnishings, to the amazement of the servants. "Done take a walk," was the inevitable explanation.

"This be Africa," Bonney reflected. It was the standard explanation for any shocking variance with accepted Euro-centric norms from torture and mutilation to the mysterious disappearance of everything from a nail to a roof. He watched one of the quick little light green lizards run diagonally up the wall and dart its tongue at an unseen insect. Several globules of rainwater found their way down the unused chimney to smack onto the bricks of the firebox. From across the hall came quavering laughter. But for hot words spoken after too much whiskey and adolescent stubbornness preventing retraction, Bonney reflected, he would have been in his father's Baltimore law office instead of this mummer's parody of a capital, and he would have been bored stiff.

*   *   *   *   *   *   *   *   *   *

What attracted Nevis to Ma Fletcher's rest house was its significant privacy. Behind her single-story clapboard home, raised off the ground by short brick footings to discourage termites, were three one-room cabins. Several indentured tribal girls cleaned the little structures and ensured the guests' comforts, sometimes in ways that the minister at the Protestant Episcopal Church would not endorse. Banana trees provided some shade and rustled pleasantly in the fairly constant breeze. Chickens and guinea fowl scratched in the dirt yard and a sow nursed her piglets not far from the whicker-fenced enclosure at the back of the property that served as the privy. Nevis despised the place, but it met his needs and was close to the semi-fortified Parkins Family compound at the eastern end of Monrovia's main street.

Cautiously Nevis slunk from the Fletcher property to Parkins' home. He really did not have to be so secretive, but it came naturally to him when engaged in conspiratorial undertakings. He was admitted through a back gate and ushered into the Minister's study at the back of the house where Parkins waited behind a mahogany table.

Their meeting was brief and all business. Indeed, they had only met a few times before and those also had been brief, secretive occasions. To Parkins' relief, Nevis reported that Nathaniel Cabot was now in power in Greenville and Gabriel permanently removed. Thus, the Minister of the Interior was free to negotiate renewed relationships between their business venture and the up-country chiefs seeking markets for the human profits of their incessant raiding and endless little wars. All that would change was the identity of the agent at Greenville and of the profiteers exporting chained humanity.

They were eager to address the political implications of all this. Injured in power and wealth, Manley would be irate, actively seeking revenge.

There were numerous factors to consider. At the moment, Cabot commanded a well-armed, but undisciplined force making a Liberian Government foray against Sinoe County a very uncertain affair. Manley would not be able to convince the Cabinet to undertake such an operation, even though he controlled the Republic's minimal naval force. However, *Quail* could cause problems were Manley to post her off the Sinoe or San Pedro rivers.

Manley clearly was out of favor with President Benson and former President Roberts because of the Drapers, but such things could pass, if politics required it. Better, Nevis urged, to co-opt Manley than to oppose him. The slave ship presented possibilities. Nevis had hoped to acquire it for their use through a questionable court proceeding in Greenville, but Justice Draper had confounded that. What if they formed some joint venture including Manley to acquire the ship? He would have an incentive to keep *Lively Quail* away from their trade routes and accept the new order.

Parkins was enthusiastic. Such an alliance could include most of the men of power in the Republic and yet preserve the profits of their slave-exporting agency for Parkins and Nevis. But what of the Americans who presently controlled the vessel?

Nevis suggested including them in the venture, if they could be kept ignorant of the eventual use of *Angel* as a slaver; possibly get them to pay for the acquisition of the ship, though it would make things more complicated. Parkins approved, unaware that Nevis already had made such a proposal to Charles Sweet.

*   *   *   *   *   *   *   *   *   *

The incessant rain drummed upon the metal roof of the three-story structure at the head of the path that ran diagonally across the face of the bluff down to the wharf. Over the mud track passed all goods landed at or shipped from Monrovia. The McGill Brothers office-warehouse-chandlery-home dominated the river side of the muddy main street. Sweet was impressed, both by the McGills' extensive facility and by its strategic position dominating all Monrovia, including the Executive Mansion, two lots (empty to preserve the Presidential view down river) to the southeast across the street. To the northwest and on the same (north) side as the McGills' was the United States Consulate.

Upon *Angel's* arrival at Monrovia, Charles Sweet had been even more impressed, surprised really, by Nevis's appearance on deck the instant Bonney and Talliaferro had gone ashore with the Drapers. The lawyer had materialized like some voodoo apparition behind Sweet as he stood watch and had invited him to the transom to discuss a matter of greatest importance. Nevis had made a dramatic proposal. Sweet leapt at the chance to reestablish his status with his peers after his near catastrophic meeting with

Justice Draper. The only negative in the plan was Sweet's nagging knowledge that he really did not have the authority to commit Sweet & Sons to the arrangement proposed by the African attorney. He *thought* his father would approve, would honor it, but…. But that was why he was here at the McGills'.

The men around the large table had to raise their voices over the clattering rain. "I know of your family business, Mr. Sweet." The hard faced mulatto stated soullessly.

"President Roberts' father, Mr. James Roberts of Norfolk, Virginia, owned four barges in the carrying trade on the James River," interjected Urias McGill, patriarch of both firm and clan.

"I am aware of that, thank you, Mr. McGill," replied Sweet with a nod. "Believe my grandfather had dealings with your father; unfortunately before my time, Sir."

"Doubtless so," Roberts answered in the lifeless monotone that fully justified his nickname, "Old Gruff."

"How the fates weave the woof and warp of men's lives down the generations," intoned Nevis. "But time is fleeting and we must of necessity bring our discussions to some clear denouement before court."

The lawyer shuffled papers and began to summarize the agreement reached by the men in the room. Under the name "Liberian Packet Company," the firm of McGill Brothers and their co-adventurers Messrs. Roberts, Benson, Parkins, and Nevis, had entered into a correspondent relationship with the firm of Sweet & Sons of Norfolk, Virginia. Under the terms thereof, The Liberian Packet Company could draw upon the credit of Sweet & Sons at its correspondent firms, to wit: LeMat *et fils* of New Orleans, and Nantes, and Bostwick, McKenzie & Gibson, Ltd. of London, Halifax and Hamilton, to the limit of 5,000 pounds sterling *in toto*, as guarantees *vice* advances. Further, the various firms were empowered to act as agent and surety each for another and could acquire shipping space and vessels upon the instructions, one to another, to be possessed or received at a future date or upon future occurrences. Due to the unsettled circumstances of the world, the relationship was to be held in strictest confidence, and not be disclosed to any third party, private or public, other than the correspondent firms. The requirement of confidentiality went to the heart of the agreement and breach thereof constituted grounds for immediate renunciation by any or all parties. The agreement was to be construed as made in the City of London, in the Burrow of Cheap, jurisdiction thereover residing in Her Britannic Majesty's courts, either of law or of equity, as the case might be.

Nevis had hoped for more control of the vessel, but between Sweet's surprisingly stiff negotiating abilities and the determination of President Roberts to launch a Liberian-flagged carrying trade, the lawyer had had to forego any idea of continuing *Angel's* life as a slave ship. He looked around

170

the room. "President Roberts, Mr. McGill, President Benson, Minister Parkins, Midshipman Sweet?" All concurred.

*   *   *   *   *   *   *   *   *   *

Baston found the whole thing displeasing, although admittedly a necessary evil in Liberian politics. The U.S. taxpayers paid a pretty penny for the information from inside the Parkins Compound. His distaste was mollified some by Manley being a despicable character with his presumptions of propriety overlying his absolute venality. It gave Baston rare pleasure to confound both Manley's and Parkins' schemes. Diplomacy sometimes demanded, indeed excused such an untruth. He simply wished he could witness Manley's reaction to the bogus correspondence he was about to transmit to him.

*   *   *   *   *   *   *   *   *   *

"All rise" intoned the bailiff as Chief Justice Draper and the two Associate Justices of the Supreme Court of Liberia, presently sitting as a prize court, entered the nearly square hall that served the republic as both judicial and legislative chamber. Several rows of legislators' desks and chairs faced the bench in a shallow arc. Across the concave front were two counsel tables. Behind and separated by a balustrade, were a dozen rows of pews either side of an ample center aisle. Above and around the three sides of the chamber not behind the bench, were balconies with, Bonney estimated, eight rows of benches. The chamber could accommodate several hundred spectators. But for The Rains hammering on the inevitable tin roof, the acoustics might have been fairly good as well. It all put Bonney in mind of Faneuil Hall in Boston.

Bonney shook his head at this latest twist of fate. He had distanced himself so completely from his father's profession, from The Law, and now he was about to practice it without a license in this surreal land. He, Talliaferro, Sweet, and Daniel (dressed in Sweet's 'second bests') sat at the right-hand table facing the bench. At the other was The Honorable Roland P. Baston, United States Consul at Monrovia, who would oppose Liberian jurisdiction over the prize. Failing that, he would represent her owners' interests.

Baston rose. "If it please Your Honors," he began by rote. *Ebony Angel* was an American vessel of the port of New York commanded and crewed by United States citizens. Though somewhat irregular, she was seized by United States officers under color of American law. Under that law, she might be libeled only in her homeport. Thus, the Liberian court lacked jurisdiction over the vessel. To assert such would be to attack the sovereignty of the United States, something neither desired nor intended by their honors.

171

Chief Justice Draper hesitated to allow Baston to continue; he did not. The Justice recognized the Officer of Marines. Carefully avoiding eye contact with Nevis, Bonney recited how *Ebony Angel* was apprehended in the mouth of the San Pedro River well within Liberian territorial waters. Her only cargo was 287 chained Liberians intended for slavery in Cuba. Because of the condition of the vessel, it had been necessary to repair in consort with a vessel of the Royal Navy directly to Sierra Leone. Subsequently, the slave ship proved unseaworthy for a trans-Atlantic crossing, conducted hither (no mention of the detour via Greenville), and this honorable court asked to dispose of claims to her in order that she might be sold and the proceeds distributed in accordance with American law.

Baston was on his feet instantly. "If it please the Court, there is absolutely no competent evidence that this vessel is in an unseaworthy state. Before…."

Justice Draper interrupted him. "I done sail on this ship, done got judicial note."

Baston gulped. "But Justice Draper, judicial notice does not apply in a situation…."

"I judge that!" Draper looked to his fellow justices. "How say y'all?" Both his associates held for jurisdiction. "Unanimous. Proceed, Mr. Bonney."

Through Daniel's testimony, Bonney introduced Hillary's secret log and ledger. Daniel also testified to the nationality and nature of the cargo. Having established that she was a slaver caught in the act and thus subject to seizure under both Liberian and United States law, Bonney rested.

Baston began questioning the documents and testimony. "You done already objected at all that," interrupted Draper. "Where y'all's witnesses?"

"I don't have any actual witnesses Justice Draper, but…."

"Be no witnesses, be no case. Where be the captain of the ship, the mate?"

"If it please," replied Baston, "I ask this honorable court to take notice of the death of Captain Hillary and allow me to speak on behalf of the owners in his stead."

"You not be there," responded Draper. "How you testify to what you not see?" Baston started to respond, but the Justice silenced him. "No way! Not to testify, you not be there." Justice Draper looked to his colleagues. They nodded. "*Ebony Angel* stand condemned as slave ship and go to bid sale, *one time!*" He smacked his gavel.

"Now," continued Justice Draper, "who make a bid for this ship?"

"Fifty Pounds" called Halcyon Nevis from just behind the bar.

"Sixty Pounds" an elegantly dressed Liberian snapped instantly. Baston fought to control his glee. Manley had believed the false report and was bidding against Nevis.

Bidding proceeded rapidly: Sixty-five pounds from Nevis; Seventy-five from Manley; Eighty – Ninety - Hundred Pounds - Hundred-twenty-five - Hundred-thirty.

"Two Hundred," snapped Manley. Nevis looked shocked.

"Pa Manley," interrupted Justice Draper. Bonney could swear the jurist had a sparkle of triumph in his eyes. "Whyfore you make bids for a slave ship?" He did not give Manley an opportunity to answer. "Your bid be no good," he ordered thumping the gavel.

Manley leapt from his chair. This proved beyond doubt that Nevis had double-crossed him. Instead of being his agent to acquire shares of the Liberian Packet Company, the lawyer obviously had promised to sell his share to Justice Draper just like Baston had said in his report to the U.S. Department of State, a purloined copy of which was in Manley's coat pocket. "You a thief, certain!" he yelled, though it was unclear whom he was accusing. That saved him from instant arrest and instead got him a stern warning from Justice Draper. As several bailiffs began to close in upon him, Manley controlled himself and sat down.

Draper looked at Nevis and questioned, "Fifty pound?"

Baston was horrified. The sails alone were worth several times that amount. It was judicial piracy. The United States was entitled to half of the net on the sale and was being swindled in open court. "Two Hundred Pounds!" Baston rasped.

"Two-Fifty," replied Nevis coldly.

"Three Hundred."

"And fifty."

"Four Hundred."

"Bid, to be paid by all cash money," announced Draper.

Baston looked stricken. "Mr. Justice Draper, I've a draft on The Merchants' and Seamen's Bank of Mystic, Connecticut. Good as gold; certainly the Court will…."

"Cash money only; that be the law at Liberia."

"But, *Your Honor*! I have but three hundred pounds cash!" whined Baston. To expend that sum on the ship would leave the consulate in penury for several months to come.

"Three-fifty," Nevis responded with a rather bored exhalation.

Baston looked around at the sea of blank or grinning faces. He realized that this had been a good day's entertainment and had taken everyone's minds off The Rains. Draper looked inquiringly at Baston who shook his head, then he slammed down his gavel. For whom had Nevis acted, asked the clerk?

"Liberian Packet Company," he replied producing a wad of ten-pound notes. Damned if he would transfer half of his and Parkins' shares to Manley as promised, he resolved.

Sweet sighed with relief; passage home was secure. Actually, Nevis was counting out Sweet and Sons' 350 pounds, advanced by the McGills. The Virginia firm had the option to take title to *Angel* at any time within the next two years for an additional 500. To Charles' surprise, that clause had been a struggle to include in the agreement over Nevis's opposition. Potentially he had bought a fine ship.

*   *   *   *   *   *   *   *   *   *

"Shut your yaps, darlin's!" snapped Sergeant Banning as Marines jostled the survivors of the slaving crew into a tight mass along *Angel's* port rail. "Now *listen-up* to the Lieutenant."

Bonney stood silently, staring down each man who met his gaze. They were a fairly typical crew - a mix of Americans, foreigners, half a dozen Negroes – slaving because it paid better than whaling, or anything else. It paid better because of the insatiable demand for labor in Cuban sugar fields and the risks of ending in a situation like this, he reflected. "*Six!*" he snapped. After a pause, he continued, "Six ... of what?"

Sullen silence met his question. Banning whispered into a front rank prisoner's ear, "Lieutenant asked a civil question, darlin'. Best answer it." He drew a great breath and bellowed, "*Six! What means it?*"

The man winced and stammered incoherently.

"Ah you're a sorry lot of numb-skulled dolts! To date, darlin's, we've thrown six of your mates to the *fishes*! All Protestants, I'm hoping."

"And the ague not started," intoned Banning. "The Rains now; The Rains always bring ague on this coast." He selected an older sailor, "*Correct?*"

"Aye, Sir." All present were rightly fearful of ague, "black fever," malaria.

"Ague: shaking, sweating, out-of-your-head fever, and *Death!* 'White Man's *Grave*' they call this coast. Be raining the next several months; plenty of time to catch the ague." The Sergeant paused. "Still-and-all, might be worth the risk. Liberians be glad to help a Jonathan with no jingle in his pocket, glad to reward you for giving their family free trips to Cuba to learn the sugar trade. And old shipmates from San Pedro River will help."

Banning glared at the older sailor. The man averted his eyes, as the Sergeant continued, "You anxious to get ashore and there's some fine Liberian soldiers on the pier to help you settled-in. But some of y'all might hanker to see more of the world. We're for England; can only use a few...." He paused until the tension seemed painful. "So any man that wants to sign with us step *slowly* to the starboard rail abaft the foremast ... *NOW!*"

It was a general scramble, elbowing and shoving, to be closest to the rail. "Not the officers," called Bonney. Marines prodded the unhappy mates back to the port side.

"Mr. Peck," Bonney said casually.

As the Boatswains Mate moved forward, Banning bellowed, "*Two ranks … NOW!*"

Peck took his time examining each man. The first and second he passed without comment, stopping at the third. "Don' like your thoughts. *Port side! NOW!*" Peck bellowed and jerked the fellow forward. Banning gestured with his musket, choking off the sailor's protest. He shuffled dejectedly across to join the officers. Peck continued his examination, occasionally inquiring as to experience, homeport, and number of voyages. At the end of his promenade, he had rejected seven of the twenty-eight sailors.

The accountant's clerk, a youth of perhaps sixteen had shrunk from his gaze with watering eyes. Peck motioned for him to join the rejects, but Banning intervened. "Need a clerk in the Detachment." He pushed the trembling lad toward Orrin. "See if you can put some backbone into the *colleen*, Orrin." He disregarded the lad's sobs of gratitude.

"All as I need, Lieutenant," Peck concluded.

CHAPTER TWENTY-TWO

From his office window Baston watched *Ebony Angel's* "Congoes," her tribal cargo, land on Bally Island across the river. The new flagship, the only ship of the Liberian Packet Company had just returned from a run to Turtle Island to retrieve these people. Perhaps the Liberian Packet Company had some validity to it, he reflected. After all, the ship could easily have gone to Cuba where its "Congoes" would fetch a pretty price. It was consistent with American policy to unload captured cargoes at Monrovia. It was less consistent to have marooned them on Turtle Island, while purported members of the U.S. Navy toppled the Greenville government.

"Now, Sir," Nevis ended Baston's musing, "cargo landed, we may conclude settlement." Baston dreaded implication as some sort of accessory in this farce. "Naturally, keep of the cargo is chargeable against your Government," Nevis continued, fishing out a list. "Could be itemized for ship's biscuit, salt meat, fruits, etc, but no need. Feeding, clothing, and shelter – sailcloth tentage – came to 63 pounds, 9 shillings, 8 pence." Nevis swallowed. "Charter for Liberian Packet Company's vessel, 50 pounds the trip, plus 10 pounds per day for three days over normal length of voyage totals 80 pounds. Your share court costs, 5 pounds. Harbor duties at Sherbro 10 pounds, at Monrovia 15 pounds. That's 173 pounds, 9 shillings, 8 pence. Then the lighterage, 6 pence per head times 182 – 4 died at Turtle Island – 4 pounds, 12 shillings; 178 pounds 1 shilling total. Your Government owes the court 3 pounds, 1 shilling."

Somehow, the actual costs payable to the Liberian Packet Company had been entered twice on the American bill. Nevis would pocket 75 pounds after deducting a *dash* to the Court Clerk for diverting the overstatement in his direction.

Baston's jaw dropped.

"Such difficulty accounting for such a paltry sum," Nevis continued. "Permit the Liberian Packet Company to absorb the overage. We shall simply call all square and include your court costs with our own." He smiled his understanding best.

Baston drew breath to protest, but the barrister cut him off. "Of course, if you disagree, liens must be filed against the American share and the matter docketed for hearing. It could be some time and cause considerable public interest. However, I do not presume to tell a consular official his duty."

"Shyster!" muttered Baston.

"Pardon?"

Baston's visions of continuing under the Republicans became foggy. Yet, to make a contest of the matter promised only further embarrassment. "Right. Certainly simplify matters for all involved … Right."

"Presuming agreement, Mr. Baston, I took the liberty of preparing these mutual covenants and releases." Nevis grinned, pulling another document from his coat.

*　　　*　　　*　　　*　　　*　　　*　　　*　　　*　　　*　　　*

The frockcoated men watching the longboats discharging passengers on the northwestern bulge of Bally Island ranged in pigmentation from light tan to boot black. Color aside, thought Bonney, they looked *and sounded* like caricatures out of Mrs. Stowe's inflammatory propaganda piece, *Uncle Tom's Cabin.*

"Don't know about these *Bush Niggers*, Joseph. Close enough to home for them to make a run," observed a light-complected man of about thirty, shaking his head.

"Not a worry, McGill," replied the grim faced older man, glowering from under the brim of a straw panama. "From far away enough to be lost hereabouts."

A tall, linear-featured young man addressed the grim fellow in the panama. "Prefer a bunch from Congo River, President Roberts. These more like to run, I'm believing."

"James Payne!" Roberts snorted dismissively, "Don't run, y'all keep them tuckered." The first President of the Republic projected a stream of tobacco juice onto the rain-saturated soil. "Y'all sounding like that over-schooled *Bush Nigger*, Crummell."

"Did not mean that," retorted James Spriggs Payne, unsettled by the allegation. "Got no truck with the holdings of Crummell, Roye, or the like."

Bonney turned away hiding a cynical smile. Alexander Crummell was a famous figure in abolitionist circles throughout the English Speaking World. At thirteen the young boy of the Timinee tribe had been enslaved and imported into the United States. Through a series of adventures rivaling those of Frederick Douglass, he obtained his freedom, with his wife, Sarah, found his way to England, earned a bachelor of arts from Cambridge University, and arrived in Liberia in 1853. A minister in the Protestant Episcopal Church and a faculty member at Liberia College, he was an outspoken critic of the dominant mulattos' treatment of tribal peoples. Crummell's ally, Edwin J. Roye, also of pure African blood, was Speaker of the House of Representatives and possibly the richest man in Liberia. No gathering of Cotton Belt planters could be more contemptuous of these highly intelligent and accomplished African equivalents of American abolitionists.

Payne suggested sending *Angel's* cargo back to the San Pedro, to which Roberts snorted, "Come-on, Payne. Y'all know how it goes up-country, 'Man come up slave one time, be slave all time.'" Roberts spat more tobacco. "Like them silly British sending Congoes back to their homes with a paper saying they British subjects! Just taken up and sold again by first man they meet on their way home! Same for these *Bush Niggers,* just be back here or sold to Cuba again. Ain't no manumission in Africa."

The arrival of another party headed by President Benson and including Justice Draper interrupted the conversation. Hats were raised and greetings exchanged in imitation of American courtesies. As was natural, Bonney admitted; after all, Roberts had been born a free Negro in Newport News, Benson the same in Bonney's own state of Maryland. Did that explained why Benson had been so intent to add the independent colony-state of "Maryland" around Cape Palmas to Liberia? Because his father was a major participant in the Maryland Colonization Society that had sponsored the settlement of some of that state's free Negroes in West Africa, Bonney was familiar with the story of Maryland Colony. In 1856 the Grebo and Kru natives had revolted against Marylander colonization of the Cape area. The following year, Roberts passed at least the trappings of power to his Vice President, Stephen Allen Benson, Delcina's uncle. As President, Benson orchestrated the joint Liberian – Marylander campaign that broke the tribes and facilitated the assimilation of the Maryland colony into Liberia.

A White American, John Says, the United States Agent for Freed Cargos, inspected the arrivals. They appeared well and fit. Fit, thought Bonney, but not happy. He realized the need to ensure order, but the number of Liberian soldiers in their old Napoleonic shakoes, rather sorry blue wool tunics, white trousers, and bare feet seemed a tad more numerous than necessary. The first boatload of "Congoes" - all males - was quickly processed and escorted to a stockade on higher ground inland from Stockton Creek.

The boats arrived at a good pace, *Angel's* craft supplemented by boats from Monrovia and from one of the McGills' schooners anchored in Montserado Roads around Ashmun Point. Females, Bonney observed, were assigned to another stockade. The process and organization had all the trappings of a slave barracoon.

"Bad luck Rains start," sighed young Payne watching another load wade through Stockton Creek. "Mostly just sit until Dry Season."

"I'm working mine, James," responded Urias McGill. "Find enough to keep busy."

"I be certain you do that, McGill, most certain," a new speaker interjected from behind the group. All turned to see a very dark figure; impeccably dressed in frockcoat, silk vest, and cotton trousers, and sporting a cane and gray low crowned top hat.

"Mr. Speaker," McGill responded with a slight lift of his headgear.

The others acknowledged the arrival of Speaker of the House, Edwin J. Roye, with the minimum civilities required by good manners. Roye replied in kind; then disregarded them, turning instead to Bonney and inquiring if he were from the slave ship. He smiled slightly as he spoke. Bonney responded affirmatively, but guardedly.

"Noble of you to carry these souls from Sierra Leone after the ship sold to Liberians, surely." Roye sank his barb, "Unfortunate for these people, however, to be landed here for indentured service, but have been all free at Sierra Leone." Roye shook his head. "Indenture same as slavery, Lieutenant," Roye sneered with disgust. "British called it 'Apprenticeship,' in Sierra Leone, but just slavery there too. Those 'Settlers' - the ex-slaves who fought for the British in your Revolution and were eventually re-settled at Freetown - treated the slaves landed there by the Royal Navy, as they'd been by their masters in your country." Roye snorted and added, "Except bit meaner I guess, account they so recent to be freed themselves. Governor MacCarthy ended the system before he stepped down in 1824, but we still do it here."

"Americans land Congoes only at Liberia," Draper spoke in Bonney's defense.

"And profitable for Liberia, Praise God," responded the legislator sarcastically.

"*Praise God!*" replied Roberts harshly, staring unblinking into Roye's face.

"*HOLD* the *BO!*" McGill's bellow broke the tension.

Bonney had noticed one of the men in the last boat furtively averting his face. Obviously McGill had noticed as well, knew the lad, and had a score to settle. At his cry, the man broke from the queue sprinting northeast, as if to escape over Stockton Creek. It was a long distance across open ground. He did not get more than thirty yards, before several Liberian soldiers blocked him. One smacked him across the head with the brass butplate of his musket. The bolter crumpled.

"Your boy Doe?" Payne asked McGill.

"Same. He one bad egg *Bush Nigger.*"

Roye stepped to Bonney's side. "Amusing, Mr. Lieutenant? Liberian law requires tribal children who live with Americo-Liberians be indentured to eighteen years of age, then back to the bush. 'Bush' usually means land owned by one of these gentlemen. That *buck* made big trouble for McGills. Call him 'Doe' as always had be told '*DO*' something plenty times before he do it. Sound like 'Doe' so his name." Roye shook his head. "Likely lad, but uppity; knocked-up one of those McGill girls. McGills don't take to their daughters amalgamating with tribal people. Boy was lucky to be away with his life and limbs in tact," Roye observed. "Probably kill him now."

Bonney was thunderstruck. The American term "amalgamation," mixing of the races, obviously had the same prejudicial implications in Liberia, the "races" being tribal versus mulatto. He wished that the troublesome Mrs. Stowe could witness this. Thinking of Delcina, he asked the McGill girl's fate. The Speaker sneered. No one had seen her. She could

180

have died aborting or been sent off. Mulattoes did not cotton to being shamed so.

"I see…."

"*Do you*, Mr. Lieutenant?" replied Roye bitterly. "You do and you see a whole lot better than them folks!" he sneered with a nod toward the assembled Liberians. Looking pointedly at Bonney, he concluded, "But truly, I doubt you see slightest better."

CHAPTER TWENTY-THREE

The Draper-Sweet nuptials were held at her uncle's house, the Executive Mansion. Timing such events during The Rains was a matter more of art than of science. In other words, thought Bonney, you had to be damned lucky.

Mrs. Draper was. The inevitable louvered French windows were open on both sides of the President's second floor study allowing a pleasant breeze to stir lightly through the room. Outside, the newly emerged sun maximized the humidity so that every pore dripped to find no absorption from moisture-laden garments. Yet here he stood, Bonney reflected, in his woolen finest. At least Daniel's ability to bring off the officers' trunks from *Jamestown* meant that they were not embarrassed before their Liberian hosts, who obviously spared no effort in adorning their favorite objects, themselves.

"Should hold until supper, *enty*," sighed Justice Draper, as he looked up from a blue willow plate on which only a few crumbs remained. After delicately dabbing the corners of his mouth with a linen serviette, he flipped a fold in it and swabbed his forehead, neck, and collar. "Must go. Felice be all-overish 'bout now."

Bonney smiled. It took no excess of judicial savvy to conclude that the mother of the bride would be agitated minutes before her daughter's wedding.

"Go and God Bless," replied Benson. "Best drink up, Gentlemen. *'Cina and Dan'l.'*"

All stood, adjusting coats, vests, and toilette. "*Cina and Dan'l,*" they chorused, draining the last of what Bonney had to admit was a respectable rum punch. With the rumble of male conviviality, they trooped downstairs.

Talliaferro, Sweet, and Daniel in Sweet's second best coat already were below.

"Not getting nervy on us, now?" Sweet asked Daniel as Bonney joined them in the foyer.

"Not nervie," piped Talliaferro, "Only tad all-overish; right, Boy? … ehr … Dan'l?"

"Just hot and sticky is all," replied the groom.

"Not nothing to what you going to be!" Alfred Russell, husband of Conscience Draper Russell, loudly observed to the jocularity of his Liberian friends. "Take it from me, just-about-my-wife's-brother-in-law, these Draper gals right lather a body."

"Suppose y'all to know," Daniel replied, eliciting hoots from Russell's fellows.

"Enough of this," Benson ordered. "Washington waiting for daguerreotype making in the Salon." Slicking hair and again tugging on vests the group began to move.

The Salon, a long gallery situated like a bulbous hourglass stem between the broad matching front and back wings of the mansion, served as the audience chamber, state dining room and ballroom. Today it was festooned with braided palm fronds over every arch and window, each heavily inset with variously colored hibiscus blooms. White ribbons radiated out from the large central chandelier to the sides and corners of the chamber, providing a canopy over the nuptials.

Beneath the chandelier, the Draper family posed rigidly, all but obscured by the stooped back of the photographer, half secreted beneath the cloak-like camera hood. An acrid sulfur stench was evident; apparently the humidity was frustrating the lighting arrangements; the tribal urchin holding the powder tray wore a particularly unhappy face.

"Hold still, Boy, and do not spill," came a querulous mumble from beneath the cape.

"No spill, certain, Boss," squeaked the hapless-looking child.

Luckily for all, including the Drapers, who obviously wished a few breaths, there was a sudden, blinding flash, followed by mumbled counting beneath the cloak and a moment later the emergence of the famous *artiste*. Augustus Washington, an African-American photography pioneer, had emmigrated to Liberia in 1853, immediately establishing a thriving business among the ruling class. His handsomely framed, leather matted works were *de rigueur* in all the best homes of Monrovia. It was unthinkable that an event such as the Draper wedding could pass unrecorded by his sulphurous art.

There followed a series of groupings: bride and groom in several poses; bride and groom with supporting bridesmaids (Delcina's three sisters) and groomsmen (Sweet, as best man, Bonney and Talliaferro); the foregoing with President and Mrs. Benson and Justice and Mrs. Draper; The extended Draper Family; and Daniel with Former President Roberts, President Benson and Chief Justice Draper. After the posed imitation of the ceremony, Sweet assumed that Daniel's "Family," the groomsmen and groom, would be captured on the glass plate and he began assembling the little band. Washington, however, commenced breaking down his equipment.

"Wait. We've another group here," Sweet addressed the *artiste* peremptorily.

"And just *who* say so?" responded Washington querulously. He had come to Liberia to end being ordered around by some arrogant *buckra*.

Sweet was surprised, but Talliaferro was offended. "Mr. Sweet, does, *My Man*," the Carolinian rejoined with an edge to his tone.

"Just who be he and who be you, *My Man*?"

Talliaferro felt the steel fingers of rage tightening around his spine.

"These be my friends and shipmates and my superior officers, *Mister* Washington." Stepping between the Passed Midshipman and the society photographer, Daniel was as astonished as Sweet at his own impulsive interference in the confrontation. "I deems it a most necessary honor for y'all to record us brothers-in-arms." Washington defiantly met Daniel's stare.

"It's an old naval tradition and bad luck to ignore," drawled Bonney over the tension.

"Then, must be followed for luck, Washington," came Roberts' emotionless voice.

Washington looked into the visage of the Father of Liberia who had entered the room unnoticed during the confrontation. "Of course, Mr. President," responded the photographer and began re-assembling his machinery.

*   *   *   *   *   *   *   *   *   *

Bonney watched a double file of the best-uniformed Liberian troops he had seen form a guard of honor along either wall in the hall between the foyer and the Salon. They all were in their late-teens to early-twenties and to his surprise they all wore shoes. Commanding them was a terse major with long, rust-colored side-whiskers along his olive jaw and sparkling hazel eyes that missed nothing. For a moment Bonney forgot the rivulets of perspiration sliding down his spine as he assessed the troops.

The strains of a string ensemble recalled Bonney's attention to the Salon. The doors to the Ladies Parlor opened. Chief Justice Draper, imposing in his robes of office, stepped forth with Delcina upon his arm. The music competed with a growing murmur - admiration and prayers - as the Justice and the bride moved down the aisle. At the front of the gathering, Mrs. Draper led the exclamations.

Daniel stood his ground watching Delcina glide toward him. She seemed to glow, almost pulsate in his eyes with a beauty that constricted his chest and made his heart race. The moment of discovery on the slave deck, the soft yellow of the lantern light falling across her, presenting her body in a contrast of radiant surfaces and impenetrable shadows, filled his memory. His knees seemed to weaken; his head go light. This girl was the most holy, most perfect, most ... I don't believe I'm doing this, he told himself.

"Take a big breath and don't lock your knees," Sweet whispered.

He obeyed and the light-headedness passed. She was close now, her eyes shining, breath quick. As President Benson cleared his throat almost in Daniel's ear, Daniel realized that he must be the only slave in the history of Sweetlands to be married by a head of state, for sure by one of color. He doubted even his mother would believe this. Well, he thought with satisfaction, Augustus Washington had taken a representation.

Justice Draper passed Delcina to Daniel. She simply placed her hand over his. "Turn," Sweet coached as the two stood frozen with locked gazes. Slowly they pivoted to face the President, who again cleared his throat and opened the Prayer Book. The service was familiar. "Shall leave her father's house … Cleave only onto ... sickness and in health … 'Til death....'" Daniel noted the lack of the customary slave wedding addition, "or distance" before "do us part."

Benson closed the Prayer Book at last. "Ring?"

Confusion seized the groom. Neither he nor Sweet was prepared for the wedding band, a relatively new custom of White society unknown in the slave quarters. Apparently the Liberian gentry followed America in this as in most things. Daniel gulped air to control his panic, unaware of the fumbling behind him. Sweet reached forward, pressing into Daniel's hand a heavy gold band representing a serpent swallowing itself by the tail.

Delcina extended her hand. As Daniel started the ring onto her finger, she jerked away shrieking, "*Ahyeeee*! Gabr'l demon ring! *BAD MAGIC!* Curse certain!"

Shocked, Daniel stood uncomprehending. President Benson soundlessly opened and shut his mouth. Sweet went as ashen as Delcina. Justice Draper stepped to his daughter's side with an unintelligible rumble. Joseph Jenkins Roberts suddenly appeared beside the close-to-fainting bride. Almost roughly he seized her wrist, moving her back beside Daniel. Wordlessly, he gripped Daniel's right wrist drawing the hand and offending ring up to his face.

"Auntie Roth." There was no agitation, indeed no emotion in Roberts growl.

A beshawled, large-framed woman, wasted by years, made her way slowly forward on rheumatic joints. Roberts nodded toward the ring, still clasped between Daniel's right thumb and forefinger. Slowly the old woman took it, deliberately raising it close to her yellowed eyes.

"Ahhhhhhhhh," she gave a low exhalation. "This ring done be from Gabr'l?"

"From Halcyon Nevis, Auntie," volunteered Sweet at Daniel's side.

The old woman disregarded the White boy. "How savvy it from Gabr'l, Cina, Girl?"

"It be on his hand for long-time, Auntie Roth."

"Gabr'l done bad by you, Child?" the old woman asked Delcina in a calming timbre.

"Yes Mam, Auntie; Most bad. He done evil to me for long-time."

Auntie Roth took the ring and held it to Delcina's face. The girl shrank from the circlet. "How come this off Gabr'l hand?"

Bonney envisioned the tortured, still living, mutilated creature crucified by the fire. "Fingers cut off whilst he was alive; rings come with them, Auntie," he volunteered.

"Ahhhhhhhh," Eyes closed, Auntie Roth demanded, "Him *buck*, same time?"

Bonney recalled the writhing thing on the cross. He was certain of the answer the priestess wanted and certain that Cabot would not have left his victim's manhood in tact while lopping off Gabriel's other extremities. "No, Auntie, he were no *buck*."

"*Ahyeeee*, Devil man, no man. Devil blood done washed clean this ring. Devil *juju* be gone from ring, same time Gabr'l seed gone off him." She passed her free hand over the ring several times, spat on the circlet and placed it in her mouth. Slowly she inclined her head back, extended her arms out and up, and pivoted incrementally counterclockwise, moaning a soft noise that Bonney was reluctant to characterize as a tune. She stopped, facing Daniel. "Gold for me, *Bo!*"

Daniel stood dumbstruck, while the three Americans desperately fidgeted in their pockets. Sweet emerged first with DePue's double eagle. He would have parted with a pocketful of the twenty-dollar pieces to restore the harmony of the ceremony.

Auntie Roth took the coin from Daniel, studied it closely, pointed to the coroneted Liberty Head on the obverse, and smiled. "Queen of Heaven, certain." Turning the small slug over she guffawed loudly at the heraldic eagle on the reverse. "Best good, certain! Queen of Heaven make Devil fly away as this vulture here!" Never again would Sweet look at the coin without seeing Miss Liberty as the "Queen of Heaven" and the mighty federal eagle as a lowly vulture. She clapped the coin into her mouth with the ring, tilted back her head, and spat something toward the roof. With surprising force, she thumped Daniel's back, staggering him. "Snatch him, *Bo!*" she screeched.

All eyes followed the ring as it twisted toward the ceiling and rolled over to descend. Daniel bumped President Benson aside unknowingly, his gaze fixed on the tumbling circlet. He stretched forward, grasping the ring in his outthrust hand at the instant he lost his balance, and plunged into the potted palmettos arranged as a backdrop for the ceremony. Delcina laughed, absolutely dissolved in relief. Her peal was infectious. The entire gathering erupted. Even Daniel, sprawled on his stomach, laughed with release.

Justice Draper helped Daniel to his feet. President Benson again asked for the ring. As Delcina extended her hand, Auntie Roth intoned, "Ring best magic for you, Cina, Girl."

Delcina glowed. She knew she was married to this magical man and now possessed a token of their union declared by the high priestess to be the most potent *juju*. Had God visited Gabriel and the captivity upon her with a purpose as He had sent the Babylonians upon the Children of Israel, she wondered? In her soul she knew that he had. Fear not, Cina, for thou art blessed among women. "Amen," Daniel heard her say as he slid the ring onto her finger. "Amen," he replied as he leaned forward to kiss her with an "all-overish" feeling that had nothing to do with being uncomfortable.

187

CHAPTER TWENTY-FOUR

In the hall, the Guard of Honor came to attention as the double doors smoothly swung open. President Benson gave a nod to the quartet, which sawed away at the ever-popular "Buffalo Gals" or "Louisiana Gals," or "Bowery Gals," depending upon where the song was played. In every case, at least in Bonney's experience, the damsels in question were implored to "come out and dance by the light of the moon." While the moon was still below the horizon and the sun, low in the west, still sucking humidity into the dank air, the meaning was clear, the formalities were over and the festivities could begin.

"Come on, *Bo!*" Delcina flashed an excited grin at her husband of 90 seconds. "We the biggest toads in the puddle this time and we go first!" Snatching his hand, she pulled him through the parting crowd.

The Bensons fell in behind them, joined by the Drapers, the Roberts, and a general inward wheeling movement as the couple passed through the throng. Bonney was the first American to comprehend the protocol. For an instant he had the vision of three small white paper boats bobbing along in the ripples of a black and tan river.

As the bridal couple entered the hallway, the youthful honor guard came to "Present." Not Marines, but not bad, thought Bonney. These parade units were "of a type," similar: Richmond Howitzers, Ancient & Honorable Artillery, Philadelphia Light Horse. Social units with their breeding, uniforms, and fancy drill did not automatically impress him. "Public Duties" as the The Brigade of Guards called attendance upon Her Britannic Majesty, were one thing, but could they hold steady as a wave of lead scythed their ranks or a line of leveled bayonets inexorably moved toward their abdomens?

With nods and smiles, Daniel and Delcina led the throng through hall and foyer to the front doors to halt upon the veranda under the deep portico. At their appearance, a brass band belched into "Hail, Columbia." The oppressive humidity seemed to have no effect upon the mass of hooting, cheering people filling the street, ankle deep in the gooey, reddish-brown laterite mud. After several numbers, Bonney thought enough was enough. As the band broke into "Bonaparte's Retreat," he caught a signal to the President from the Major of the Honor Guard; the Salon was rearranged for the levee.

The Americans were in the receiving line directly before the Drapers, all five of them, who stood next before the bride and groom. Above the couple at the very head were the Bensons. Before reaching the bridal party, guests passed through the main entrance, transited the foyer where a gang of very dark children knelt with cloths to remove the worst of the clinging mud from guests' shoes. They then threaded between two files of guards, and introduced themselves to the Major, though Bonney was confident that he was thoroughly familiar with all the guests.

Attendance was open to a wider circle than simply the mulatto upper crust. Edward Roye, as Speaker of the House, obviously had to be included. So was Alexander Crummell with his Cambridge baccalaureate. The West Indian linguist, Edward Wilmont Blyden, also was present. Bonney had told Talliaferro of the open hostility to Roye and vituperative references to Crummell on Bally Island. Bonney reckoned Talliaferro would make a point to meet the Teminee legend. For all his hotheaded impetuosity, Talliaferro had a strong curiosity.

The press of people allowed only a mechanical smile and perfunctory greeting. Suddenly, Bonney confronted several white faces: Consul Baston, Agent for Captured Cargoes John Says, and Reverend Prescott and wife, sent to save the souls of benighted Africa by the good Methodists of Schenectady, New York. He was amused by the Consul's hostility and the missionaries' suspicion as they recognized Sweet's Tidewater accent and their open hostility at Talliaferro's Carolina drawl. They were less certain of Bonney, but obviously subscribed to "birds of a feather."

To the relief of all three Americans, the receiving line finally dissolved, its members allowed into the Salon. The room was in ballroom configuration, orchestra at the southwestern end and refreshments on tables around the walls attended by ebony youths. President Benson and his lady moved to the far side. His toast of welcome was on a par for eloquence and longevity with any at home, Bonney concluded. He missed a portion of it as he gathered his fellows in a hasty, whispered conversation.

"There's going to be dancing, and what would be expected at home?" Bonney began.

"Dance, of course," Sweet answered impatiently.

"So?" replied Bonney instantly.

"Sir?" inquired Sweet, suddenly suspicious and defensive. What was the Marine trying to maneuver him into doing this time?

"So you'll dance *here*." Talliaferro's entry into the conversation was an order.

"Sir?" Sweet's response was as much a challenge as a question.

"Charles, y'all were nursed on a Nigra tit, and you can damned well dance with these aunties and missies." Talliaferro was firm.

"After all, Mr. Sweet," grinned Bonney, "fair number are your business partners."

Sweet blushed and stammered. But there are rules in life, he thought, and....

"Standby," Talliaferro cautioned as President Benson reached the climax of his toast. The three officers raised their punch cups with the rest to open the festivities.

190

Talliaferro danced with Mrs. Draper and each of the daughters, except little Chastity pouting at her exclusion from the floor. He enjoyed the accomplished footwork of Jane Roberts, Old Gruff's genteel wife, and lumbered dutifully with Mrs. Benson. Delcina had been something to keep up with as she swirled around the floor.

Social obligations satisfied, Talliaferro headed for a punch bowl where Alexander Crummell stood apart with his wife. At Talliaferro's approach, the couple turned with the eagerness of those who feel out of place and are unexpectedly welcomed by one of the inner circle. It shocked Talliaferro, who considered himself very much an outsider here.

In response to Talliaferro's greeting, Crummell smiled, making the light sparkle for an instant from his hexagonal glasses. Talliaferro noted the way his hair grew over his temples, to the edge of his eyebrows nearly, and how high his full beard extended. Could the Teminee have an Arab ancestor who had engaged in the millennia-old trans-Saharan slave trade? The African intellectual introduced his wife, Sarah.

"I've been looking forward to making your acquaintance, Sir," Talliaferro began. "Your adventures rival the *Arabian Nights* and your intellectual accomplishments would be a very high achievement by many with all advantage, let be the impediments you have bested. I salute your considerable grit and brilliance."

"For a person of color, you mean, Lieutenant?" Crummell said icily.

"For anyone, Mr. Crummell," Talliaferro replied with equal chill.

"Thank you, Lieutenant, for your compliments to my husband," interrupted Sarah Crummell. "In certain circles, his abilities, indeed his sacrifices go unappreciated."

"Recently been in such circumstances myself, Mrs. Crummell," Talliaferro replied.

"Do tell, Lieutenant," she rejoined. She had his rank wrong he noticed.

"Oh, simply the result of the present unsettledness in my country, Mam."

Crummell returned to the conversation. "Had you to name a single causation of the discordant occurrences, Sir, what, or whom for the matter, would you indict?"

"Why," after slight hesitation, Talliaferro replied, "diverseness, for a certainty."

"An interesting concept," rejoined the Teminee.

"Well, it's not slavery, Reverend Crummell," Talliaferro challenged.

"I agree, Lieutenant. I have experienced the condition of servitude in America. I know the distain for the person of color common in *all* your states."

"The diverseness I'm contemplating, Mr. Crummell, results from different ways of constructuring society, the different emphasis each section puts upon freedom of the individual compared against coordinating society."

Crummell nodded contemplatively. "There is substance to what you opine, Lieutenant, but I would employ another word to identify the basis for your unfortunate national condition." Crummell paused, then added, "Fear, Lieutenant, Fear."

"*Sir?*" Talliaferro bristled. "Fear is not an allegation taken lightly by my countrymen or myself."

Crummell held up his hand. "'Fear', Lieutenant; not 'Cowardice.' Please attend the specific meaning with which I employ the terms. 'Fear' is an instinctive behavior of all God's creatures. It is the response to this instinct that reflects upon one's honor. One may respond by seeking to avoid the causative factor engendering the fear, or one may respond with fortitude, action, and intelligence. The former response we term 'Cowardice,' while the latter we denominate 'Courage.' I meant no insult."

Talliaferro seemed to accept Crummell's explanation and the African continued, "Recall, Lieutenant, that I have been a slave in Africa and America; that I have been a free person of color in America and in Europe and, most tragically of all, in Africa again. As a slave in Africa, I was a bit of goods to be transferred expeditiously and in marketable condition. In your slave states, I was an integral part of the society, an accepted, an *expected* part. No person troubled to raise me up or crush me down, unless I invited such by acting outside my allotted sphere; which I was prone to do of occasion."

I should wager you were, Talliaferro thought.

"At the North, after my escape, I never felt this sense of place. I was always the odd one out and as such elicited a most forceful response. The only consistency was the complete lack of acceptance in your North. Do you know that many of your 'Free' States have restrictions or prohibitions upon free persons of color residing within their borders with severe penalties for those who flaunt them?"

"Indeed, Sir, I do. The new state of Oregon has an absolute constitutional prohibition upon persons of color residing in the state and Illinois just recently enacted a similar law."

"All wished me hence," Crummell continued disregarding Talliaferro's response. "Thus, hence I went to England, where I was a curiosity, not a part of the natural order, and I could not be by my inherent difference. Left to my studies, I actually graduated."

To himself Talliaferro admitted that Crummell probably was correct, but what did all this have to do with the causes of America's present travail?

"And so I came to the Colored Republic, the Negro Eden. Truly, I saw it, and still see it potentially as the hope, the solution for the ills of your country. Repatriation is the only viable solution. But what greets me here? Look about you, Lieutenant." Contempt did not conceal the anguish in

Crummell's heart. "They ape the worst outward boils and carbuncles of your nation. They call the tribal people *"Bush Niggers."* They enslave them. They call the landed cargoes "Congoes" and, with the connivance of your government, also enslave them under the guise of 'education.'

"Worst of all, they enforce a *color caste*. The mulatto thinks himself superior to the full African. A person, or his ancestors, may have been shipped to America and returned, but if he is not enhanced by the infusion of White blood, he is inferior to these mulattoes. That is the cruelest joke of all. They despise themselves for their African blood. Mixed blood that kept them from power in America, they believe the same logic entitles them to dominate in Africa, to tyrannize those without the curse-blessing of amalgamation."

Talliaferro started to respond that Crummell's concerns, while probably true, really were not the cause of America's crisis. Then he felt the pain Crummell did not admit and stopped himself. Was he so agonized by the internal conflicts of the Americo-Liberians, Talliaferro wondered, or by the fact that, as a non-mulatto, he was significantly excluded from their dominance and therefore had to attack it? Did he even know his motivations?

"Some punch, Alexander?" asked Sarah Crummell. This had gone far enough.

CHAPTER TWENTY-FIVE

Every male at the levee was in line to dance with Delcina, Daniel calculated. Exuberantly she passed among them, giving Daniel infrequent, tepidly apologetic glances. For his part, Daniel performed obligatory turns with the Draper women, Mrs. Benson, Jane Roberts, a host of McGill females, and numerous others. Finally, hot and breathless, he made his way to the punch bowl.

Youthful Guardsmen immediately surrounded him, eager to meet the outsider who had bested them at winning a Draper girl. Amused, Bonney watched them circling, like hounds around a new dog. The leader was an olive-hued lad, with hair more wavy than curled. On his right cuff, was a single gold chevron. Bonney meandered closer.

"Lot of lemonses," the tall youth was saying to Daniel. "Splash white Bordeaux…."

"Not the best, naturally," interrupted another Guardsman with a knowing grin.

"And good rum."

"Not enough, naturally," observed the same lad eliciting a hearty laugh.

Bonney smiled as well. A third youth volunteered that he could fix that, reaching inside his shell jacket. Daniel declined, allowing that what he had was fine enough.

"Not fixin' be all corned for Cina?" leered the leader. Again, Bonney observed, the Liberians used an American idiom, "corned" for inebriated, originally by corn liquor.

Daniel responded evenly that he liked the lemon taste, it being close enough to lime to be a partiality for sailors. The last was added to defuse any hint of confrontation.

"Let be, Munro," cautioned the second Guardsman, winking dramatically. "Man not want no brick in his hat for his wedding night."

Munro took a different tack. "What kind of sailor you be, Mr. Dan'l?" he drawled. "Y'all acting a big bug, but I ain't heard of no *buck* officers, in no *buckra* navy."

"Ain't no officer, Munro is it?" responded Daniel evenly. "I be a Volunteer."

"What that?" Munro reposted with a poorly concealed note of contempt.

"Ain't introduced," the youth Bonney had nicknamed "Naturally" hastily intervened. "This Cadet Corporal Munro Manley. I be Nathaniel McGill. That Thaddeus Warner, with the flask, y'all change your mind, and Richard Henry Roberts; all 'FFM' might say," he flourished.

"Fist Families of Monrovia," Bonney interpreted the play on "FFV" or "First Families of Virginia." Was it a dig at Daniel or merely humor? The introductions did confirm Bonney's supposition that the Cadets were escutcheons of Liberia's elite. Manley's father obviously was the Minister of Trade who opposed Cabot over Sinoe County. McGill and Roberts were self-evident and Bonney had heard the name Warner before.

"Dan'l Sweet, United States Naval Volunteer," the groom replied with a nod.

Manley started to question Daniel, only to be cut off by Nat McGill's explanation that the youths were Presidential Cadets. Nat's announcement was made using a hard "C" and long "A" so that it came out "Kaydet." With real pride he explained that they were students at Liberia College and the honor guard for the President. Daniel edged Manley out of interrupting by asking if the Cadets wore uniforms all the time.

"Just for ceremonies," Warner replied.

"But we set to be officers in the militia, once we past graduation," added Nat proudly.

"*The Militia!*" announced Manley raising his punch cup.

"Is a Bottomser," Rich Roberts hinted to Daniel, who dutifully drained his cup until the bottom faced the ceiling.

"Another," Warner directed, his hand on Daniel's cup before it was fully lowered.

"*Ahyeee,*" exclaimed Roberts. "Look at Doma and *buckra!*" All eyes turned to Sweet sashaying with gusto, Freedoma Draper beaming and breathless in his arms.

Manley, the ever-present distain in his voice, admitted Sweet danced fair for a White boy. In reply, young Roberts teased that Sweet's performance was as good as Manley's.

"'Cause Munro too-bright-by-half to be worth a flip for a dancer," McGill chortled.

"Brighter than you, Boy!" snapped the Corporal with unintended loudness at the sudden cessation of the music as the dance ended.

"What you use, Munro?" McGill reposted, ducking the instant backhand that was just a smidgeon too quick to be fully in jest. Warner called their attention to the young tribal waiter proffering their refilled cups. Warner personally passed Daniel his. He missed the questioning look McGill gave Warner; Bonney did not.

"*United States Navy,*" Manley toasted immediately.

"Bottomser!" added Roberts as the music started again.

"What be a United States Navy Volunteer do?" asked Manley lowering his cup.

"Anything needs doing," Daniel replied evenly, an edge to his voice.

"As be?"

Daniel hardly noticed Warner take his cup. "As captain a gun crew; kill a chance of folk at Greenville; stop mutiny; kill a poke of White men as needs killing," Daniel drawled. He silently acknowledged using Delcina's appraisal of the forecastle events.

McGill whistled softly. "Sure bests bitching about how a body be holding a musket, Munro. 'Pears Volunteer done seen the elephant plenty more than Cadet Corporal."

Bonney shook his head and smiled. "Seen the elephant"- the American colloquialism for experiencing life, combat in particular.

"Just right place, right time," smiled Daniel. He had won that round.

"Life all set by luck and *juju*," observed Manley with petulance as Warner handed Daniel his refilled cup.

"Gentlemen," announced Roberts, "*Cina!* most cap-the-max girl at Liberia!"

"Bottomser!" commanded Warner. How could Daniel not comply when his wife was being toasted as "cap-the-max," better than the best?

"What be you to that *buckra* Sweet?" Manley challenged.

"He is an officer on my ship," Daniel responded evenly. He was sounding more relaxed than he knew he should. This time he was aware of Warner taking his punch cup.

"*Buckra* officer, *buck* volunteer, same ship, same name?" drawled Manley.

Bonney sensed the palpable hostility. He looked around for Delcina. It was not difficult to spot her. She was half of the only couple on the dance floor. Under the grim stares of the Drapers, Bensons, McGills, Roberts, indeed almost every mulatto in the room, she began to dance stiffly with Mr. Speaker Roye as the music re-commenced.

Bonney knew better than to interfere. He looked, but could not find Sweet, strange, since he should be obvious. Talliaferro, deep in conversation with the Crummells, was too distant to summon without attracting attention. He swept the room looking for inspiration, a way to extricate Daniel from the jolly blades of the palace guard. Inspiration struck when he saw Chastity, the six-year-old Draper daughter, stamping her feet at her nurse, in obvious resistance to her bedtime. Bonney moved to them.

"Chastity," he said surprising both girl and nurse. "I need your help."

"Mistress say pickan for bed, *one time*, Marse," the nurse mumbled.

"It's all right, Girl. Just be a moment. Chastity," Bonney said squatting down to her level, "you do something for me?"

"Certain, Pa 'Tennant," she replied with a sheepish grin and averted eyes. She was still in awe of the man who had burst through the door to rescue her and her family.

"Would you go out and tell Cina, time she danced with her husband?"

"*Enty!*" responded Chastity with a bob and sprinted out upon the dance floor, oblivious that all eyes suddenly were upon her. She went right up to the dancing couple and yelled above the music, "Cina! Pa 'Tennant say, time you to dance with Pa Dan'll!"

Delcina stopped precipitously, nearly tripping Mr. Speaker Roye in her hem. The music stumbled to a halt. A second's flash of perturbation crossed the parliamentarian's face, quickly replaced with an uncle-like smile.

Extricating herself, Delcina turned to her little sister. "Certain sure, Chastity. Enough partying with other folks." She looked to Roye, "Pleasure, certain, Mr. Roye." With a quick curtsy she left him alone in the middle of the floor.

At that instant, rumbling thunder shook the building, saving her actions from being a cutting snub. The storm had been muttering its way toward the town for some time, its pronouncements unheard under the music.

Joseph Jenkins Roberts stepped forward to command the moment in tones that would appear pompous if spoken by a lesser mortal. On behalf of all present he thanked the Bensons for their hospitality, Justice and Mrs. Draper for including all in celebration of their beautiful daughter's nuptials, and invoked God's blessing upon Delcina all her days wherever she might wander. He charged Daniel to protect and keep "our dear child," and promised, come what may, the couple had a place and home at Liberia. Interrupted by a thunderclap so close that the concussion put the chandelier in motion, Roberts observed that, if the President did not want his guests sleeping the night on the floors, they best take their leaves and beat the storm to their homes. He gazed across the crowd and regally swept his extended arm toward the entrance. Who could resist such a command from the father of their country? With surprising quiet, the guests began to move.

As Roberts turned for the door, he stood face-to-face with Bonney. To ignore each other would have been a deliberate snub that neither man wanted. Roberts ended the hesitation, "How long it take to establish an 'old naval tradition,' Lieutenant?"

Bonney was amazed to see a wisp of a smile playing at the corners of Roberts' mouth. "Varies, Your Excellency, but I thank you for supporting that tradition."

"Old Gruff" actually grinned. "Welcome, I am sure." Roberts sighed. "Washington being no-account, but did not come here to take orders from a bunch of White boys." The smile vanished. The Father of Liberia reached forward grasping the Marylander's bicep. "Cina, as we say hereabouts, '*close my stomach*,' really fond of that girl; goddaughter, you understand? Watch over her, Lieutenant. I appreciate it more than you know."

The depth of sincerity touched Bonney. "My word, Mr. President."

"Trust that from you more than most White men, Lieutenant; an air about you; loyal to that word." Bonney flushed with embarrassment, wondering if his recent actions reflected the fidelity Roberts thought he possessed. Roberts read his reaction to the compliment as humility, squeezed Bonney's arm again, and stepped past him with a determined stride.

Dazed, Bonney was awakened by the voice of Urias McGill urging Talliaferro to stay ashore as his guest rather than be caught in The Rains. Another slamming roll of thunder shook the building, momentarily stifling speech. With all his officers ashore, Talliaferro regretfully declined; he had to be with his ship in this weather. McGill agreed, observing, he was part owner of *Angel*. Both men chuckled as Bonney joined them, but Talliaferro instantly sobered when asked if he had seen Sweet.

"Not for some time, now I think on it." Talliaferro's eyes swept the room. "Can't spend the night waiting on him, Clave. Need to be aboard, case this storm worsens."

"Certainly, Mr. Talliaferro," Bonney replied formally, "But hate leaving him ashore."

"I can handle things aboard, Clave, y'all want to find Sweet."

McGill smiled. "Stay at my home this night, Lieutenant, and find Sweet come day."

"Shouldn't say this, but *sure* you can handle this weather without another officer?"

"Hell, yes. Stay ashore and bring Sweet aboard at morning." Talliaferro marched off.

"Appears I'm your guest tonight, Mr. McGill," observed Bonney.

"*Enty!*" McGill's pleasure was genuine. Nice to be welcome, Bonney concluded, but he wondered what the mattress was host to?

CHAPTER TWENTY-SIX

Face flushed, heart hammering, Sweet skipped to the left holding Freedom's hands. *Damn*, he thought, this girl could *dance*! At the head of their respective lines, men in one, women in the other, they locked arms, circled clockwise twice, separated to pluck their opposite numbers from the lines, circled once with them, rejoined to circle once together, and spun back to the next in line. Passing from arm to arm, Sweet was amazed at the variety of hues. Everyone was all pleasantries, yet he felt an awkward outsider present on the Liberians' tolerance; it was an unaccustomed, vaguely unpleasant sensation, even dancing the Virginia reel.

Slightly dizzy, they reached the end of the lines, circled, and backed away to let the next couple sashay. As they tapped feet and clapped in unison, Sweet was amused by the way her hair bobbed. Like most Americo-Liberian women, Freedoma wore a very familiar style, parted down the center with the strands running straight and flat to either side. Over her ears it exploded into coils hanging to her collar, or rather where her collar would have been. Her very stylish gown left her shoulders and indeed a rather risqué amount of her upper torso undraped by anything other than the light from the chandeliers. At the back of her head her hair gathered into a large coil held by a "snood," a net of lavender silk matching her gown. Sweet caught a glimpse of matching slippers and, shockingly *yellow* stockings. Would that be all the scandal in Norfolk, he thought. In the soft light her shoulders glistened from the exertion. Her bosom heaved distractingly as she too fought for breath. He checked himself; hoped he had not been ogling.

It was amazing how his cheeks flushed, sort of a light pink. She could not decide whether she was attracted or repelled by it. She certainly was fascinated by the pulse throb in his temple as he kept time and how his hair matted to his scalp. Unlike the straight-haired boys she was used to, his had been all soft and billowy earlier, not slicked down before the evening began. And that skinny little nose, she wondered if what her oldest sister, Conscience, had told her was right? She liked his longer uniform coat. The Cadets' waist-length shell jackets made some boys' backsides look too big, like that Thad Warner, she reflected; not Munro Manley's problem, his backside was fine shaped. He had other problems, that boy did. Oops, she had been dreaming. It was time for a last whirl, then a chance to rest. Freedoma skipped to meet Sweet. Once more she thrilled to the giddy centrifugal force as they hurled into the reel.

To Sweet's relief, and regret, the set ended with a flourish. His line bowed to Freedoma's curtsying a couple of yards away. As if on order the male line straightened and stepped to the female formation. Sweet did not want to be swept immediately into another celebratory exertion. Any future partner most assuredly would be less vivacious, less sprightly, and definitely much less appealing. He was pleasantly surprised when Freedoma announced, "Pshaw, Mr. Sweet, I be souring on all this dancing and suspicion y'all be too. I've a hankering for some punch and allow you might help me to it?"

"Certainly, Miss Draper; pleasure," he responded, automatically extending his arm.

He started toward a group of Cadets gathered around Daniel, but Freedoma gently guided him northward. Punch cups charged, they found seats by French doors opening onto the Presidential Gardens. Freedoma turned her chair obliquely toward the garden. Sweet copied her action.

She slid down in her seat sighing, "Lawd! I is flat tuckered."

"Rather blowed, myself," rejoined Sweet; then wondered if Tidewater equestrian references had meaning in a land where horses died within one, at most two sickly years and thus were all but nonexistent.

She squirmed upright, half-turning to face him. "Like the punch?"

Her enthusiasm startled him. "Ehr, ah, yes'm, right nice, I do say."

"Ain't no fuss on it. Just did not know as y'all have lemons and such."

Sweet grinned. "No lemons; apples a-plenty, but no lemons or limes. Further south they do, but Virginia is a bit too northerly." He paused. "Had limes, be favorable for my family's business. We sell lots of supplies to the Navy." Sold, he corrected his thought.

"Do tell." She hesitated, separating the business, about which she cared not a whit, from the question she really wanted answered. "What is an apple like, Mr. Sweet?"

"Why," Charles paused momentarily to gather his thoughts, then continued, "Come to think on it, seen nary an apple in Africa. No wonder you asking. They are, well, about the size of a good mango, but not quite as hard and nowhere as sticky. Skins red, green, sometimes yellow. Meat is white and the good ones are real juicy and sweet, though times are a body can get some right sour ones." He looked at Freedoma's face. "Guess I did not make it all that clear, huh?"

"Why, Mr. Sweet, I intellectualizes it, but not taste it, quite."

They laughed freely. Sweet had just caught his breath, when suddenly he was gasping. Freedoma had ended her laugh by leaning forward and putting her right hand on his left thigh, the fingers gently settling along the interior surface.

She giggled as he tensed. "Everybody as is my friend calls me 'Doma', Mr. Sweet. Y'all can too, have a notion."

He swallowed to clear his clogged throat. "Ahh … Thank you, Miss, err, Doma."

She twittered, squeezing lightly, "Now, what people close call you? 'Sweetie'?" Lord, she realized, it was fun teasing this shy White boy.

202

Sweet was flummoxed. "No, Mam, err, Doma. No, they sure not call me that!"

"Well, what then?"

"'Charles,' mostly. Can call me 'Charles,' have a mind."

She giggled, leaning, drawing his eyes to her cleavage. "Charles; I like that." She sat back, hand lightly on his leg. "Now, tell about this Dan'l brother-in-law I *catched*."

"Dan'l's a fine boy; with me all my life...." *Damn!* Sweet thought; said too much, completely the wrong way. "I mean ... known Dan'l all my life. We are close neighbors (forty yards, he reflected); went to sea together. Sort of brothers, catch my meaning?"

"He your Nigger?"

God in Heaven, thought Sweet. "*No!* Dan'l nobody's Nigger. He is a fine person of color, Volunteer in the Navy, and my best friend." The last was said with a force that surprised both Freedoma and Sweet. At least that last bit was the truth, he admitted. Daniel had shared more of his life than anyone, Harry DePue and Charles' brothers included. Daniel's mother raised him, nursed him if the tales were true. Sweet was shocked at this epiphany in the stifling humidity of a West African night as a little Liberian coquette played with his dignity. How in the Eternal had he come by this fix?

"Miss ... ehr, Doma, know where the necessary is?" It was not the most original means of separating from a girl.

She giggled and squeezed his leg again. "Y'all gots to pee, or what?"

"Ehr ...Yah."

"Ehr, which?"

"Pee," he whispered. This was not the way the conversation was supposed to unfold.

"Well now I know," she cooed giving him the calf eye up through her lashes. "Me too. Come on," she ordered moving her grasp from his thigh to his left wrist.

She stood and opened the door to the garden. Roiling with uneasiness, Sweet prayed that no one saw her dragging him into the night. She led him through the thick growth; a place of sprawling palmettos, spreading hibiscus, and other unknown flora concealed in the dank darkness. To the east, inland, magnificent webs of lightening slivered across the horizon, followed by ominous rumblings. A hint of wind began to enliven the humid night; bringing sudden refreshment as the lightening momentarily illuminated their surroundings, then buried them in dazzled night blindness.

Freedoma drew up short. Sweet bumped against her and mumbled for her pardon. Along the back of the garden a border of low plants separated the slightly graveled path from the wall. Freedoma marched directly to the shrubbery, hiked her skirt, and stepped into the verdure dropping from view. "This be Africa," he muttered taking several strides to his left before stepping from the path and laboriously undoing most of the eleven buttons on his broadfall trousers. Another explosion of lightening and thunder rent the humid night giving Sweet a dazzled impression of flaking whitewash on the garden wall. As the world snapped into inky nothingness, he was stupefied to hear her trilling giggle. "*Missy!*" Sweet gasped.

In the dark he heard her voice, light with innocence, "Conscience ain't right."

"Wha…."

"She say *buckra* boys got little old pencil pricks thin as they noses. Ain't much, but bests that."

"*Damn*, Girl!" No lady of his acquaintance would have *ever* verbalized such a thought; White women, he was certain, were incapable of contemplating such matters. And, he thought angrily, no Nigra wench would have the effrontery, the uppitiness, the *stupidity* to say such a thing to…. He was jolted back to breathing by a staggering concussion, another eruption of thunder and lightening directly overhead. With it came a wall of water.

"Come on, Sweetie," bubbled Freedoma through the deluge as she grabbed his wrist. Gasping, embarrassed, Sweet stumbled after the girl toward the official residence of a head of state with his broadfalls open and … Oh, God have mercy, he thought with alarm.

As they slithered through a small door at the back of the mansion, Freedoma hardly checked her stride. "This way," she gasped, making a sharp right up narrow service stairs in complete darkness. At the top she froze and, just audible, whispered, "Hush."

Sweet complied, but there was no need for stealth; the rain was hammering on the tin roof like a thousand drummers. He tried to recover some dignity by adjusting his clothes.

"Forget that," she ordered. "Walk *soffle*," and, holding his wrist in an amazingly strong grip, started forward along a wide hall with rooms off either side, doors closed, mostly dark as indicated by the lack of light through the louvers. "We in here," Freedoma whispered, guiding him left through a door, closing it, and shooting the bolt.

Fumbling to button his trousers, with his back to her, Sweet began, "Now just one minute here, Girl. What you think you doin'?"

"Well do tell," she giggled. "What you think I think I doin'?" As she spoke she took his arm, pivoting them face-to-face. Without further preliminaries she planted her full lips on Sweet's and, to his shock, reached down with her right hand to seize him. With total disbelief, he fell backward onto a thick sack mattress. "Better than pencil already," Freedoma giggled flattening herself upon him.

In a floundering of waterlogged silk, wool, and linen, Sweet responded. The hammering rain hid any sound of straining ropes or human excess. Spent, breathless, sodden, he crumpled upon her welcoming warmth.

She stroked his head cradled against her neck and right shoulder, his breath exciting her nape. She fought to calm her unsatisfied hunger as he gasped, "Whe … 're ... your … folks? … I ... best ... be … going…."

For a moment she silently caressed his head. Finally, her barely audible whisper, a sigh really, "Sweetie, you ain't through," followed immediately by a sharp nip on his ear.

He winced and rolled right; she followed with him maintaining contact. Before he could answer, she wriggled down his body to bring them face-to-face. "Conscience off doing same we do with that Russell *buck*. Cina and Dan'l doing what we doing, sure. Mama got her ear to the wall listening at them. Pa Draper off drinking and palavering with President and them other sure-enoughs. Be rain for plenty time yet, and you ain't finished, *Buckra* Sweetie." Sweet felt himself responding as she wriggled. He always enjoyed the sound of heavy rain on a metal roof.

*   *   *   *   *   *   *   *   *   *

He snapped awake, instincts alert, fight or fly. Rain, it had stopped drumming on the tin. Freedoma responded to his movement with a feline stretch, levering herself onto an elbow. Slowly, she pivoted toward the emerging grayness through the louvered window. "Time you be going, Sweetie," she purred with a touch of sadness.

Sweet felt absolutely wonderful, totally used up, thoroughly indolent. He stretched back into a reclining position face-to-face against Freedom's copper skin, joining her in a languorous kiss. Breathless yet at rest, he looked into her eyes. She smiled beautifully. "Sweetie, time you gone," she silkily whispered and barely touching stroked his chest with her fingertips. "Here," she encouraged, uncoiling herself from the bed to stand above him. Taking his hand she raised him to his feet. He sought his dank clothes in the general tumult across the bedroom floor. His things were clammy, his mouth sour. Her magical little giggle brought his eyes to hers with a look of puzzlement.

"Just thinking about boys and them say we the vainful ones."

"Well?" questioned Sweet, trying to turn his ankle-length drawers rightside out.

"Well," she drawled. "Y'all cream color round your butt and all, and near a brown on your face and hands. Where be, that gone-on-his-self Munro Manley almost cream on his face and hands and plenty dark at his rump and privates." She giggled. "Recon he lightening his self, sure." She poked teasingly at Sweet. "Y'all use lightening here?"

"*No, Mam!*" he hissed flinching away.

"Y'all see I not use none," she purred, stretched her arms above her head, rose on the balls of her feet, and slowly pirouetted. From what Sweet could observe, she was entirely of one hue.

"Y'all want me leaving, Doma, better stop that!"

"You walk *soffle* on the stair, Sweetie," she responded with a pout.

Looking like he had gone through a mill wheel, Sweet moved to the door. Wordlessly, she took hold of his coat and softly faced him to her for a kiss. When they eventually parted, she hissed, "Now off with you, *Buckra* Sweetie," and gently pushed him out the door that closed quietly but finally behind him.

*   *   *   *   *   *   *   *   *   *

Sweet stole down the back stairs, through the garden, and out the side gate. In his few previous experiences, he had felt slightly guilty slinking into the early morning light. This was different, he castigated himself; this time he had broken a commandment, acted contrary to fundamental law, trespassed upon a principle underpinning of civilization. His guilt was irrefutable, he admitted, and he writhed with self-loathing at his failing.

He pictured so clearly his father standing with his back to the tall windows opening upon the little bay, the Nansemond River, with the gardens and gently descending lawns going down to the pier. They had moved speedily through the birds-and-bees part. His entire life he had been around horses, cattle, dogs, and all of the other beings that constituted life in the country. Between that and Daniel's whispered reports of goings-on in the Quarters, he would have had to be a complete dolt, deaf and blind in the bargain, not to understand male and female. But Edward Sweet had gone further with the transfer of the wisdom of the ages.

> "This land, our life here, society in all of its facets, Charles," his father had said, "depends upon everyone performing properly their appointed role. We depend upon each other, cannot function without each other." He had paused to insure that the fourteen-year-old was attending. "At the bottom of it all is Trust, Charles, confidence that everybody else will act within certain understood limits. You follow?"
>
> "Yes, Sir," he remembered answering rather cautiously.
>
> "Good," his father had responded, then paused. "Our society, like every society before it that amounted to more than a Hobbesian scrabble for the next meal.... You know Hobbes, don't you, Son?"
>
> "Yes, Sir. Hobbes and Locke."
>
> "Right. That school is doing some good. Rome, Greece, Babylon, Egypt, the Israelites ... all of them had, and today, though some choose to use

206

different terms, have an underlying stratum of society that performs the drudgery of life. 'Hewers of wood and drawers of water,' the Bible calls them. And, Charles, in their way and place, they are just as important as planters and presidents, kings and counselors, to the order of things, be they Russian serfs, Pennsylvania miners, or hands here at Sweetlands."

"Yes, Sir."

"We are luckier than most, Charles, because our hewers and drawers are distinct, unlike many places, though people in those other places claim there are distinctions there as well. Ours are of a different species, like horses and burros, so the idea of disrupting everything is not there, because everybody involved knows we're different and that by God's will from the Day of Creation." Edward's eyebrows rose in question.

Charles nodded. "Yes, Sir, Sons of Ham. Ours are Nigras."

"From Africa, originally, yes, Charles. And . we all work together to make life go along in a civilized way, rather than, 'cruel, brutish and short.' I see you know the quote, good. And to do this we must *trust* each other. Some people try to replace trust with fear, but that never works in the long haul. Up North the factory workers fear being turned out to freeze and starve, but here we have our laborers to care for good times or bad. Some masters, and too many overseers think that if their people fear them, they will perform to escape punishment. Too often they just try to escape. That leads to excessive reliance on physical punishment or splitting families by selling south. It is stories of these folks that get the Abolitionists all riled up and believed as well.

"So what we tell our people we shall do, we do: assure that they have clothes, food, houses, garden plots and seed, religious guidance, some ability to gratify their wants and whims, and most of all that they trust us, *so that we can trust them.*" Edward Sweet held his son's gaze a moment.

Satisfied that the pubescent boy-man before him recognized that what he had just said was the kernel of the fruit of his thoughts, he continued.

"I must be away from here to Portsmouth
for the chandlery, Richmond for the Assembly, First
House or farther, just to check on crops. I must leave
my family – you, your mother, your sisters – here
surrounded by our people. I must trust them to
respect what is dearest to me of the entire world.
And, Charles, *I do*." He paused, but only for a second.
"I do, because they do, they trust me. I extend *to*
them the same respect that I expect *from* them. I do
with regard to their most cherished things in the
world, their families. Sweets have never broken
families by sale or service, have never disrupted
families as punishment, most importantly, have never
allowed lust to drive us to the sin of amalgamation."

In the West African morning, Charles felt the sweat begin along his
back. At that point, those years ago, his father had paused again and sighed
deeply, before continuing.

"Doubt you will believe me, but I was a randy
colt once, too. I understand the fires that push, pull,
and pursue one of your age. Dance your dance and
court your fate with the girls of your own kind. I'll say
nothing about any frolics with an adventuress, other
than to remind you that Doctor Johnson wrote of
seeing doggerel, 'a night with Venus, a lifetime with
Mercury.'"
Sweet had looked at his son for reaction.
"You do know of what I speak? Mercury, the treatment
for the French Pox?"
Charles' nod confirmed his understanding of
syphilis and the father continued, "What I do tell you is
this. I *never* expect you to exploit your race and status
by forcing or accepting carnal contact with any of our
people, or any other children of Africa, here at
Sweetlands or at the ends of the earth. For to do so,
Charles, whether the favors appear freely given or not,
is to violate God's will and our people's trust, to
disrupt the order of things upon which all depend, to
jeopardize all civilization."

He shuddered. He was back in Africa, slinking from the Liberian
Executive Mansion. He was surprised that there were no obstacles to his exit,
no security. At least he got out of the Presidential Grounds before the

208

inevitable West African dogs began barking. Flustered, Sweet hurried onto the main street toward McGills'. He felt confusion in addition to his guilt. He sensed that Freedoma had taken somehow, not given. Scurrying by the back of the McGills' building he started at a sharp voice, "As a thief in the night." Bonney stepped into the road beside him. "I shall not even ask."

"Hah ..." spluttered Sweet.

"Was a young sailorman in a foreign port once myself," Bonney grinned. "Not another word, you damned fool! Come on, we have work before us."

*   *   *   *   *   *   *   *   *   *

From her window Freedoma watched his self-conscious progress toward the bluff. He was older than she, she reflected, but mighty young in ways. She knotted the thread that held the small Moroccan leather wallet against her abdomen, shut her eyes, and envisioned the future that Auntie Roth predicted. She just had to get one of the "Eligibles" liked Nathaniel McGill or Henry Roberts up here. Long as it was not Manley, she would be satisfied. With the powerful *juju* pouch above her womb, she knew he would be the brightest pickan in Monrovia. Either Nathaniel or Henry would be proud to strutting with such a child; might even have those see-through glass eyes of its daddy.

CHAPTER TWENTY-SEVEN

With a mixture of amusement and concern, Bonney watched Talliaferro drum his fingers on *Angel's* landward rail and exhale slowly through pursed lips. Rather than blindly rush to a Southern port, they had decided to take the ex-slave ship to Britain for the latest news of American affairs and then determine what their next action should be. Talliaferro accepted the logic of the decision, but chaffed at the delay. Most Southern officers in the U.S. Navy would resign and seek service in the navy the South inevitably must create, a navy of few ships. Those present at the creation would receive the best, perhaps *only* berths on those rare vessels. Talliaferro desperately wanted one; he could envision no life other than that of a naval officer.

Only with great reluctance had Talliaferro agreed to sailing for Britain rather than immediately for a Southern port. Then Sweet had nearly made him apoplectic. While Talliaferro commanded *Angel*, Sweet effectively owned her. Young Charles had insisted Sweet & Son's newest investment not depart Africa "in ballast," nautical terminology for without a cargo. The McGills had scrambled together an assortment of goods Sweet intended to trade in England for items useful to the Southern war effort. Sensible, Bonney admitted, so long as the added delay did not send Talliaferro stark raving mad. The "Captain" seemed to be compensating by relentlessly driving Sweet to load the ship in an impossibly short time.

In addition to pressuring the midshipman, Talliaferro had done his best to expedite matters. *Angel* lay at the foot of the path from McGills' down to the river in one and a half fathoms, nine feet, by the chart. Ordinarily, she drew nine feet or better in ballast. With the weight of the palm oil tumbling down the ingenious bamboo piping into her four large water tanks, she would settle significantly. To reduce *Angel's* draft, Talliaferro had employed a "camel." Two McGill schooners had been maneuvered alongside, partially flooded, and lashed together by numerous hawsers running from *Angel's* masts to the outboard sides of the schooners and under all three hulls. When the water was pumped out, the schooners floated higher in the river lifting *Angel* on the cables slung beneath her.

Bonney did not know if the name "camel" derived from the two outboard vessels resembling a bactrian camel's humps or that, like the "ship of the desert," a cameled vessel could continue her journey with little water. Whatever the derivation, it was a precarious undertaking, especially with hawsers of questionable age, hulls of questionable condition, and charts of questionable accuracy. Dubiously, Bonney examined the awkward contraption the sleek ship had become. Trussed like a turkey in a pan, he knew she would not steer worth a Dutch *dam*.

The report of a musket snapped everyone's attention to the bluff. Smoke drifted from the McGill Factory. Sweet excitedly started for the entryport clearly intending to investigate and, Bonney thought, in the process have some respite from Talliaferro's continuous pestering. Bonney knew Talliaferro would never tolerate Sweet leaving his duties in such a manner.

"Not so fast, Mr. Sweet," Bonney cautioned, blocking his path. "As *Angel's* First Officer your duty is supervising the load, not chasing wisps of smoke." He almost added "or anything else," but forbore; the lad was sheepish enough about the night ashore.

"*Damn it,* Mr. Bonney," Sweet snapped in frustration; he had had more than enough this morning of people criticizing his every move. "If it's all gone to Jessie up there, the loading is disrupted! That *is* my business, and I'll thank you to mind your own!" Just when he began to think the Marylander was a good fellow and friend, Bonney had to go pushing him around again. Hell, it had been Bonney's demand that he dance at the wedding and look how that had turned out!

He has a point, Bonney realized. The bearers on the path were looking toward the bluff breaking the smooth progression of goods down to the ship. Maybe Sweet wasn't just trying to avoid Talliaferro's hazing, Bonney concluded. Shocked at the thought, Bonney suddenly wondered if he were projecting his own reactions to Trueman's goading of the watering party in Freetown upon Sweet's situation in Monrovia? He made a note to give Sweet more credit in future. Aloud he added, "True, Charles, but makes more sense for me to investigate and you to supervise the stowage aboard here."

"*Mr. Sweet,*" Talliaferro called from the quarterdeck. "Get them moving!"

Sweet's exasperation was evident as he barked his "Aye, aye, Sir," to Talliaferro and hurried off to chivvy the bearers into movement. Bonney called to the "Captain" that he would investigate and started to slurp toward the bluff, the red laterite mud sucking at his brogans as he sidled by the bearers again plodding down the path in an unbroken chain.

Although winded by the climb, Bonney wordlessly brushed past the McGills' clerk, and took the stairs two-at-a-time. On the veranda overlooking the river, a group of Americo-Liberians gathered around a seated figure hunched forward over a table, his eye to the telescopic sight of a rifle. The man raised his cheek from the piece, his sigh of exasperation quickly vanished when he recognized the Officer of Marines. Nat McGill rose with a greeting and met the Marylander with an extended hand.

"Mr. McGill," Bonney began, "We need to clear for action?" The instant he said this, Bonney realized how ridiculous it was to suggest *Angel* with her one archaic cannon "clearing for action," readying for battle like a man-of-war.

McGill laughed heartily, "No enemy near, just doing justice Liberia-style." The humor rippled through the rest of the group: Daniel and Delcina

"Sweet," Freedoma Draper, two of the McGill Brothers, and a couple other Cadets with their belles. Bonney noticed an uncomfortable forced jocularity in Daniel's laugh and a pained discomfort in his features.

Bonney eyed the table. McGill was well equipped for competitive shooting. Beside the weapon were a beautifully adorned brass powder flask, a colorfully labeled box of specially cast bullets, a small tin of lubricant, another of fine silk patches, a tin of percussion caps, and a pair of binoculars. Bonney raised the leather-wrapped glasses and asked the target. Nat indicated Carey Island Rock, a low bump of land in the middle of the Montserado River. Bonney swept the mound of mud and rock, passed a large boulder and swung back to it. The glasses trembled in his hand. Spread upon a bamboo frame erected over the largest bolder was a naked African, that fellow Doe who had tried to escape on Bally Island. His limbs were extended so stiffly that they formed a perfect line with the raffia ropes binding them to the four corners of the frame. Greenville all over again, Bonney thought; God, he was sick of Africa's fascination with torture.

"*Bush Nigger*, Doe," Nat spat. "You know him. He shame my sister; then *make a run*." Nat grinned. "Come back a slave on your ship. Bad luck, *enty*!"

Seemed so, Bonney responded, eyeing the rifle. It resembled the Model 1853 British service musket, but for the beautifully checkered wrist and forearm of the fine-grained stock and the brass telescopic sight above its barrel. Bonney asked to handle it. Nat beamed. "Only *soffle, soffle*. Not to shoot that one, just close enough to fear him."

"Just playing with the boy?" Bonney nodded. He hefted the gun: excellent balance, well and carefully tooled and fitted. He looked down at the man stretched upon the rock several hundred yards away, the sun directly in his face, unable to scratch, swipe away insects, or defend against the vultures that would come when dehydration weakened him sufficiently. "How long you going to leave him like that?"

"'Til Uncle Urias say," shrugged Nat. "Maybe for day; maybe 'til he *done-live*."

Obviously, Doe was fated to *done-live*, either as a latter day Prometheus chained to his rock for the birds to peck or in some even more fiendish manner. Bonney yearned to raise the rifle and blow out the captive's brains as an act of mercy, or, he had to admit, just to spite the Liberians. But, he recalled, he had higher priorities than subverting local justice. He suddenly struggled to control a nascent grin; just maybe…. "Whitworth?" he asked hefting the weapon.

"Same!" Nat giggled with pleasure. "Shoot!" he urged Bonney.

"Now, I miss and damage the boy, you not expect me to buy him?"

"Ain't slave-mens here, Lieutenant," challenged an older McGill.

"I know; Just indentureds learning to lead civilized lives." Bonney's sarcasm went unnoticed. "I meant to say, I injure him so he can't work, you not claim damages?"

"Certain no," the older Liberian laughed heartily. "He nothing but *Bush Nigger.*"

Bonney snapped the weapon to his shoulder, inhaled deeply, exhaled, and, shutting his left eye, squinted into the four-power scope. His right hand closed around the weapon's checkered wrist; his left supported the walnut forearm. He thrilled to the rifle conforming perfectly, naturally to his body, becoming a part of him and he an extension of it. He progressively tensed his right forefinger against the .451-pound trigger resistance. The recoil rocked him, the report chimed his ears, and smoke obscured his view.

Nat followed the shot through the binoculars. "Maybe hit a stick," he suggested, disappointment evident. He doubted Bonney even hit the boulder. He missed the shocked surprise on Daniel's face. Actually, Bonney had established that the four-power scope facilitated precise shooting at that range. His bullet had done significant damage to the upper left-hand corner of the bamboo frame upon which the tribesman was splayed.

"Not as good as Dan'l, gospel," the Marine apologized, recalling the slave's proficiency on Tower Hill. That day he had used a Whitworth just like Nat's.

Nat took the bait. "You try, Dan'l?"

Daniel glanced at Bonney. "Go on, Boy," the Marine encouraged, "*Doe* show them the sort of shooting that, as they say, '*Freed* America.'" Daniel caught Bonney's twisted pronunciation and read an order in the eyes of the expressionless face. Now it was his turn to control a grin; he did not care for African justice much either.

"Wager give this some excitement," observed Bonney extracting his timepiece, a larger than usual gold case. Offhandedly opening the watch, he passed it to Nat. In awe the Liberian examined the chronometer's face. At the top in a cobalt sky speckled with stars hung a yellow moon positioned to show the phase of the lunar cycle as it moved behind a rounded cloud. The white face marked hours in golden roman numerals. At the nine and three o'clock positions respectively, the month and date were in Arabic numbers. The days of the week appeared at the six o'clock position in two letter abbreviations. Holding it to his ear Nat heard the tick of numerous small gears. The thing was quite heavy. Between the gold of its manufacture and the complexity of its mechanism, it had to be.

"My watch against that Nigra," urged Bonney. "What do you say, Nat?"

"No can do," groaned Nat. "*Bush Nigger* to *make-a-die,* say Uncle Urias." He glanced at Bonny adding, "Dead," to ensure clarity. Nat really wanted the watch. He paused in momentary reflection; then grinned. "Chance my rifle, *enty?*"

214

Bonney hesitated; he had no desire to risk his grandfather's unique watch for a rifle he could buy by mail. He glanced quickly at Daniel, who licked his lips and nodded. He wants the bet, Bonney concluded, assuming Daniel had understood his intention to win Doe. Now that it was impossible, what did the boy have up his sleeve? Bonney decided to trust his instincts and Sweet's slave. "A bet," he agreed, "but Dan'l's shooting. He wins, he gets the rifle."

"Marse Clave...." Daniel started to protest the wager of the watch. He did not want to be responsible for losing Bonney's family heirloom. Besides, what would he do with a rifle?

"Thing's too heavy by half to tote around, Daniel, and I been thinking on being shut of it," Bonney interrupted.

Something in Bonney's tone told Daniel not to protest. "Affeared, but alive, right?" Daniel asked.

Nat nodded agreement.

"What say to one round under each heel, one at the tip of each hand, one centered as close to the top of his head," Daniel proposed.

Nat added with glee, "And one as close up his crotch as can be."

"All without drawing blood," Bonney added. "Draw blood, other man wins."

Again, Nat nodded.

Bonney carefully swabbed the barrel with a lightly oiled cloth, then a brush, and then another cloth. With exactitude he measured 70 grains of FFFg black powder into a brass dipper and tipped it down the muzzle. From the box, he removed one of the elongated bullets made to match perfectly the five .577 caliber lands and the five .593 caliber groves of the Hexason Whitworth Rifling. He lubricated the bullet, wiped the excess grease, and fitted the projectile into the bore. With the brass-tipped steel ramrod he drove it down, hefted the piece at the balance, half-cocked and capped the weapon. Finished, he passed it to Nat, who courteously extended the rifle to Daniel offering him first shot.

Daniel removed his coat, wiped his hands on his trousers as he had asked Charles Sweet countless times not to do, and settled at the table. Along the bank of Barrett Creek southeast of Big House at Sweetlands, "Old Marse" Edward Sweet, Charles' father, had taught his son and Daniel to shoot. Recalling the hours of patient instruction, Daniel settled the rifle butt into his shoulder, found his sight picture and went through the rifleman's creed, "Breathe, Relax, Squeeze." The report was as much a surprise to him as to anyone. The figure across the water flinched as the rock spalled at the tip of his right hand.

The competition progressed, Daniel and Nat alternating. Doe's right hand, balled into a fist, was a tie. The African winced and screamed defiance as their shots chipped rock fragments below his right heel. That round was Nat's. Daniel took left heel and left fingertip. Bonney suggested the head next, fearing Doe would writhe after the groin shot, spoiling chances for a careful headshot. Daniel's left a crease in the thick mat of the tribesman's hair perfectly in line with his nose. Nat's shot was almost two inches above Daniel's. Young Roberts suggested that the contest stop, since Nat could not catch Daniel in points.

However, Freedoma coquettishly sighed, "One them boys may just take the *Bush Nigger's* whatzims off and it be Dan'l, why Nat win."

Bonney chuckled. "Dan'l do that, he'd best head *northwest* 'til he's home, less Urias *corner* him for ending the fun too early." He pretended not to notice the Africans' quizzical looks in response to his comment.

Daniel understood. His shot was unobserved, but Bonney thought rock spalled beneath the upper-left, i.e. "northwest" corner of Doe's torture rack, the corner Bonney had hit with his shot before the contest. He moved to reload the rifle, but Nat took the weapon and proffered it to Daniel. "No chance for me to best you, you not hit that *bo.*"

"God smiled on me today; on you next. I not take your rifle, Nat."

It was a fair win Nat argued extending the weapon. Again Daniel refused with evident regret. To take it would be pointless, he reminded himself. As an enlisted man, he could not keep it aboard ship and slaves obviously did not enjoy the right to "keep and bear arms." Delcina was puzzled. She would have to teach this boy not to turn down his winnings.

Thunder to the east drowned Nat's reply. The evening Rains had arrived. All present looked skyward, their gazes sweeping over the river mouth. A horizontal cloud of black smoke seemed to erupt from Cape Montserado, pass from west to east low above the peninsula, and obscured the roadstead. Around Ashmun Point in obvious haste under steam and staysails, *H.M.S. Tourch* churned the reddish-brown water with her paddlewheels. As the gunboat entered the river, her sails came in and her way slackened. Then, with renewed purpose she continued upstream. Commander Parker must have seen *Angel* and decided that *Tourch* could stay above the mud as well. Not tempting fate as brashly, he anchored opposite Kroo Point in three fathoms by the chart, four or better in the flood. Before *Tourch* lost all way, a boat was lowered, rapidly manned, and pulling for *Angel.*

Through the glasses, Bonney recognized Paltier's muttonchops. Brits were not in the habit of hurrying for hurrying's sake, especially in the tropics. Something was afoot. He made quick farewells and started for the stairs, scooping up his timepiece on the way. Daniel needed no picture. Gently he took Delcina's arm and started after Bonney.

$*$ $*$ $*$ $*$ $*$ $*$ $*$ $*$ $*$ $*$

Aboard *Ebony Angel*, Lieutenant Paltier, Royal Marines, was in earnest conversation with Talliaferro and Sweet when Bonney and his companions arrived. To Bonney's surprise, Delcina appeared enthusiastic for whatever adventure had excited the Americans. To his even greater surprise, Sweet seemed to have forgotten to be testy.

Talliaferro hushed them as Paltier resumed his description of the United States West African Squadron's call at Lagos the week before, and Commodore Inman's declared intention to take his command home to enforce the blockade. Additionally, he had dispatched a brig to Monrovia, via Harper, Greenville, and a couple of other points, to assure the Liberian Government and any American missionaries or merchants that the rebellion was not a serious threat to the United States nor to its policies in Africa. Commander Parker had pushed *Tourch* hard to arrive sufficiently ahead of the American warship and warn the Southerners in time to avoid a clash. Clearly, Bonney decided, the British were still uncomfortable with the entire *Ebony Angel* affair.

"Brig has to be *Bainbridge*," observed Sweet. "Armed with two medium 32-pounders and ten carronades, 32's as well."

"Considerable sailer," mused Talliaferro. "Winkler had her, last I knew."

"Lieutenant Winkler," whistled Sweet. "Death on room inspections my plebe year. Thank the Almighty he went to sea."

"Not a dashed room inspection concerns us, Mister," rebuked Bonney.

"I am certainly aware of the difference, Sir!" Sweet snapped back.

Damn, Bonney thought, I've ruffled his feathers again. He chose to ignore Sweet's response, asking, "When was *Bainbridge* to move this way, Lieutenant Paltier?"

"Directly. Most directly we left, I am quite certain."

"Drat!" snapped Talliaferro. "Be here any time; Sweet, those tanks close onto full?"

"Close, Sir." The response was sharper than necessary. Sweet recognized that he was bordering upon disrespect and added more calmly, "Not rain us out, should be finished by candle-lighting or close thereon."

"Well, hurry it." Sweet took Talliaferro's gruff response as a rebuke. Unaware, the "Captain" turned to Bonney. "Be so kind as to go ask the McGills to load the cam wood and ivory, fast as they can." Then to Daniel, "You and Miss … err, your missus be aboard directly, y'all not want to miss our sailing. Sorry Mrs … err, Sweet." Talliaferro was catching himself just in time.

"One other matter," Paltier cleared his throat. "I am constrained to repair to England on rather short notice. As your departure is imminent and your transit will be without intervening ports of call, might I beg passage? It would be significantly faster than leaving *Tourch* at Freetown and waiting for a homeward bound vessel that would make several intermediate stops."

Talliaferro looked to Bonney, about to climb the riverbank once more. The Marine's expression clearly indicated that he considered the matter the "Captain's" decision alone. "You are more than welcome, Lieutenant Paltier, but *Bainbridge* might delay us."

"I shall have to risk that," smiled Paltier. As he spoke another crash of thunder followed by the swooshing of torrential rain over Bally Island hastened all from the deck.

CHAPTER TWENTY-EIGHT

Doe could hold his breath no longer, so he relaxed his diaphragm expelling the oxygen-robbed air. With a heave, he gulped a moist, fresh breath, savored it, reveled in it, almost relaxed with the pleasure of it. Then the anguish seized him. How could the spirits and God have let him come to this? He had been far from the village gathering plants, molds, and a few tiny creatures on the list he had memorized for his uncle, the Head Devil of the Poro Society. It had been framed as a task to be performed, but Doe had known it was a test to see if he understood the magical values and dangers of the various specimens he was to collect. Success would mean full apprenticeship to his uncle and a career as healer, sage and wielder of great political as well as magical powers. He had been so intent upon the spider he was hunting that he had not heard the approach of the tribesmen. Only when they were a dozen yards away had he become aware and bolted away from them into the arms of their hidden companions. They had not hurt him. If they had, he would not have been able to walk to the coast and the barracoon on the San Pedro River. His captors had treated him with the greatest indifference, so long as he obeyed them swiftly and completely.

It had changed the day they were taken from the pallisaded camp, shackled at wrists and ankles and with numerous companions shuffled to boats ten at a time to be rowed to the schooner. They had been yelled at in strange tongues, rushed below decks, made to crawl onto shelves and secured by iron collars to the framing so that they could roll over, but not leave the platform. He did not remember how many days he had spent like that, lying in his own excrement, eating mush from his cupped hands. The vessel had changed motion, titled heavily and creaked and groaned for a long time as he listened to the water gurgling along the hull, the creaking of the timbers, and occasionally the increasingly fearful shouts of the crew. Then the ship had stopped, righted herself, and gone quiet. There was noise on the deck above and strange men with guns and swords had shown lights about the hold. Then for a long time the ship had gone back to moving along at an angle with the water gurgling along the hull. The next time it stopped Doe and the rest of the cargo had gone ashore on Bally Island and his real misery had begun.

The McGills had taken their quota of the cargo and sorted them according to their needs and the responses of the Congoes to a few rudimentary questions. Young Doe had been seen as a likely houseboy. Not understanding Liberian English and from a privileged background himself, though in a less complex civilization, he had not comprehended that he was a servant and not a guest. His behavior was seen as rebellion and met with a whipping that only hardened his resistance. For three years he had survived in the McGill household, an increasingly surly and troublesome servant, but an increasingly attractive and quick-witted young man.

For some reason, a daughter of the house took pity on him and the two young people had let their mutual attraction progress to its natural culmination that after three months was obvious to all. Doe had fled for his life, swimming across the Monsorado to Stockton Creek and heading inland. Wondering in the hills, he had gone beyond the reach of Liberian authority and been welcomed by a tribal community with whom he stayed through The Rains. His shamanistic learning had earned him some respect when he was able to cure several sick members of the community. With the Dry Season, however, came the slave traders and Doe found himself awakened one night and tied into a wooden yoke attached by a light chain to the yoke of the man in front of him as they continued the long walk to the San Pedro.

Now he was back in Monrovia, strapped to this damnable rock, and he had no illusions of his intended fate. The bastards were playing with him, he thought with rage. At some point, he knew, the near misses would become surgical amputations, a finger or toe, progressing slowly toward his vitals. He doubted that they would do him the blessing of splattering critical organs. No, they would wound him just enough to guarantee an agonizing death. As he weakened, the vultures would come and begin pecking at his eyes, genitals, and abdomen. "*Curse Them!*" he wanted to scream as he tensed for the next shot.

Nothing. No report. No impact spalling rock into his skin. There had been time to reload. Through closed lids he sensed the sky darkening. He opened his eyes by miniscule progressions to limit the pain of looking directly into the lowering sun. To his surprise, it was obscured by the great thunderheads of The Rains. A second later, the wall of water smacked upon him, drenching, cooling his sweating body. Open-mouthed, he attempted to drink of the downpour to replace the fluids lost to the tropical sun and skillet-hot stone. He writhed to let the water trickle beneath him and cool the rock.

AHHHAYEEE! Pain knifed into the stretched muscles. His right arm, still rigidly extended, came round in front of him. The frame gave a cracking sound disintegrating under the unequal pull. As the edifice of torture crumpled upon itself, the surprised African slithered down the rock to land in a stiff, painful collection of bamboo, raffia, laterite mud, and rigid limbs.

*   *   *   *   *   *   *   *   *   *

"Gentleman make a bet," Freedoma scolded, looking down her nose at Nat McGill, "he no gentleman, he not pay when he lose."

He was sitting uncomfortably in one of the whirl-footed Louis XV chairs in the Ladies' Parlor as The Rains hammered the tin overhead. Blast it, he thought, he had offered the rifle and Daniel had refused it. "*Eeeby,*" exclaimed the unhappy youth, "Daniel not want to take my rifle, Doma, certain not."

"Be so what?" she replied. "Dan'l, *my brother*, shoot best than you!" The story of Daniel's marksmanship had swept throughout Monrovia winning him deep admiration.

Frustrated at her attack, Nathaniel pleaded, "I done tried; Dan'l not taking that rifle."

"Dan'l *swanga buckra* aside of you, Nat."

"You be best girl I know and worst for making trouble." Shocked, he realized he actually believed it. She was the best of the Monrovia beauties: spirit, looks, family … and, worse luck, she knew it. "What you want I do?" he demanded.

With a flip of her skirt showing a flash of yellow-stockinged ankle, she threw up her right shoulder and crooned, "Boy, make that rifle be a wedding *dash* to Dan'l."

Yes, Nat thought, Daniel would have to accept his rifle as a wedding gift. Nat would do anything to please her, to end this discussion. There were plenty of rifles, but just one Freedoma and he wanted her more than he could stand, even more than that fancy watch.

*   *   *   *   *   *   *   *   *   *

For a time Doe lay in the mud battered by drumming rain accepting that he no longer was crucified upon his boulder. Slowly he moved his rigored limbs until mobility returned. He crawled back upon that damnable rock to avoid being swept from the rapidly submerging island by the rain-swollen river. He knew that it would recede with the end of the storm, probably after dawn, leaving him in full view, at the mercy of his tormentors, who would tie him back on his bolder, or worse. His progressive weakness was as obvious to him as the sharp ache of hunger. He had to move, to eat.

He lashed together a pathetic float from the ruins of his torture frame and slipped into the churning river. The water carried him with minimal effort and less sense of course blindly through the wall of rain. Without warning, he found himself heading between two hulls toward an eddy a few rapidly diminishing yards ahead where the two masses merged. Doe kicked with all his remaining energy to pass to the outside of the smaller vessel. He almost made it and was able to grasp the schooner's stem. As the current pushed him back between the hulls, he watched his raft surge into the broiling eddy, break apart, and disappear. He faced downstream. Bouncing on the current was a line from the schooner's gunwale. Releasing his grip, he let the water carry him to the rope and grabbed it as he slipped by. Doe was horrified to feel the line play out. The schooner was riding high and the barnacles sliced him as he bumped along her side. His strength was going;

even his anger that had sustained him to this point. He was going under again.

He almost lost his grip as the rope came taut, the current lifting him against the resistance, forcing his gaze up to the rigid hawsers holding the schooner to the bigger vessel. They ran through ports at deck level. He tried, but could not reach them. His effort added significantly to his lacerations and entangled his legs in the line extending beyond his grip. He floundered free. He could not climb the schooner's side. He did not have the strength to pull himself back to the bow. Would he cling here, he wondered, until his strength failed and he was swept between the hulls to drown in the eddy?

The rope entangled his leg again. It must be rather long, he realized. How long? Frantically Doe pulled at the trailing rope. He took a turn around his body, freeing both hands. Finally it ended; ten, fifteen yards of it. He forced himself to look up into the downpour. By will alone, he forced his body up in the stream and tossed the coiled line over the first of the large cables. He eased himself along in an aquatic belay until he had hold of the dangling rope. He ran it back under his left arm, across his raw back, and under his right armpit where he laid it along the rope already holding him in the current. Gripping the lines together with the pressure of his bicep against his side he took the line before him in both hands and began pulling. As he brought line in, he inched it forward under his right armpit and clamped it in place. Slowly he ratcheted himself upward toward the hawser, inch by inch, willing his endurance not to fail, willing the rope to move across the hawser like a line through a block.

Finally he was able to place an arm over the hawser. He fought desperately to raise his leg over the great hemp shaft. He pulled himself along the taut rope. Slowly, Doe inched his way through the gun port. Like some great lizard, he wriggled forward indifferent to the smacking rain on his back or his flesh galling as the decking worked his lacerated torso. Cover, hide, protection, disappearance, he thought disjointedly. His head impacted a great cold rim, but he felt no pain. He groped. Open. Hollow. Dry. Doe wriggled as far as he could into the dismounted carronade barrel, and passed from consciousness.

*   *   *   *   *   *   *   *   *   *

Sweet jerked awake. The hammering rain had stopped; time to continue loading. As he exited his cuddy, Bonney was already in the wardroom donning sword belt and pistol. Sweet started to extract his watch, his parents' graduation gift. It was gone. *Damn*, he thought after a moment's confusion. He last remembered looking at it during the levee. With a sinking heart, he realized where it was. He could not go back *there* for it.

"Just shy of four o'-the-clock, Charles," Bonney said as if he knew his troubles.

Sweet gave Bonney an angry glance, then added coldly, "Thank you, Sir." If he had not danced.... Sweet let the thought die unfinished.

"Hope those people up the hill are wakable," Bonney answered conversationally.

Sweet's extended silence before answering expressed his resentment better than words. Finally he replied, "Expect so ... Mr. Bonney."

"Well, best get after them, *Mr.* Sweet."

"My intent before stopping to converse, Lieutenant." Sweet hurried for the ladder.

Bonney watched him go with a shake of his head. Touchy as a long-tailed cat in a room full of rocking chairs, he concluded and deliberately finished dressing to put an interval between them. Maybe Charles would cool down with the climb?

On deck Bonney saw no hint of dawn, no need to be up. Sentries on the forecastle, the quarterdeck, and at both entry ports were sodden despite their gum rubber panchos. He questioned the wisdom of soaking them and their equipment in conditions that prohibited any hostile action against the ship. Still, they were manning duty posts and that obligation was not restricted to good weather. He sensed the river's force along the hulls straining on the hawsers. Light shown through the forward hatch; Peck rousing the hands. Bonney strolled forward to the open railing where the hawser came aboard. He was sailor enough, though he would never admit it to the Navy, to be concerned about the hawsers chafing. He tested the cable tension with his foot; not the slightest give. He bent to examine the hemp. In the faint light from the hatch he saw no fraying. A variation of hue in his peripheral vision attracted him, the lightly pigmented sole and heel of an African foot protruding from the muzzle of the dismounted carronade.

Bonney hissed at the sentry by the portside entryport. At Bonney's motion the Marine came to the ready and stealthily ghosted to his lieutenant's side. It was young Schmidt, Bonney recognized and signaled silence, motioning the New Jerseyite to lean his musket against the rail. Pointing to the foot, he pantomimed seizing and yanking. Schmidt nodded as he bent forward. Bonney slid his Colt Navy revolver from its holster and placed his thumb on the hammer. With his left hand he held up three fingers. Schmidt nodded again. Bonney closed his fist and began the count: forefinger; fore and middle fingers; fore, middle and ring fingers.

The sentry jerked the black ankle, hurling his body weight into the process, his brogans fighting for purchase on the sodden deck. Bonney thumbed his revolver to full cock. Doe snapped into consciousness as he sped feet-first down the carronade's bore. There was no way to grip the smooth sides in the second it took the Marine to snap the tribesman from his hiding place. As Doe's head plumbed onto the deck, he felt his skull uncomfortably pinned to the planking by the hard hexagonal muzzle of

Bonney's pistol. Struggle and he knew that his head would explode like a melon. He lay still.

Bonney slowly reached forward and seized a handful of Doe's hair. Without breaking contact, he scraped the muzzle of the pistol across the stowaway's face and jabbed it into his ear. By the hair he levered Doe's face down on the deck. "Understand English?"

"*Enty.*"

"Crawl to the hatch, real slow." The awkward creature created by the two men crab-walked into the light. Bonney bent back Doe's head none too gently. Doe recognized the American soldier-officer; he must be bad cursed to be back on that slave ship.

Bonney was surprised and satisfied by the blue-black face he had last seen through the binoculars. So the harebrained idea had worked. This fellow would not be where he was, had not Bonney's and Daniel's bullets weakened the bamboo frame and the raffia binding the captive to his stone; fine shooting, he had to admit. Bonney was aware of activity up the bank at the McGills' Factory and around the foot of the ladder on the berth deck. He had a second's reflection. Why did he care a tinker's damn what happened to this wild man? He thought of Greenville, the shrieks from around the fire cutting the night as Gabriel and his lieutenants died so slowly. But Gabe was no saint. No, it was the arrogance, the fiendish glee these people took in torture that made him want to frustrate their intentions.

"Welcome to the *Angel* of your deliverance, Boy," whispered Bonney in what, even in his uncomfortable posture and through hearing impaired by the muzzle of a .36 caliber Colt revolver, Doe understood as a friendly tone. Easing his pressure on the weapon, Bonney whispered into Doe's unobstructed ear, "Listen, Boy, I'm your friend." Bonney sincerely doubted that the African would accept that assertion on his word alone. "Promise to keep still, I'll have this pistol out of your ear." Doe gave a miniscule affirmative nod. Bonney helped him to a sitting position. "This ship is leaving real soon. We can get you ashore up the coast; you stay low until then. Savvy?"

"Savvy," Doe mumbled.

"Come quiet. Better places to hole-up than that gun barrel," Bonney ordered.

He assisted the African to his feet. Exhausted, Doe nearly collapsed. Unbidden, Schmidt caught him by the left bicep and, taking his lead from Bonney, helped the tribesman to the aft hatch. They stumbled below to the wardroom. Soon, the ship would be crawling with Liberians. Bonney could think of no place to hide Doe, other than his own cuddy. The Marines half-carried Doe into the small cubicle. Reticently, Bonney pulled the blanket from his cot, tossed it open on the bit of deck, and eased Doe onto it.

"Y'all lie here, quiet, understand?" Bonney glanced around the small cubicle. "Schmidt," he commanded, "fill my canteen from the scuttlebutt and give it to him. There's some ship's biscuit in the bread safe yonder on the for'ard bulkhead. Grab him a handful as you pass." Poor devil must not have eaten for more than a day, Bonney calculated. He growled to Doe, "Stay hidden. Stay quiet."

Schmidt returned with the canteen and hard bread. The two Marines stepped from the cuddy and started for the ladder. Bonney suddenly stopped, turned to the bulkhead and, scooping up a fire bucket, retraced his steps. He opened the cuddy door. Doe was gnawing on the biscuit. Bonney could not help grinning. "Soak it a bit, Boy, or you'll break a tooth," he advised. "Y'all have to pass anything, use this, hear?" he added and thrust the wooded pail inside.

"Savvy," Doe responded through a mouthful of biscuit.

Bonney returned to the ladder. "You smiling, Schmidt?" he growled. "NO, *SIR!*"

"Didn't think so. Not a word to anybody about this, hear?"

"Aye, aye, Sir."

"Back to your post. Carry on."

225

CHAPTER TWENTY-NINE

Sweet ran the back of his hand across his brow. It did little to stop the stinging rivulets of sweat oozing into his eyes. For an hour the sun had been sucking moisture from *Angel's* sodden decks and every other surface within one hundred miles of the coast. Palm oil gurgled down the bamboo piping. A steady train of bearers, bundles of cam wood and some ivory on their heads, cycled down the ankle-deep rust-red laterite soup of the path, deposited their loads, and returned to the warehouse for more. In the hold the hands, most newly recruited from the slaver crew, stowed the cargo. For a Sunday morning, loading was progressing better than he had any reason to expect.

"Mr. Sweet." Talliaferro brought Sweet from his reverie. "Our newly weds?"

Sweet shook his head. "Not as yet, Sir." Was Talliaferro blaming him for this too, he wondered before asking, "Shall I fetch them?"

"Best so, Mr. Sweet." Talliaferro's mood was much improved, now that departure was imminent. He hauled his watch from his waistcoat pocket. "Seven of the clock now. Have your people aboard by one bell the latest to weigh at nine of the clock."

"Aye, Sir," Sweet answered, relieved at the agreeable timbre of Talliaferro's speech. Surely he could have Daniel and Delcina aboard by half after eight.

Talliaferro moved beside Bonney who was intently scanning the bluff. "Had Orrin and a couple signalmen on the headland since dawn with a glass," the Marine reported.

"May they be ever disappointed."

"Amen," answered Bonney. "By the way, 'Captain,'" he began his report of Doe's arrival.

Talliaferro's reaction was resignation, but not opposition. It was too good a morning, now that they finally were departing, to let one stowaway spoil it. "Just keep him out of sight until we sail," sighed the Carolinian.

*   *   *   *   *   *   *   *   *   *

Sweet's reticence to awaken the household of a head of state was apparent even to the somnolent doorman. Yapping dogs appeared to be the only security for Liberia's chief magistrate. Given the lack of harmony in the republic, Sweet was appalled by this indifference. Had the canine alert roused Freedoma, he wondered with an unsettling tingling of animal excitement? He shook his head to clear the thought. The porter ushered him into the foyer to wait while "Mr. Sweet" was informed.

I am "Mr. Sweet," he thought. Damned if he was going to cool his heels in the hall, he decided, while his slave took his own good time. He brushed past the servant into the Presidential Parlor, yanked on the bell pull, and casually stretched himself on a divan. These "pussuns" could fetch him some coffee, he irritably resolved.

*   *   *   *   *   *   *   *   *   *

Baston closed his telescope. All seemed normal, worse luck, aboard the cameled ship. His thoughts were in turmoil. These people were incapable of acting with any immediacy. His silk dressing gown stuck to him uncomfortably; most definitely a white linen morning, he decided. Eight in the morning by the Thomas clock on the sideboard under his late wife's portrait, he confirmed with a quick glance. All he need do was detain the slaver until *Bainbridge* appeared. The inevitable morning offshore breeze would do little to delay *Bainbridge*, he reasoned; a magnificent sailer, she could tack into almost any wind. Still, he reflected, it was exasperating that his meeting last evening with Minister Manley had not borne fruit.

To Baston's amusement, they had met upon the Minister of Trade's initiative. Baston was surprised by Manley's news of the brig's imminent arrival. The efficacy of the "Bush Telegraph," the magical unknown means by which news moved about West Africa without explanation frustrated and fascinated the diplomat. *Bainbridge* had called at Harper and the news flashed to Monrovia within a matter of hours. Baston suspected Manley had a system of drummers that thumped out code from settlement to settlement along the coast. It was the only logical explanation. At least here was a possible solution to the embarrassment of the entire *Ebony Angel* affair. So long as she was returned to the American flag, the rest of the debacle would be quickly forgotten among the more pressing issues of the Southern rebellion.

Baston was even more amused and supremely gratified at Manley's vehemence that *Ebony Angel* not put to sea before *Bainbridge* apprehended her. The minister was urging Baston to act, rather than Baston having to cajole the Minister into preventing the slaver from sailing before *Bainbridge* cut off her escape. If he only knew that I fooled him into this new animosity with Parkins, Nevis, and the rest of the members of the Liberian Packet Company, Baston reflected. It certainly was advantageous to have such an ally in his efforts to repossess the slaver, but, glancing again at *Angel*, Baston wondered why the failure to produce results? Could this be some kind of a trick, a trap? Baston suddenly experienced a rising panic; Manley had that copy of his fictitious report to Washington.

*   *   *   *   *   *   *   *   *   *

"Come on, Cina; you has to get up." Daniel recognized his own exasperation.

"Say who?" Delcina answered querulously, more asleep than awake.

"Say I."

Daniel snapped back the sheet. She did not respond. The light air over her moist skin was soothing, inviting sleep. Daniel slapped open the louvers, sunlight exploding into the room. Delcina moaned, buried her face in the crook of her left elbow, and wriggled down into the mattress. Content to let the sun work on her, Daniel turned to his ablutions deliberately sounding like an elephant floundering through cane. Delcina lay unmoving.

"Cina, that ship going sail without us."

"Not."

"Why not?"

"My father boss of that ship." Raising her head, Delcina smiled triumphantly. "He done bought Pa Nevis's share in the Packet Company."

Daniel sighed in frustration. Delcina would learn. Even chief justices could not control ship's captains. "Not so, Girl. Marse Talliaferro captain that ship and say it going most soon. Y'all get up and moving, *one time.*"

She levered herself up onto her elbows and looked at him. The curve of her breasts, the arch of her back down into her tensed buttocks excited him. He was glad that he had just knotted the cords at the ankles and waist of his drawers. A man could not argue with a woman aware that she had him aroused. His infatuation vanished as she spoke. "Boy, my father own that ship. Ain't no *buckra's* slave Nigra say what time I going on boat."

The smack of his palm on her bare rump startled Daniel almost as much as Delcina. She yelped more in outrage than in pain. Before she could respond further, he was kneeling on the bed holding her jaw in his left hand. "Listen good, Girl." His eyes held hers. "I be your husband. Ain't no never-mind what I be to nobody else. I love you beyond countin', but you not know for nothing how life be for sailorman or house people. I want you by me for life, but you got to flow with the stream; not be no rock bust-up my boat. Y'all be a rock, just stay here; cain't have no rock in my river."

Their eyes locked. Each noticed the moisture in the other's. Each sensed the hostility ebb, saw the fire die in the opposing pupils, the bodies relax. "I gots to pee," announced Delcina rising from the bed.

*　　*　　*　　*　　*　　*　　*　　*　　*　　*

Tourch's gig had deposited Paltier and his dunnage on the McGill Brothers' pier just after 7:30 that Sunday morning where he was met by Bonney. The Briton dashed one of the bearers a three-penny bit to move his sea chest aboard *Angel* and deposit it in the cuddy Bonney indicated on the starboard side of the slaver's equivalent of a wardroom.

"Not up to Royal Navy standards exactly," the American observed with a grin.

"I should be pleased with an open boat were it my speediest means to raise England," Paltier responded.

Bonney frowned. "None of my business, Paltier, but you excite my curiosity. What can be so critical that you must leave your ship and dash for home in such haste?"

The Briton fixed the Marylander with a cold stare. "You most certainly are correct, Lef'tenant Bonney; my personal matters are none of your concern."

Bonney recoiled as if struck. His face went ashen and he struggled to apologize for assuming to pry into Paltier's personal affairs. A thought flickered through his confusion, was Sweet correct in believing he boorishly interjected himself into other's private matters?

Paltier was shocked at the confusion, the alarm on his friend's face. After all, Bonney had certainly responded openly to Paltier's inquiries about the American's personal crisis in Freetown. Paltier even had hoped that he had assisted Bonney in sorting out what path to take simply by enabling him to verbalize his concerns. Now that Bonney was offering to return the favor, Paltier realized he had insulted him in response to the proffered friendship. "Bonney, I beg your pardon. I spoke from anger at my situation, not at you." He placed his hand on Bonney's shoulder. "Thank you for your concern. It is a bit of a long and sordid story and I shall spare you the details. I am constrained to go home to prevent my elder half-siblings from evicting my mother from her home and living."

Bonney experienced a surge of relief at Paltier's sudden remorse. His offer of kindness had been recognized and received as such and their friendship remained firm. "As I said, Robert, none of my concern, other than I wish to be of service if you wish it. No need to explain. Just recall that I am here to assist as I may."

Paltier nodded his thanks. "The entire matter makes me a bit testy, obviously." He dropped his hand from Bonney's shoulder. "Bit of a bother, airing family matters through barristers, and the sides are a bit uneven, what with my half-brother having the title and all."

Bonney was curious, but not about to inquire. "Now, I best be on deck," he responded shifting the conversation. "Make yourself to home," he added with a smile, "but I warn you, you start idling on deck and we'll find you something to do."

"That would be a blessing on many levels, my friend," Paltier responded matching Bonney's smile. The American nodded and turned to the ladder. After Bonney left, Paltier thought better of going on deck. His presence aboard if observed by the Liberians and reported to the United States representatives might be construed as British endorsement of *Angel's* actions. Best to remain below until *Angel* was under way, he concluded.

Talliaferro snapped his watch shut in disgust, twenty-nine past nine and no sign of Sweet. *Angel* was not a blasted yacht for the Midshipman and his self-important servants, he fumed. Even he recognized that his mood was changing. Word that *Bainbridge* had been sighted at Harper made immediate departure imperative. He had stopped the loading. The palm oil tanks were full. Sizable quantities of cam wood and tusks were aboard. Not a full cargo, but it would turn a nice profit for the run to Liverpool; if they got to Liverpool rather than New York in chains, he reflected.

The schooners' crews awaited his command to let the bows swing into the current. He had examined the "freeboard," the height of their sides still above the water, of all three vessels and there should be no problem staying out of the mud. Maintaining steerage was the challenge. The vessels would move at the river's speed, preventing the rudders from leveraging the bows. To have steerage, he needed the offshore wind to move the cameled contraption faster than the current. They had to be away before the wind shifted. Where in Billy Blue Blazes were those people? Three bells chimed as if to emphasize his frustration.

CRUMPH! The musket report drew all eyes toward the cape. Bonney instantly looked to his signalman stationed on the northeast corner of the McGills' veranda to relay signals from Orrin. The Marine with the yeoman was writing something - thanks to New Jersey's free public education Schmidt was literate – which meant that the shot was part of Orrin's message. Absent Midshipman Sweet, the message would be Bonney's to decipher. Not that he would need much expertise, the only message to justify firing a weapon would be "ENEMY IN SIGHT."

The signalman at McGills' lowered his glass, grasped his flags, and turned toward the ship. Then he hesitated and turned back toward Monrovia. At the same instant, Bonney heard the thump and blare of a brass band.

"*For Heaven's blessed sake!*" growled Talliaferro. "No time for shilly-shallying."

"Easter and a New Orleans funeral," added Bonney as the procession came into view rounding the McGills' corner.

Several barefooted little girls in calico led, spreading flowers in the reddish-tan mud. Then Daniel and Delcina appeared supported by most of Monrovia's aristocracy. Behind them all, the Liberian Army Band puffed away at "Columbia the Gem of the Ocean." Last, a score of bearers headloaded Delcina's necessities. Sweet's pale face stood out in the throng. Talliaferro promised himself that none of them would be so very happy once aboard. "The signal, Lieutenant Bonney," he snapped.

"A moment, Mr. Talliaferro," Bonney replied, irrationally irritated by Talliaferro's authoritative tone. As he spoke, the veranda became a-swarm with spectators, swamping the signal party. "We have been overrun, Mr. Talliaferro."

"So I observe, Mr. Bonney. 'Those whom the Gods would destroy....'"

"'They first make mad.'"

"And this is pure madness," rejoined Talliaferro. His good mood had vanished.

The band halted to the north of the pathway, serenading the descending dignitaries. Clearly the President intended to come aboard. Bonney hastened to the entryport, bellowing for Sergeant Banning. Banning understood and had the Marines in two short ranks on either side of the port before the visitors arrived. For a moment Bonney thought that the entire mob intended coming across and quaked at the "goat rope," to use Banning's phrase, that would produce. Mercifully, they crowded onto McGills' veranda or stopped along the shore.

The flower girls, however, came on until they were spreading petals among the Marines. Sergeant Banning brought his detail to "Present Arms" with the usual slapping of musket stocks as Daniel and Delcina stepped upon the gangplank between the schooner and the ship. The terrified children dumped their remaining petals and fled. The farcical undertones were not lost upon Bonney. Delcina and Daniel, supported by Midshipman Sweet, halted just inboard and aft of the Marines. As the Presidential Party and the Drapers spilled forth onto the deck, Sergeant Banning stepped through his ranks closing the entryport with his frame. The bull-like bellow "Order ARMS!" froze all but the band on the bluff. Talliaferro seized the moment to welcome the President and the rest to the Liberian Packet Company's ship, *Ebony Angel*.

Bonney recognized Marine Schmidt squeezing through the crowd. He also observed the bearers with Delcina's "necessities" working their way along the landward rail of the schooner inshore of *Angel*. Bonney moved beside Thoms and impatiently ordered him to stow Delcina's dunnage.

Schmidt continued squirming through the press. Benson was speechifying about sending a daughter of Africa and America to that country of great travail, this time as a free woman of color on a ship owned by her family. Delcina's mama planted that idea, Bonney reflected absently. Leaning across the rail, he received Schmidt's report. A Yankee brig was visible hull-down to the south-southwest-by-south.

Bonney conducted a quick estimate. Orrin's designation as "Yankee" had nothing to do with sectional prejudices; it identified the easily distinguishable characteristics of American naval architecture. It had to be *Bainbridge*. She was to the south and somewhat west of Cape Montserado tacking to the northwest. Once she had the sea room, she would come about and run down on Monrovia in a position to cut off any vessel bound for Europe and, with enough time, to prevent any sortie at all from the

Montserado River. Once the onshore flow began, less than three hours from now, she would have the weather gauge, be upwind, of any vessel trying for sea. Could they clear the river and castoff the schooners in three hours, Bonney wondered?

Bonney squared his cover, then marched forward to where President Benson addressed the multitude. As he moved, he became aware of scuffling at the entryport, Banning jostling with a young Liberian, Nat McGill holding the Whitworth rifle. Bonney changed course. At the entry port, young McGill announced his intention to "make Daniel a wedding *dash*" of his rifle. Bonney had to suppress a smile; with all that was happening, how could this boy be so damned serious about something so trivial?

Together they moved forward as President Benson leaned to kiss his niece. Nat turned to Daniel, but had to wait while Benson shook the bridegroom's hand, then embraced him. As the President and his Lady turned to depart and Sergeant Banning returned the Marines to "Present Arms," Nat handed Daniel the Whitworth with its numerous accoutrements. Bonney stepped between Talliaferro and Justice Draper, muttering that if they did not want to see the Liberian Packet Company's only vessel repossessed by the United States Navy, it was time to get the blazes out of the Montserado River. Draper understood and began shooing his family ashore.

Nat stopped by Sweet and pressed something into his hand. "'Doma say tell you, make for good time." Cheeks reddening, Sweet accepted his watch.

"*Mr. Sweet!*" Talliaferro's voice was cutting.

Sweet mumbled thanks to Nat and turned to face his commanding officer. "I must apologize, Sir. Didn't have my watch...." Sweet realized he was holding it in his hand. Talliaferro must think him a bald-faced liar.

"Later," interrupted Talliaferro in disgust. "Get this gaggle under way. Y'all explain this evening," he paused, "*if* we're still alive and free this evening."

Bonney was concerned. Those blasted people still were not off the schooner. *Orrin!* He realized with a shock; he had to get Orrin and the signalmen back aboard. Desperately, Bonney looked toward the bluff. Three blue-clad figures slithered down the bank, sun glinting off Orrin's musket, the others awkwardly encumbered with signal flags. Bonney expelled a sigh of relief.

*   *   *   *   *   *   *   *   *   *

"Not stay in this," Delcina snapped, standing aghast in the sleeping cabin hatch.

Sweet did not care a Dutch *dam* if Delcina thought the accommodations below her. "This is where you *are* staying until we get shut of that damned Yankee brig!"

Delcina jerked her head around. "Whatfore, say Yankee brig?"

"Cina!" Sweet thundered in exasperation. "There is an American Navy brig in view from Thompson Town heading this way fast. It has more cannon than we got men and unless we get the Sam Hill out of here *now*, you be lucky to be put back ashore and Dan'l and me and the rest of us will either drown or hang."

"*Dan'l*, you no say such." She looked at him with reproach. "Sweetie," she let out a giggle as Sweet cringed. "Mr. Sweet, we perfect here. You and Dan'l make this ship to go." She turned to her three maids, "*Set!*" Like obedient bird dogs, they settled to the deck in silence.

Sweet and Daniel exchanged looks; then made for the ladder. For the first time since coming aboard Sweet really *looked* at his servant and realized that Daniel was armed to the teeth with the rifle and accoutrements.

"Nat McGill; weddin' gift," Daniel explained apologetically.

"Under my mattress, quick," Sweet ordered and continued to the weather deck.

On deck confusion reined, as the bowlines were cast off, the last Liberians hurried ashore, and worried porters hustled Delcina's trousseau across the rails. What in tarnation could she need all that dunnage for anyhow, Sweet wondered; then realized in horror that somehow it all was supposed to fit into the Quarters at Sweetlands. Slave with his own rifle, slave's wife with more stuff than his sister-in-law, and her own three maids.... What was the world coming to, Sweet mused with a shake of his head?

Daniel watched in fascination as the bows made an accelerating swing through the panorama of the Montserado River: the Carey Island Rocks where Doe had been crucified, the expanse of Bally Island with its dominant hill, the mouth of Stockton Creek red-brown with soil washed down by The Rains, Kroo Point at which the flood was ripping, and finally the view down river to Montserado Roads and the sea. He could see activity on *H.M.S. Tourch* pulling at her cables opposite Kroo Point and at the Liberian battery covering the river mouth. The wild excitement of the departure set his heart to racing. Life had been grand, almost a fairytale since they left the old *Jamestown*.

"Let go aft!" Talliaferro bellowed. There was no slacking the lines over cleats in this current. Loosened before the strange composite craft began its swing, the hawsers simply were allowed to play out and remained behind.

Would the awkward combination of vessels steer? Peck deployed the jib as soon as the bow angled away from the shore, but it was a steering sail, not a driver. *Angel* was not answering her helm; she needed to increase her speed beyond that of the river current.

"Loose the foretop, Mr. Sweet," Talliaferro's voice had an urgent tension.

"Loose the foretop, Mr. Peck!"

"Aye, Sir," Peck answered automatically.

A pandemonium of shrieks and shouts erupted through the aft hatch.

"For *Christ's sake*, Mr. Sweet!" exploded Talliaferro, "What's all that?"

Sweet, Daniel, and Bonney tumbled into the wardroom upon a scene reminiscent of bear baiting. Through the cuddy bars, Delcina's maids were attacking Doe with parasols, and a belaying pin. Delcina was about to take an axe to the dowels so the vixens could get to him. Backed against the hull, Doe was parrying the thrusts, but clearly tiring.

"*HALT!*" Bonney's bellow froze the scene. "What in the Sam Hill is going on?"

"We going fix this *Bush Nigger, one time!*" Delcina shouted, murder in her eyes.

"*Stow it!*" retorted Bonney. "He sure as salvation is not attacking you! What has got into you, go poking at the poor savage? Not much count as ladies acting…."

Delcina's counterattack drowned out Bonney's words. "He done shamed McGills and run off to bush. How he get free off Carey Rock, I not savvy." If she only knew how he escaped, Bonney mused. "*Same-same* he die this day!" she concluded resolutely.

"Not on this ship!" Bonney barked. "I've seen your torture. Boy is in my cuddy, my protection, hear?" Bonney stared down the indignant young woman and turned to Daniel. "Get him some clothes and keep her off him, or by Jesse a cowskin will open her back!" His face within an inch of Delcina's, he demanded, "Savvy that, Girl?"

She knew the difference between a man promising rather than merely threatening violence; it was in the eyes. Bonney's eyes said he would use the cowhide whip without hesitation. "Savvy," she responded with surprising calm.

"You better!" Bonney turned back to Daniel. "Get him dressed and on deck," he snapped indicating Doe. Then ordered, "Mr. Sweet! Obliged, you keep your Nigras under control, remainder of this voyage. Now, get back to your post."

For the first time since Greenville, Delcina felt real fear. No one since Gabriel had threatened her with bodily harm. And Bonney had referred to her as one of Sweet's 'Nigras" like she was his property, his *slave*! Her stomach felt like it was falling through her abdomen as she realized that *Angel* no longer was tied to Africa. Had she made a terrible mistake? She closed her

235

eyes and clenched her jaw, resolving to trust Daniel, absolutely convinced that he would keep her from harm, from sorrow. Suddenly she realized how serious the threat of *Bainbridge* must be for everyone to react so. She discovered with a start that she was terrified, not for herself, but for Daniel.

Sweet shot Daniel a glance and followed Bonney up the ladder. On deck, things were not going well for Talliaferro. Lashed to her consorts, *Angel* was little more than a large raft. The wind, in the doldrums, could not propel the cameled contraption significantly faster than the current. Not answering her helm, *Angel* bobbed along like driftwood on a collision course toward Kroo Point.

"Didn't intend for *all* officers to desert the deck," Talliaferro censured.

After an awkward pause, Sweet suggested "More canvas?"

"Tarnation, Charles," Talliaferro was beyond tolerance for suggestions. "No speakable wind, just make her more uncertain at her helm." Just got to ride this to whatever."

"Well, Captain, we better get some...."

A concussion like a cannon shot drowned Bonney's voice as the hawser running from the main mast to the McGill vessel to port recoiled like a whip smacking the ship's side. The camel began to disintegrate. The remaining two cables parted, also slamming into *Angel*. No longer balanced by the pull of the ropes to *Angel's* masts, the hawsers running down the outboard side of the schooner to port, beneath *Angel,* and to the schooner to starboard slowly rolled the portside schooner away from the black ship dragging her keel up *Angel's* side with gargantuan screeching. As she rolled, the hawsers under *Angel* slackened, lowering the larger ship bow-first into the mud. The angle of her strike brought *Angel* to a gradual, rather than a jolting halt. The portside schooner was almost on her beam's end, deck nearly vertical to the river surface, before some quick-acting souls took axes to the remaining hawsers. Slowly the endangered vessel righted herself. Stern-first, she gathered speed downstream toward the roadstead.

From his window, The Honorable Roland P. Baston, United States Consul at Monrovia, smiled and lowered his telescope. Manley had come through, though by Jesse he had taken his sweet time.

CHAPTER THIRTY

Sweet stood immobilized by melancholy disbelief. Talliaferro held his breath Heaven only knew how long. Bonney scanned the ship, the schooner to starboard, and the river generally; pursed his lips; and drawled, "We're in the pisspot now."

At Bonney's vulgarism, Talliaferro resumed breathing. His eyes seemed to focus again as he growled, "Let's get this black-hulled harlot out of the mud."

"*Sergeant Banning!*" Bonney bellowed.

"*Mr. Peck!*" copied Sweet.

Parted from the countervailing force of the cables running beneath *Ebony Angel* to her opposite number to port, the buoyancy of the starboard schooner forced her keel up and away from the slave ship. The hawsers connecting the vessels' masts frustrated the separation, producing a vicious grinding of the hulls and tangled rigging. Something had to be done or *Angel* would be dismasted.

*   *   *   *   *   *   *   *   *   *

"Here, out-the-way, you, 'til Marse Bonney want you," Daniel ordered Doe to the starboard rail level with the mizzenmast. "I's for doing and can't stand watch of no *Bush Nigger*. You be from here without Marse Bonney say, I cut your bullocks off." Doe returned a level stare; he had evaded more serious threats of castration. Daniel thought of teaching this savage some respect, but Doe might resist and a scuffle would impair efforts to re-float *Angel*. Giving stare for stare, Daniel sneered; then turned away.

*   *   *   *   *   *   *   *   *   *

Talliaferro had no difficulty finding the schooner's master. He was at his own port rail searching *Angel's* deck for Talliaferro. "*Capitaine,*" he greeted Talliaferro with a semi-bow. Mustachioed after the style of the Emperor of France, he had a spread that would put the third Napoleon to shame. A clean jaw differentiated him from the monarch as did his olive hue and slight heaviness of lower lip and nostril, a genealogy caressed by the tar brush, Talliaferro surmised; Cape Verde or Fernando Pao Portuguese. "We must separate our vessels, *Seniore,*" the master continued. There was no time for pleasantries.

"That would put you against the Point," Talliaferro hailed. "What's the bottom there?"

The Portuguese spat contemplatively upon his own deck. "Muck and mud. We can do," he assured the American. "Re-float past rain," he continued, dropping the corners of his mouth in an expression of accepting the unavoidable. Despite his concerns, Talliaferro observed with amazement the arc described by the tips of the man's mustache; it had to be twenty degrees. "Well it is of you, *Tennante*. May God smile for you. I wave my hat, so." The master pulled off the broad-brimmed straw and vigorously circled his head, paused, smiled, and recovered his shining bald spot.

Talliaferro looked for Peck. Instead, a large bronzed fellow in full-flowing beard and pigtail confronted him. The apparition grinned tobacco-yellowed teeth and rumbled, "Samson, Sir. Boatswain of this here, before you took her."

The smile was genuine. "Samson" did not seem to hold his changed circumstances against Talliaferro or the *Jamestownes*. Talliaferro hoped that the rest of the score of former slave ship hands, now constituting the majority of his crew, shared his attitude. Samson explained that Peck had him heading the axe crew to sever the lines. Talliaferro saw men, axes in hand, by each mast.

"Very well. Standby," he ordered.

*   *   *   *   *   *   *   *   *   *

Daniel watched as several seamen struggled to leverage the plank out of the forward portside gunport. Thoms already straddled the jib boom twirling the lead line in a vertical circle to build momentum before launching it as far forward as he could to test the river bottom. Daniel had the great pleasure of making a similar determination to port. He literally would walk the plank as far from *Angel's* side as possible before taking his sounding. That he was unenthusiastic was gross understatement.

Sweet ordered Schmidt, the Marine bracing Daniel's plank under the remains of the forward pivot mount, to hold it steady. It was not necessary; all the old *Jamestownes* knew how close Mr. Sweet was to his servant. Sweet gritted his jaws as Daniel moved along the sixteen-foot board extending from the ship. He wanted to take the sounding himself, but it was not an officer's task. Besides, Daniel could pitch the lead farther than he. Still, he felt guilty. As Daniel neared the end, the plank evidenced considerable flex.

"*Dan'l!* whyfore you go there?" Delcina was three-fourths out of the forward hatch when she saw her husband bobbing over the river and shrieked, startling all hands.

Sweet spun toward her. Schmidt looked up, the plank shifting with his weight. It was not much movement at the deck end, but it produced major springing as Daniel pivoted to look at his wife. Body already out of alignment, he over-corrected for the unexpected movement, going off balance to his left. In reaction he flung up his arms as he shifted right and slapped the back of his head a glancing blow with the six-pound lead.

"*Damn!*" Schmidt cursed, clutching the plank desperately, but too late. As Daniel crumpled, Sweet started for the board. He did not stop to factor the effect of his one hundred-forty pounds running out the plank. Before he reached the rail, a powerful shove felled him. Sweet rolled onto his chest and looked desperately toward Daniel, his view totally obscured by bloomers and petticoats. Delcina, still in her Sunday finery, had flattened herself along the board.

"Catch my feets, Sweetie," she screamed from somewhere beyond the crinoline.

Sweet rolled painfully across his sword hilt and gripped her ankles. "Move with me, *Bo!*"

"Hold steady, Schmidt!" Sweet ordered. Delcina came to his eyebrows, five foot-six perhaps, he estimated. Arms out she might reach six foot tip-to-toe. He was five foot-eight, say seven feet arms extended for simplicity's sake. Daniel was not quite at the end of the plank, assuming he was still on the plank; Sweet could observe nothing save Delcina's small clothes. The two of them alone might barely reach Daniel and would have no steadying effect. "Somebody grip my ankles!" Sweet bellowed.

*   *   *   *   *   *   *   *   *   *

"Parker is a good fellow, Bonney. Assist howsoever you require," Paltier was certain that the Royal Navy could extricate the Americans, if they would only ask.

"Once the Navy has the bees from its bonnet, we can suggest that, Paltier, but I am not about to interrupt Talliaferro at this…."

With a loud hallo in some unintelligible tongue the schooner's master swatted his hat in a great circle above his head. Neither Bonney nor Paltier saw Talliaferro's nod to Samson, but everyone within a half-mile heard the ex-Boatswain's order to "*PART CABLES!*" As the axes began to beat a rhythm through the thick hemp, Bonney realized that the tribal fellow, Doe, was standing beside the port through which the aft hawser ran to the mizzenmast. In seconds the cable would part and recoil like a great whip capable of slicing a man in half. Doe was looking at the schooner, not toward the source of the danger, even if he could comprehend it, which Bonney doubted.

The Marylander responded on reflex, three strides and a leap. He caught Doe just above the waist. Together they tumbled aft along the deck. Above them the parted hawser, as thick as a man's thigh, shot back from the mast like a recoiling snake, whapped against the rail leaving a six foot long, inch deep indentation in the oak. Energy spent, it slapped to the deck and slithered through the port.

Once again Doe had been surprised from behind. He writhed around to fight whomever or whatever it was. His motion put Bonney into the rail. Doe's face was not an inch from Bonney's. The African recognized his benefactor and stopped struggling. Then Doe noticed the destruction the cable had wrought. "Szeee," he whistled. "*Swanga mamba!* Plenty powerful be that rope snake."

"Well, Boy, help him up," Paltier spoke with exasperation. "You do owe him your bloody life." Bonney was too valuable to be sacrificed for this bush fellow, Paltier fervently believed; even the Jonathan Marines did not always use good judgment.

*   *   *   *   *   *   *   *   *

Paltier steadied Bonney and walked him to the binnacle. Sweet, straightening his disheveled uniform, was making his way aft. Forward, several Liberian women clustered about something or someone on the deck. No matter, Talliaferro dismissed the scene, there were more important issues for him to address.

"Soundings?" he demanded as Sweet limped into the group.

"Fathom-and-half to two, mud bottom, forward, Sir. Not got one for the portside as yet. Little accident. Damned near lost Dan'l."

" When y'all planning to have it?" Talliaferro snapped.

Sweet bristled at Talliaferro's dismissal of Daniel's plight. "Thoms getting it now," Sweet hesitated just a fraction before adding, "Sir."

Talliaferro overlooked Sweet's hostility. "All right. Schooner is free. Other one is no help, ass-backwards for the roadstead. We are poked in the mud by a tolerable current. *Bainbridge* with enough firepower to blow us all to Jesse is due any minute."

"*Sweetie!*" Delcina shouldered her way into the group of officers.

"Awh, *Hell*," moaned Talliaferro.

"Dan'l be bad hurt. Best fetch him to land. He needs go doctorman, *one time.*"

Sweet saw the blood on her hands and dress. She was right, he knew, but how? Sweet sighed and started to explain that in this current a boat would never make the pull to the McGill landing even manned by half the crew.

"*You not be friend to Dan'l.*" She pushed her young copper face an inch from Sweet's. "My father treat *Bush Nigger* better, than you treat Dan'l!"

Not from what he had seen of Justice Draper's attitude toward tribal people, thought Sweet. "*Damn it,* Cina! I love him like a brother; just not able to get him ashore."

"Lie! You say *LIE!*" she shrieked. "Make boatman's carry. You no good sailormans. You dumb same as *Bush Nigger*. Boatman's carry, easy to do."

"What is this?" demanded Paltier. "'Boatman's carry?' What do you mean, Girl?"

240

"*Aahyeee!*" Delcina wailed. "*Buckra* brains like Carey Rock," she demonstrated by pointing toward the few boulders, all of Carey Island that remained above water. "Watch!" she ordered.

She skipped to the taffrail and seated herself upon it sidesaddle, holding her hands beside her head like a girl grasping the ropes of a swing. "Be rope here." Right hand extended above her head, she made a long chopping motion fore and aft. "Rope same here." Bouncing on the rail she added, "Dan'l, here him be." She leapt down to the deck and scampered to the ship's rail facing the McGill Factory. "Man pull boatman's carry to Monrovia for doctorman." She faced them, hands on her hips.

"*Boatswain's chair,*" exhaled Sweet. "They must rig a boatswain's chair from McGill's to the landing."

Graceful as a hanging turkey, Bonney reflected, but it avoided tolerable amounts of mud. His brogans had a definite reddish hue from his trek to McGills' the preceding day.

"Well, Missie," Paltier joined in, "it is a meritorious suggestion, but no boat can carry a line to the opposite shore, even given sufficient line to rig the affair."

"Shoot the son-of-a-bitch."

All eyes snapped to the latest speaker, Sergeant Banning.

He eyed Delcina with some uncertainty that instantly resolved into action. Casually saluting her, he added, "Pardon for the expression, Missie."

"Whom?" demanded Paltier.

Banning came to attention as the Lieutenant spoke. He was a damned Pommey, but an officer of Pommey *Marines*. "The line, Sir, certain I'm thinking. Put something in that damned great gun there," he inclined his head toward the long-nine, "with line to it and shoot the damned thing to the nig … err, to the buggers on the bluff."

"You only *buckra* be smart on this boat," Delcina smiled at Banning.

"Thankee, Missie," he responded.

God in Heaven, thought Talliaferro, between the enlisted Mick and the darkie girl they have solved our problem. "*Congratulations* you two," he verbalized. "Mr. Sweet. Crew that gun. Load and secure something, a rammer, a bar, a spar … something with light line, and get it to McGills', through the wall, you must, to get their attention." Turning to the rest he added, "They got anybody ashore can read signals?"

"Better, Mr. Talliaferro," Paltier spoke up. "*Tourch* certainly can understand signals and is close along shore to land a rigging party. This suggestion has promise indeed."

"Not just Dan'l, gentlemen," responded Talliaferro. "'Big enough lever and I can move the world.' We rig the right line and blocks and we can pull this black-hulled adventuress out of the mud."

241

CHAPTER THIRTY-ONE

While Paltier supervised the signalmen requesting assistance from *Tourch,* Sweet loaded the long nine 32-pounder with a half charge, several layers of rope-mat wadding, and an iron spacer bar with light line to the ring at one end. In theory, the line would play out from a coil by the weapon's muzzle and accompany the bar on its flight. When the Royal Navy rigging party was in position north of McGills', Talliaferro ordered the line shot. The gun belched whistling the bar and line across the river like a harpoon. Bonney marked its strike just under the brow of the bluff, the line parting and recoiling down the bank. One of the British sailors secured the rope just before it was sucked into the river.

"Bravo!" erupted Paltier. "Jack Tar's not as clumsy ashore as I suspected."

"Mr. Sweet, make to *Tourch,* 'Well Done. Obliged,'" ordered Talliaferro.

Sweet was surprised to receive a response of substance. "My Pleasure. Brig topsails nor'-nor'west-by-north." *Bainbridge,* northward reach completed, was coming down wind toward Montserado Roads. An hour, two at the most, Sweet calculated, before *Ebony Angel* would be bottled-up in the shallow narrows of the Montserado River.

It would take considerable time to complete rigging the lines to extract *Angel* from the mud. For a second Sweet thought it was hopeless. He looked around in despair. Banning had abandoned his hard-earned dignity as a Sergeant of Marines and was hauling on a rope like an Ordinary Seaman. Peck had lowered himself over the stern to hurry threading the hawser through the block on the sternpost.

Thoms looked up from splicing more hawser onto the line that would go back to the shore and announced, "Bugger them *Bainbridge* lubbers; we *Jamestownes!*"

If the hands had not lost faith, how dare he as an officer give in. "Damned right, Thoms!" Sweet shouted. "Now make certain that splice'll hold!"

*   *   *   *   *   *   *   *   *   *

Talliaferro nodded as Sweet reported all weight possible had been shifted aft. He gazed absently at the dismounted carronade lashed above the transom, then toward McGills'. The two large double blocks had been rigged with heavy cable, the outboard one pulled across to the bluff and secured Heaven only knew how by British riggers. He leaned over the stern looking down at the other block lashed to the sternpost, the great upward thrusting extension of the keel, the ship's spine. The rigging would not fail at *Angel's* end without shivering the ship like a barrel.

The landward end of the cable was secured to the eyebolt on the block ashore. From there it ran through the block at *Angel's* stern, twice more back and forth through the block ashore and the block on the ship, finally back through a hawsehole in the ship's stern and along the berth deck to the capstan forward of the mainmast. The arrangement reduced the pull necessary to extricate the ship to twenty-five percent of direct effort. Talliaferro hoped that it was enough. All hands were at the capstan bars on the weather and berth decks, save the officers, petty officers, and Daniel, not as *in extremis* as Delcina first thought, but still woozy.

Talliaferro ordered Peck to take up the hawser on the capstan messengers.

"Aye, Sir," Peck replied and bellowed, "Bring her in, Lads!" He and Thoms began to sing:

In the Virginia lowlands I was born,

The men at the capstan bars answered:

Low lands, low-lands, away, my John.
I worked all day down in the corn,
My d – ol-lar and a half a day.
I packed my bag and I'm gone a - way;
Low - lands, lowlands, a - way, my John.

"Sing *John Brown's Body*, if it pluck us out," Talliaferro said to no one in particular.

I'll make my way to Mobile Bay.
My dollar and a half a day.
In Mobile Bay, where they work all day,
Lowlands, lowlands, away, my John,
A-screwing cotton by the day,
My dollar and a half a day,

"Coming taut," reported Sweet from the transom.

Five dollars a day is a White man's pay,
Lowlands, lowlands, away, my John,
A dollar a day is a Nigra's pay,
Lowlands, lowlands, away, my John!

244

The singing died as they met full resistance. Necks bulged beneath scarlet faces as men strained into the capstan bars. Peck finally ordered, "Belay!"

Wordlessly, Bonney shed his sword belt and frockcoat and stepped to the capstan. Paltier nodded approval and followed. Sweet, Talliaferro, and Daniel copied the movement. Talliaferro, however, peremptorily ordered the dazed servant from the bars. While his head wound had stopped its copious bleeding and much prodding and pressing established that his skull was intact, Daniel clearly was too wobbly to man a bar.

Delcina watched the vignette and turned to her three servant girls. "You help, *one time!*" she commanded leaving Daniel's side to take a place at the capstan. Coquettishly, the three maids hurried to join their mistress at playing sailor.

"When they have their breath back, Mr. Peck," commanded Talliaferro.

"Aye, Sir." The Boatswain paused, inhaled deeply, and bellowed out:

Sal – ly Brown was a gay old la – dy

The hands chorused:

Way –ay, roll and go!

Peck responded:

Oh, Sal – ly Brown was a Cre – ole la – dy,

He was answered by the chorus:

Way –ay, roll and go!

The chantey died as the straining men and women met solid resistance. Necks bulged, faces flushed, and feet slipped on the decking, all to no avail.

"*Bloody* bother!" gasped Paltier. "Steamer would have us off in jig-time."

Talliaferro called his officers to him and said, "Not for certain more muscle be a help. Suction holding her. Need to wiggle her some."

"My father bring plenty *Bush Nigger*," volunteered Delcina.

"Thank you, Miss Drap … err … Mrs. Sweet," Talliaferro responded with laudable self-restraint. "Have to be smart swimmers to reach us."

"Pass a cable to the *Seniore* on the schooner, Sir," suggested Sweet, "perhaps they could pull the stern round enough to break the suck."

"Or pull them off and be banging against us again," replied Talliaferro. "I doubt they are as smart riggers as the Brits; not much savvy in them rigging something ashore."

Paltier's raised voice cut into the discussion. "*Tourch* has steam winches and all that. If she got a line over the cables at midstream and did a bit of tautening – relaxing, might it not break the hold of the mud?"

"Worth trying," mused Talliaferro. "But take more than flag coordinating, I fancy."

"No bother, 'Captain'," responded Paltier cavalierly. "Let us work the details and I shall go ashore by boatswain's chair to coordinate with Commander Parker."

"If she is still stubborn, *Tourch* might pull on the cable as well," added Bonney.

"I can request a chair from the rigging party at McGill's, Sir," volunteered Sweet.

Talliaferro looked about at the taut hawser, the rushing river, the willing but stymied crew, and the industrial outline of the British gunboat, and ordered, "Make it so."

*　　*　　*　　*　　*　　*　　*　　*　　*　　*

From the forecastle of *H.M.S. Tourch*, Lieutenant Ryder reported "All Ready," to Commander Parker standing upon the catwalk between the paddleboxes. Parker had watched with amusement the usually dignified person of Lieutenant Paltier gyrating unpredictably as the rigging party jerkily pulled the boatswain's chair to the bluff. Parker wondered if those daguerreotype chaps could record such a thing? Ashore, Paltier had barged through the mass of Liberians gleefully celebrating his arrival and hurried aboard *Tourch*. Parker had made a rapid assessment. Whatever her legal status, *Ebony Angel* was a ship in distress entitled to assistance. He had to admit that the idea had merit, despite coming from a barely grown Jonathan and a lieutenant of Bootnecks. Utilizing the boatswain's chair, riggers had secured a hawser from *Tourch's* machinery over the cables between *Angel* and the bluff.

Now, on Parker's order, *Tourch's* steam windlass commenced turning, bowing the tackle, straining *Angel's* stern away from Kroo Point. "Ease," commanded Parker and the pressure lessened as the winch reversed. "Haul," and the hawser came taught again. He caused the process to be repeated at least a dozen times.

On *Angel,* Talliaferro prayed fervently for the stresses to break the suction holding his ship. He felt the strain, noted the creaking timbers, but no sudden release, no increased buoyancy. The change was too subtle for that. The alternating pressures worked the bow enough to create a channel for the surging river water where the mud contacted the hull's copper sheathing. As *Tourch* strained and relaxed her pressure upon the cable, the channel widened, deepened, broiling water hollowing a space between hull and earth insufficient to break Africa's hold, but weakening her grip.

Concerned, Parker noted the thunderheads forming inland; evening Rains gathering to dump more water, swelling the river's force against *Angel's* hull, blinding communication between the two vessels. If it were to be it had to be now, he decided and ordered his signal midshipman to make to *Angel*, "Shall haul you off."

On *Angel*, Talliaferro ordered Sweet to acknowledge and through Peck prepared his crew. The report of a distant gun followed by an answering shot from the Liberian battery at the river's mouth froze his heart; *U.S.S. Bainbridge* had arrived. Talliaferro needed no glass to see *Tourch's* stern slowly swing out into the river. She had been tied bow upstream, and now was going astern out into the current steering with her paddlewheels. The hawser Parker had run from his vessel to the bluff and spliced onto the last length of hawser running to *Angel*, was losing its slack. Forward by the main hatch, Peck looked expectantly at Talliaferro. Talliaferro held his breath as he watched the cable draw taut.

"Execute! Sir," announced Sweet.

The "Sir," was drowned by Talliaferro's bellow, "*NOW!*" that Peck repeated.

On the berth deck, Samson swung the great wooden maul driving the wedge from the capstan pawl, slacking the cable between the capstan and the block on the bluff. That, however, was the only section of the parallel hawser lengths to relax. The others tensed as the pull changed from the muscle-powered capstan to the steam-powered winch and paddlewheels of the gunboat.

Sweet balled his fists. Bonney held his breath as he trained his field glasses on Parker, then on *Tourch's* winch. Delcina prayed for *Angel* to be plucked from the mud as God had plucked Daniel from the lions and fervently rubbed the serpent ring to excite its good *juju*. Daniel, forgetting his throbbing head, watched mesmerized as the hawser took the strain. Talliaferro, unmindful of his clenched jaw, strove to determine what would give first and what immediate response would be required. He thought he sensed a tremor under his shoes, but nothing happened to confirm what he so ardently hoped for. *Again!* Had the deck dropped a bit? *Again! YES!* There was a slight up and down movement. *Angel* was coming alive, inching back from the mud, beginning to stir. *Tourch* was gathering sternway. With a geometrically increasing velocity the ex-slave ship moved toward the center of the river, deeper water. Her bows, freed from the land, swung downstream, yet she moved astern as the great wheels of *Tourch* churned the water and the iron drum of the winch turned upon its gears.

"Anchor Party!" Talliaferro ordered.

Peck and several seamen rushed forward, positioning themselves to let go the starboard anchor, the "small bower." *Angel's* movement stern-first across the river put her in a posture that would swing her in an arc to the west if her head were secured and the pressure on the hawser released. She would present her bows to the river flow and the debris churning along in it.

With a sound like hail, the great drops of The Rains began to hammer the decks. Both Parker and Talliaferro knew that they had just moments before losing visibility between their vessels. At least *Angel* was well afloat in the rising river.

"Let go, Mr. Peck," hailed Talliaferro. As the anchor splashed into the broiling brown torrent, he turned to Sweet. "'Execute.'"

"Aye, Sir, 'Execute'," the midshipman replied with a nod to his signalman.

Across the water Talliaferro saw the forward surge of *Tourch's* port paddlewheel die and a great thrashing astern commence. Parker was taking his vessel forward, easing the tension on the cable. "'Thank you and God Bless,' Mr. Sweet."

Sweet acknowledged and called for the appropriate flags. The solid wall of rain was speedily obscuring the gunboat, the bluff, and the river mouth. Sweet caught wavering movement atop the bluff as onlookers fled the deluge. *Angel* swung rapidly, aligning herself with the current. He watched as the great block, freed from the *Angel's* stern, bounced across the river's surface in response to *Tourch's* winch. The Brits could keep all the cable and blocks, an embarrassingly small price for deliverance.

"Ready, sir," announced the signalman. Sweet ordered the flags aloft, dubious that *Tourch* could read them. Looking toward the gunboat, he spotted some flapping bit of red and white down river above the outline of a ship's boat, white-hulled, pulling to the Liberian battery. The flag left no doubt; *Bainbridge* was across the river's mouth.

CHAPTER THIRTY-TWO

"Ship's no more Liberian than I am," snapped Lieutenant-in-Command Winkler of *U.S.S. Bainbridge*. Wearing Baston's best dressing gown, he toweled vigorously at his shoulder-length hair. The probable ruin of his uniform had him in a foul mood. The shoes definitely were all-in, saturated and packed with the pasty red mud of the path – he would not honor it with the appellation "road" – that he had followed from the Liberian battery uphill through the shanties of Thompson Town to reach Baston's consulate.

"As I was observing, Lieutenant," replied Baston, "purported disposition by Liberian courts has no legality, whether or not she was taken by American naval officers."

"Who?" demanded Winkler, excavating at his left ear with a twisted towel corner.

"Marine lieutenant Bonney and two midshipmen, Talliaferro and Sweet. Parted from *Jamestown* at Sierra Leone."

"Parted? *Balderdash!*" snapped Winkler, his ear forgotten. "*Jamestown* rejoined the Squadron sometime back. Trueman charged them and two dozen sailors and Marines, with mutiny, treason, and desertion." Winkler paced excitedly. "By the Powers, I'll have them for hanging." Turning, he demanded, "Aboard the slaver now?"

"Why," the Consul hesitated, "I assume so; certainly so."

A strong gust beat rain against the windows. Winkler searched through the water-distorted glass for *Angel*. Sweet was a snotty at the Academy when he was on staff, Winkler mused aloud. Talliaferro was a North Carolina hothead from Wilmington just up the Cape Fear River from the South Carolina border and tainted with the same strong secessionist prejudices as their southern neighbor. He was not acquainted with Bonney, but Marines would not tolerate mutiny, let alone by an officer, he assured the consul. By Billy, he fantasized with glee, if he acted quickly, take them and overhaul the Squadron, Inman could hang the lot at sea, no politics and clemency then.

Baston abjured mentioning the political chaos produced by a similar drumhead court martial some years earlier on *U.S.S. Somers*, *Bainbridge's* sister ship. Instead, he cautioned, he could see doing nothing quickly. The ship flew Liberian colors. A Liberian shore battery was between the brig and *Angel*. She was owned by an unknown combination of what had to be some of the most powerful men in the country. Winkler also should know that President Benson's niece, daughter of the Chief Justice, was married to an American person of color, Daniel Sweet, servant of one of the midshipmen. Baston enjoyed taking some swagger out of his guest.

"'Person of color,'" Winkler said, sneering. "Damned slave."

"For a certainty?" Baston's eyes narrowed.

"Certainly; 'Daniel', Sweet's Nigra at Annapolis. Had to stay on my toes to keep him from doing all that little FFV's work preparing for inspections."

"Interesting," beamed the Consul, "These Liberians are a snobbish bunch. Not likely to accept a slave into the family, especially if hoodwinked into it."

"Do say," responded Winkler. "They all came from slaves."

"Certainly, Sir, but the closer one is to something, the more one must differentiate."

"So what is our course, Mr. Consul? You supposedly know these minstrel majesties."

"I must give it thought, Lieutenant. In the event, we can do naught until the storm passes and your uniform is renewed."

*   *   *   *   *   *   *   *   *   *

It poured all night under spectacular celestial pyrotechnics and rolling barrages of thunder. The storm lifted slightly before nine that morning, Monday, the 15ᵗʰ of July 1861. Through the Consul's telescope Winkler got his first good look at *Ebony Angel*. She was a serious threat, speed etched in her every inch. She could chase down the proud clippers carrying America's most valuable cargos and evade naval vessels, except in a light wind when steam would give the advantage to men-of-war so equipped.

After a knock and pause, Baston entered, followed by an African girl with a tray and an African youth with towels and razors. The Consul thought the Lieutenant-in-Command might enjoy coffee and a shave from Noah, the houseboy, while Baston sent for their audience with President Benson. Winkler's uniform, renewed as best it could be by his host's staff, would be up directly and, Baston added mentally, the pushy sailor could get out of his best dressing gown.

Winkler forced a smile, mumbling something about the thoughtfulness of his host, while concealing his thoughts; he would decide when he would shave, drat it. Rather vain about his firm jaw and high cheekbones, Winkler wore only a mustache not wishing to deny the rest of the world the chance to share in his enthusiasm. Extremely careful about who put a sharp edge against his fine visage, he examined Noah. The boy seemed steady, competent to wield the razor and Baston was clean-shaven without scars. The steaming towels on the tray would be relaxing and the Yardley's in the small bottle bracing afterward. He accepted the offer. Tilted back in Baston's desk chair, he missed Bonney and Sweet come dangling ashore to meet the Drapers at the President's House.

*   *   *   *   *   *   *   *   *   *

"Honorable Mr. Baston, American Consul at Liberia, and Lieutenant 'Winker' of American ship '*Bandage*'," resonated the major domo.

Winkler tugged at his coat and, Baston on his right, stepped through the doors of the receiving hall into the state chamber. To his surprise, the gathering consisted of nearly as many White men as Liberians.

President Benson greeted the Americans by name, stepping forward two paces, then waited for the newcomers to make the longer march. Saying he is boss man from the get-go, Bonney observed. Benson was forewarned; Draper had consulted his brother-in-law.

What a pleasure it was for the Consul and the Lieutenant-in-Command to be there, Benson observed, half-turning toward his original group. He assumed they were acquainted with The Honorable Mr. Roberts. Roberts and the two Americans exchanged bows. And The Honorable Chief Justice Draper; The Honorable Mr. Parkins, Minister of Interior; and Mr. Urias McGill, President of the Liberian Packet Company. More bows and expressions of pleasure at the acquaintance were exchanged. Benson began deftly leading the newcomers toward an assemblage of uniformed Whites: Commander Parker, RN - more bows and mutterings - Lieutenant Paltier, Royal Marines - again the courteous formalities. Now the dicey bit, Benson thought.

"You must know …" he began.

Winkler cut him short. "I know these men, Sir; who and *what* they are."

"Yes, Your Excellency, we all are acquainted," Baston interrupted.

Talliaferro and Bonney held Winkler in defiant stares. "'Men,'" Talliaferro greeted, blatantly suppressing any hint of the "gentle" prefix.

Peremptorily Winkler demanded to know where, "that spoiled little Charlie Sweet … and his *slave*, Daniel," were. Talliaferro replied with saccharine smoothness that Sweet was standing watch aboard *Ebony Angel* to insure no dishonorable rascal took advantage of Talliaferro's absence to try to seize the ship. Mockingly Bonney wondered who would do that? Benson chuckled inwardly. Perhaps, the *buckras* would go at each other immediately, avoiding any need for diplomacy.

Winkler had stomached enough of the insolence. As senior officer present, he ordered Talliaferro and Bonney, along with Sweet and any and all United States Navy or Marine personnel in their company to report aboard *Bainbridge* immediately. Bonney icily refused, extending a handful of envelopes to Winkler, resignations of every officer, sailor and Marine Trueman had "marooned" in Freetown. Bonney knew full well that the "resignations" of the enlisted men were meaningless under Rocks and Shoals, but made the gesture with the thought that it might provide an argument in some third nation's courts and the knowledge that it would irritate Winkler.

"You have not heard, Bonney," Winkler retorted triumphantly, "April 23rd a Board held all so-called resignations worthless. Some senior officers were dismissed the Service. Others are in custody for their foolishness, *and* their treason. You are under arrest, both of you. I order you to accompany me to *Bainbridge*."

"Being a spot hasty, Lef'tenant, what?" Paltier interrupted the Americans.

Winkler pivoted. "This affair is no concern of yours, Sir."

"Not so, my good man," replied Paltier through a mirthless smile, stepping to within six inches of the Lieutenant-in-Command.

Winkler bristled with all the primeval indicators of animal hostility: shallow breath, red face, forward stance. "These men are *mutineers, deserters* and *traitors*! And, by Gad, Lieutenant, I do not need any assistance from the British in deciding their fate!"

"You, Sir, are a *liar* ..." Paltier paused for effect, "or terribly misinformed," he concluded deliberately.

Winkler's face drained pale. "Lieutenant-in-Command Elias Trueman of *U.S.S. Jamestown*, commanding these *persons*," Winkler snapped, "has reported fully and charged them with instigating mutiny, desertion, and treason." Winkler paused; then growled, "And you, Sir, shall retract that most insulting remark!"

"Oh," responded Paltier with a mirthless chuckle, "Lef'tenant Trueman is an *incorrigible liar*, as you, a man of *supposed* minimal intelligence, must know." Paltier shook his head with mock sadness. "Thus, Sir, either you are such a *fool* as not to recognize the obvious, or I must judge you a *liar* as well."

"By *GOD*, Sir," Winkler bellowed, "You insult me, my colleagues, and my country!"

"Quite," Paltier agreed. "Issue remains, have you the bezants to do aught about it?"

Winkler understood; every seafarer knew the "three Bezants Or," the three gold balls of the pawnbroker's sign. Furiously, he struck Paltier an openhanded blow, Paltier's muttonchop side-whiskers muffling the slap.

"Lef'tenant Bonney," Paltier spoke calmly, "would you be so kind as to second me?"

"With the greatest of pleasure, Lieutenant Paltier," responded the Marylander. He felt the excited rush a challenge always gave him. "Yours, Lieutenant Winkler?"

"Baston?" Winkler questioned the Consul.

"Oh ..." the politician-diplomat stammered, "It...." He caught Winkler's tone. It was not a request, but an order. "Yes ... Yes, of course," Baston's voice died away.

"We are all gentlemen of the sea, affairs in order, with no time to waste," announced Paltier, supposedly to Bonney, but in a voice that carried beyond the double doors into the hall. "Tomorrow dawn, if no objection. *Epees;* there is a pair in my kit."

With that Paltier stepped back a couple of paces and Bonney moved forward to face Baston. "As you must have heard, Sir, the choice of weapons has been made, *epees*." Controlling a cold contempt at Baston's large-pupiled consternation, Bonney continued, "'Waste not a moment' is a saying of the Royal Navy, that I subscribe, Mr. Baston. Dawn tomorrow should be convenient for all?"

Baston realized that a response was expected. "Ah … I … But.…"

"Say 'Yes', damn it," Winkler snapped.

"*Yes!*" exhaled Baston. "Yes. Agreed."

"Given our usual morning rains, this season," all eyes shifted from the tense group to Former President Roberts, "might I suggest the contest be here, in this room; providing President Benson agrees?"

"Certain," responded the head of state.

"Here, then. Six of-the-clock agreeable?" Bonney spoke to Baston in a flat voice.

"Ah … Oh.…" the Consul stammered.

"*YES*, for God's sake," Winkler answered for his second in evident exasperation.

"Yes," parroted Baston.

"As a matter of form, Sir," Bonney addressed Winkler through Baston, "I must inquire if your principal wishes to withdraw his challenge and admit the truth of the statements."

"*HELL No!*" came Winkler's instant bellow.

Silence held for a moment. "Again, as a matter of form, you should inquire if my principal wishes to retract his statement, Sir," Bonney prodded.

"Ah.…"

"Don't bother," instructed Winkler.

"He does not compass doing so, in any case," added Bonney.

"Not so hasty, Mr. Bonney." It was Commander Parker of *H.M.S. Tourch.* "Before you cut Lef'tenant Paltier's cables, I am obliged to emphasize to all present that he acts *solely* in an individual capacity and not as a representative of Her Majesty or of the Royal Navy or the Royal Marines in any form whatsoever." Parker's eyes swung across the crowd, fixing each man in turn. "Secondly, Lef'tenant Paltier, as your compatriot and one who has great respect for you, both professionally and personally, I am obliged to remind you that dueling has been specifically prohibited within the Navy. To proceed with this inauspicious chain of events indubitably will produce a negative impact upon your professional standing. As your senior, I caution you, Sir."

"I thank you, Commander Parker," Paltier addressed his superior with a slight bow. "Regretfully, there is little that could further degrade my prospects, but I am honoured by your sentiments." Paltier looked across the assemblage. "I most earnestly confirm the Commander's statement that I am acting in a purely personal capacity and not as a representative of my Queen or of my Service." He looked directly at Winkler. "I reiterate that Lef'tenants Winkler and Trueman of the United States Navy are *liars* and *knaves* and I anticipate with the deepest pleasure proving so in the morning."

The principals glared at each other until Baston broke the spell. "Mr. President, we requested an audience to discuss the American ship, *Ebony Angel* that at this moment is anchored...."

"Yes, Mr. Baston," interrupted President Benson. "I am aware of your desire to discuss the Liberian Packet Company's ship, but time for such is past." His Excellency extracted an open-faced timepiece from his waistcoat. "Cabinet meeting directly, most here must attend. Perhaps another day, say Thursday, would suit?"

"But Mr. President," pleaded Baston, "the unsettled status of *Ebony Angel* combined with the unsafe conditions of the river and the presence of the United States Brig-of-War *Bainbridge,* all conspire to produce a most dangerous situation that threatens the peace of Liberia and her relations with The United States."

"That case, Consul, best you send away that warship," Benson responded with a tone of warm helpfulness. "Must thank y'all for coming and turn to matters of state." The President gestured to include all foreigners in his dismissal.

"Thank you, Your Excellency," responded Commander Parker as the second senior foreigner present, while Baston, the most senior, stood dumbly staring into space.

CHAPTER THIRTY-THREE

Shaded from The noonday sun by the canvas awning rigged above *Angel's* poop, Bonney puffed heavily urging the humid tobacco to respond to the smallish flame. Daniel and Doe stood by the transom willing the cigar to light. Daniel sighed. Doe had been all thumbs lighting the friction match and had blurted, "*Eeeeeheee, Devils!*" at the first ignition. To make Doe any account, he realized, would be a long row to hoe. Still, Daniel had to admit, the tribal youth had made amazing changes since yesterday morning. Daniel's thoughts wondered back over the previous day:

> While clothing Doe after his combat with Delcina and her maids, Daniel had recounted how Bonney goaded young McGill into a wager, first trying for Doe's freedom, then so that Daniel could shoot Doe's bonds. He did not mention his own contribution to the plot. A slow smile had spread over the blue-black features, expanded into a grin, then a laugh. "*Aahhee, Bo*! Make fools them McGill *swanga bucks.*"
>
> After the incident with the recoiling hawser, Doe had been reflective, then determined. Upon Bonney's return from the President's House, Doe had approached him, knelt, and placed the Marine's hands upon his tightly curled scalp. "I work for you this time, all time. You be *close my stomach* all time. You go trip, I go same. You *done-live*, I die that day. You *dash* me life; my life I give you, *one time*, all time. *Enty!*" Doe remained kneeling holding Bonney's hands to his scalp.
>
> "Doe want to be your Nigra, Marse Clave," Daniel had volunteered. "You in his heart for always. Y'all go traveling, he go too. You die, he die. Says y'all gave him his life and now he give it to you for always."
>
> Bonney had protested, denied, and ordered Doe away, all to no avail. Doe stubbornly clung to Bonney's hand pressing it into his coiled mat of hair and repeating his protestations of fealty. Finally the embarrassed Lieutenant agreed to place Doe on a form of probation under Daniel's tutelage, confident that Doe would reassess his obligations and welcome being put ashore if they ever got free of Monrovia.
>
> That had been at five bells of the forenoon watch, 10:30 a.m. Half-an-hour later, the officers had settled to dinner that Daniel had served with the "assistance" of

Doe. At least the savage had not spilled anything on anybody, Daniel recalled with a mental sigh. He was a fairly quick study in clearing and cleaning, probably done some before when at McGills. Daniel had let him sample the mutton and pudding, but had denied Doe's request to finish the wine. Bad business, liquor, Daniel knew; one road to perdition he would block for Doe.

"At last," mumbled Bonney around his cigar as a yellow flame flared at its end, then subsided to a red-embered glow. To Daniel it sounded more like, "A' lass," as Bonney tried to annunciate with the cigar in his teeth.

Back from his reverie, Daniel gave Doe a slight pressure on the elbow and nodded to the splinter of kindling. Doe stepped forward, took the fire from Bonney, and passed it to Paltier, patiently waiting to ignite his cigar.

"Good choice," observed Bonney after removing his smoke from his mouth. "Winkler does not appear to have done much with *epee's*."

"But is one helluva pistol shot," announced Sweet stepping past the skylight. "Not bad with the sword, either."

"Well, you should know," answered Bonney, while Paltier merely nodded his greeting, continuing to puff on the stubborn cigar. "Smoke?" offered Bonney.

"Thanks no, Sir; new plug." Sweet shifted a bump of tobacco inside his left cheek.

"Finally," muttered Paltier as his cigar caught. As Doe, at Daniel's direction, took the kindling and tossed it over the side, Sweet observed that Winkler always had been a bit of a dandy, but able to back it up. Paltier pursed his lips in thought.

"Really not have to fight our battles, you know," Bonney admonished Paltier, who removed the cigar and demanded to know if Bonney were attempting to make this an affair of honor? "*Hell....*" Bonney checked himself, joining Paltier's laughter. "Just not wanting you Brits thinking we are unable to mind ourselves." His comment amused Sweet; he believed that Bonney had exactly that problem.

"As I said above," Paltier gestured toward the bluff, "a purely personal matter." Momentarily interrupted as Talliaferro joined them, Paltier explained that there were two reasons to personalize the affair. The Briton had delivered the letters of resignation to Trueman and had seen him pitch them unopened onto the deck. That Paltier found insulting. Secondly, he was in a rush to return to Great Britain and *Angel* seemed his fastest way home. He would not have that arrogant Winkler delay him. Paltier looked in turn at the three Americans, three friends he realized. Surely, he asked them, they must understand that he was obliged to forestall any protracted legal questioning as to the status of the vessel or her officers and simply had taken the obvious course? He resumed puffing his cigar, admitting to himself that he really could not explain the impulse that had propelled him to challenge Winkler. The probable truth was, he simply had developed an instant, intense dislike for the arrogant cad.

"Why the all-fired hurry to get to England?" Talliaferro ended Paltier's reflections.

"Longish tale of sordid family history, I am afraid, 'Captain,'" responded Paltier. "I'm Irish, you know, Anglo-Irish." Talliaferro apologized, having no intent to pry and no understanding of how Paltier being Anglo-Irish explained anything. "But enough of my concerns, Gentlemen," Paltier changed the subject. "Best attend to exiting this great mud slew," as he phrased the Montserado River, "and passing that troublesome little gun-brig."

Talliaferro welcomed any ideas. Sweet expectorated into the river before suggesting a dramatic dash close alongside *Bainbridge*, dismasting her with the aft pivot, their solitary gun of any significance. Talliaferro looked dismissive, Bonney amused, and Paltier respectful of brash youth. Gently for the circumstances, the Briton questioned their ability to achieve the requisite surprise, while admiring the dash and all that. His supposition, he declared, was that the Jonathan, or rather, the *Yankee* would be aware of their movements before *Angel's* bows were turned seaward. Further, they needed to consider the problems of territorial waters, the flag they flew, the presence of the Royal Navy, and the pickle they could place their Liberian friends in, were "their" ship to initiate hostilities.

Would Commander Parker put to sea with *Angel*, Talliaferro asked? Sweet's face brightened with a new idea. Great Britain and France were co-guarantors of Liberian sovereignty along with the United States. If *Bainbridge* took action in Liberian waters, the Brits would be bound to intervene.

Paltier questioned what would happen beyond the one-mile limit. Sweet's face fell as Bonney observed that he could not see the Royal Navy going at it with the United States in the circumstances. From Her Majesty's perspective, it certainly was a passel more involvement than Lord Palmerstone's Government would appreciate. It came down to a boat race. Talliaferro cautioned them not to be all that confident. *Angel* had hit the mud and done who knew what to herself. Full sail might produce some bitter surprises.

If they exercised the purchase option, raised the Southern flag, and demanded the Liberians enforce neutrality, would they keep *Bainbridge* in port for twenty-four hours after *Angel* sailed, Sweet wondered?

"Were I Winkler," Paltier paused, "or whoever commands the brig after tomorrow dawn, I doubt that those ancient rusting relics the Liberians have the audacity to address as a shore battery would deter me from sailing from an open roadstead."

257

"I do not think Liberia recognizes the South as a belligerent," observed Bonney. Thus, all the British concerns for the niceties of neutrality did not exist at Monrovia.

There followed two minutes of smoking and chewing in a silence that seemed to last two hours. At least, Bonney observed, Sweet accepted the observations of shortcomings in his suggestions as discussion and not personal insults. Maybe the boy was maturing? Slowly Bonney became aware that Paltier was humming and gave him a quizzical look. Incrementally, Talliaferro and Sweet joined the audience. Conscience of their united attention, Paltier broke into song:

> If I should swim along side of the Spanish enemy,
> And sink her in the Lowland, Lowland, Low,
> Sink her in the Lowland Sea?

"What if you would?" asked Bonney.

> Why, I should give you silver
> And I should give you gold,
> And my own fairest daughter,
> Your bonny bride to be,
> If you should swim along side of the Spanish enemy
> And sink her in the Lowland, Lowland, Low,
> Sink her in the Lowland Sea.

Paltier stopped. "Elizabethan chantey. In the end the cad sails off and leaves the cabin boy to drown after, 'with his brace and auger, in her side he bored holes three.' Not the proudest moment of British nautical tradition, ashamed to admit."

"One powerful swimmer to get down this river," observed Sweet.

"No go river," Doe interjected. His presumptuous interruption shocked Daniel; servants were not participants in masters' conversations.

"What?" Bonney turned to Doe.

"Go swim from beach," responded the tribesman. "I swim to boat, certain."

"Y'all understand what we talking about here, Doe?" interrogated Talliaferro. "Swimming out to the Yankee brig and doing something to her under the water?"

"Can do," replied Doe matter-o-factly.

"Doe did make it here from Carey Rocks," observed Bonney. "Y'all swim a lot?"

"All-time swim," Doe responded with pride. "How I get free from Monrovia one time, two time. This be three time." Doe was smiling roundly.

Daniel could not stay silent. "What he going to do; drill a passel of holes in the old *Bainbridge*? Not hardly! *Bush Nigger* probably not even know how to drill no holes." *My Dan'l is not about to be shown up by any tribesman*, Sweet concluded.

"Point well taken, Daniel," observed Paltier. Turning to the officers, he continued, "I trust you Americans sheath your hulls with copper? We have, I believe, from around the time of your innovations in colonial administration, 1780 say, if not before?"

"Sometimes, Paltier, y'all's sense of humor gets tiresome," Bonney drawled in exaggerated imitation of Talliaferro.

"Ahh, since you recognize it as humour, there is hope for amity and understanding."

"Not drill holes, exactly," mused Sweet. "Sir," he continued addressing Talliaferro. "If *Bainbridge* lost her steering, *Angel* could dance away under plain sail."

The brig's steering was all internal responded Talliaferro. They would have to board her to get at it, and even then it was not all that demanding to repair.

"Rudder ain't so easy to fix," observed Daniel, thinking that if that tribal savage was part of this council of war, so was he.

"Rudder?" asked Doe in puzzlement.

Rudder!" replied Daniel. "Don't you know from nothing, Boy?" Doe still looked blank. "Steering oar," Daniel went on, motioning as if manipulating a canoe paddle and turning his front in response to the imaginary alterations of paddle angle in the water.

"*Aaaayeeee*," Doe trilled as his face beamed with understanding. "Go there; go here," he expressed mimicking Daniel's pantomime.

"Ain't dumb as you let on, Boy," Daniel half-complimented.

"You not so smart you make to be, *Bo*," replied Doe. His smile was too much for Daniel. The Virginian grinned back.

Sweet and Bonney struggled to avoid joining in as they watched their servants edge toward mutual respect. The two had best become compatible, Bonney reflected, or life could be miserable for all four of them in the confines of a ship.

Talliaferro ended his daydreaming, demanding details of *Bainbridge's* rudder. Sweet summarized the facts from memory: She was sister ship to *Somers*. There was a scale model of the latter at Annapolis. Sweet shut his eyes in a squint. Four, yes four hinges held the rudder. No top or bottom pivots. Pinned? Yes, pins through hinge tongues on the rudder and tongues to the sternpost.

"Play Jesse pulling those pins," Talliaferro mused envisioning the corrosion of the iron fittings.

"Like to just blast the dern thing off her," Sweet snapped in frustration.

259

"Or tear, rather," Paltier drawled. "I have a thought."

CHAPTER THIRTY-FOUR

Doe swam upward until his head broke the surface of Montserado Roads. Through the sheets of rain he impatiently sought his bearings. The river current had taken him somewhat to the northwest. He adjusted his heading for the starboard side of *Bainbridge*, faintly identified by her riding lights some distance in front of him; it was impossible to make any accurate assessment in the pelting rain. Daniel surfaced nearby. The Virginian thought it ridiculous to be swimming under water this far from the brig; in this downpour no one would see them. Still, that was how Marse Clave wanted it. Bonney's head appeared between them. He barely could see his two companions in the beating rain. The Marine nodded and Doe submerged, heading again for the brig.

The light line connecting the three by their waists was no impediment. Daniel and Bonney, however, were slowed by the bag of trapped cocoanuts floating a couple of feet below the surface supporting a collection of tools dangling like jellyfish tendrils. He thanked Heaven that the Liberian schooner released from *Angel's* port side had anchored two cable's lengths, some 480 yards, from *Bainbridge*. She provided an excellent staging platform for their hasty preparations that afternoon. Shielded from observers by her hull, the swimmers had experimented with the buoyancy of the cocoanut float, amassed tools required for Paltier's plan, and significantly reduced their swimming distance to the brig.

Once more they surfaced. Daniel could hear the rain hammering *Bainbridge's* deck. Bonney thought of his sentries on *Angel* the night Doe came aboard. All the watch would hear, sheltering as best they could on the flush deck, was the drumming rain. Daniel had to give Doe his due, downright unnatural how he found his way in this storm. Doe took his bearings and submerged again.

The outward rise of the brig's stern protected them from observation as they surfaced against her hull. Sheltered from the rain, they conversed in hoarse whispers, trying to be heard over its hammering. Daniel and Doe rested easily holding to the rudder for the little support needed in the salt water. Bonney cautioned them not to let the float bump the brig's side, then he submerged again. Squinting at Doe, Daniel felt a grudging respect for the African. There was more ability in this savage than Cina and her family and friends let on. Hoarsely he complimented Doe upon leading them to the brig. Doe nodded.

Suddenly Bonney's head bobbed up beside them. He tapped Doe on the shoulder and motioned him to follow as he dived again. Moving down along the angled rudder, feeling the way, Bonney maneuvered Doe into position beside the second of the great hinges. The massive pin was secured by a nut and cotter on its lower end. Bonney had a hacksaw in his hand that was still connected by a line to the submerged float. He placed the teeth on the pin and began the slow process of sawing against the resistance of the metal and the surrounding water. Doe nodded his understanding and took up the job. Bonney seized another saw from the dangling tool collection and went to summon Daniel. In short order, all three were sawing at the cotters on the three submerged hinge pins.

Progress was slow, as they had to surface for breath every several strokes. Doe's pin was the first to give way and he triumphantly extracted it from its hole. His reward was to have Bonney leave his own sawing and assign the African to Daniel's job on the pin second from the bottom. Doe's budding resentment vanished when Bonney immediately put Daniel to drilling a hole in the toe of the rudder halfway between the third and fourth hinges. Daniel was right; Doe had to admit, he had never used a brace and auger.

After Doe and Bonney finished with the remaining pins, the Marine retrieved a pair of large wrenches from the dangling collection of implements. With Doe's assistance he fitted one to the enormous nut. The other gripped a flattened surface on the hinge pin just above the nut. Through the outboard jaws of the wrenches Bonney attached the opposing hooks of a "come-along," a pulling device employing the principles of the lever in its handle, the block and tackle in its rigging, and the capstan palls in its brake. Bracing his feet against the rudder, Bonney strained at the handle until he thought his lungs would burst, but felt no give in the adhesion of the nut to the pin. Suddenly, Doe was beside him adding his strength. Bonney thought he heard the crack as the rust gave way. He had to reposition the wrenches several times, but at last the nut dropped between their feet to settle forever in the mud of the roadstead, two to go.

They had to rest twice before three of the four nuts were all deposited in the coastal mud. Next came removal of the pins. The constant movement of the rudder had prevented them rusting to the hinges. Using a selection of dowels from a bag kept below the cocoanuts by the weight of some tools, Bonney drove the lower three pins up from below to follow the nuts to the bottom. Only the top pin, exposed above the water, remained.

While Doe and Bonney worked on the pins, Daniel finished his boring and rigged a pulley to the hole by a short length of chain. Through the pulley he passed the line from the schooner that had trailed behind the swimmers.

Bonney's limbs were leaden, his energy slipping away. The others must be tiring as well. Focus on the mission, the job at hand, he reminded himself. All three bobbed in silence and inaction for an uncertain time before Bonney handed the end of the line to Doe. "Back to Mr. Sweet."

*   *   *   *   *   *   *   *   *   *

Sweet had thrown himself into his duties to drive away his guilt. He was not the best of swimmers and, of the two officers engaged in the operation, was the more knowledgeable about rigging. Thus, his natural lot was to handle operations on the schooner. Regardless, he was embarrassed at staying in such safety, while Bonney and their two servants risk themselves in the shadow of the enemy. *The enemy!* He was aghast that he could think of a *United States Ship* in such terms.

At Sweet's direction, the schooner had all three of her anchors deployed, connected to each other by heavy chain and to one end of a hawser most of which was still coiled in the schooner's hold. The massive rope seemed stout enough, but Sweet still wished he had some of the steel rope just coming into use at sea.

"Be swim man, *enty,*" announced one of the Krumen huddled beneath the awning. Sweet saw nothing in the wall of rain and leaping ocean. Another Kru suddenly stepped through the entryport and down the cleats, bent, and grasped a fawn-palmed hand. Breathing heavily, a weak-kneed Doe was pulled aboard.

He stumbled forward and supported himself against the mainmast, chest heaving. Two Krumen helped him free himself from the line about his waist. They swiftly dropped from sight through the main hatch. Forward, under more awnings, men manned the capstan. The two with the line re-emerged hauling after them the free end of the hawser that had been worked into a great loop, a rope eye. They secured it to the line Doe brought from the brig. "Be ready, *Seniore,*" reported the Portuguese-speaking Master. Sweet nodded. The Master gave an order. The hands lowered the end of the cable into the water and started the first twenty yards over the side as the capstan pawl began to click. The hawser with its single eye put Sweet in mind of a great hemp snake as it disappeared into the rain and swell toward *Bainbridge.*

*   *   *   *   *   *   *   *   *   *

Exhausted from his time in the water, Bonney felt so light-headed that he thought he might trip over his sodden feet climbing the few steps of the Liberian President's House. Behind him Corporal Dyer carried a long box draped in an oilskin. In front Lieutenant Paltier was entering the foyer and unclipping his boat cloak. Water poured from all three as they handed sodden capes to the unusually quiet servants. The entire house exuded a heavy sense of expectancy, the impression that it and all within were holding their breath in anticipation of drama, of danger, of death.

The major domo, obviously on duty at an unaccustomed hour, advised that Winkler's party was yet to arrive, motioned them into the President's Parlor, and offered coffee. Bonney nodded in gratitude. Paltier said nothing as he entered the room. Settling onto one of the horsehair sofas, he finally asked Dyer for the bag. Dyer passed a carpetbag to the Briton.

263

Paltier removed his sodden shoes, extracted a rolled pair of white cotton knee breeches, and, standing, removed his dripping trousers. With what Dyer thought was extreme care, the Briton toweled his wet legs and donned the archaic garment. He sat, as carefully dried his feet, and replaced his footwear with stockings and fencing slippers. He spent extra time on the lacings. "One quarter in the hand, three-quarters in the footwork, Corporal," he volunteered.

"Aye, Sir. Thank you, Sir," responded Dyer as if caught eavesdropping.

"The weapons, Clave," Paltier suggested to the exhausted Bonney.

The box was of highly polished rosewood, over three feet long by eight inches deep and 18 inches wide. In his stupor, Bonney did not examine the silver escutcheon centered on the lid. The case had the aura of lovingly preserved antiquity; the Marylander felt a sense of receiving a holy relic. He opened the two latches and lifted the lid. Bonney's pulse quickened; before him were a matched set of *epee's*, the French dueling sword, descendant of the rapier, tapered triangular blades on hilts shaped to fit the hand protected by large hemispheric bell guards. Resting in supporting puzzles of blood red velvet-covered bracing, they sparkled in the lamplight, romantically entrancing like the swaying dance of the cobra.

"My maternal grandfather's," Paltier said softly. "Bit of a wild goose."

A knock followed by the slowly opening door announced the coffee's arrival. As the waiter left, Bonney heard subdued conversation in the foyer; the challenger had arrived.

Paltier was lying upon the sofa, eyes shut. "Not asleep, Clave; just contemplating the fate of man."

Suddenly Paltier sprang from the couch and began flexing his knees, then moved into a lunge, springing slightly upon the vertical plane. Holding an imaginary blade he executed several advances, retreats, and lunges; then imaginary parries, reposts, and beats. Turning to Bonney, he suggested, "Best inquire of the other side, Clave. God forbid they think us reticent."

*   *   *   *   *   *   *   *   *   *

The challenger already had taken position at the far side of the Salon. The assemblage shocked Bonney; half of the anybody-who's-anybodies of Monrovia were present, even if it were just short of six in the morning: the Drapers, including their eldest daughter and her spouse and their third daughter on the arm of that young McGill; the Roberts; the Parkins; of course the Bensons; a host of McGills; and others. Glaringly absent were the Manley tribe and any of the liberals. Cynically, Bonney imagined them thinking, "What fun; we are going to see a *buckra* die."

Dyer placed the sword case upon a table centered and to one side of the length of the room. Bonney walked to it as Winkler said something to Baston, who nodded and scurried to meet the Marine Lieutenant. For the slightest instant, Bonney felt sympathy for Winkler who must be frustrated to tears by his incompetent second. Dyer open the lid as the two seconds stood before the table. They continued to stand.

"You first, as we had choice of weapon type, you get choice of individual weapon of that type," Bonney let his voice trail off, as the Consul stood mesmerized before the blades. "Baston, you hear me?"

God, Baston thought, how did he ever get embroiled in this barbaric idiocy? With a momentary flash of anger he wished both fools would kill each other. Aloud he said, "Oh … Certainly. Why, yes…." He looked at Dyer. "I'll take that one," he said pointing.

"Very well, Mr. Baston, pick it up," urged Bonney.

"Oh … I…." Sweet Jesus, Baston thought as his knees seemed to vibrate, I cannot touch the bestial thing! "Could he hand it to me?" he concluded.

"*Pick it up*! You're his second; have the gumption to touch the darned thing!" Bonney urged.

Cowed, the Consul reached into the case and gripped the sword by the hilt and slightly more than halfway up the blade. As he lifted it from the box, a slight trickle of crimson ran between the fingers of his left hand to fall upon the velvet lining.

"Leastwise, you don't shirk from testing the edge, Mr. Baston," chuckled Bonney.

Baston, shocked, released the blade. "*Christ*! I have lacerated myself!" he gasped as the point bounced upon the floor.

Paltier snapped his gaze toward the sound. Fool will ruin the point, he thought, but checked any comment. Winkler had an expression of absolute disgust. Bonney helped the diplomat raise the sword point toward the ceiling. "Give it to Winkler; then put your handkerchief around your hand," Bonney whispered. Baston nodded and stepped woodenly toward his principal.

Armed, the protagonists moved to the center of the chamber and faced each other. Unusual for a party's second, Bonney assumed control of the situation in the absence of another considered qualified and willing to conduct the contest. He announced that at first blood he would halt the proceedings and determine the desires of the parties and their abilities to continue. There was no objection or question. "Ready, Gentlemen?" Both nodded. "*En guarde!*"

For a moment neither moved. They simply stood in the *en guarde* position: knees bent with each foot directly below its respective shoulder giving the ability to spring backward or explode forward by simply tensing the leg muscles; torsos turned; heads facing the opponent over right

265

shoulders; right arms advanced with elbow flexed ending in a yard of tapering steel. Slightly overlapping points made small unpredictable circles.

Paltier made a sudden short beat on Winkler's blade. The American instantly retreated one pace, letting his blade move with the force of the beat to circle under Paltier's coming back on line in its original position. He knows something, Paltier thought.

Paltier sensed Winkler gather himself; slight recoil of the arm, flexing of the back leg signaled his intention. Winkler executed the attack well. Unannounced by any prior foot motion, his right hand propelled the blade forward with the first of a pair of sharp beats against Paltier's *epee* intended to knock it aside enabling the sailor to get "inside" the Marine's defense for a scoring thrust on his chest. Paltier, anticipating the attack, without conscious thought revolved his wrist clockwise, so that Winkler's second beat found only air and Paltier's blade came up over the American's forearm threatening his chest. Winkler had committed to his lunge. His momentum carried him forward, his blade passing "outside" behind Paltier's back.

Paltier did not retreat, but countered with a short half-step advance, rotating his sword upward until at its zenith he laid a razor edge against the right side of Winkler's head. As Paltier pirouetted around Winkler, circling to face his opponent from the other side of the room, Bonney was aware of something falling to the floor. Winkler recovered himself in the reversal of field and came to *en guarde.* Suddenly Paltier dropped his point to the floor and did a shortened advance. Winkler instinctively retreated. Bonney was as shocked as Winkler to see the top half of the Naval officer's right ear skewered on the tip of Paltier's rising blade.

As Bonney announced, "*Reste,*" Winkler erupted with the most ancient of Anglo-Saxon expletives, launching himself upon Paltier. The blind rage gave force to his attack, but the Royal Marine easily parried the heavy lunges, Winkler's point ringing bell-like as several times it was turned by the guard of Paltier's *epee'.* "Damn it! *HALT!*" bellowed Bonney without effect. Exhaustion of breath finally stalled Winkler's charge. "To the center. Blood is drawn. Are you satisfied, Sir?" Bonney questioned Winkler.

"Hell *NO!*"

"Pity. All your daguerreotypes must be from the *left* side," goaded Paltier.

"*BASTARD!*" Winkler unleashing a storm of beats and thrusts upon the Briton.

Paltier had to be light on his feet and exceptionally quick of hand to counter the attack. He gave ground for four or five lengths until Winkler's breathing slackened his assault. Paltier immediately countered with a series of beats and advances, sending the pair back to the east end of the room. Again Winkler came on forcing Paltier to retire. At one point, Winkler beat Paltier's blade and followed with a thrust that was too fast for the Briton to circle and deflect. A red line appeared along Paltier's right bicep.

266

"*Reste!*" commanded Bonney. "Second blood. Are you satisfied, Lieutenant Winkler?" Bonney controlled a grimace at the blood running down Winkler's neck from the mutilated ear, soaking the right shoulder and side of his shirt.

"Ear for an ear! *NO!*"

"*En guarde!*" ordered Bonney unnecessarily as Winkler attacked.

He is better than I imagined, thought Paltier, tactics, my boy. Paltier began a pattern, two beats right-to-left against Winkler's blade, followed by disengagement under and around to the outside. He did it twice. Each time Winkler raised his weapon in time to parry the movement. Paltier then varied his approach, but returned to the beat-beat-disengage several times. He could sense Winkler becoming familiar, anticipating it.

Winkler initiated a series of beats, then an attempt to maintain contact while circling Paltier's blade in the hope of loosening it in the Briton's grasp. At the end of Winkler's attack, Paltier again went into the familiar beat-beat. Starting a lunge, he disengaged below the American's blade, but instead of continuing to circle it to the outside in an attempt to reach Winkler over the top of his weapon, Paltier snapped back his hand almost to his right shoulder. Winkler's parry to the outside met nothing but air as his point passed short of the Englishman's near vertical blade. Paltier's blade flashed forward and down, digging into Winkler's face just below the left cheekbone laying open a gash slightly over an inch wide extending nearly to his jaw. As he recovered from the lunge, Paltier drew his blade along Winkler's head causing a flap of skin to hang dripping from his clean-shaven chin.

"Rather seems you've 'turned the other cheek' not won 'an ear for an ear,' what?"

Bonney called "*Reste.*"

Winkler dropped the point of his weapon and put his left hand to his bleeding face. Baston was in shock, jaw hanging, eyes bulging. "Mr. Baston," hailed Bonney. "Will you not concede for your principal? I doubt he should continue."

Baston seemed to awaken. "Ah … Yes…. Certainly, yes, I agree. This must stop!"

"*FUCK YOU!*" bellowed Winkler eliciting a shocked gasp from the assemblage.

"I am fully satisfied," announced Paltier dropping his sword point. Winkler would be incapacitated for several days. The change of command aboard *Bainbridge* would inevitably cause some confusion and reduce her as a threat to *Angel*. "I've no desire to dissect the Lef'tenant." He said and turned toward the sword case.

Without a sound Winkler lurched forward leveling his blade at Paltier's back. Instinctively, Bonney sprang to intercept. Winkler sensed the movement and parried whatever was coming from his right, the point of his weapon rising in defense. It caught Bonney under his right collarbone, penetrating the flesh as if it were air, striking against the shoulder blade, deflecting toward his spine, but exiting before reaching it.

Bonney felt no pain, just a strange pulling sensation as if he had been thrust through with a large sewing needle. His momentum carried him forward onto the blade, his head lowering toward Winkler and the floor. As he stumbled, he was aware of a blue pole coming over his right side connecting loudly with Winkler's devastated face, a soggy noise surrounding a muffled crack. He hit the floor and rolled onto his left side the pain building as the blade quivered in his right shoulder. At least Winkler had released it, was not trying to rip it from the wound. Bonney realized why as Winkler fell heavily to the floor near him, his nose flattened across his face.

Above him, Corporal Dyer, legs spread and fists clenched, shouted, "Fuck *You*, Sir."

CHAPTER THIRTY-FIVE

Much to his own surprise, Bonney remained conscious as Dyer and Paltier tenderly carried him to the northeast corner of the hall. They left the blade sticking through him; its removal would have produced a great rush of blood. He felt little pain. The *epee'* was so sharp, he reasoned, the cuts were so fine as to be minimally insulting to the nerves. He admitted to himself that he had absolutely no basis for such an opinion; what the Hell, his body and he'd hold any opinion he liked.

Was he losing consciousness or merely coherent thought? Dyer was pulling chairs together, making a narrow and, from appearances, none too comfortable couch. Cannot use the parlors, Bonney decided groggily, not to bleed on the fine furniture. Whoa, he responded to being lifted, traveling again. Numerous arms raised him to Dyer's improvised operating table. No, he thought foggily, it should be made of sea chests, officers' sea chests; at sea operating tables always had been, why change now? "Out it go," he heard a Liberian say, but it was distant, fuzzy. Suddenly there was pain, great pain. He was falling, down, down.... Bonney passed into unconsciousness.

*   *   *   *   *   *   *   *   *   *

To staunch the blood, the Liberian doctor packed the wound with a bit of cloth; then wrapped it in a figure-eight bandage. It was nine o'clock before the weather cleared sufficiently to transport Bonney to the boatswain's chair, rig a sling, and slowly lower him to *Ebony Angel*. Doe, although exhausted by his night in the water, had attached himself limpet-like to Bonney and refused to be relieved, even by Delcina. Much to his own surprise, Daniel intervened on Doe's behalf. To his even greater surprise, Delcina casually conceded the matter and worked harmoniously with the tribesman.

Now, Daniel was on the periphery of a conference among Talliaferro, Sweet, and Paltier. Bonney's fate seemed inevitable, death from infection, gangrene. There was no surgeon aboard. The penetration wound was the vicious three-cornered type, unlikely to close. He had lost significant blood. They could not remain in Monrovia, not that the unhealthy climate and ministrations of a questionable doctor promised much benefit. Talliaferro shifted from Bonney's plight to the larger situation. They had missed the morning tide, but would leave on the ebb about four bell of the afternoon watch. The 'Captain' asked Mr. Paltier to see if Commander Parker would accompany them down river with *Tourch*. All silently assumed that Bonney would be buried at sea.

Daniel had not realized how attached he had become to Bonney. He recalled Bonney's attempts to guide Sweet away from trouble, the way the

Marine Lieutenant had championed his marriage (he had been eavesdropping during that conversation as he so often did), how Bonney had acted to save Doe…. Daniel felt an instant of consternation. "You *done live,* I die that day," Doe had sworn to Bonney. Crazy *Bush Nigger* might just do it, too, Daniel thought with alarm. Slowly he moved behind Doe who was kneeling by Bonney's bunk and rested his hand on the African's shoulder. Doe looked up, sensed the empathy, and slowly rose to follow Daniel to the far corner of the captain's cabin.

"Marse Charles and them others say ain't much hope, Doe. Just want y'all to know, so not make you go to sunders, he die." Panic sparked in Doe's eyes. "Ain't your fault…."

"Whyfore, say *make-a-die?*" Doe demanded defiantly.

" Infections and such." Daniel was certain this savage had no idea of such things.

"'Fection? 'Fection no *make-a-die,* certain. Who say such?"

"Drat, Boy, everybody know that. Maybe we get lucky and he get laudable puss draining, and maybe Marse Paltier or someone can bleed him or such."

"Bleeded plenty. Not to make him bleed more," Doe snarled. He looked quizzically at Daniel. "For American *buck,* you no savvy much you think." Daniel let it pass. "I go land, *small time,*" Doe announced.

"What you mean 'go *small time,*' Doe? About three-and-half hours, whole ship going down river, *one time.* Ain't got time, even y'all get past them Liberians this time."

"Go," responded Doe, starting for the ladder.

"Damn," muttered Daniel. "Wait-up. I go just to get y'all back. Just best hurry, *one time,* Doe, hear?"

*   *   *   *   *   *   *   *   *   *

Winkler fidgeted, writhed. The combination of pains, especially from his broken nose, drove him to continuous motion fruitlessly seeking some position of relative comfort. More agitating, he admitted, was the memory of how that damned Brit had played with him, teased him, humiliated him in front of all those damned Africans and those two traitors, Bonney and the enlisted man, Dyer. *Dyer!* He would hang that bastard if it took his entire life to catch him, he resolved. *They had ruined his face!* Then, he recalled, that clumsy darkie doctor had bound him up like some bale of cotton and sent him off with this cowardly idiot Baston, who kept driveling about eradicating dueling. Hell of a lot of good that would do! His face was ruined, might get infected, kill him. His only hope, he decided, was to have that lummox of a surgeon's mate clean and stitch the wounds. Stitch! Christ, he knew that the sail maker could do a better job, but the earlier the better, because the less drunk the surgeon's mate would be.

270

"Enough of this," he snapped at Baston through his bandages. "I'm to the ship."

*   *   *   *   *   *   *   *   *   *

Doe leading, his face hidden by a so'wester hat, they moved with purpose past the McGills' Factory and along the main street to Lower Spring Field southeast of Monrovia's street grid. Marching directly across the large cultivated portion, Doe plunged into the bush. Here the land sloped up into a steep hill, a forward outrider of the Montserado Mountains that paralleled the coast between ocean and river.

They progressed steadily uphill. With sympathetic condescension Daniel watched the African search rapidly among the brush, grasses, and scrub trees, then pounce upon some unseen item, (animal, vegetable or mineral, Daniel knew not), and secure it in a bit of cloth or a mustard bottle. Glancing at the sun Daniel figured it was noon, or later.

"Best be going, Doe, *one time*."

"*Soffle, soffle*," Doe replied, concentrating upon sliding mold into a bottle.

"*NOW*, Boy," snapped Daniel seizing Doe's arm.

Suddenly, Daniel was flat on his back; unaware of how he got there. "Say *soffle*," Doe said levelly, kneeling beside him. Daniel let Doe finish collecting.

"Now to ship, *one time*," Doe announced.

"So *go*," Daniel responded and began striding toward the town.

They moved as quickly as they could without drawing excessive attention, as quickly as they could in the humidity of the mid-day break in The Rains. They passed the Executive Mansion, Daniel's thoughts of his wedding, Doe's of his master's wounding. Rounding the McGills' Factory they beheld *Angel* tugging on her anchor as if impatient to depart … and collided with Nat McGill.

Had Daniel had time to think about it, he could not have decided whether Nat or Doe was the more surprised as they thumped together. As Doe's so'wester fell off, Nat's eyes bulged in disbelief. "*Ahyeee*," he wailed, "he the *Bush Nigger!*"

They were only fifty feet from the boatswain's chair and safety. Doe shoved Nat away and dashed for the conveyance. The commotion confused the British sailors assigned to operate it. Understandably, they blocked the fugitive's path. In an instant numerous McGill retainers rushed from the factory, surrounded Doe, and viscously pinned him to the ground. Nat ordered them to take Doe inside and in a moment he was gone.

Daniel stood open-mouthed aware that any protest of his would be useless. Out of the mud he lifted Doe's seabag with the strange collection of plants, molds and insects supposedly able to heal Bonney. With the despair of

271

defeat, he realized that he had no inkling how to use the remedies. Doe had *done-lived* this time, he was certain.

"What was all that about?" asked a bearded British boatswain's mate.

Daniel looked at the sailor with dull eyes. There was no point explaining to him; there was nothing he could do. Daniel dejectedly asked to be returned to *Angel*.

*   *   *   *   *   *   *   *   *   *

Barely an hour after Winkler's departure, Pa Manley, Minister of Trade of the Republic of Liberia, stood in the window of Baston's office looking angrily down upon *Ebony Angel* and *H.M.S. Tourch*. The American Counsel stood just behind his right shoulder sharing both the view and the angry expression of his guest. Ostensibly, Manley had come to coordinate the anti-slaving operations of *Lively Quail* with the Americans. Both he and Baston wished *Quail* had not been dispatched northward the day before *Angel's* arrival. Perhaps she could have assisted in Manley's true purpose, ensuring *U.S.S. Bainbridge* remained capable of apprehending *Angel*.

"Be one good pirate, that boat," Manley observed. "Pa Lincoln not want such boat after Americans, *enty*." He did not care a whit about U.S. merchantmen, but knew that letting *Angel* loose upon Yankee commerce was the last responsibility Baston wanted.

"Damned British had stayed clear, she'd still be stuck in the mud," Baston whined peevishly. "They *want* her after our commerce."

"So must stop her leaving out from Liberia," Manley replied.

"You were not that effective, your first try." Baston could not resist expressing his frustration at the long wait before Manley's agents parted the cables that lowered *Angel* from the camel slings two days before.

"We done work good," Munro Manley swiftly answered the Consul. "Just British boat there to help, is all." He looked at Baston either with resentment or contempt, the diplomat could not tell which, before the minister added, "This time Britishers not to be able to help that boat." With that introduction, Munro put forth a plan that took Baston's breath away with its simple audacity. Yet it just might work, given the aversion these Liberians had to finishing off their opponents within their closed little society. And the price was outrageous, but manageable; one thousand dollars and support of the U.S. Navy in some future action by Manley's anti-slaving force. And, unlike Draper, Manley would take a draft upon the Merchants' and Seamen's Bank of Mystic, Connecticut.

*   *   *   *   *   *   *   *   *   *

"Where-all you been?" demanded Delcina as Daniel slouched to Bonney's bunk in a corner of the captain's cabin.

He explained. Her reaction was immediate and deafening. How could he let that Nat McGill take hold of Doe? Why, She bellowed, Nat was no more than an overgrown *pickan* and Daniel should be ashamed! He held out the seabag of purported remedies. Did he think she was some damned *Bush Nigger*, Delcina demanded? She had no idea what *juju* Doe was planning to use on Bonney. That sack of muck and weeds did no good without that savage! Nat probably had killed Doe already! Why....

"*Silence!*" Sweet thundered. Delcina froze, mouth open, as the midshipman pushed between the spouses. On the bunk Bonney stirred and moaned some incoherent syllables.

Charles experienced a surge of grief at the thought of Bonney dead. For the first time he recognized how much he relished resisting Bonney's guidance, but it wasn't just some game, it was much more complex. Bonney had been like an external conscience, checking his more impetuous tendencies, enabling him to express, even act-out his frustrations, but limiting the excesses toward which Sweet knew he was inclined. Ever since that first dinner at Government House, Charles had known he owed Bonney a debt, both for acting as he did and to compensate for some of the caddish ways Sweet had responded. "Debt of Honor still owin', set heavy on the soul," Uncle James, Daniel's father, used to say, and with Bonney dead Sweet knew his soul would be heavily burdened. This might well be his last opportunity to settle matters with Bonney; it might even be too late. "Come with me," he sternly ordered Daniel and Delcina.

As the boatswain's chair swayed and jerked its way to the bluff, Sweet studied the crowd – mob really – forming around the McGill Factory. Doe's tortured demise promised to be even better entertainment than the possible departure of *Ebony Angel*. He scanned the crowd for one face in particular, but did not see her. Impatiently he leapt from the chair and urged the British sailors to send it back for Daniel and Delcina as swiftly as possible. Daniel understood the hurry, for he held his wife on his lap so that they would come across in one trip. Before the chair had stopped Sweet was bellowing at Delcina to find her sister.

"Which," she demanded of the frenzied American?

Sweet realized she did not know of his intimacy with Freedoma. "Doma," he snapped. "Nat will listen to her." He hoped that he had read Nat's feelings correctly when young McGill presented him with his watch and Daniel with the Whitworth rifle.

Delcina nodded and was gone. Taller than Sweet, Daniel could see her pushing through the crowd to disappear into the Factory. It took them much longer to convince the press of Liberians to let them through, but finally they were headed up the stairs to the veranda. At the top they spotted Delcina in heated discussion with her sister.

"Y'all got your *buck*," Freedoma snapped at Delcina as the Virginians approached, "don't you be spoilin' me gettin' mine!" Delcina said something unintelligible and Doma spat back, "I don't give a flip! Damned *buckra* not nothin' to me!"

Sweet gripped Freedoma's arm and spun her around so that he was between her and her sister. "Listen careful, Doma," he growled. "Less you want Nat and everybody besides hearin' me tell how you been whorin' for a *buckra*, you best get Nat to put Doe on that ship *one time!*"

Grimacing at the pain of his hold, she triumphantly challenged, "So? Don't make no-never-mind to Nat, I been with a pencil-dick *buckra* like you, Sweetie."

"That has the French pox?" Sweet demanded viscously.

Her eyes bulged in horror. There was plenty of venereal disease in Monrovia, but none of her circle would willingly seek exposure. She wilted with dismay.

"I don't have it, Silly," Sweet relented, "But sure as Judgment I'll say I do, yell it to the rooftops, you don't get Nat to turn loose of Doe, *one time!*"

She concentrated hatred in her look, but nodded and wrenched her arm free. Purposefully, she began to push through the press of people around Nat and his captive. Delcina gave Sweet a questioning look. They could barely see Doma speaking to Nat and of course could hear nothing in the din. He seemed to be adamantly refusing, then objecting, and finally agreeing with her, though as to what they had no clue.

Freedoma slithered back through the crowd, her face one large pout. "Be at that boatman's chair *one time*," she instructed Sweet.

Nat already was moving with Doe toward the stairs. Charles had no time to question her for details if he were to make it to the chair before them. Without a word he pushed and writhed through the Africans until he was at the boatswain's chair. No one seemed to notice him. All eyes were fixed upon Nat brutally dragging the bound and bleeding Doe down the stairs and out onto the path to the river. Suddenly they were ahead of the mob, no longer ringed by Nat's supporters. Nat stopped, jerked Does head close to his face, snarled something into his ear, and gave the tribesman a vicious shove. Doe stumbled, caught his balance, and made a dash for the chair.

Doe's dash took the British sailors by surprise as much as it did the Liberians. Without interference Sweet caught Doe by the waist and tossed him into the chair, his back toward the river. Sweet seized the cable and swung up onto the seat so that he was sitting on Doe's lap facing the bloodied, wild-eyed face. Sweet ripped his dirk from its sheath and slashed the line from the seat to the hand winch that pulled the chair up to the bluff. The chair began an uncontrolled descent down the steep incline from the cliff to *Angel*. Doe was grinning madly through the blood, mud, and sweat covering his battered face. They both began to laugh uncontrollably; relief, success, *victory*.

"Shite!" Banning snapped as he watched the overloaded chair accelerate. The lower end of the chair's cable ran over the ship's bow at an angle and attached to *Angel's* foremast. The uncontrolled descent would slam Sweet and Doe into the mast with the force of a fall from the masthead. They had not escaped, but committed suicide. "Orrin, Schmidt, quick as ye can!" He motioned them to take up clue lines for the jib. "Haul Away!"

As the chair hurtled toward the ship the three Marines feverishly hauled up the jib. Rising spasmodically, its hypotenuse pressed against the chair cable curving it up and bowing it out from the straight line to the mast. Sweet must realize the danger Banning concluded, for the midshipman was holding his feet out straight to absorb the impact, not that it would make a difference. The jib was far from fully deployed, but it was open enough to catch the chair as it hurtled across *Angel's* bow. In a cloud of canvas Sweet and Doe thumped into the mast and spilled from the chair to land in a cushion of sailcloth.

Sweet was still disentangling himself when Doe bolted for the hatch. Charles floundered after him brushing aside Talliaferro and Banning. After a moment's disorientation at descending the forward hatch, Doe got his bearings and dashed aft to the captain's cabin. Through the one eye that had not swollen shut, he saw his seabag, seized it and rushed to Bonney's side. Suddenly, caring for Bonney, he was calm as a nursing mother.

Talliaferro was not. "Where you been, Mr. Sweet? What in Sam Hill is this all about?" Not waiting for a reply, he bellowed, "We'll miss this tide, too, you don't quit your shilly-shallying!"

"Doe and Dan'l...." Sweet stalled in mid-sentence, realizing for the first time that his dirk stroke had marooned Daniel and Delcina in Monrovia. "Sir," he exploded, "Dan'l and Delcina are still ashore!" His voice was tense with immediacy. "We must retrieve them!"

"*God's wounds, Sweet!*" Talliaferro irrupted. "Your damned darkies cost us one tide; be damned to hinges if they'll do the same again!"

Sweet made to protest, but a feverish groan from the bunk silenced him. "Must leave, Charles. Dan'l understand...."

"Probably be a Liberian admiral, time we get back," Talliaferro added. "Now get under...."

"*NO!*" Sweet screamed.

"Where's your sense, your loyalty?" croaked Bonney, trying to rise onto his elbows.

"Must leave afore brig *make-a-go* and find rudder trick," Doe added trying to support Bonney both physically and argumentatively.

"*Bainbridge* finds that hawser to her rudder, we'll never get away," added Talliaferro more calmly.

"Well, Charles," Bonney rasped with labored breath, "your crew and country or your colored couple?"

Sweet balled his fists as tears welled in his eyes. "Patriotism and fidelity?" Patriotism versus fidelity, more like, he thought bitterly. Daniel would die for him without thought or hesitation, Charles knew. Now he was about to abandon him without a thought or explanation. It was shameful, despicable ... and *unavoidable!* Through gritted teeth he growled, "Underway! Aye-aye, Sir," and pushed past Talliaferro toward the ladder.

"Boy's growin' a pace, Clave," Talliaferro observed. "Don't you dare die on him; he needs you for some time yet."

Bonney released a long sigh and collapsed against Doe. He was too exhausted to give voice to his intended response, "Balderdash!"

*   *   *   *   *   *   *   *   *   *

On the cliff, Daniel and Delcina went limp with relief at the successful escape. Then Daniel swore foully. Without a means of winching the chair back to the bluff, they could not return to *Angel.* A white shot of steam surged upward between the twin stacks on *Tourch.* All on the bluff jumped as the gunboat's great brass whistle gave a long and two short blasts. "Right, Lads. We're for it," bellowed a British boatswain's mate. His party rapidly dismantled the rigging of the boatswain's chair, grabbed their gear, and began to lope toward *Tourch.* Below them *Angel* rushed stern-first with the current, small figures quickly circling the capstan taking-up the slack of the aft anchor cable. Suddenly the line went rigid, *Angel* began to swing. Accelerating by the second, she pivoted upon her stern until she pointed toward the river mouth, the sea.

"We doin' the same," snapped Daniel to his wife and they scrambled after the British Tars.

No one paid them any mind until they reached the gunboat. At her brow, a petty officer barred their way. "Sorry lad, no need for more woolies at present."

"We from *Angel*" gasped Daniel.

"Look the Devil to me," persisted the sailor.

Delcina did not debate. She simply hiked her skirts to her waist and vaulted to the holly-stoned deck.

"*Right!*" stammered the petty officer in embarrassed confusion at Delcina's obvious distain for undergarments. "Stand where you are, Girl," he added stepping toward her. Behind him, Daniel leapt aboard as the gunboat paid-off into the stream. "Now behave, *kaffir,*" the petty officer commanded, turning to face him.

"Steady, all." They turned to confront Lieutenant Ryder, First Lieutenant of *H.M.S. Tourch.* "Problem?" he demanded.

"Not as can't be made right, Sir. Couple darkies trying for free passage is all, Sir."

"More to it, Dockering. They're daughter and son-in-law to the Chief Justice of Liberia." Ryder smiled, "Welcome to Her Majesty's Gunboat *Tourch*, Mr. and Mrs. ... Sweet is it not?"

Daniel relaxed, tried to breathe normally. "Yes, Sir," he said adding after the slightest pause, "of the Nansemond County Sweets of Virginia, Sir."

*　　*　　*　　*　　*　　*　　*　　*　　*　　*

Angel was moving at the speed of the river, not answering her helm. Talliaferro tried to keep her in the deeper water along the Thompson Town bank. Thank Heaven the stream was so high in flood. He glanced at *Tourch,* swinging into the stream, paddlewheels churning the muddy Montserado. He shared the late Captain Pennington's aesthetic preference for sail, but maneuvering that way definitely had advantages.

"Deck, there!" It was Thoms from the foretop. Talliaferro could see the signal rocket streaking skyward from the American Consulate. *Bainbridge,* your fox is breaking cover. Now we shall see if those Liberian anchors hold, Talliaferro reflected.

He was surprised by the flurry of activity at the Liberian battery on Ashmun Point. A bugler was blowing an insistent call, gunners swarmed about their guns, and up the flagstaff rose a holiday flag so large that the pole barely kept it from brushing the parapets. Lord, Talliaferro thought, first a band and flower girls, now a formal salute; these Liberians ever tire of celebrating? He turned his attention to more serious matters, getting downriver without sufficient steerageway and fickle winds. The jarring report of a large artillery piece came as no surprise as they passed the battery, but the rhythmic whooshing of chain-shot passing overhead caused his heart to skip. That was no salute, he realized; the bastards were trying to dismast *Angel!*

As the Liberian shot whirred by, Sweet did not recognize the peculiar sound of the two half-cannonballs connected by a length of chain designed specifically to destroy a ship's masts and rigging; he had only seen the archaic round in static displays at the Academy. But he did realize that the battery was firing live ammunition at his ship. He grabbed the watch telescope from beside the binnacle and sprang to the port rail. Smoke obscured the gun that had fired, but he easily caught the reflection from the uniform brass of a figure hurrying toward the next weapon downstream in the battery. He had a chevron on his right cuff; it was Cadet Corporal Munro Manley waving his arms, giving orders to the gun crew. The second weapon discharged and another whooshing projectile spun across *Angel's* path. With an oath, Sweet dashed for the aft hatch.

"*Mr. Sweet!* " Talliaferro was aghast; his second-in-command was a coward.

Sweet had no time to correct Talliaferro's conclusion. He thrashed his way into his cuddy and yanked Daniel's Whitworth rifle from beneath his mattress. Frantically he tore open his sea chest and rummaged for the ornate powder flask, bullets, and percussion caps Nathaniel McGill had given to

Daniel. Daniel.... His conscience flayed him like a lash. How could be desert Daniel?

He smacked the butt of the weapon onto the deck and poured a measure of powder down the muzzle. Fumbling and sweating, he finally started the hexagonal bullet into the lands and grooves of the barrel and rummaged some more to locate the small brass hammer used to start the projectile down the bore. He jerked the ramrod from its keepers below the barrel only to have it stop halfway out when it hit the overhead. He kicked the cuddy door open and tilted the rifle into the wardroom so that the rammer would clear its groove in the walnut stock. Viciously he beat the bullet down the barrel – he'd not taken time to lubricate it - grabbed the box of rounds, flask, and caps and charged up the ladder.

As he emerged on deck, a third shot savaged through the rail demolishing the nested ship's boats forward of the mainmast. Flying splinters felled a seaman, one of the old slaving crew. Peck was bellowing orders to get the man below and repair several parted lines.

Sweet rushed to the port rail and saw Manley hurrying to the fourth gun in the battery. He rested the rifle in the mizzen shrouds, tried to get his breathing under control for a halfway steady shot at an animate target roughly five hundred yards away. He thumbed the hammer to full cock, found Manley in the eyepiece of the four-power sight, and squeezed. The cap exploded, but the charge did not. "*God* damn it!" Sweet bellowed. He had neglected to snap a couple of caps before loading to clear the oil from the nipple.

Frantically, he fumbled for another cap, fitted it, and tried again. Misfire. He spilled caps across the deck as he took another with fingers that seemed like sausages. Once more he had Munro Manley in the scope. Make it count, he urged himself. He cleared his mind, controlled his breathing, and took up the slack in the trigger. Munro's arrogant face filled the sight. Sweet squeezed. Just as the Whitworth recoiled into his shoulder, his vision of Manley became a cloud of smoke as the Liberian cannon fired. He had no idea if he hit his target, but there was no more firing from the battery.

*　　*　　*　　*　　*　　*　　*　　*　　*　　*

"She's on the move, Sir," *Bainbridge's* first lieutenant crowed excitedly to his miserable, heavily bandaged commander seated in a chair abaft the brig's wheel.

"Well, damn it, *you move* then," Winkler mumbled through the bandages swathing his head, the laudanum fogging his brain. "Your show; too damned befuddled."

"Aye, Sir," the lieutenant responded; then forgot Winkler in his excitement. What a great time to take command. "Boatswain, the cables. All hands to make sail."

278

Anticipating *Angel's* dash to sea, Winkler's first priority was to rapidly sail in pursuit. Because of the river current surging into the roadstead, it took both the brig's anchors to hold her in place. To speed getting underway, Winkler had run *Bainbridge's* cables to buoys chained to the anchors. The cables could be slipped from the buoys, the anchors left in place. Once *Angel* was apprehended, *Bainbridge* would return for them.

To the southwest the Liberian schooner also got under way. Ordinarily, the schooner abandoning her anchors would be cause for comment aboard the brig, but focused upon *Angel,* the men on *Bainbridge* did not even glance toward the coaster.

"Limey moving as well, Sir." Winkler heard the voice speaking in synchronization with the throbbing laudanum. The speaker was distant he reflected; the world a pulsating cotton bowl. Life was … well, fuzzy. Winkler wanted to sleep.

"Let go!" bellowed the master's mate and the topmen let fall the sails. "Sheet home!" and the line handlers hauled the clew lines taut securing the lower corners of the sails. *Bainbridge* heeled increasingly to port as she gathered way.

Half a mile from *Bainbridge, Ebony Angel* cleared the seaward headland, Ashmun Point, her sails drawing, beginning to generate headway as the river current dissipated in the open water. Several hundred yards behind the black-hulled vessel, *Tourch* churned the mud-red waters like some Oriental sea monster. Too close for the Yanks to risk a shot, observed Talliaferro. He owed Parker an even larger debt.

Bainbridge rapidly gained speed pushing out a frothy bow wave as she surged across the roadstead. In the murk of the silt-filled water, the hawser like an awakening hempen sea serpent roused itself from the ocean floor, its chain jaws sunk into *Bainbridge's* rudder. Through the hemp snake, the force of the brig's momentum progressively transferred to the Liberian schooner's best bower, the biggest of her three anchors.

Summoned by *Tourch's* whistle, Baston's rocket, and the battery's "salute," Liberians of all stations rushed to view the spectacle. It was beautiful, Freedoma thought as she stood between her father and Nathaniel McGill. The Americans, rather the American and the Liberian vessels were like big sea birds opening their soft-white wings taking flight, while the British boat was all fire and power belching out black smoke obscuring parts of Kroo Point. She brushed against Nathaniel whispering, "My brother-in-law be there with my sister and I be left without nobody save a pickan sister and old folks, Nat. I *so* bored." She had admitted to the strongest feelings of affection toward young McGill, but had threatened that they would be shattered if he did not release Doe. He had complied as willingly as he had with her wishes concerning giving his rifle to Daniel. Thought himself in the catbird seat, Freedoma concluded, but still she might as well make Nat yearn for it.

He took his eyes from the spectacle. "That so, Doma?" he answered. Her admission of affection more than compensated for Doe's freedom. "Well, I fix that, directly."

"Best you speak to me first, Nathaniel," interjected Justice Draper, unaware of their newly explicit relationship.

Beneath the roadstead the Liberian schooner's biggest anchor tilted and began to drag. The chain between it and the two others tightened. Then one of the spade-shaped flukes of the largest anchor buried itself in the mud. Nathaniel McGill lifted his gaze from Freedoma to her father about to respond, when the crowd gave a great exhalation. The youth faced the roadstead and his jaw dropped.

*   *   *   *   *   *   *   *   *   *

On *Bainbridge's* quarterdeck, the lieutenant was ecstatic. Water gurgled along the brig's side. *Bainbridge* began a gentle pitching, her deck canting as she heeled with the wind. Heavenly Days, thought the lieutenant, she soon would be....

The brig stumbled in her career across the roadstead. Men staggered along her length, accompanied by the loudest rending screech Winkler had ever heard, at least heard in his laudanum half-world; metal and wood protesting some force. The helmsmen lost their balance as all resistance left the wheel. Without the countering pressure of her rudder against the water, answering only to the onshore wind in her full sails, the brig whipped upright, snapping her bow downwind toward the shore. Men tumbled to the deck. Winkler's chair flipped on its side.

Looking up from the scuppers, the lieutenant struggled for his bearings. Lord, he thought, she was heading straight for the shore northeast of Kroo Point! He scratched for a foothold, cursing the bewildered helmsmen. On the sailors' third attempt to communicate, he finally understood, no steerage. He had to get the way off her. "*Let go all sheets!*" he screamed. Men struggled to comply, simply to let-go the lower corners of all the sails and dump the wind. Then, he decided with relief, he could drop the anchors; *the anchors* left behind in the roadstead. *DAMN*!

On *Tourch*, Commander Parker was astonished by the brig's sudden course alteration. She instantaneously went from running parallel to careering across his path. "*Bloody ...*" he left the curse hanging. "Port your helm. Chief! Starboard paddle all ahead; Port paddle full astern!" The steamer began to pivot seaward on her central point between the great paddlewheels, a point moving forward toward collision with the sailing brig, thanks to her own momentum and the river current.

It would be a near thing, this, reflected Lieutenant Ryder gauging relative speeds, angles, and turning progressions. As the American's silhouette grew larger, he watched the Union Jack at the gunboat's jack staff flutter along the brig's starboard side. *Come on, Old Girl, turn*, he willed. Ah, he felt a moment's relief, the jack was clear, nothing behind it, save a backdrop of open water. Now the great starboard wheel had to turn past an angle of intercept. Looking merely at the line of the gunboat's forward movement and the distance, it seemed impossible to avoid contact, but that was without calculating the portside paddles, which Parker ordered "Full Ahead." *Tourch* gathered way to seaward and by the slightest of margins her transom slid past *Bainbridge.*

On the brig's quarterdeck, her First Lieutenant sighed in relief that the danger of collision was past. The sheets had been let go and she should be losing way, but would it be enough? He turned to the rapidly approaching shore. She was going to strike. He imagined great submerged rocks shivering *Bainbridge's* hull. Were there rocks on this part of the African shoreline, he wondered? The river current swollen by The Rains should wash sediment away exposing rocks....

At several knots, *Bainbridge* struck the shelving mud bottom. The impact was sufficient to snap the foretopmast forward beyond its sustainable arc. It broke like a twig and, loose sail flapping, cascaded down to loll over the bow.

Again all aboard tumbled to the deck. Sprawled upon his face, the Lieutenant felt tears of frustration pressing at the backs of his eyes. In command less than an hour, he had run his ship aground, the biggest disaster for a sea officer, aground in front of every person of importance in Liberia. Why did this happen to him, he demanded of the open sky? Why could not Winkler have been in command at this ignominious moment? Why?

Aboard *Ebony Angel*, Sweet turned to Talliaferro. "Now, Sir?"

"Make it so, Mr. Sweet."

At the ship's gaff a series of signals broke out.

"Tough luck, friend" was flying under *Bainbridge's* recognition number.

On *Tourch* Ryder snickered and then smiled. "Well?" demanded Commander Parker.

" 'Thank you, Mother,' from the ... err ... *ship*, Sir."

"Not quite finished with favors for the...." Parker looked perplexed. "What are they to be called, Mr. Ryder, these rebels, these former Jonathans?"

Ryder looked at his commanding officer. "From 'John Bull' came 'Jonathan,' then from 'Jonathans,' ... 'Johnnies' Sir?"

"Johnny Rebels," Parker chuckled. "Yes. Well, advise the 'Johnnies' that we have cargo to transfer at their convenience." Parker hesitated. "Better make that 'persons' not 'cargo', Mr. Ryder; don't want the *Guardian* getting ideas we're trading flesh."

EPILOGUE

Bonney's knowledge derived solely from what others had told him. He had been brought aboard the black-hulled ship in a sling and moved to the captain's cabin, a third of which had been screened off for him. Essentially, he had been given-up for dead. Doe alone had adamantly refused to accept the obvious and had taken suicidal risks to return ashore for a collection of Lord-only-knew-what native remedies. But they had worked! Doe had attached himself to Bonney's unconscious, feverish form and refused to leave. Delcina had been amazed at, as she said, the "powerful magic what have this *Bush Nigger*!" Her condescension translated into awe for the remedies Doe had employed. Slowly her contempt for tribal Africans had melted into respect, for this one at least, then blossomed into a form of camaraderie, much to everyone's absolute amazement. After all, just days before she and her three maids had done their best to beat him to death.

As feared, Bonney's wound had become badly infected. The fact that it was open at both ends, and Doe kept it so permitting it to drain freely, had been a great advantage for Bonney. From a mustard bottle, Doe had extracted mold-covered rotting bits of vegetation that he had gathered in the last hour before *Angel* sortied from Monrovia. Much against Delcina's and Daniel's advice, the African had packed it into the wound. As the flesh putrefied, Doe introduced maggots from another collection in his magical seabag. Sweet came close to banning Doe from Bonney's presence upon hearing of this treatment, but Daniel by then had developed an instinctive faith in the tribesman and convinced his master not to interfere. A tea Doe brewed from a collection of leaves and bark unknown to Delcina or any of her maids seemed to give Bonney strength and reduce his fevered ravings. On the 23rd of July, his fever broke, the delirium passed, and, pale and weak, he rejoined the world of the living.

The thralldom of Doe's powers had not included Bonney's alter ego, Sergeant Banning, who with almost as much rejoicing as Doe had greeted his lieutenant's recovery. "Sure, Sahr, and what really done t'was myself and a few other Christians what said the rosary to the numbing o' our fingers and the dryin' o' our throats. If the savage had ought to do with ye returnin' from the dead, t'were by holy intervention, none other."

However, Daniel had witnessed and reported to Bonney Banning's other statement to Doe as he left the Lieutenant's bedside, "Gawd bless and keep ye for the marvels and what ye done the Lieutenant, Bucko." Daniel thought better than to report that he had had to retrieve from Doe the better part of Banning's rum ration that the sergeant had "dashed" Doe later the same afternoon. The end result, Bonney knew, was that Doe was now a fully accepted member of their company.

Now Bonney was standing at *Angel's* port rail watching the little dory glide across the Mersey toward Liverpool, Paltier sitting calmly in her stern. Bonney felt a loneliness coming-on; he would miss his "fellow Marine," Royal though he be.

"Sir." Sweet's voice beside him brought Bonney's thoughts back to the ship.

"Mr. Sweet?"

"Don't really know how to say this, Sir," Sweet began.

"Charles...."

"But I'm makin' a stab at it, Mr. Bonney," Sweet interrupted Bonney's interruption. "You pretty much saved my bacon on several occasions, and, well, I wasn't always rightly appreciative of it and kind of acted the ass, so...."

"Charles," Bonney repeated holding up a hand for silence. "You saved my life, you along with Doe and Daniel. Seems pretty damned appreciative to my reckoning."

"Well, I'm trying to apologize and thank you, not looking for argument...." Sweet stalled in his speech and grinned. "And I promise to be less touchy about advice or orders in future."

"And I'll not be so forward in minding *your* affairs, Mr. Sweet," Bonney said smiling.

Standing by the lee rail, Daniel turned to Doe. "New plug navy cut chawin' tobacco, don't take three days, they be back at each and other."

"*Ahyeee, Bo,*" Doe responded. "I no give you bet on that!"

WHO'S WHO
&
WHAT'S WHAT

"Abaft": A naval expression meaning "behind" as in "abaft the mast."

American Hotel (Historical): An eating establishment run by a Liberian in Freetown, Sierra Leone. Its exterior appeared as described according to Sir Richard Francis Burton in his 1862 book, *Wanderings in West Africa*. The fare, interior, and details regarding its proprietor are the author's suppositions and creation.

APPLETON, Ralph Quincy (Fictional): Lieutenant, USN aboard *U.S.S. Jamestown* on West African Station, spring 1861. Thirty-three years of age, shorter than average, ample girth, fair complexion, jolly, clean-shaven, of New York State. Unmarried, he is immature for his age and has made his place by being agreeable and accommodating.

ARMOND (Fictional): Master of *U.S.S. Jamestown*. A bluff character in his late forties with full sidewiskers, weathered face, and inflexible personality given to life "By the Book." At sea since his early teens, he got his start whaling and entered the Navy during the Mexican War. Briefly married, he lost his wife to childbirth while he was at sea and has carried a morose attitude toward domestic life ever since. He would rather be at sea than on land any day and rather commune with his ship than his shipmates.

BANNING, Cullin (Fictional): Sergeant, United States Marine Corps, Senior Non-Commissioned Officer of Marine Detachment, *U.S.S. Jamestown*. An Irish immigrant as a child, he was reared in the Pennsylvania coalfields working in the mines from the age of eleven. His father tried to free the family from debt bondage to the mines by enlisting for the Mexican War, but deserted to the Mexicans, was captured, and was hanged as the Stars and Stripes appeared above Chipaltipec. After his mother's death, he and another brother fled to Philadelphia and joined the Marines. The Corps gave him acceptance, self-respect, and purpose for the first time in his life, which he repaid with absolute devotion to every facet of Marine Corps culture. Standing five-feet-ten-inches, he almost magically maintained an impeccable uniform in the world of tar and sweat that was a sailing man-of-war. A committed bachelor, he was known for establishing quick liaisons within twenty-four hours of arriving in any port, but never letting them or anything else interfere with his duties.

BASTON, Roland P, The Hon. (Fictional): United States Consul at Monrovia, Liberia. A slender, clean-shaven man of average height with spectacles that he avoided wearing giving him a perpetual squint. He was a former Democratic political operative in Mystic, Connecticut, whose loyalty to President Buchanan had been secured with promise of a diplomatic posting under the new administration. He had married the daughter of the President of the Merchants' and Seamen's Bank of Mystic. A widower despised by his former father-in-law for taking his daughter to die in West Africa, Baston was bitter at the possibility of being replaced by the Lincoln Administration and alternatively at being retained in his post in a society he had come to loathe.

"Belay": A naval expression meaning to "stop" as in "belay hauling" meaning to stop pulling on a rope.

"Bend-on": A naval expression used as a verb meaning to "attach" or in the case of sails to "set."

BENSON, Stephan Allen, The Honorable (Historical): President of Liberia and previously Vice President under Roberts. Born in Maryland, he is thirty-five years old at the time of this story and the author has made him the brother of fictitious Mrs. Draper. His physical description is taken from photograph by Augustus Washington.

Stephan Benson

BLYDEN, Edward Wilmont (Historical): West Indian linguist, resident in Liberia.

BONNEY, Aaron Claverton (Fictional): 2nd Lieutenant of Marines aboard *U.S.S. Jamestown*. Twenty-six years of age, clean-shaven, he was of average height at five-feet-six-inches and well proportioned. The eldest son of a distinguished Baltimore attorney who also was a leader in the Maryland Colonization Society sponsoring repatriation of freed slaves to Liberia. Bonney had attended Princeton College intending for the law. A late night debate at his eating club over slavery led to an early morning duel and his departure from New Jersey rather than face manslaughter charges. After an heated confrontation with his family, he presented himself along with a letter of introduction to a friend of his father's who also happened to be Commandant of the Marine Corps and began a career as an Officer of Marines. While experiencing continuing guilt at disappointing his family, Bonney reveled in the life of the Corps and felt delivered from the confines of an office and the routines of the law. His devotion to his Corps had enabled him to view the building national political crisis with detachment, confident that whatever happened, the nation, the Naval Service, and The Corps would continue unchanged.

BONNEY, William (Fictional): Younger brother of Aaron killed in the Baltimore resistance to Federal troops moving through the city to Washington.

Bostwick, McKenzie & Gibson, Ltd. (Fictional): Correspondent firm with Sweet & Sons of Portsmouth, Virginia. Of London, Halifax and Hamilton with branches in Liverpool, Kingston, and Cape Town.

BOUNCE (Fictional): Commander, Royal Navy, Captain of the Port of Freetown, Sierra Leone. A veteran of nearly four decades at sea, this graying, corpulent man of average height, ample girth, and flourishing brown beard, was soldiering on toward retirement maintaining order in Her Majesty's principal port in West Africa. He avoided the mundanity of his daily existence by emphasizing the myriad formalities of Naval Life and social mores, making him pompous in the opinion of many. Before Christmas 1861, he would retire, return to his wife and teenage daughter in Poole in Dorset, and begin a new career as agent for a small shipping firm struggling to maintain a coasting trade in the face of competition from the railroads.

BOYLE, Sibyl (Historical): African shopkeeper in Freetown whose establishment is as described by Burton and whose name was derived as described according to Burton. A light-skinned middle aged Creole of medium build with gray hair and muttonchops sidewhiskers which he maintained despite the heat and humidity, Boyle was noted for the variety and quality of his wares and his educated and enlightening conversation that accompanied his sales efforts.

Bullom Boat, (Historical): Small sailing craft combining Northern European clinker-built hulls and triangular Mediterranean sails, these vessels were introduced to West Africa by the Portuguese during the 16th century and named for the Bullom Peninsula that forms the northern bank of the Sierra Leone River. See picture *infra*.

BROOKE (Fictional): Surgeon of *U.S.S. Jamestown*. Short, heavyset, balding, and on the far side of middle age, his veined nose and cheeks reflected his love of drink and disappointment at life.

CABOT, Nathaniel (Fictional): Liberian owner of the American Hotel in Freetown, Sierra Leone. A well-fed, well educated, large framed Americo-Liberian claiming roots in Massachusetts before that state abolished slavery, he was influential within Creole society that dominated Freetown and Sierra Leone. He maintained his extensive family and numerous wards in the two floors above the public rooms of the American Hotel and an adjacent building that also housed a mission school.

CHERRY (Fictional): Gunner aboard *U.S.S. Jamestown*. Graying and lanky, this slender six-foot petty officer had been at sea so long that it was rumored even he had forgotten his home of origin. He never spoke of family, childhood, or any life beyond his naval career impossibly rumored to have begun off the shores of Tripoli. He loved whist, but had trouble finding those willing to play with someone who seemed to remember every card played throughout the night. Careful of his money he was believed to have amassed a fortune stashed in some unknown New York bank. A light eater, he was famous for occasionally venturing to the galley and producing exceptional puddings delivered in wondrous shapes such as swans, human visages, and on special occasions naval ordinance.

"Close": A naval expression meaning "to approach" or "to narrow the distance between," as in "close with the enemy."

CRUMMELL, Alexander (Historical): Timinee boy taken as a slave to U.S. at age thirteen. He found his way to England, where he earned a B.A. from Cambridge. He was a Protestant Episcopal Church minister, a faculty member at Liberia College, and an outspoken critic of Mulatto dominance in Liberia.

Alexander Crummell

CRUMMELL, Sarah (Historical): wife of Alexander.

Dam, also Dutch Dam or Two-Penny Dutch Dam: A sixteenth century Dutch coin worth two English pence, used by the British as a figure of speech for something of little value. The phrase shortened over time to Rep Butler's, "I don't give a damn," though the modern spelling wrongfully evokes damnation rather than the coin.

DANIEL (Fictional): Slave of Charles Sweet. Between 20 and 25 years of age, tall at five-feet-nine-inches, well muscled, light complected. His mother, Celia, was head of household slaves at Sweetlands. His father was head groom at Sweetlands. Taught by Charles Sweet's father along with Charles to read, write, and shoot. Accompanied Charles to Episcopal High School in Alexandria and on to the Naval Academy, where he acted as steward in the Officers' Mess and served Charles to the extent permitted by Academy Regulations. He followed Charles aboard *U.S.S. Jamestown* as officer's servant and wardroom steward with rating of "Volunteer" on the ship's books. Charles once described Daniel as his "brevet older brother" and their relationship was one of companions as much as master and servant.

DePUE, Harold C. (Fictional): Midshipman twenty-two years of age, average height of five-feet-six-inches, black haired with fine features and slender build. From New York City where his family owned a furniture factory, he was four days junior to Charles Sweet at Annapolis, his close friend and Academy roommate, and served aboard *U.S.S. Jamestown* with Sweet.

DOE (Fictional): Tribal African formerly indentured in the McGill household where he reportedly made a daughter of the house pregnant. As a result the McGills would see him dead. He escaped from Monrovia, only to be kidnapped and sold to the slave crew of the *Ebony Angel*. He was fiercely resentful of his treatment by the Americo-Liberians.

DRAPER, Chastity (Fictional): Americo-Liberian six-year-old daughter of Justice and Mrs. Draper.

DRAPER, Conscience (Fictional): Americo-Liberian 22 year-old daughter of Justice and Mrs. Draper. Fictitious wife of historical personage, Alfred Francis Russell.

DRAPER, Delcina (Fictional): Americo-Liberian nineteen-year-old daughter of Justice and Mrs. Draper.

DRAPER, Freedoma (Fictional): Americo-Liberian sixteen-year-old daughter of Justice and Mrs. Draper.

DRAPER, Felicitous Benson (Fictional): Americo-Liberian wife of Chief Justice of Liberian Supreme Court and fictitious sister of the President of Liberian Republic.

DRAPER, Jefferson, Honorable (Fictional): Americo-Liberian Chief Justice of Liberian Supreme Court.

DYER (Fictional): Corporal of Marines aboard *U.S.S. Jamestown*.

ELLIOTT, "Pa" (Historical): African Pilot at Freetown. Competitor of "Pa" Johnson, according to Burton. Their competition for pilotage of *Jamestown* is similar to that for pilotage of Burton's ship *Blackland* in 1862.

"E'PHANT" (Fictional): African Bailiff of Freetown Magistrate Court.

FLETCHER, Ma (Fictional): Proprietress of Monrovia "rest cabins" approximating Twentieth Century American motel cabins, without running water, electricity, insulation, or any other modern amenities. Dr. Hibberd Kline, Jr. stayed in similar accommodations, absent the maids, on the Banana Islands off Sierra Leone in 1954.

FLINT (Fictional): Purser, *U.S.S. Jamestown*.

GOODE (Fictional): Boatswain, *U.S.S. Jamestown*.

GABRIEL (Fictional): Half-brother of Nathaniel Cabot by tribal woman, about thirty-five years of age, dark, with slight beard and tending to fleshy.

290

Assumed control of Greenville and Sinoe County, Liberia after death of his father and butchered entire Cabot household except for Nathaniel who was in Monrovia at the time.

Head: Naval term for latrine.

HILLARY (Fictional): Captain of slave ship *Ebony Angel* of New York.

HORNBY (Fictional): Secretary to Governor Porter of Sierra Leone.

JACKSON, "General" (Historical): African "guide" in Freetown described by Burton.

JENNINGS (Fictional): Captain, Royal Navy, commanding *H.M.S. Falcon*, steam-sloop, senior officer of the Northern Division of the West African Squadron.

"JESSIE" or "By Jessie": Common 19ᵗʰ Century euphemism for "Jesus."

JOHNSON, "Pa" (Historical): large, light-complected African Pilot at Freetown. He piloted the African Steam Ship Company vessel *Blackland* into Freetown Harbour with Burton aboard in 1862 after winning a race with his competitor Pa Elliott in much the same manner as described for the *Jamestown's* arrival in Sierra Leone.

JOSHUA (Fictional): Slave servant of Captain Pennington aboard *Jamestown*.

"JUMBO" (Historical): African guide in Freetown, competitor of "General Jackson." Jumbo was retained as guide both by characters in this story and in fact by Burton during his visit to Freetown in 1862.

LaMat et Fils (Fictional): Correspondent firm of Sweet & Sons with offices in New Orleans, Louisiana and Nantes, France.

LeMat Revolver (Historical): The invention of a New Orleans doctor, the pistol had nine .42 caliber cylinder chambers and 16 guage smoothbore barrel under the pistol barrel, which fired by tipping down the hinged hammer.

Laudanum (Historical): A medicinal opiate, usually in liquid form, used to treat a wide range of conditions.

Liberian Packet Company (Fictional): Firm formed among Sweet and Sons, McGill Brothers, President Benson, former President Roberts, and Halcyon Nevis, Esq. to own and operate the *Ebony Angel*. Nevis sold his interest to Chief Justice Draper.

MANLEY (Fictional): Americo-Liberian Minister of Trade. He was a silent partner with Nevis, Parkins the Minister of the Minister of the Interior, and Superintendent Cabot in a slave exporting enterprise run out of Greenville, Liberia. He organizing a coup in Greenville that resulted in the exile of Nathaniel Cabot to Freetown. He also was responsible for the captivity of the Draper family in Greenville.

MANLEY, Munro (Fictional): Americo-Liberian son of Minister of the Trade and Cadet Corporal of the Presidential Guards from Liberia College.

McGill Brothers (Historical): Trading company owned by four Americo-Liberian brothers in Monrovia.

McGILL, Urias (Historical): Head of McGill Brothers.

Urias McGill

McGILL, Nathaniel (Fictional): Americo-Liberian son of one of the McGill brothers and member of Presidential Guards from Liberia College.

MUNRO, ISSA (Fictional): Young Americo-Liberian male aboard slave ship *Ebony Angel*, identified as "cousin" of Nathaniel Cabot, proprietor of the American Hotel.

"Necessary": 19th Century term for latrine.

NEVIS, Halcyon, Esquire (Fictional): Creole lawyer in Freetown.

ORRIN (Fictional): United States Marine serving aboard *U.S.S. Jamestown*.

PAGE-NORTON (Fictional): Captain, Second West Indian Regiment, Officer Commanding, Freetown Garrison.

PALTIER, Robert (Fictional): 1st Lieutenant, Royal Marines serving aboard *H.M.S. Falcon*. Twenty-nine years of age, mutton chop side-whiskers, Anglo-Irish.

PARKER (Fictional): Commander, Royal Navy of *H.M.S. Tourch*, paddlewheel gunboat of Northern Division, West African Squadron.

PARKINS (Fictional): Americo-Liberian Minister of the Interior of Liberia.

PAYNE, James Spriggs (Historical): Americo-Liberian. In his twenties, tall, fair skinned. Photographed by Augustus Washington. Later he was President of Liberia.

PECK (Fictional): Boatswains Mate of *U.S.S. Jamestown*.

PENNINGTON, James Carlyle (Fictional): Captain, United States Navy; graying, in his early sixties, five feet–eight inches tall. He was a Virginian and a longtime friend of the Sweets. He arranged to have Midshipman Charles Sweet serve aboard the *U.S.S. Jamestown* under his command.

PORTER, James D. P, Honourable (Fictional): Governor of Sierra Leone. Clean-shaven, athletic, he had been in India during the Mutiny posted to a native court and had failed to gather indications of the coming revolt. His career had been side-stepped to Africa as a result with the "promotion" to Governor thanks to his wife's family connections.

PRESCOTT Reverend Doctor Horace (Fictional): Methodist missionary from Schenectady, New York in Monrovia with his wife.

PREWITT, Samantha (Fictional): Schoolmistress of the private day school attended by Bonney as a child. Miss Prewitt kept Bonney informed of happenings in Baltimore and among the Bonney family after his breach with his father and estrangement from his family.

PORTO NOVO (Historical): Native African settlement and slave exporting center in modern day Nigeria ruled by King "Soji" laid waste by the Royal Navy April 22, 1861 as described herein and reported by Burton.

RAMSEY (Fictional): British Commissioner of the Court of Mixed Commission at Freetown created pursuant to treaty to dispose of alleged British, Spanish, and Brazilian slavers seized by the Royal Navy along the West African Coast.

ROBERTS, Jane (Historical): Wife of Joseph Roberts. Genteel, light complected, she wore her hair in numerous curled tails like Mrs. Lincoln according to a photograph by Augustus Washington.

Jane Roberts

ROBERTS, Joseph Jenkins, Honorable, "Old Gruff" (Historical): First President of Liberia. His father, James Roberts, was a free African-American owner of four barges on James River. He was photographed by Augustus Washington.

Joseph Jenkins Roberts

ROBERTS, Richard Henry (Fictional): Son of Joseph Roberts. Member of the Presidential Guard from Liberia College.

ROTH, "Auntie" (Fictional): Liberian voodoo queen.

ROYE, Edwin J. (Historical): Of pure African blood, he was the richest man in Liberia. Speaker of Liberian House. Ally of Crummell and opponent of mulatto domination.

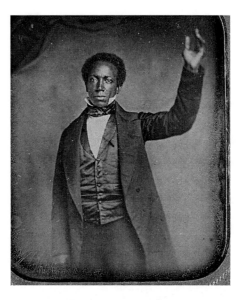

RUSSELL, Alfred Francis (Historical): Americo-Liberian. Supported, then turning upon Mr. Crummell. President of Liberia 1883-84. Husband of Conscience Draper.

Alfred Russell

RYDER (Fictional): Lieutenant, Royal Navy, and First Officer of *H.M.S. Touch.*

"SAMSON" (Fictional): Boatswain of American slave ship, *Ebony Angel.*

SAYS, John (Historical): United States Agent for freed slave cargoes in Liberia.

SAWYER (Fictional): Lieutenant, Royal Navy of *H.M.S. Falcon.*

SCHMIDT, Marine (Fictional): Nineteen-year-old private from New Jersey aboard *U.S.S. Jamestown.*

Ships:

U.S.S. Bainbridge (Historical): Gun brig built at Boston Navy Yard in 1842. Lost off Cape Hatteras, 21 August 1863 with all hands save one. Her presence on West African Station is the author's creation. In 1861 she was laid up at Boston Navy Yard until re-commissioned to enforce the Blockade. Characteristics are as found in Chapelle, *The History of the American Sailing Navy.*

Blacklands (Historical): African Steamship Company's vessel Sir Richard Francis Burton sailed upon in 1862.

Buenaventura Cubano (Historical): Spanish slaver captured in the Gallinhas River by the Liberian vessel *Lively Quail* as found herein and as reported in Burton.

Cortez (Historical): American slaver seized by the Royal Navy off Cuba as described herein and as found in Thomas, *The Slave Trade.*

Ebony Angel (aka: Black Jonathan) (Fictional): Ship-rigged purpose-built American slaver. She is entirely the author's creation. Her characteristics are based upon those of similar vessels used in the "Trade" at this time when over 70 percent of slaving vessels were American flagged. See Thomas, *The Slave Trade.*

H.M.S. Falcon (Historical): Steam sloop-of-war in the Northern Division of the Royal Navy Anti-Slaving Patrol as reported by Burton in 1862. Her characteristics are the author's conjecture, but conform to vessels of this type.

L'Audace (Fictional): Gaff-rigged cutter the Sweet boys sailed about Hampton Roads area as teenagers.

U.S.S. Jamestown (Historical): 1st Class ship-rigged sloop-of-war built at the Norfolk Navy Yard 1843-44. She was laid up in Ordinary at Philadelphia Navy Yard in 1861. Her presence in the West African Squadron at that date is the author's creation. She was re-commissioned in 1861 and served in the Atlantic Blockading Squadron making several captures. She was destroyed by fire at Norfolk Navy Yard on 3 January 1913. Her characteristics are as found in Chapelle, *The History of the American Sailing Navy*.

U.S.S. Jamestown late in her career.

H.M.S. Tourch (Historical): Gunboat in the Northern Division of the Royal Navy Anti-Slaving Patrol as reported by Burton in 1862. Her characteristics are the author's conjecture.

Lively Quail (Historical): Small patrol vessel given to Liberia by Great Britain prior to 1862. Her activities regarding the Spanish slaver *Buenaventura Cubano* are as reported in Burton.

Pachita (Historical): American slaving ship out of the port of New York seized by the Royal Navy off West Africa in 1857, as found in Thomas, *The Slave Trade*.

SOJI, King (Historical): "King" of African slave exporting community of Porto Novo, Nigeria, destroyed by the Royal Navy, April 22, 1861.

SWEET, Charles (Fictional): Midshipman aboard *U.S.S. Jamestown* in the West African Squadron. Twenty-two years of age, of Sweetlands, Nansemond County, Virginia. Attended Episcopal High School, Alexandria, Virginia 1855-56 and US Naval Academy 1856-59, graduating 12th in that class. Family owned Sweet & Sons shipping firm and chandlery in Portsmouth, Virginia, a longtime supplier to the Gosport Navy Yard. Had difficulty recalling names and was only a fair swimmer.

SWINTON (Fictional): Older Briton, passenger aboard African Steam Ship Company's *Blackland* and guest at a dinner given by the Governor of Sierra Leone.

TALLIAFERRO, Henry Lawton (Fictional): Past Midshipman, USN, twenty-six years of age, of Wilmington, North Carolina. Tall at five foot-nine and redheaded despite the Mediterranean origins of his name Talliaferro was extremely sensitive of his honor and brooked no slight from anyone regardless of rank. Reticent to speak of his family or past, Talliaferro was reputed to come from circumstances unable to maintain the social position of his august Tidewater name. Rumors stated that the Midshipman's father had been unaccounted for during much of his upbringing and his mother had married for a second time during his boyhood to a Wilmington merchant. The intercession of distant relatives in Virginia had won him his appointment to Annapolis and his temper had not scuttled his career so far. Having passed the examination for promotion to lieutenant, he was only waiting in order of seniority for a vacancy in the authorized number of lieutenants to assume his new rank.

THOMS (Fictional): Captain of the Foretop, *U.S.S. Jamestown*, Swedish nationality. Walrus-like mustache. His infatuation with a Gosport barmaid was a cause of much mirth and teasing aboard *Jamestown*.

TRUEMAN, Elias Welles (Fictional): Lieutenant aboard *U.S.S. Jamestown* In his forties, severe, tall (5'11"), thin, dark, of Massachusetts. Abstemious in regard to food and drink. He was deeply resentful of what he perceived to be a Southern cabal that kept him from the recognition and professional advancement he felt he deserved.

WARNER, Daniel Bashiel (Historical): Americo-Liberian.

WARNER, Thaddeus (Fictional): Son of Daniel Warner, and member of Presidential Guard from Liberia College.

WASHINGTON, Augustus (Historical): African-American photography pioneer who emigrated to Liberia in 1853 and became photographer to the elite of that country. Thanks to him, excellent images of the Liberian upper classes of this period are plentiful.

WATCHES:

> Middle (graveyard watch): midnight to 0400 hours
>
> Morning: 0400 to 0800 hours
>
> Forenoon: 0800 to 1200 hours
>
> Afternoon: 1200 to 1600 hours
>
> First dog: 1600 to 1800 hours
>
> Second, or last, dog: 1800 to 2000 hours
>
> First: 2000 hours to midnight

WINKLER (Fictional): Lieutenant-in-Command of the brig-of-war *U.S.S. Bainbridge.* Was on staff at Annapolis when Sweet was a student.

WHAT'S WHAT

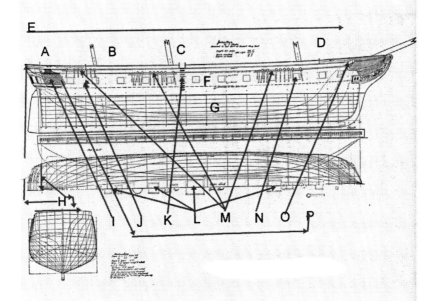

U.S.S. Jamestown Hull Diagram

(A) Poop Deck (B) Quarter Deck (C) Waist or Spar Deck (D) Forecastle
(E) Weather Deck (A, B, C & D inclusive) (F) Gun Deck or Berth Deck
(G) Orlop or Hold (H) Transom (I) Captain's Cabin (J) Wardroom
(K) Cleats and Entryport (L) Hatches (Fore, Main, Aft & Captain's)
  (M) Chains (Fore, Main & Mizzen) (N) Gunport (O) Cathead for Hoisting
Anchor (P) Officers' Quarter Gallery or Head (Toilet)

Sloop-of-War *U.S.S. Jamestown*: Masts, Spars & Principal Rigging

A. Main Mast **B.** Main Top Mast **C.** Main Topgallant Mast **D.** Fore Mast **E.** Fore Top Mast **F.** Fore Topgallant Mast **G.** Mizzen Mast **H.** Mizzen Top Mast **I.** Mizzen Topgallant Mast **1.** Main Spar/Main Course Spar **2.** Main Topsail Spar **3.** Main Topgallant Spar **4.** Main Royal Spar **5.** Fore Spar/Fore Course Spar **6.** Fore Topsail Spar **7.** Fore Topgallant Spar **8.** Fore Royal Spar **9.** Crossjack Spar **10.** Mizzen Topsail Spar **11.** Mizzen Topgallant Spar **12.** Mizzen Royal Spar **13.** Boom **14.** Gaff , **15.** Main Gaff, **16.** Fore Gaff.

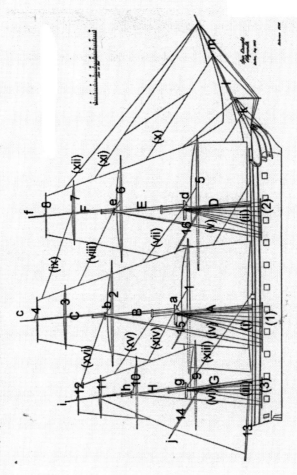

a. Main Top / Main Fighting Top **b.** Main Crosstrees **c.** Main Truck **d.** Fore Top **e.** Fore Crosstrees **f.** Fore Truck **g.** Mizzen Top **h.** Mizzen Crosstrees **i.** Mizzen Truck **j.** Gaff Head **k.** Bowsprit **l.** Jib Boom **m.** Main Chains **n.** Fore Chains **o.** Mizzen Chains **(i)** Main Shrouds **(ii)** Fore Shrouds **(iii)** Mizzen Shrouds **(iv)** Main Backstay **(v)** Mizzen Backstay **(vi)** Mizzen Backstay **(vii)** Main Forestay **(viii)** Maintop Fore Stay **(ix)** Main Topgallant Stay **(x)** Fore Forestay **(xi)** Foretop Forestay **(xii)** Fore Topgallant Forestay **(xiii)** Mizzen Forestay **(xiv)** Mizzentop Forestay **(xv)** Mizzen Topgallant Forestay **(xvi)**

302

U.S.S. Jamestown: Sail Plan

Square Sails

Mainmast:
(1) Main Sail /Course
(2) Main Topsail
(3) Main Topgallant Sail
(4) Main Royal

Foremast:
(5) Fore Sail/Course
(6) Fore Topsail
(7) Fore Topgallant Sail
(8) Fore Royal

Mizzenmast:
(*Jamestown* had no Mizzen Course)
(9) Mizzen Topsail
(10) Mizzen Topgallant Sail
(11) Mizzen Royal

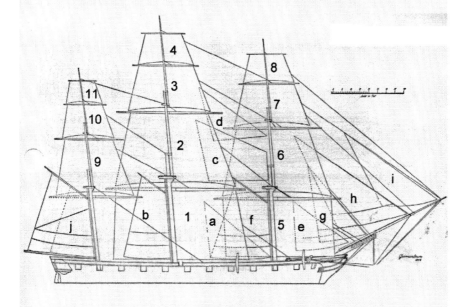

Fore-and-Aft Sails

Mainmast:
(a) Main Staysail
(b) Main Driver/Spanker
(c) Main Topmast Staysail
(d) Main Topgallant
    Staysail

Foremast:
(e) Fore Staysail
(f) Fore Driver/Spanker
(g) Fore Topmast Staysail
(h) Jib
(i) Jib Topsail

Mizzenmast:
(j) Mizzen Driver/Spanker

303

U.S.S. Bainbridge

Hull Diagram

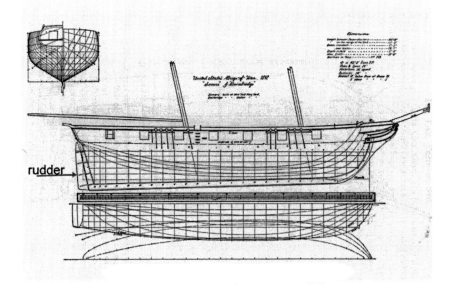

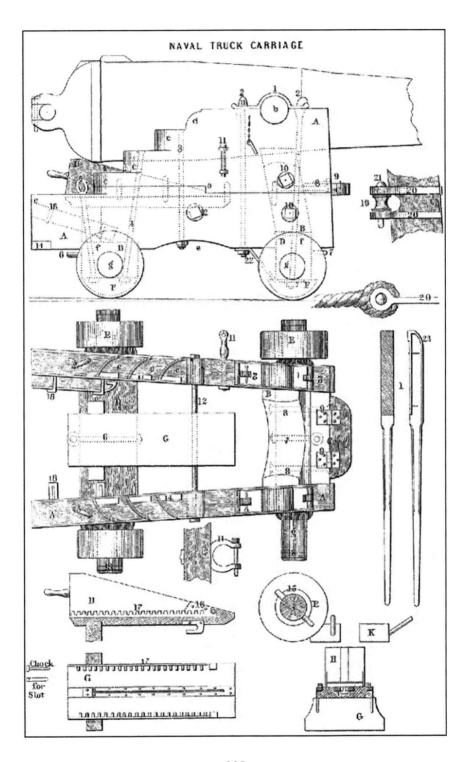

Pivot Gun Mount

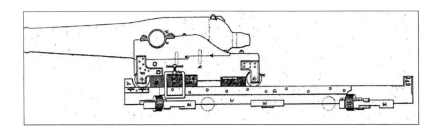

CARRIAGE		SLIDE	
WOODEN PARTS	**METAL PARTS**	**WOODEN PARTS**	**METAL PARTS**
A. Brackets of two pieces, with jog 'a', and dowels 'b'.	d. Cap squares.	C. Rails.	G. Shifting trucks.
B. Transoms, projecting beyond the rails; front middle, and rear, jogged into brackets.	e. Trunnion plates.	D. Compressor battens.	H. Training trucks, both with journals and eccentric axles.
	f. Compressor, with screw and lever.	E. Transoms; front and rear each in two parts, middle in one part.	
	g. Rollers and journal plates.	F. Hurters, front and rear.	

Seal of Her Britannic Majesty's Crown Colony of Sierra Leone

Gulf of Guinea & Bight of Benin

FREETOWN, SIERRA LEONE 1852

From a Drawing by Letitia Jervis Terry

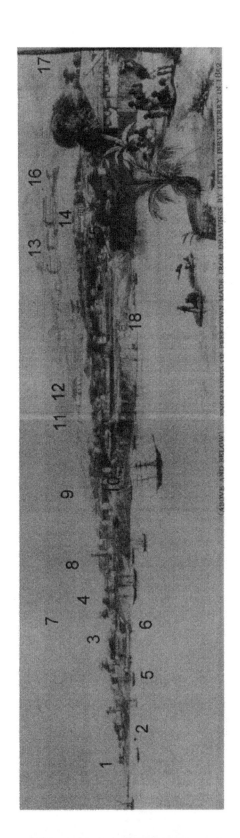

(ABOVE AND BELOW) DRAWINGS OF FREETOWN MADE FROM DRAWINGS BY LETITIA JERVIS TERRY IN 1852

1. Fort Falconbridge
2. Port Captain's Wharf
3. Commissariat
4. Haddle's Warehouse
5. Government Steps
6. Slave Steps

7. Cottonwood Tree
8. St. George's Cathedral
9. Law Courts
10. Market
11. Gun Position, Ft. Thornton
12. Government House

13. Tower Hill Barracks
14. Colonial Hospital
15. King Jimmy's Bridge
16. Mt. Oriole
17. Sugarloaf Mountain
18. Fish Market Beach

Bullum Boat in Sierra Leone River and **Fish Market** below **King Jimmy's Bridge**

These Mid-Twentieth Century views hardly changed from the Mid-Nineteenth Century.

Liberia 1858

Monrovia, Liberia

Montserado River Soundings
Carey Island
Kroo or **Kru Point**
The Path from McGills' Warehouse

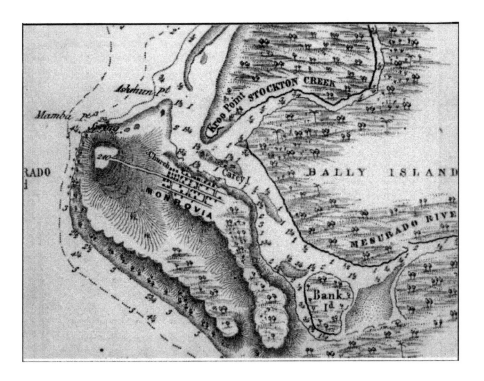

Monrovia, Liberia Showing Bally Island

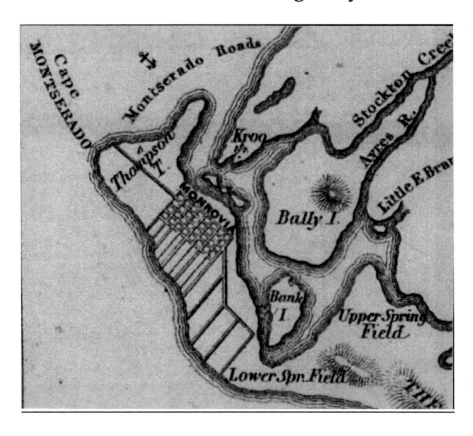

Monrovia, Liberia Showing Montserado River Soundings & Carey Island

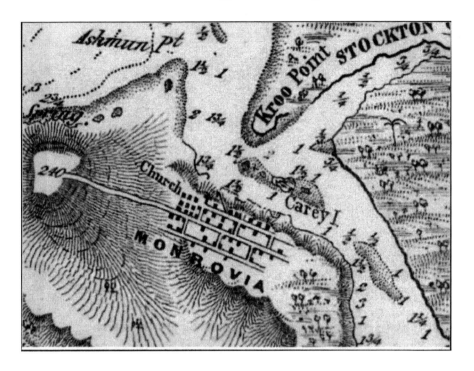

The Author at Drewry's Bluff, Virginia, May 2012

About the Author

Hibberd Van Buren Kline, III, Colonel USMCR (Ret) brings a variety of experiences and training to his writing of Civil War naval fiction. He is an honors graduate in History from Harvard College, where he was starting saber on the Freshman Fencing Team and founding President of the Harvard Polo Club. Subsequently, he earned a Juris Doctorate from the University of Virginia. Colonel Kline served thirty years active and reserve, ashore and afloat, as an infantry officer and intelligence officer in the United States Marine Corps, including active service during Vietnam and the Gulf War. Colonel Kline has been a War Between the States re-enactor on-and-off since 1962, including participating as a Marine in the movie *Gods and Generals*. When he writes of amphibious landings from whaleboats or firing large caliber 19th Century naval guns he actually has done so. The first novel in his **Navy Gray** series is set in West Africa where he lived for a year as a child. Hibberd currently is a practicing attorney, an adjunct college professor, and a Civil War re-enactor. He and his wife Christine have a home in Kansas City and a farm in nearby Centerview, Missouri.